REBEL WARRIOR

Regan Walker

REBEL WARRIOR

Paperback ISBN: 978-0996849531
Print Edition

"Here," he said reaching toward her, "take my hand and allow me to help you out."

There was fire in her eyes but she took his hand while holding on to her shoes, soaked with water.

He pulled her from the stream, sodden and shivering. It was the first time they had touched and even dripping wet, the feel of her skin caused a surge of desire to course through him. The wet gown clung to her body, revealing her nipples hardened to small buds and her curves in vivid detail. Wet, she was even more alluring than before. He wanted to pull her close, to feel her softness, but instead, he merely steadied her with his hands. "Did you not see the moss that grows on the log? 'Tis quite apparent."

Her brow furrowed. "You might have warned me."

"You fell before I could."

Wiping water from her face, she looked up at him. Her eyes were the green of the forest around them. Light filtering through the trees added a soft glow to her pale, damp skin. His gaze dropped to her lips, the color of wild roses. He ached to kiss them.

Bending his head, he moved his lips closer to hers.

Water suddenly dripped from her hair onto her nose, causing her to sniff and step back.

Still holding her shoes in one hand, she shivered. "I... I must look a mess."

"Indeed not, but you are pale." Recognizing her predicament, he said, "I wear no cloak to offer you, but I can give you the heat of my body." Taking the shoes she carried and dropping them to the ground, he pulled her into his arms and held her against his chest, ignoring the water soaking into his tunic. Her breasts pressed into his chest, warming him as his body responded to the nearness of the woman he could not dismiss from his thoughts.

AUTHOR'S NOTE

Steinar of Talisand, the brother of the heroine in *The Red Wolf's Prize*, belonged to that generation of young Englishmen who were not yet twenty at the time of the Norman Conquest. They were old enough to understand what was happening and to feel keenly the loss of family and lands, yet powerless to do anything about it. Young Anglo-Saxon nobles forever exiled from their country. Where should they go but to Scotland?

In the eleventh century, Scotland was a wild country where warlords vied for the throne, and the cultures of the Gaels (the Irish who became the Scots), Norse and eventually Saxons and Normans melded together. In 1057, Malcolm Canmore, the son of a king, murdered his way to the throne to become King of Scots, but he did not reign over all of Scotland. The Norse and the Irish Gaels still controlled parts of the north and west.

A decade later, William the Conqueror's harsh actions in England sent Saxons in Wessex and Anglo-Scandinavians in Yorkshire fleeing to Scotland. King Malcolm welcomed them and, in so doing, received a boon. For when he cast his eyes upon the beautiful Saxon Princess Margaret, whose family sought refuge at his court, he was smitten. By 1072, when my story begins, they were married and she had already given him the first of six sons and two daughters.

Queen Margaret was a woman of faith who saw her marriage as a calling from God to help shape Scotland's future and to move the Scottish church closer to Rome. For her efforts she was ultimately made Scotland's only royal saint. While not all Scots welcomed the changes she brought, none could criticize the character of their new queen, for she was kind and charitable to all. That her rough, warrior husband deferred to her, at least in matters of their family, can be seen in the names given their sons: Edward, Edmund, Ethelred, Edgar, Alexander and David, the first four from the English royal dynasty. Perhaps, in agreeing to such names, Malcolm saw the potential for his sons to one day claim the throne of England, for as long as Margaret's younger brother, Edgar Ætheling, the Saxon heir to the throne, remained unmarried and childless, his rights would be transmitted through Margaret to her children. Certainly William the Conqueror did not fail to note this.

At the time of my story, the borders between Scotland and England were not well defined. Malcolm often raided into Northumbria. That he had claims to the region cannot be doubted, but I believe he was also making a point to the Conqueror. It was a bit like poking a stick at a wild boar, for William would ultimately seek to rein in the powerful King of Scots and his support for the rebels in England.

In all this, what did Steinar, a rebel warrior and the exiled son of a dead English thegn, have to offer a woman? What chance was there for him to find love in a foreign land when he had lost everything? Ah, but this is the Scotland of long ago where a bold warrior king won the heart of a pious Saxon princess.

There is every chance in the world.

Scotland
1071-72

Orkneys

North Sea

SCOTLAND
Atholl

Dunkeld

Abernethy   St. Andrews
             Fife
Dunfermline   Firth of Forth
Loch Lomond
          Vale of
          Leven
                    Lothian
Strathclyde

                Northumbria

IRELAND   ENGLAND

CHARACTERS OF NOTE
(BOTH REAL AND FICTIONAL)

Steinar of Talisand

Catrìona of the Vale of Leven

Angus, Catrìona's guard

Niall, Catrìona's younger brother

Domnall mac Murchada, Irish nobleman, Catrìona's intended

Matad of Dunkeld, Mormaer of Atholl, Catrìona's uncle

Fia of Atholl, Catrìona's cousin and daughter of Matad

Rhodri ap Bleddyn of Gwynedd, Welsh bard, master of the bow and friend of Steinar

Malcolm Canmore, King of Scots

Margaret of Wessex, Queen of Scots

Edgar Ætheling, brother to Margaret and Saxon heir to the throne of England

Machar, King Malcolm's falconer

Maerleswein, English thegn of noble Danish blood and former Sheriff of Lincolnshire

Giric, orphan boy

Audra of Fife, daughter of Duff, Mormaer of Fife, and one of Queen Margaret's ladies

Isobel of Ross, one of Queen Margaret's ladies

Elspeth of Loch Tay, one of Queen Margaret's ladies

Davina of Lothian, one of Queen Margaret's ladies

Isla of Blackwell, one of Queen Margaret's ladies

Cristina of Wessex, Queen Margaret's younger sister

Colbán of Moray, captain of the king's guard

Nechtan, the king's steward in Dunfermline

Gormal, the king's steward at Ballingry and Nechtan's brother
Bishop Fothad, Bishop of St. Andrews, a Culdee
Caerell, Culdee monk in St. Andrews
Paul and Erlend Thorfinnsson, Jarls of Orkney and Malcolm's stepsons
Ivar Kalison, a Northman from Norway
Duncan, Malcolm's young son by his first wife, Ingebiorg
Deidre, handmaiden to Catrìona
Cillyn ap Cynfyn, Rhodri's uncle

Wretched and sorrowful, bereft of my homeland,
Far from my home, far from my noble kinsmen,
I long ago hid my lord in the darkness of the earth,
And, laden with cares and weary, crossed the waves,
Sought a giver of treasure, far or near
Where I might find one in the mead hall who knew my people,
Who would foster a friendless warrior, and treat me to joys.
He who has tried it knows how cruel a companion is sorrow
For one who has few beloved friends;
The path of exile holds him, not wrought gold,
A freezing heart, not the bounty of the earth.
He remembers warriors, the hall, the giving of treasure,
How, as a youth, his lord honored him at feasts,
All joy has perished!

From the Anglo-Saxon poem *The Wanderer*

PROLOGUE

The Vale of Leven, Strathclyde, Scotland 1071

Catrìona stepped to the edge of the crag perched high above the vale. Wind whipped her auburn hair and umber cloak behind her as she raised her gauntlet and let the falcon fly free.

Spreading his long wings, Kessog soared into the air over the blue waters of Loch Lomond.

Her heart soared with him.

This land of tall peaks and deep lochs was her home. Gray clouds might hover over the tops of the mountains, but bright yellow wildflowers graced the steep slopes and the foothills were clothed in the green velvet of spring.

In the distance, the falcon shrieked as he arrowed toward the loch's crystalline waters, then flew in tight circles over a flock of teals, seeking his prey. The clouds parted and a golden shaft of sunlight reflected off the ducks' wings and shimmered in the waters of the loch.

Thoughts of her future filled her mind and her excitement rose in anticipation of the arrival of her intended, Domnall mac Murchada. This very day he would come by ship from his family's lands in Leinster to meet with her father and seal their betrothal. Domnall's home in Ireland was a place she had heard much about, but had never seen.

In her mind Domnall appeared a most handsome man, except for his nose, which was thin with a high ridge. His wavy light brown hair was always neatly combed and his darker beard invariably neatly trimmed. His eyes were pale blue. But it was not his appearance that had made her father choose Domnall. It was his noble Irish lineage and the trade between Leinster and the Vale of Leven.

During Domnall's visits, she had been keenly aware of his pale blue gaze following her. In his eyes, she had glimpsed desire, flattered he wanted her and not just the trade with her father. Her cheeks flushed to think that one day she would bear his children.

In the distance, Kessog streaked toward a duck, but missed his strike.

Catriona watched the falcon for a while until a sharp gust of wind made her shiver. She had a sudden urge to return to her father's hillfort.

Whistling Kessog back to her uplifted hand, she fed him a bit of meat from the small leather pouch secured at her waist.

Not far away, Angus, her faithful guard, waited patiently next to the horses. His craggy face broke into a smile. " 'Tis best we go back, milady. Yer mother will be wantin' to see ye about the final packin' fer yer journey."

"Mother did not want me to fly Kessog today," she said with a smile, "but I had to, just one more time." She set the falcon on his perch affixed to the pommel of her saddle. Fastening the velvet hood over his head, she stroked his breast feathers and secured his jesses.

Angus helped her to mount and as she turned her pony toward home, her heart warmed as she thought of her trip east to visit her cousin in Atholl. This time she would have Domnall's escort for the journey.

The garrons she and Angus rode over the mountain pass were sure-footed ponies and easily found their way over the rock-strewn path.

As they approached the last ridge where they would begin their descent to the River Clyde, instead of the quiet she expected, men's shouts, cries of terror and women's screams rent the air.

Urging her pony forward, she reached the crest and slid her feet to the ground. Wide-eyed, she stared into chaos fifty feet below where two longships with dragonheads carved into their stems were belching forth silver-helmed warriors wielding axes, swords and spears.

Northmen.

The longhaired raiders shouted what sounded like battle cries as they ran across the sand toward her father's hillfort, ruthlessly cutting down her father's men as if butchering cattle.

Men moaned as they fell, pierced through with spears and swords, grunting their last as blood spurted from their bellies.

Unarmed servants shrieked as axes sank into their backs.

Panicked women ran in all directions, shouting for their children.

Catriona's heart raced and her mouth gaped as she watched the unfolding terror. She gripped the seax at her waist. "*A Dhia m'anam!*" God preserve us! "I must go to them!"

Angus pulled her back from the crest. "Keep away from the edge lest they see ye. The bushes provide scant cover." Grabbing up the reins of the horses, he led them away from the ridge.

"But—" She looked toward the crest, unable to see but desperate to know if her father's men prevailed. "I want to help…"

"Ye can do nothing fer them, milady," Angus said in a low voice as he returned to her. "Stay down. We can only await the end of it."

Fear of the brutal Northmen warred with the desire to help those she loved. Rising panic nearly overtook her as she remembered what she had heard of Norse raids. But what help could she offer? In the face of so many bloodthirsty warriors, she would only become another victim. Angus, sworn to protect her, might die trying to prevent her death.

With the sounds of the mayhem ringing loud in her ears, Catriona dropped to the ground and crawled on her belly to the edge of the rise, pulling her hood over her flame-colored hair to blend with the shrubs.

Angus came to join her, lying on his stomach in the grass. "Are ye certain ye want to see this?"

She peered down at the scene below, not wanting to witness the bloody fighting, yet unable to turn away. "Somewhere down there is my family." Tears streamed down her face as the women's screams pierced her like knives through her heart. "I cannot look away."

Huge Northmen grabbed screaming women and dragged them over the sand and pebble-strewn beach to one of the longships.

Men fought and continued to fall. Some of the fallen were Norse but most were her father's men. Bowing her head, she prayed God would give the men of the vale the strength to defeat this horde from Hell.

Raising her head, she winced as a Norse raider swung his axe, severing a man's head. It flew through the air to land on the ground while the man's body dropped where he had stood. Sickened by the sight, her gorge rose in her throat, choking her. She closed her eyes tightly against the sight of it. The man was father to one of her friends. Only that morning he had wished her and Angus good hunting.

Forcing her gaze back to the unfolding horror, she searched for her father, her mother and younger brother, but did not see them. Niall had gone hunting that morning, his bow and arrows slung over his shoulder. She prayed he had not yet returned.

Suddenly, a tall giant, covered in the blood of those he had slain, shouted orders as he cut a path through her father's men guarding the palisade gate. His greater height and long black hair contrasted sharply with the other Northmen.

He must be their leader.

Her father, strong and robust, his fiery hair so like her own, suddenly appeared at the gate with sword raised.

Catrìona cringed in fear for him and her mother who she knew must be in the hillfort behind him. Cormac, Mormaer of the Vale of Leven, would give his life for his family.

Lord, protect them.

Closing her eyes, she sobbed. She could not watch. *Not this.*

Angus laid his arm across her shoulder. "I would go to his aid, milady, but yer father swore me to stay by yer side and I will nae leave ye. Either Cormac will prevail or God will take him."

The shouts and screams died away and she opened her eyes, her gaze darting to where her father had stood. He lay on the ground in front of the gate, blood dripping from a gash in his tunic. *Nay!* He could not die, not her powerful father.

Mother... where was her mother?

Tears filled her eyes and coursed down her cheeks. She wiped them away and surveyed the scene below.

The fighting was nearly over.

The ground in front of the hillfort was littered with bodies from the palisade fence to the river's edge.

The Norse raiders, splattered with the blood of those they had slain, retrieved their dead and wounded and carried them to the longships. At the top of one mast flew a banner, a black raven on a field of yellow. Stirred by the wind, the raven appeared to fly. The eerie sight made her shudder.

Having struck and killed, the invaders now descended like a flock of vultures to pick clean the corpses, gathering prized swords and treasures accumulated over a lifetime, hauling them to the longships.

The sound of women sobbing drew her attention to one of the ships where a small group of women huddled together at the base of the mast. A harsh command from one of the Northmen cut short their wailing. A crimson gown worn by one of the women caught her eye. It was one of Catrìona's own gowns she had given her handmaiden, Deidre, that morning to wear to the festivities planned for that evening.

Oh, Deidre.

A terrified bellow sounded from a cow as one of the Northmen prodded the animal up a boarding plank onto the ship. Another raider followed, leading her father's stallion.

Suddenly, a Northman appeared with a blazing torch. Holding it high, he strode toward her father's ship, climbed aboard and set the flaming brand to the furled sail. It burst into flame.

My father's ship! Catrìona sobbed, watching in horror as the hemp and sailcloth burned, sending great billows of smoke into the air.

Once the oars and the hull caught fire, the Northman jumped to the sand and carried the torch to the palisade fence. Another of his band joined him to splash what looked like pitch onto the timbered posts. Lit by the torch, the wood began to burn.

The two Northmen walked to the palisade gate, stepped over her father and headed toward the hillfort, their terrible task not yet done.

"Nay!" she whispered hoarsely. "My home."

"Best ye not look," said Angus, his dark eyes filled with torment.

"I will look," she said, determination turning her voice hard. "I want to remember their leader, their ships and their banner." The terrible events of this day would be seared in her memory forever.

A short while later the Northmen climbed aboard their ships, rowed out to the middle of the river and raised their sails. The wind filled the square canvases, carrying the ships toward the Firth of Clyde and the open sea beyond.

The determination Catrìona had felt only moments before drained from her, leaving in its place the shock of what she had witnessed. Her eyes burned from the tears she had shed.

She cast a defeated glance at Angus who seemed to have aged since they had arrived at the crest, the creases in his face etched deeper than before, making him look older than his thirty summers. He had no wife or children to lose, but he had served her father for ten years and could count many friends among the fallen.

With a deep sigh, Angus got to his feet and helped her to rise before walking toward the horses.

Mindlessly, Catrìona brushed dirt from her cloak. "To where do those heathen dogs sail?"

"I canna say fer sure, milady, but I would guess the Orkneys from the raven banner. They claim it assures them victory. They were young, mayhap an errant band out fer mayhem and plunder."

She trudged to her horse and Angus helped her to mount. Steeling herself for what lay ahead, she said, "We must hope some of our people yet live."

What they found when they reached the bottom of the hill confirmed what they had seen from the crest, only now they could smell the stench of bodies ripped asunder. Covering her nose, she stood staring out at the field of dead.

Slowly she walked forward, stepping around bodies strewn upon the blood-soaked ground, listening for a groan or a sound that would tell her some still lived. She avoided looking at their faces, for she would know them and that would be worse. But she scanned the dead for auburn hair like her own and sighed with relief when she did not find Niall.

She went next to her father where he lay in front of the palisade, knowing by the blood covering his chest and the vacant look in his eyes he was dead.

Catrìona wanted to scream but no sound came from her throat. Her heart sank with her knees as she dropped to his side. She kissed his forehead and closed his eyes, paying her last respects to the father she loved. No one else called her "little cat". In her mind she heard his voice as he told her the stories of Ireland from long ago.

She stood. Inside, she felt numb and hollow. Her eyes burned from crying and the still rising smoke.

"I will see to him," said Angus coming alongside her.

She looked back at the bodies. "There are so many…"

"Aye, but Domnall's men will help bury them when he arrives."

Nodding, she stumbled forward to the gate. The palisade's timbers still burned but the flames had not yet reached this point. The acrid smell of smoke filled her nostrils and stung her eyes, but she forced herself to keep going. She had to find her mother.

As she stepped through the gate, she spotted her lying on the ground in front of the hillfort, a knife not far from her open hand. Her skirts were crumpled to her waist, her bare legs outstretched. Her dark hair was loose and tangled. Her throat had been slit.

Oh, Mother.

Refusing to give in to tears, Catrìona pulled her mother's gown down to her ankles, covering her shame, and kissed her forehead before rising. Retrieving her mother's knife, she saw the blade was still clean. Now it was Catrìona's. Securing it in her belt, she vowed, if given the chance, to draw Norse blood with it.

Wrapping her arms tightly about her waist, Catrìona held in the emotions threatening to overwhelm her, the sorrow, the despair and the anger for all that had been done here. In one morning she had lost her parents, her home and her people.

Stumbling back through the palisade gate, she searched for Angus, wanting to be assured he was close.

Movement drew her eyes to the edge of the trees next to the palisade. A figure ran toward her, bow and arrows slung over his shoulder, his bright auburn hair flying out behind him.

"Niall!" She broke into a run. When she reached him, they embraced. She clung to him as tears she could not hold back poured from her eyes. "Thank God you were not here."

He pulled back to face her. "Who did this, Cat?"

"Northmen." She looked around but saw none of the dead raiders. "They took their wounded and their dead. Oh, Niall, 'twas ghastly. Angus and I had just reached the crest when we realized the hillfort was under attack. I can still hear the screams of the women."

"Father? Mother?" His voice faltered as he looked toward the bodies scattered upon the grass between the river and the palisade.

"Dead with the others. Father fought bravely, as did his men, but they were greatly outnumbered." When the rush of words ended, she paused, then added, "All the men were killed." Remembering the small bodies scattered among the others, she said, "Even the children. The only ones taken were some of the women. The young ones."

"Deidre?"

"Aye, taken with the other women." Her pretty handmaiden had lived sixteen summers, older than Niall by only a year. The two had grown up together as friends. Catrìona could still see Deidre's smiling face when they had talked of their coming journey to Atholl.

Niall clenched his jaw and shut his eyes as if to gain control. When he opened them, his face was set in stone, much like her heart.

Angus approached, wiping soot from his forehead with the back of his hand. " 'Tis glad I am to see ye're safe, Niall."

Her brother's face twisted in anger as he clenched his fingers around his bow. "I wish I had been here to fight the whoresons."

"Cormac would not have wanted that. He would want ye to live to protect yer sister and one day father yer own sons." He turned to Catrìona. "None who lay on the grass are alive, milady. I have moved yer mother away from the burning hillfort to lie next to yer father, just there." He pointed to a patch of grass some distance away where two bodies lay apart from the others. Angus had covered their faces. "The wind will feed the fire," he said. "Soon 'twill all be consumed."

The pungent smell of burning wood filled the air. Dark smoke rose into the air from the palisade. The taste was bitter on her tongue.

Glancing at the bodies of their parents, Niall said to Angus, "I will help you bury them." To Catrìona, her brother seemed older than his years.

Some time later, she and Niall stood over the two graves that he and Angus had dug, as Niall spoke the words from the Psalter they had learned as children. Catrìona barely heard them. She was consumed with anger and pain and the regret for being unable to help those she loved. Images filled her mind: her father smiling at her as he had wished her a good hunt; her mother reminding her not to be long; and Deidre excited for their journey.

She could not believe they were gone and that she and Niall had been spared. She took a deep breath and closed her eyes as guilt overcame her for remaining unscathed while so many had died horrible deaths.

After the Northmen had killed, they had plundered, even taken her dowry. She had seen them carrying to the longships the chest in which her father kept his gold. They had taken the weapons of the fallen, her mother's goblets of silver and Catriona's new gowns, leaving nothing of value.

Soon her home would be reduced to a mound of ashes, a black scar on the land.

Turning her back on the sight, she went to sit on a rock near the river. Niall joined her, putting his arm around her. She leaned against his chest, drawing comfort from his male strength. He understood her as few did and now he was all she had left.

After a short while, Niall rose. "I must help Angus in digging more graves."

By the time Domnall arrived late that afternoon, the fire had died to smoking embers but there were still bodies to be buried. She raised her hand to shield her eyes from the sun as she watched him sail into the small bay, his ship like her father's, a trading ship with plain stems.

His men jumped out to pull the ship onto the shore and once the plank was set in place, Domnall strode down to the sand. She walked forward to meet him. He had come richly attired for his meeting with her father, a meeting that would never occur.

Domnall looked first into her eyes and then behind her to the ruins of the hillfort. A deep crease formed between his brows. "My God, Catriona, what happened here?"

"We were attacked by Northmen." She yearned for him to hold her, to comfort her, but instead, he took her hand and led her toward the charred remains of her home, a sight she had no desire to see again.

"How did you—?"

"Angus and I were hunting with Kessog and Niall was in the forest or we would have died with the others." She did not add that she might have been taken with Deidre.

"Cormac?"

"Dead with my mother." She looked toward the new graves. "All the men were killed and the women, too, save for the young ones they took as captives."

Niall and Angus came to join them. The guard was the first to speak. "Milord."

"Angus, Niall," Domnall said shortly in acknowledgement to the two men.

"There's naught to be done now," said Angus, "save to bury the rest of the dead. We could use the help of yer men."

As if waking from a trance, Domnall blinked. "Certainly." He gestured his men to draw close and ordered them to help.

It was not the joyous meeting she had envisioned. Not a betrothal to be celebrated. But at least Domnall was here and alive. And he still held her hand.

CHAPTER 1

Dunkeld in Atholl, a year later

Catrìona approached Kessog's perch just as Fia stepped into the dim light of the mews, lifting her skirts to avoid the feathers strewn about the earthen floor.

"Make haste, Cat," her cousin urged. "The cart is loaded and Father is anxious to depart."

Catrìona hurriedly untied the falcon's jesses. "I just have to retrieve Kessog. I'd not leave him behind."

Fia brushed a feather from her gown and ran her fingers over her long dark plaits threaded with ribands the same color as her deep blue eyes. "I do wonder if Margaret's ladies have time for falconry, Cat. 'Tis said they spend more time in prayer than aught else."

Catrìona heaved a sigh of resignation and set the hooded falcon on her gauntlet, stroking his breast feathers with the back of her finger. She had prayed little this past year, but since her uncle had accepted the invitation for her and Fia to join the ladies attending the devout queen, she would go.

In the last few months, except for flying Kessog, she and Fia had dedicated themselves to the sewing of gowns and practicing the Saxon tongue. They had been told the queen spoke Saxon and Latin, but only a little Gaelic.

"I could not pray all day in a damp dusty chapel, Fia. Besides, I want to fly Kessog as much as I can before his molt begins."

With a sympathetic smile, her cousin said, "If the hawk will make you feel more at home in Dunfermline, do bring him. When you and I are praying with the queen, the king's falconer and Niall can see to the bird."

Catrìona considered Fia's words. Mayhap it was for the best that Niall took charge of Kessog if the queen kept her ladies busy with duties all day. The king would have a master falconer, but she would feel more comfortable if Niall checked on the falcon. "Kessog is trained to my brother's hand as well as mine."

At her urging, Niall had come with her to Dunkeld. There was nothing for him in the vale save scorched earth and sorrow. They had mourned together in the months that had followed, taking long walks in silence when they could not bear the company of others. In recent days, the terrible dreams she had at first experienced had diminished, but they had not disappeared altogether. Even now, she had to force the calm demeanor she displayed. Inside, she harbored a gnawing ache for the loss of her parents and friends and worry over the fate of the young women taken captive. What kind of a life must Deidre be living?

But today, Catrìona set those worries aside, determined to allow Fia's enthusiasm for their new lives to carry her along.

She followed Fia out of the mews into the bright sunlight where Uncle Matad and his men waited with the horses in a field of bluebell flowers. The guards in her uncle's service were men-at-arms who wore knives and swords of various sizes. Angus carried a seax and a longer sword, Niall his bow and arrows.

Placing Kessog on his perch in front of her saddle, she accepted Angus' help to mount.

She had bid the faithful guard to go more than once in the last year, but he had refused to leave her.

"I made a solemn oath to yer father," he had told her. "I will nae leave ye, not until ye be wed and another becomes yer protector."

Accepting his decision, she had finally let him stay. In truth, she was glad for his presence. Along with Niall, Angus was the last tie to her past and the vale.

Fia rode across from her on a handsome gray palfrey. Excitement sparkled in her eyes. "Just think, Cat. By day's end we will be in

Dunfermline dining with the queen!"

"So we shall." Catrìona had never met Margaret, the Saxon princess who was now Queen of Scots, but her uncle Matad had told her about the beautiful pious woman who held the king's heart in her hand. While Catrìona knew little of the queen, she had heard many things about Malcolm Canmore. A ruthless warrior, he had seized the throne a dozen years ago by killing the former king and his heir. She could not imagine such a man married to the pious Margaret.

As they rode south toward Dunfermline, Catrìona's thoughts turned to Domnall. On the journey from the vale to Dunkeld a year earlier, she had been an empty shell with naught but tears to offer him. He had been kind but distant, respectful of her loss, asking little of her.

They had arrived in Dunkeld and conveyed the horrible news to her uncle, her mother's brother. Matad, a widower who had not remarried since losing his wife, was protective of both his daughter and his niece, now the only women in his life. And for Catrìona and Niall, he and Fia were their only family.

Consumed with grief for his sister's murder, Matad had said nothing of the betrothal to Domnall. Catrìona saw the wisdom in waiting. One could hardly have a celebration in the midst of so much sorrow.

They had all needed time to grieve.

Domnall had lingered in Atholl only a few days that first time. He and her uncle had spoken together often but always out of Catrìona's hearing. It was only after Domnall left for Dunfermline that her uncle told her he was postponing any discussion concerning the marriage contract.

Forlorn, she had merely nodded her acceptance.

In the last year, Domnall had been to see her twice. He had been polite and deferential each time, expressing his understanding of her sorrow. Now that the year was over, she looked forward to being with him at King Malcolm's court. Finally, their life together could begin.

*   *   *

Dunfermline

Sunlight fell on the bluebell flowers lying on either side of the path Steinar took through the woods. Eager to be about his errand, his long strides ate up the ground, his soft leather boots making no sound. The years he had spent as a warrior in England had taught him to tread lightly.

His right leg ached with the dampness in the air. The wound he'd received from a Norman sword left him with a limp and stiffness in the leg when he sat for too long. Still, it was better than the alternative. For a time, they had not expected him to live. Even with the ministrations of his sister, Serena, recovery had been slow. When he and Rhodri had left England, the bones were still knitting together, the withered muscles that had been pierced through still weak. For a long time, he could not walk without assistance. And after, he had limped badly even with a walking stick.

Fortunately, when he arrived in Scotland, King Malcolm had been in need of a scribe. Educated to one day succeed his father as thegn, Steinar filled the role of a clerk well, his duties requiring him only to sit on a bench and labor with parchment and quill.

When Malcolm raided Northumbria, he had not asked his crippled English scribe to accompany him. But now, his leg grew stronger and the limp was fading. As long as Steinar rested the leg, he could use it with ease. One day he hoped to be more than a scribe.

Rhodri teased him about his unsteady gait, saying he wobbled like a cart on a rutted road. Steinar took it in stride, knowing his friend would have said nothing were it not for the miraculous way the leg had recovered.

Whenever he could escape his duties, Steinar belted on his sword he kept hidden in his horse's stall and took to the forest to spar with imagined foes. Sometimes his opponents were remembered Norman knights, clad in mail and helm, sometimes he sparred with Theodric, the captain of Talisand's guard, who now served the Norman who had claimed Talisand as well as Serena.

Each time Steinar wielded his sword, his arm gained strength and his movements became more agile. Now his sword arm was nearly as sure as it had been that day near Stamford Bridge when he fought with King Harold's army turning away the Norse king, Harald Hardrada. And as sure as that day on Senlac Hill, not long after, when he'd survived the onslaught of the Conqueror's knights only to watch his father and the

Saxon King Harold fall. Steinar's escape north with some of King Harold's elite guards, the huscarls, had been all that stood between him and death that day.

His last battle had been in York with Edgar the Ætheling, rightful heir to the English throne. Steinar well remembered the vicious fighting, for it was there he had received the wound that all believed had left him a cripple.

Once he arrived in the clearing, he set about his practice in earnest.

In one smooth arc, he slashed his steel blade through the air, the flash of sunlight on metal sending a surge of strength coursing through him. He could feel the power return to his arm that for so long had lifted only a quill as his ink-stained fingers attested. Soon he would wield a sword as well as his sister, Serena, wielded her bow. If only his leg would perform as it once had, he would be whole.

In his mind he fought the Norman knights on Senlac Hill, deflecting their blows and ripping through flesh. Swinging his sword wide, he saw his father fall. The remembered shock caused his right leg to crumple and he stumbled. Muttering an oath, he wobbled to one side of the path to lean against a tree, wiping the sweat from his brow, his chest heaving from exertion.

He hissed a curse. Had he fought a real enemy, he would be dead. The leg was not yet at full strength and mayhap not his mind either. He vowed one day 'twould be so. He would yet be the warrior he once was.

"It seems you have been keeping secrets from me. I should have known that muscle you have been adding to your arms did not come from tossing about a quill."

The deep voice was Rhodri's and with his words, Steinar relaxed and looked around for his friend. Dressed in hosen, tunic and leather jerkin in the colors of the forest, Rhodri blended in with the foliage so as to be near invisible where he stood against a tree, his arms crossed over his chest. The bard was slight of build but strong with a bowman's muscled arms and a head of black curls and deep-set brown eyes.

"Do you battle your demons, Steinar?"

"Some. But I also spar with teachers who once sharpened my skills. As you can see, I am not yet there. The leg fails me often."

"But you will be strong again. You were once the best swordsman at Talisand, or so Theodric claimed." Leaving the tree, Rhodri came closer. "When you are recovered, what then?"

Steinar slid his sword into its scabbard and limped to his friend, his leg telling him he had pushed it too hard. "When that day arrives, we will see. For now I remain the king's scribe. Malcolm seems content with my service."

"Aye, he is. But you came here to prove something and I'm thinking 'twas not just that you can again wield a sword."

"You may be right," he admitted, looking down at the forest floor covered in the green grass of spring. Lifting his head to face his friend's expectant gaze, he added, "I would test my resolve to fight the Bastard Norman again. After all, Malcolm has faced William's knights more than once and come away the victor. But for now I remain a scribe."

Rhodri gave him an assessing glance. "You can be more than one thing," he said, adding in an amused tone, "I am."

Steinar grinned. " 'Tis why the king has his bard training his archers."

"I do not mind. Like you, I need the practice."

Together, they slowly walked back to Malcolm's tower where they shared a chamber, the limping English scribe and the Welsh bard, each harboring a secret.

*　　*　　*

To Catrìona's relief, the ride to Dunfermline had not been as long as the journey to Dunkeld the year before, nor so sad. It was oddly comforting to leave behind her past and set forth on a new adventure, one that would lead to her future with Domnall. With every mile she traveled, her spirits had risen knowing she would see him that evening.

Midday they had stopped at the River Earn to water the horses and eat a hasty meal of bannocks, cheese and berries before resuming the journey south. There were eight of them with Angus, Niall and her uncle's three guards.

Their small company arrived in Dunfermline at day's end, passing tall stands of trees to cross a stream, before riding up a long path to a rocky plateau where they dismounted. Facing her was a massive square tower made of hewn stone blocks. Catrìona tilted her head back to take in its height, so much greater than either her father's hillfort or her uncle's home in Atholl. The tall tower, the like of which she had never seen, seemed a fitting fortress for the king, impregnable in its appearance. And it would be her new home, at least until she and Domnall were wed.

Two men flanked the large carved wooden door that led into the tower, their gazes fixed on the new arrivals. From their muscled bodies, sheathed swords and proud stance, she judged them to be guards.

Suddenly, the large oaken door opened and the king and queen stepped outside.

Catrìona would have known Malcolm, King of Scots, even if he had not been wearing a gold crown and royal attire. Tall of stature and noble of bearing, his dark hair fell to his broad shoulders and he wore a well-trimmed mustache and beard. His eyes exuded power and intelligence as his gaze roved over the small group standing with the Mormaer of Atholl. For all his elegance, the king's hardened face told her he was a warrior still.

The king smiled widely and strolled up to Matad greeting him and her brother, as men are wont to do, leaving his queen to deal with the women. It was the same way her father had treated men of rank and their wives visiting the vale. Malcolm and her uncle easily conversed, making it apparent to Catrìona they were good friends.

The queen walked towards Catrìona and Fia, her movements graceful. As fair as her husband was dark, Margaret was serenely beautiful in a gown of yellow silk, finely embroidered with blue flowers at the neck and wrists. She appeared delicate and slight of form despite that her slightly rounded belly suggested she was with child. Her long flaxen plaits hung below her headcloth encircled with a delicate, gold crown. The blue ribands wrapped around her plaits matched her sky-colored eyes.

Margaret quickly put Catrìona at ease with her warm smile. "Welcome to Dunfermline," she said in Gaelic. Then looking from Catrìona to Fia, she said, "I understand you two are to be my new ladies and I am told you both speak the Saxon tongue."

Catrìona and Fia curtsied. "My Lady," they said in unison with downcast eyes, Catrìona adding in the Saxon tongue, "Aye, we speak both languages as well as Latin."

"That is most agreeable," said the queen. "I know you must be tired. Your chamber has been made ready to allow you to change ere we dine. The servants will escort you there and see your chests are brought to you."

Taking her leave, the queen joined her husband and Matad. As Catrìona watched her walk away, she could not help but wonder if beneath the delicate exterior the queen possessed an inward strength. Else how could she deal with a hardened warrior like Malcolm?

Fia started to follow a servant who beckoned them toward the tower.

Catrìona stopped her with an outstretched arm. "I must see Kessog settled."

"While you see to your falcon, I will see to our chamber. I am anxious to know where we will be lodged." Excitement once again danced in Fia's eyes as she hurried to follow the servant. Catrìona was happy for her cousin. It had been Fia's dream to be one of the queen's ladies; she had talked of little else.

Disappointed that Domnall had not been there to meet her, Catrìona waited for Niall who was coming toward her. "Want to come with me to see the mews?"

Niall nodded and walked with her to her horse where she lifted Kessog from his perch.

"The king's house is large," he remarked, looking back at the tower.

"Aye, 'tis the royal seat."

In response to her inquiry, a servant pointed them in the direction of the mews, which lay just beyond the stables. The wooden building that housed the king's hawks was twice the size of the mews maintained by her uncle, but then a king would have a large house for his many birds.

Stepping over the threshold of the dimly lit structure, she glimpsed rows of perches on which were settled many hooded birds.

A smoothed-faced young man with a prominent nose and kind eyes introduced himself.

"Welcome. I am Machar, the king's falconer."

"I am Catrìona, one of the queen's new ladies, and this is my brother, Niall."

She extended her gauntleted hand, passing the falcon's jesses to Machar. "And this is Kessog."

Machar carefully lifted the falcon to his own gauntlet, murmuring soothing words and calming the bird with practiced strokes. "A fine tiercel," he said, using the term for a male peregrine. "He is most welcome to join the hawks I tend for the king and his chiefs."

Niall and Machar exchanged a few words as Niall told the falconer of their home in the vale where Kessog had been raised and trained, not disclosing the tragedy they had survived a year earlier. They did not often speak of that time except to each other.

Even in the dim light from the single window, Catrìona could see the many perches held a gyrfalcon, several peregrines and various other hawks. "So many falcons," she said in awe. "The king must love to hunt."

"Aye, that he does, from the time he lived in England before he claimed the throne. King Edward was fond of the sport. Some of Malcolm's men also hunt to the hawk." With a smile he added, "You will frequently dine on roast duck."

"Kessog has not flown this day, but I have fed him," she advised the falconer. "We traveled from our uncle's home in Dunkeld."

"I will see to him, my lady," he said confidently. "Mayhap you might like to join me in flying him?" he asked Niall. "The days are long and there is still good light."

"Tomorrow, aye. But tonight we are expected at the king's table."

"Are many of the hawks you tend owned by ladies?" Catrìona interjected, suspecting the answer would not be to her liking.

Machar laughed, but sobered when he saw her frown. "There are not many ladies that care to risk their skirts and their lives up on yon crags, scrambling to catch themselves a chick to train. Owned, no. The ladies of a few visiting nobles can fly birds, but when they're here, they fly the king's hawks."

Catrìona remembered well the lengths to which she had gone to catch and then train Kessog. Winning his trust had taken time, getting him accustomed to her voice, her touch. Feeding him was a constant task, made easier by her father's falconer, as Kessog was trained to hunt for sport and did not eat his kill.

At her look of disappointment, Machar explained, "The ladies here-abouts—that is, the queen and her ladies—busy themselves mostly with prayer and needlework. They might wave at the men riding out to hunt, but they do not ride with them."

Niall shot her a glance, amusement dancing in his eyes.

"Well then," she said, "mayhap 'twill be my brother who will fly Kessog most often in the time remaining before his summer molt."

Catrìona felt better for leaving her falcon in the care of another, knowing Machar and Niall would keep Kessog happy when she could not attend him.

With a nod toward her brother, she left them to seek out her cousin. Her uncle had told her that she and Fia would likely share a small chamber in the tower, as did the queen's other ladies.

She entered the tower and stopped to admire the great hall. Two long trestle tables flanked a central hearth. At the head of the two tables was another table set upon a dais. *The king's table.* All the seats were benches save two high-backed chairs on the dais where she imagined the king and queen would sit tonight.

A servant, observing her looking around the hall, told her the ladies' chambers were on the second floor as were the chambers of the king and queen and offered to show her the one assigned to her and Fia.

Catrìona climbed the stairs behind the servant, who stopped on the second story where a long corridor with a window at the end contained many doors. When she asked, the servant told her the corridor wrapped around the square tower.

The servant stopped in front of one chamber midway down the corridor and gestured to the door. Catrìona thanked her and entered to find Fia bent over her chest, digging through garments.

Lifting one of her gowns, Fia looked over her shoulder to where Catrìona stood appraising the room. "They brought your chest," Fia said, pointing to the end of the other bed. "There are pegs for our cloaks, too."

The chamber was sparsely appointed but more than adequate to Catrìona's mind. Two narrow beds took up most of the space. Atop them were well-stuffed bed cushions lain with blue woolen covers. The only other furniture was a small table between the beds, a brazier for warmth, a side table and a stool. Catrìona walked to the one window. Its shutters open, she looked down on the burn that flowed around the king's tower on three sides like a moat.

" 'Tis not as large as your bedchamber in Atholl," she said, "but will serve us well."

"Aye," Fia agreed. " 'Tis clean and at least we are alone."

Catrìona sat upon the bed that would be hers, the one closest to the window. " 'Tis comfortable."

"Mine, as well. Oh, a servant brought us water to wash." Fia pointed to a pitcher and a bowl sitting on the side table.

"I passed quite a few servants speaking English to each other on my way here," Catrìona remarked. "I wonder why there are so many."

"Some English fled the Normans," said Fia, "and thankfully, the ones I spoke with can speak a bit of Gaelic as well as the Saxon tongue."

Feeling quite gritty from the day's ride, Catrìona walked to the side table and proceeded to wash the dust from her face. "I would love a bath but I suppose 'twill have to wait."

Fia refolded her gowns into the chest. "With so many lodged in the king's tower, even with a great number of servants it must be difficult to provide baths for all."

"Mayhap there is a stream that affords privacy." Catrìona spoke her thought aloud. The water would be cold but at least she would be clean.

"With so many men around, only you would think of bathing in a stream."

Catrìona opened her chest, mumbling to herself about preferring to be clean even if she had to wash in the woods surrounded by men.

Soon they were both somewhat refreshed and had helped each other to don proper gowns.

"We do not really need a servant to help us dress," observed Catrìona, "and I doubt one will be provided. Here, I will help you do your plaits and you can help me with mine."

By the time they arrived in the hall, the cavernous room was filling with those attending the evening meal. Torches set in sconces, a fire in the stone hearth and candles provided ample light.

Catrìona and Fia stood to one side watching those assembled. Boisterous conversations erupted in laughter, some in Gaelic but others in the Saxon tongue. Most of those in attendance were men but some women mingled among them, which was a comfort to Catrìona. Spotting the queen surrounded by several other women, Catrìona tugged on Fia's sleeve.

" 'Tis the queen and her ladies. Let us join them."

They launched forth, passing clusters of men and drawing interested stares. Catrìona attributed their curious gazes to the fact she and Fia were new. Or, it could be her bright auburn hair. Her father had once told her, "Anyone would know you are mine by that thick head of dark red hair, little cat." She felt, but did not return, the men's stares as she guided Fia through the throng to where the queen stood.

Margaret had changed into another beautiful gown, this one azure silk embroidered in golden thread at the neck and sleeves. Seeing Catrìona approach, the queen raised her head to greet them. "My new ladies... did you find all you needed in your chamber?"

"Yea," said Catrìona, "and we thank you, My Lady, for your kindness."

Margaret gestured toward the women standing with her. "These are your fellow ladies. I will allow them to introduce themselves."

First came Audra with light brown hair and hazel eyes. "I am the daughter of Duff, Mormaer of Fife. I bid you welcome."

The woman's pleasant face and unassuming air contrasted with what Catrìona knew of the Mormaer of Fife, the warrior who led the king's army. Since Dunfermline was in Fife, to make conversation, Catrìona said, "You did not have far to travel."

"Nay, not far," Audra said with a smile.

Next in the circle of women was Davina. "I come from Lothian to the south." Her sweet smile was set in a round face with brown eyes framed by honey-colored hair. By her expression, Catrìona judged her to have a genial nature. "Welcome," was all Davina said.

Mayhap she is shy.

Isobel, darker in both hair and skin than the others, was quick to inform them she had served Margaret since she became queen two years ago. Catrìona thought she heard Isobel say she was from Ross in the north.

Lastly, there was Elspeth. "I am from west of Fife near Loch Tay." To Catrìona's mind, by her giddy demeanor, Elspeth appeared to be the youngest of the ladies, especially after seeing the flirtatious looks she flung at the men with her large brown eyes that were the same color as her hair. *A charming imp.*

"We passed Loch Tay as we traveled to Dunkeld a year ago," said Catrìona. " 'Tis very beautiful." She resisted the urge to say Loch Lomond was far more resplendent. She was very proud of the beauty of the vale.

"Aye, Loch Tay is grand," said Elspeth, stretching out the word "grand".

Catrìona thanked the women for their welcome. She could scarce recall their names, much less which one came from where. *In time I will know them well.*

Fia had told her the queen's ladies were rumored to be pious to a woman, making Catrìona wonder if she would be accepted into their company. Pious was not a word she would have used to describe herself. What little faith she had possessed had been shaken by the attack on the vale and the deaths of her parents.

"We lose ladies from time to time," offered Audra once they were all acquainted.

"Lose them?" Fia repeated, startled.

"Yes. Lose them to their new husbands," she said in a teasing manner, "as one of us is married off by the king. You two replace ones we lost in such a way."

The others laughed but the queen remained quiet, leaving Catrìona curious as to whether Margaret considered herself one of those who had been "married off".

Catrìona was inwardly relieved that her own betrothal was soon to be secured, sparing her from such a fate. She had no desire to be bartered to one of the king's men she did not even know.

When those gathered in the hall began to take their seats, the queen bid Catrìona and Fia to follow her to the dais, explaining as special guests, along with Matad and Niall, they were invited to dine with the king and his family.

The queen introduced them to her younger sister, Cristina, whose fair coloring was like Margaret's, and then seated Catrìona beside Edgar, Margaret's brother, with Fia on Catrìona's other side. Niall took his place beyond Fia, while Matad sat on the king's left with the queen's sister. The queen then joined the king in the place of honor on his right.

Smells of roast game and spiced vegetables filled the air as servants set platters and bowls before them laden with food. Bread, smelling fresh from the oven, was added to the table along with goblets filled with red wine.

Casting an indifferent glance at the trencher she shared with Edgar, Catrìona tried to muster an appetite and found she was more weary than hungry. Voices rose around her but her mind wandered and she did not attend the conversations. She was relieved to see Edgar conversing with his sister, the queen, and Fia occupied with her meal. Niall, on Fia's other side, was staring into the hall.

Catrìona's gaze drifted over the men and women conversing in low voices as they ate. The variety of those in attendance surprised her. Some, who must be the king's warriors, had a rough appearance, their long hair and beards unkempt. Powerfully built with swords dangling from their belts, their arms displayed bulging muscles. Their tunics were in shades of brown, dark blue and green, more suitable to hiding from their enemies than for a king's court.

Other men stood out like brightly plumed birds in fine velvets and woolens of rich colors. Among them she spotted Domnall, her intended, and her heart sped. She tried to catch his eye but was not successful. It was clear he had not changed much in the months since he'd last come to Dunkeld. Always richly attired, tonight he looked the part of the successful trader with a noble lineage. One with like apparel sat next to him: a man of middle years with sun-streaked hair to his broad shoulders. When they had first taken their seats, she had heard the king address him as Maerleswein and wondered if he was a Dane as his name suggested.

Her eyes paused on a servant woman setting dishes before the men. One of the warriors wrapped his arm around the woman's waist and she pulled away. Like many of the servants in the king's hall, this one appeared to be Saxon in both style of tunic and speech when she chided the man. Some of the female servants carried themselves like ladies, making Catrìona wonder where they had come from.

Edgar urged her to eat, gesturing to their shared trencher that he had piled high with meat and vegetables. "You must be hungry after the journey from Dunkeld. 'Tis a far ride and hard on a woman, all day in the saddle."

Catrìona swallowed a defensive reply. He must not be accustomed to women who rode. She mustered her strength and reined in the nagging concerns she harbored about what her uncle had committed her to. Edgar is just being polite, she chided herself. *Tonight I must be agreeable.*

"You are right, of course. I expect the queen will have much for us to do on the morrow."

Edgar burst into laughter, nearly spewing his wine. Wiping his mouth with a cloth, he said, "My sister will have you up to pray while 'tis still dark. Trust me, to keep pace with her, you will need your strength. Best eat while you can."

"You persuade me," she said, smiling at the handsome young man. For the first time, she noticed the golden curls and blue eyes so like the queen's and the way he held his head, as if he wore an invisible crown. She had heard that two years prior, thousands of rebels fought the Normans in York to try and win the throne of England for Edgar. But they had failed.

How disappointed he must be.

With her eating knife, Catrìona speared a small piece of roast boar and brought it to her mouth. The combination of aromas from spices and herbs and the taste of the succulent meat roused her appetite. " 'Tis very good."

"Aye," Edgar said, spearing a piece of meat with his eating knife. "Margaret demands a well-run kitchen. 'Tis what she was used to before we came here."

Turning her goblet in her hand, the light caught the intricate gold and silver pattern on the vessel. "These are silver trimmed in gold. Do you drink from such goblets every evening?"

"Aye. That, too, is Margaret's doing," said Edgar. "She cares little for worldly goods, but she would have the king's house and the chapel adorned in kingly dignity. 'Tis why you see bright colors here in the hall. She has changed even the way the king's subjects dress, well, except for the men-at-arms."

Catrìona's eyes roved over the people eating and talking, noting the bright reds, blues and greens worn by some.

"My sister encourages them to buy the brightly colored cloth from the merchants she beckons to Scotland's shores. 'Tis what she expects in a king's court and she would not have Malcolm appear less than a king."

Catrìona glanced at the subject of Edgar's remarks. Margaret was speaking to her husband, Malcolm's head inclined to his wife's. While their words could not be heard in the noisy hall, she could see Margaret was most attentive to the king. Curious to know more about her new mistress, she asked Edgar to tell her how his family came to Scotland.

Fia leaned in to listen.

Edgar took a sip of his wine, then stared at the goblet as if remembering the deep past. "Margaret was only ten and I younger still when we left Hungary where our father was in exile."

"Why did you return?"

"King Edward summoned Father to England as heir to the throne. But days after we arrived, my father died." Edgar's voice dropped to a whisper. "My mother suspected poison."

Catrìona gasped. "Treachery?"

He nodded. "For years, we lived in England, sheltered by King Edward. But then the king died and Harold Godwinson was named king. He did not reign long. You know, of course, the Normans killed him at Hastings. As the last male in the Wessex line, I was named king. I was fifteen, about the same age as your brother," he said to Catrìona. "Did you know that?"

"I knew you were England's rightful heir," she said without hesitation, "but I did not know you had been named king."

He shrugged. " 'Twas only for a brief time after King Harold's death. The Norman Conqueror lured away my supporters making sure I was never crowned. 'Tis still in my heart to rule England, yet sometimes I am forced to consider it may not be God's will."

"I am sorry for all that has been taken from you," said Catrìona. Ruthless men had robbed him of his father and his home just as they had robbed her. But unlike her, Edgar had lost a kingdom.

"Two years ago we had great hope," he said wistfully. "I fought with the rebels in York and with the Danes' help, we took the city." He glanced around the hall and she and Fia followed his gaze. "Some of the men here tonight fought with me. But when the Danes left and the Conqueror laid waste to York, my family and I fled England and Scotland became our haven." He let out a deep sigh. "Malcolm's bid for my sister's hand changed whatever else might have been."

Anxious to know, she pressed him. "And your sister, Margaret—"

"Did not want to be queen of anything. But I prevailed upon her when Malcolm pressed his suit. She would have preferred the cloistered life, but there was little to be done except to agree to Malcolm's wishes. After all, we had already accepted his protection." His gaze drifted to where the king sat listening intently to Margaret. "It was not a bad decision, I think. He adores her and now she is a queen."

As she reached for her wine, pondering Edgar's words, Catriona had the feeling she was being watched. She turned her head toward the trestle table on the right where a man not fifteen feet away gnawed on a leg of roast fowl while devouring her with his eyes. He had the face of a hawk, eyes alert and his gaze piercing, making her feel like prey. She knew she should look away but she could not tear her eyes from his strong well-defined features, his long golden hair nearly the color of flax, and the hint of a beard lining his square jaw.

At her perusal, his mouth twitched up in an impudent grin.

Her cheeks flamed and she abruptly turned her attention back to her trencher. Beneath her lashes she shot a glance to where Domnall sat, but he was talking to the one called Maerleswein and did not appear to have noticed the exchange.

CHAPTER 2

Steinar shifted his gaze from the trencher he shared with Rhodri to scan the hall when suddenly his attention was arrested by a blaze of auburn hair reflecting the light of the torches.

Who is she?

Reaching for a roast leg of duck, he chewed on the savory meat as he stared at the woman sitting beside the queen's brother on the dais. She was as beautiful as the queen but her features more striking. Redheaded women, he remembered, had a reputation for spirit. *And passion.*

Leaning in to Rhodri, between bites he asked, "Do you know those dining with the king?"

Rhodri turned his eyes to the front of the hall. "The dark-haired man of middle years is Matad of Dunkeld, Atholl's mormaer. He is a powerful relation of the king but mayhap you do not recall his last visit. I was told I would be entertaining him and his party this eve."

Steinar assessed the king's nobleman. "He is just as I would imagine Atholl's mormaer." Of stern countenance, his dark eyes looked out on those in attendance as if suspicious of all. But Steinar was not so interested in the man as the woman sitting next to the queen's brother. "Who is the woman with the red hair sitting next to Edgar?"

"I assume the two females are Atholl's relations," offered Rhodri. "The auburn-haired lad sitting on the other side of the girl with dark hair must be brother to the woman you ask about. They look much alike."

In truth, he had not noticed the youth, but now Steinar looked again, seeing the resemblance. "Aye, 'tis possible."

"The dark-haired young woman," Rhodri murmured, "could be Welsh. Mayhap I will sing my first song for her. 'Tis a Welsh love song."

"You would offer your song to *her* when all the women at Malcolm's court, save the queen and her ladies, willingly fall at your feet? 'Tis a shame to give up what is offered to seek what is not."

"Ah, but that is ever the way of it. A bard's task is to sing of the love that eludes a man. And what of you? Your eyes wander not to the available females in the hall, as is your wont, but alight on only a single, flame-colored flower."

Steinar watched the auburn-haired woman as she spoke to the queen's brother, her face lit with an inner glow. "Not a flower, I think, but a firebrand." Not since he had come to Dunfermline had he encountered a woman who, even at a distance, captured his interest like this one. Nothing could ever come of his interest in one the king's guests, however, for he had naught to offer a woman. No title, no lands and little coin. But watching the redhead in the days ahead would provide a welcome diversion.

"Do not let her fiery hair deceive you," said Rhodri. "If she is to be one of the queen's ladies, she may be as devout as Margaret and the others who serve her, compliant women who will not question to whom they are given. Rich dowries all, but the king will wed them only to men he favors."

Steinar was certain Rhodri was wrong about the redhead being compliant. "After growing up with Serena, I could never desire a woman who lacks spirit."

Rhodri chuckled. "The Lady of Talisand is unique. Your sister was the best of all the archers I trained, though she did not wield a longbow."

"Aye, she did well with that bow you made her." Remembering their happy times together before the Conqueror came, he let out a wistful sigh. "I miss her and our sparring with words. In truth, I would wish for one like her."

"There is little challenge in a woman who never questions, never speaks her opinion. One could fall asleep with all the 'Yea, my lords' one hears from the women at Malcolm's court."

"True, but now that I think on it," Steinar pondered aloud, "the queen is not as meek as she appears. Mayhap we should not be so quick to judge her ladies."

"Aye," said Rhodri, fingering his scant dark beard. "The queen has her say and the king supports her. They have argued a time or two."

Steinar noticed his friend's gaze kept coming back to the companion of the redhead. "You find the dark-haired one to your liking?"

"I like the look of her, yea. Hair the color of a dark night on the Irish Sea and skin like fresh cream. I wager her eyes are as blue as the waters of Llyn Tegid."

"Llyn Tegid?"

"The lake of beauty, 'tis near my home," Rhodri said, a faraway look in his eyes.

"You sound like you are missing the shores of Gwynedd."

Rhodri shrugged, admitting nothing.

"You'd best tread carefully," Steinar cautioned. "If she is related to the Mormaer of Atholl, she'll nae have a bard for a husband."

"Stranger things have happened," Rhodri said with feigned annoyance. "Doubt it not."

Amused, Steinar let his friend have the last word and resumed chewing on the leg of roast duck, his eyes never leaving the woman with the bright auburn hair.

When she looked his way, pausing to consider him, his mouth left the duck to hitch up in a smile.

She had noticed him, too.

Immediately, she looked down at her trencher. A moment later, she lifted her head to gaze about the hall. He wondered what she was seeing. Was she impressed? Had she seen the great room before Margaret's changes, she would have been appalled.

Steinar thought back to when he and Rhodri had first come to Dunfermline. In those days, the tower was mostly the abode of men, the floors of the hall strewn with dirty rushes where the hounds lurked, waiting to grab a fallen bit of meat or a bone cast aside. But once King Malcolm had convinced Margaret of Wessex to become his queen, all had changed.

Now the wooden floors and tables were clean scrubbed, the rushes fresh and herbed and the whitewashed plaster walls were graced with tapestries from the queen's dower chests. Even the hounds were confined by the king's command to one corner when meals were served. Margaret could be a tyrant when it came to appearances.

The presence of the new queen brought many nobles to Dunfermline wanting to pay homage to the Saxon princess who had become the Lady of Scotland. And not all of those who had come to Malcolm's court were Scots. The king's prior marriage to the widow of Thorfinn Sigurdsson, the Jarl of Orkney, had sometimes brought the Norse to Dunfermline. He scanned the hall, but saw none of the Orkneymen. However, he did note the presence of the Irishman with roots in Leinster who had come this past year and stayed.

The blond heads in the hall reminded him many Saxons were now at Malcolm's court, driven north by the Conqueror's ruthlessness. There were so many in Dunfermline, the Scots had to wonder if their country was being overrun. Still, Malcolm could hardly complain when he had dragged many English captives back to Scotland as slaves, plunder from his raids.

Steinar chuckled remembering how the queen had intervened to ransom as many as she could, pilfering the king's treasure to free the English. How Malcolm had railed about that. She had even sent spies throughout Scotland looking for any English slaves who might be mistreated. Those she could not ransom, she cared for and put to work. There was hardly a cottage in Dunfermline that did not have an English servant.

From across the table Maerleswein lifted his hand in greeting. Steinar raised his goblet to the former Sheriff of Lincolnshire, who had shifted alliances with the coming of the Conqueror and now vowed allegiance to Malcolm.

In their conversations over the hearth fire, Maerleswein had confided his regret that his daughter, Emma, had chosen to wed a Norman knight. Deep in his cups, Steinar had told the former sheriff of his sister, Serena's marriage to the Norman called the Red Wolf, but unlike Emma, Serena had been given no choice. As the evening had worn on, the two men realized that Emma was at Talisand, Steinar's home, and her Norman husband was Sir Geoffroi, the Red Wolf's most trusted knight.

Steinar sighed, trying not to wallow in self-pity nor allow his desire for revenge to consume him. He could not look back.

The meal drew to a close as servants set plates of small honeyed cakes before them. More wine was poured and the hall quieted in anticipation as Rhodri reached for his harp.

⋆　⋆　⋆

Sipping wine from her silver goblet, Catrìona's eyes followed the bard as he carried a small harp to the front of the dais.

"Matad," the king addressed her uncle, "do you remember this Welshman?"

Matad nodded.

"His music is wondrous and his tales fascinate," the king continued. "He is also the best of my archers. Mayhap before you return to Atholl, you might test your skill against his bow."

"Your bard is an archer?" Matad asked incredulous.

"Not just any archer," the king said with a grin. "Rhodri is a master of the bow. He *instructs* my archers."

Matad dipped his head in acknowledgement before turning his attention to the bard, who bowed to the king and queen and took his place on a stool.

The bard wore a tunic of dark green over brown hosen, his clothing plain but well fitted. He plucked the strings of his harp and ethereal notes filled the hall. The bard's head of ebony curls cascaded over his face as he bent his head over the instrument, his long fingers working their magic.

"The Welsh bard is well favored, is he not?" Fia whispered into Catrìona's ear.

She turned toward her cousin to see Fia staring at the bard, transfixed. "Aye, I suppose…" He *was* handsome in a boyish way, she silently conceded, his features finely carved. Were it not for his close-cropped beard and slight mustache, she might have thought him pretty.

The enchanting music continued, lilting into the air, instilling a peace in Catrìona's soul still damaged from the events in the vale.

"He first sings in the Welsh tongue," the king said to her uncle, "but then he will change to Gaelic."

As the bard began to sing, a hush came over the hall. His dark eyes alighted on Fia and he fell silent, pausing in his song while his fingers continued to pluck the strings. The bard and Fia locked gazes for a moment before the Welshman dropped his head to focus on his harp.

Catrìona knew bards to be charmers but she would not have believed one could be so bold as to flirt with Fia in front of her father. Catrìona sneaked a glance at her uncle but he did not appear to have noticed what transpired between his daughter and the bard.

A moment later, the Welshman lifted his head and began singing in Gaelic. The song told of a young heir to the throne denied his rightful place and a brave warrior's stance against the Norman Conqueror who had seized lands that were not his. From her father, Catrìona had heard King Malcolm's story, how, from his youth, he had wanted the throne of his father, Duncan. But that throne had been denied him. As she listened, she wondered, did the bard sing of Malcolm or the queen's brother, Edgar?

The song ended and the bard began to tell a story. His deep voice wove a tale of ancient Cymru, land of the mists, where one Rhodri ap Merfyn, called "the great", defeated the pagans who stormed the shores of Gwynedd from their dragon ships in search of plunder. The bard sang of the fierce battle and the Welsh victory that turned the pagans back.

Listening to the bard's story, Catrìona's mind filled with images from that horrible day when the life she had known had been so viciously torn from her. She saw the Northmen storming ashore, her father's lifeless body, the knife just out of reach of her mother's hand and the young women dragged away.

Her heart sped and her brow grew damp. Unconsciously, she closed her eyes, clenching her fists, bidding the terrifying scenes to go away.

Fia must have sensed her distress for she reached out her hand and placed it over Catrìona's, squeezing gently.

Grateful for the comforting gesture, Catrìona smiled her thanks and forced her heart to calm, letting out the breath she had been holding.

The bard's story ended and he stood and bowed to the king and queen, receiving praise from all. Setting his harp on a cushion placed to one side, he returned to his seat beside the blond warrior who had stared at Catrìona earlier. *Mayhap the two are friends.*

Margaret rose and turned to the king. "With your leave, My Lord, my ladies and I will retire and find our beds."

Malcolm took his wife's hand, kissed it and pulled her down to whisper something in her ear. Margaret blushed, pulled her hand back and, without a word, turned to walk gracefully from the dais.

Matad shot a look at Fia and Catrìona, a signal they should depart with the queen. Exhausted after the day's travel, Catrìona was only too happy to comply. She had a feeling that once the queen was gone from the hall, the atmosphere would degenerate to a masculine swagger of ribald jests from too much wine.

Rising from her seat, Catrìona bid Edgar good eve and stepped from the dais, Fia just behind her. She tossed Domnall a look of regret as she passed him and then hurried after the queen, joining the other ladies trailing after Margaret like cygnets after a swan.

She felt Domnall's gaze following her as she and the ladies crossed the hall. When she reached the stairs, Catrìona looked back, seeing many heads turned in their direction. Among the men whose eyes flickered with interest were the blond warrior and the Welsh bard.

★   ★   ★

Domnall's gaze never left Catrìona as she and her cousin followed the queen from the hall, her long auburn plaits hanging below her narrow waist. A fetching woman, but not as attractive to him as she had once been now that she was without her rich dowry and her father's lucrative trade with Leinster.

In his message telling her he would be at Malcolm's court, he had not mentioned that his grandsire, the King of Leinster, had recently died.

There would be more than one man in Ireland who desired to reign in his grandsire's stead and Domnall was one of them.

No longer could he afford to seek the hand of the woman who made him the envy of other men. Now he must marry for wealth and position. But that did not end his lust for the comely redhead. He still wanted Catrìona in his bed.

CHAPTER 3

The door of their bedchamber suddenly opened, jarring Catrìona from sleep.

"Arise! The queen departs!" a raspy voice shouted.

Catrìona heard the command in her mind, instantly aware the harsh voice was not Fia's. Since the attack on the vale, Catrìona slept lightly. A whisper could bring her awake, but the servant who had hissed the command could not know that. "I am awake," Catrìona mumbled, knowing Fia was not, for her cousin slept like a rock.

The door thumped closed. She opened her eyes and sat up in bed. Darkness surrounded her, the only light in the chamber a soft glow from the brazier's banked fire. Edgar's warning had not been an idle threat. They were summoned before first light to pray.

God must be fond of the dark.

She fumbled on the small bedside table to find the candle, knocking it over at her first try. Finding it with her fingers, she righted the small tallow column in its stand. Once she was certain the flame had caught, she turned to see her cousin still asleep.

"Fia! Wake up. Else we will be late for the queen. One of the servants already shouted as much."

Fia groaned and tried to cover her face.

Catrìona pushed herself off the bed and crossed the few feet to her cousin, shaking Fia's shoulder. "Hurry. 'Twill get easier once we are used to the unholy hour." The irony of praying at an "unholy" hour made her smile.

Leaving her cousin, she reached for the water in the bowl on the side table and splashed it onto her face. The cold water brought her alert as the servant's shout had not. She dried her face and lifted the clothes she would wear today from the peg where she had hung them the night before.

Slipping her gown over her linen undertunic, she darted a glance at Fia, who, she was pleased to see, was finally stumbling out of bed.

As quickly as they could, they made themselves presentable, donned their cloaks and descended the stairs to the hall. Torches set in sconces along the walls lighted the large space and a fire blazed in the hearth set in the middle of the cavernous room. The servants were obviously well trained to their mistress' odd habits.

Catriona stifled a yawn as she spotted one of the queen's ladies waiting near the front door, a candle in her hand.

"I am Audra," the woman reminded them. "The queen bid me stay to show you the way to our place of morning prayer."

Catriona was tempted to tell the woman it was not yet morning, but she refrained. She was now in the queen's service and at Margaret's disposal. Moreover, Audra's pleasant manner at so early an hour told her that this one might become a friend. "Thank you," she said.

They passed through the open door, Catriona and Fia following Audra as she hurried along.

"Where are you taking us?" Catriona asked. In the predawn light, she could see little.

"To the new chapel," said Audra. " 'Twas where the king and queen were wed. Margaret had it made larger. Now 'tis a fine place to pray. Some afternoons the queen goes away to a cave to pray alone but in the mornings we attend her here."

"A queen who prays in a cave like a hermit," Catriona mumbled under her breath as she stepped carefully over the rocks and tree roots she felt through her leather shoes.

Fia was having the same trouble making her way and reached for Catriona's hand to steady herself.

Eventually, they came to a small building on the other side of the tower. Inside, Catriona glimpsed the queen on her knees before an altar lit by a single candle. The three other ladies were beside her, their heads bent in prayer.

Audra knelt next to the queen and, not wishing to disturb the queen's prayers with an apology for being late, Catrìona took her place next to Audra. Fia quickly joined her.

The small chapel was silent except for the women's whispers as they prayed, the smell of stone and dirt strong, the stillness nearly tangible. It was not unlike the chapel at her home in the vale, only larger.

Catrìona hesitated. Should she say something to God before beginning the ritual Latin prayers? She had not spoken to Him since the day her parents had been killed. When Angus and Niall had laid them in the ground, she had prayed for their souls. But even then, she had questioned how a God who cared about His children could permit something so horrible to happen. How could He allow pagan savages to rampage unchecked and unpunished?

What kind of God lets innocents suffer while evil triumphs?

When she had asked the priest at Dunkeld, he offered only pious platitudes. "We are visitors here on earth, my child. Heaven is our eternal home. Your parents are in a better place now, with the holy saints and angels." His words brought scant comfort. The Northmen who had murdered her parents and her people still roamed free. The cry for justice burned in her heart like coals stirred to a fierce blaze by her memories.

But now, she served a devout queen, one who apparently lived like a nun when she was not with her husband. Catrìona knew she must find a way to pray. And so she began by reminding God who she was until the absurdity of it gripped her. Of course, He knew who she was. But it was the only way she could think to reestablish some kind of a connection with a God she had dismissed as uncaring.

Unwilling to say the old Latin prayers and unable to find words of her own, she remembered the Psalter.

Domini pascit me... The Lord is my shepherd...

She had only finished the last line, *et ut inhabitem in domo Domini in longitudinem dierum. ...in God's house forevermore my dwelling place shall be,* when she heard the queen rise.

Even in the faint light, Catrìona could see the face of her mistress shining with an inner light and she felt ashamed of the turmoil within her.

The queen's ladies stood as one.

Margaret turned to Catrìona and Fia. " 'Tis your first day among us and so you do not know our practice. We begin each day with prayer. Then we feed the orphans and those in need before breaking our fast."

"Yea, My Lady," Catrìona said, bowing her head, hearing the command in the queen's voice and wondering how they were to feed the orphans. "Please forgive us for being late."

"As I said, 'tis your first day."

"If I may ask, My Lady..." began Catrìona. She heard the sudden intake of breath from the other women at her effrontery, but she genuinely wanted to know. "Why do we pray before the sun rises?"

The queen gave her a look as if indulging a young child. "Have you never heard that when it was still dark, our Lord got up and left the house and went away to a secluded place to pray? Before He chose the twelve, He prayed all night. There is much to be gained from His example if we would have our prayers answered."

"Surely He will answer yours, My Lady," said Catrìona. "You are so... good."

"Nay, not good, just a woman."

The queen turned and left the chapel, her ladies following, leaving Catrìona and her cousin alone.

In the light of the candle, she saw Fia roll her eyes. "Now you are questioning the queen herself?"

"I suppose I am. 'Tis hard to think of a woman who rises in the middle of the night to pray as 'just a woman' no matter what she says. But if she is just a woman, surely she can answer another woman's questions."

As they left the chapel, dawn made its glorious appearance, lighting the sky in shades of blue and heather. Catrìona paused to admire the colors in the clouds, deep rose with the bright color of foxglove flowers in the center. Below the clouds, the sky was streaked in gold. Mayhap the beauty of the dawn was worth the early rising.

Her stomach rumbled, reminding her she had eaten little the night before. She whispered to Fia, "I cannot fault the queen for her devotion to God and the orphans, but my stomach objects to so much activity before breaking my fast."

"The priest would say serving others before ourselves is a virtue," said Fia.

"Aye," Catrìona agreed, knowing Fia was right and the queen a model of devotion. "We serve a queen who shames us all."

They arrived back at the tower and stepped through the door to find the queen and the other ladies standing inside. Wafting through the air was the smell of fresh-baked bread. Catrìona's mouth watered.

A woman wearing a headcloth and carrying a babe came toward Margaret. Handing the babe to the queen, she said, "Good morning, My Lady."

Margaret cradled the sleepy child in her arms. "Did Edward sleep well?"

"Yea, My Lady, 'tis a sweet lad ye have."

Margaret kissed the babe—who Catrìona realized was the queen's young son—before releasing him back to his nurse.

An older man with gray hair, who had been standing to one side, approached. Catrìona assumed he was the king's steward.

"My Lady, the orphans await you and your ladies."

"Thank you, Nechtan," said the queen.

Audra leaned in to Catrìona and Fia. "Before she takes any food for herself, Margaret will see the orphans fed. They come to the tower door each morning, usually nine or ten of them. 'Tis her way and we do the same."

Just then, the king stomped down the stairs, his heavy feet sounding like drum beats on the wooden planks. Frustration emanated from his grunts as he struggled to pin a large brooch to his scarlet cloak. His dark hair, thrown back from his face, fell to his shoulders in wild abandon. A golden-handled sword hung in a sheath at his side. A man of great height and presence, his entry drew the attention of all. Catrìona could not help but stare.

Spotting his queen, Malcolm went straight to her.

" 'Twould seem I am in need of your deft hand, *mo cridhe*." He grinned mischievously at his wife.

The queen raised her hands to his shoulder and with efficient movements, secured the brooch to his cloak. The king bestowed a kiss on her cheek. As Margaret turned toward her ladies, Malcolm slapped her affectionately on the bottom before striding toward the door, snapping his fingers at two hounds lying in the corner. The hounds immediately rose from the rushes and followed at their master's heels as he swept through the door.

Margaret seemed flustered for only a moment, then a smile flickered on her face.

Catrìona felt a stab of envy at having witnessed the exchange. Malcolm had called his wife *mo cridhe*, my heart, and in his eyes she had seen the adoration he held for Margaret that was whispered of at court. To be loved by such a warrior, to be touched in such an affectionate and possessive way. 'Twas not unlike the love that had existed between her father and her mother. The love she hoped to one day share with Domnall.

The king swung open the door and before it thumped closed, Catrìona heard the king's men, gathering outside, greeting him in a loud chorus.

She turned her attention back to her mistress. At one of the trestle tables, a group of children stood wearing broad grins and simple tunics of earthen colors. They greeted Margaret with noisy expressions of delight, pulling at the queen's gown.

"Wait your turn," Margaret gently reproved one very insistent young boy who could not have been more than four summers in age.

Servants bustled about, setting the table with bowls of gruel and bread. Others poured milk into small cups and set them before each place.

Margaret sat down on a bench in the middle of one table and beckoned a small girl to her. "You first, Bridget." The child was not shy but came directly to the queen and climbed onto her lap. As Audra had told them, the queen did not eat. Instead, she picked up her own silver spoon and began to feed the girl from a bowl of gruel.

Catrìona and Fia joined the queen's other ladies as they took their places at the table around Margaret and began to attend the remaining children clamoring to be fed from the bowls set before them.

Looking up at Catrìona and Fia while still feeding the young girl,

Margaret said, "I try to give them something a child would like, sweetened with honey and raisins."

Catrìona nodded her understanding as her rumbling stomach reminded her she was hungry. She was about to point out it was not just children who liked honey and raisins when the queen said, "I am rather fond of them myself."

Off to the side, Catrìona saw a boy standing by himself and called him to her. Older than the others, he was slight of body, ruddy of complexion with beautiful wide set brown eyes and straight brown hair to his nape.

He came toward her cautiously, wearing a serious expression, mayhap because he did not know her, but she sensed there was more behind his reluctant demeanor. The boy's being orphaned young and having no one made her all the more grateful for Niall. Without him, she would be as alone as this boy.

When he reached her, she invited him to sit beside her. "My name is Catrìona. How are you called?"

"Giric," he said crawling onto the bench.

Thinking he was about six or seven summers, she handed him a spoon. "I expect you feed yourself."

He nodded vigorously and took the spoon, dipping it into the bowl. Between mouthfuls of gruel, he said, "Yer hair is pretty."

She could not help but smile. He was adorable. "Thank you."

He squinted up at her. "Art new?"

"Aye. My cousin, Fia," she pointed to Fia sitting across from them feeding a young girl, "and my brother, Niall, and I have just come from Dunkeld. Like you, Niall and I are orphans."

"Ye're older," he said as if that was entirely different and she supposed it was.

"Aye, but orphans still." He did not ask how it had come to be she had no parents and she did not wish to ask about his own circumstances, knowing it would cause each of them pain to speak of it. She had only wanted him to know she and Niall understood his loss.

The sounds of eating and occasional exchanges between the children echoed about the hall. For a while, she let Giric eat. Then she thought of something that might please him. "Do you like falcons?"

His eyes lit up and he put down the spoon, wiping his mouth on his tunic sleeve. "Aye, lady! Do ye have one?"

"I do. His name is Kessog and he lives in the mews. Mayhap we can visit him this afternoon."

He frowned. "The queen's ladies do their sewing then."

"I will ask the queen if she will allow me to show you my falcon. I am not so good at needlework that I will be missed. Can you be outside the door to the hall at midday?"

He nodded. Licking the last bit of gruel from his spoon, he reached for a piece of bread. "I will be there." Taking the bread with him, he slipped from the bench and raced toward the door to join the other children who were leaving. Just as he went outside, he turned and waved to her.

She returned the gesture. *Giric.* Smiling to herself, she thought to ask Niall to go along on their afternoon adventure.

When the children had gone, a score of men and women came into the hall and were greeted by Margaret. They were simply dressed like the servants. All of them seemed to know the queen and warmly responded to her words of welcome. Catrìona wondered who they were. She had not seen them the evening before. Their clothing was modest but clean. Some looked more like Saxons than Scots, fair-haired and blue-eyed. A few children accompanied them.

They took the empty places at the same table where Catrìona, Fia and Audra sat with the other ladies.

Catrìona was puzzled.

As if reading her mind, Audra said, "They come each morning, the poor in Dunfermline. Many are English. The queen offers them food and provides them clothing."

"The queen does much good," Catrìona observed as a servant filled her bowl with the warm, cinnamon-scented gruel. She was happy to see raisins sprinkled on top.

"I love her for her goodness," said Audra. "We all do. You have not seen the half of it."

"Will the queen eat now?" Catrìona asked. She would not eat before her mistress, but truth be told, the smell of fresh bread and the thought of the honey and raisins on her tongue made her ravenous.

Audra glanced at the villagers and then turned back to Catrìona and Fia. "Once Margaret is certain the poor have been fed, then she will eat. But much of the time, she consumes little. We must remind her each day that she eats for the babe she carries or she would waste away to nothing. She fasts often."

Catrìona felt shame for her own selfishness. At her father's home in the vale, any in need had been welcomed but they had never placed the poor above themselves like Margaret did. No wonder the king loved her.

The queen walked to the dais and took her place at the high table. Not long after, the tower door burst open and Malcolm strode into the hall, his men trailing behind him, sending up a great din, laughing and speaking in loud voices of the hunt they were planning. From their eyes fixed on the bowls of gruel, Malcolm and his men appeared eager to break their fast and take to the woods. They must have been accustomed to seeing the poor in their midst, for they did not remark on it.

The king and Catrìona's uncle joined the queen at the head table. The king's men found places at the trestle tables, most of them sitting at the table across from where Catrìona and the queen's ladies were eating with the poor.

Among the men were the golden-haired warrior and his companion, the bard.

Catrìona picked up her spoon and scooped a helping of gruel into her mouth, the honey and raisins as tasty as she had imagined.

"There's the Welshman," said Fia, looking up from her own bowl and turning to glimpse the bard.

Catrìona broke off a piece of bread and glanced at the handsome blond with broad shoulders sitting beside the bard. "And his friend."

As if he sensed her eyes upon him, the fair-haired warrior turned and smiled at her.

Instantly, she looked down at her gruel, embarrassed at having been caught at his game of staring. *What must he think?* It was Domnall she should be looking at but she had not seen him come into the hall with the king.

A moment later, with a one-word command, the king summoned the warrior who had smiled at her. "Steinar!"

The warrior immediately responded, rising from his place to stride to the king, his hair catching the sun's light flowing through the open shutters. He walked with a slight limp.

"Who is that one?" she asked Audra.

The queen's lady followed Catrìona's gaze. "The king's scribe."

A scribe? She would never have believed it. His body was that of a warrior, not a man of the cloth. Though he carried no sword, she could not imagine him as the king's clerk. It meant he was educated, a man of letters, as few warriors were. Even the king was unlettered. Mayhap this blond scribe, who looked like a Saxon, had fled to Scotland, or been dragged there by the king as a slave. *Could this man be a slave?*

At the sound of the tower door opening, she turned. Domnall strolled inside with Maerleswein. Gesturing his companion to proceed without him, Domnall came toward her.

Her heart began to race in her chest. She was glad to see him. He looked very handsome. He might intend to hunt with the king, but first he was coming to speak with her and she was pleased he would do so.

His features, sharp as always, softened as he approached.

She stood to greet him. "Domnall."

He gazed at her with obvious pleasure. In his pale blue eyes, she saw the desire that she had seen there before. Inwardly, she warmed to the idea they would soon be man and wife.

"Catrìona, I regret I have not been able to see you until now. How do you fare? How was your journey from Dunkeld?"

She drew him aside so they would be out of earshot of the others. "I am well, sir. The journey was uneventful, the weather fair. And you?" She had missed him and longed for him to say he had eagerly awaited her arrival and looked forward to their betrothal now that her mourning period was over.

But he said none of those things. Instead, he spoke of the king. "Malcolm has been a most gracious host. I have lingered long in his hall and hope to trade with him."

Unwilling to let him see her disappointment, she let her gaze drift to the floor. Gathering her resolve, she raised her head, a mask of calm in place. "The queen, too, is most kind."

"Will you walk with me later?" he asked. "Mayhap before the evening meal?"

Hope sprang within her. "Aye, I will come early to the hall."

"Good. The sun will not have left the sky and we can walk to the burn."

He bid her a good day and she wished him a successful hunt, watching him walk to his place next to Maerleswein. It had not been the longed for meeting she had hoped for. He had not even taken her hand. Had time and distance changed his feelings? Yet, she was certain it was desire she had glimpsed in his eyes.

★ ★ ★

Catrìona's fingers, unused to embroidery, were red from her many missed stabs of the needle. *It has scarce been an hour. How will I survive more of this?*

Margaret, her sister, Cristina, and the queen's ladies were tucked away in one of the chambers the queen called her own, the women bent to their needlework, each embellishing a piece of cloth or a garment.

"Tell us about your home," said an exuberant Elspeth.

Catrìona glanced up from her needlework to see the youngest of Margaret's ladies looking at her expectantly and sitting forward on her stool.

Happy for an excuse to lay aside her embroidery, Catrìona began to describe her home in the vale, recalling happier days, before the Norse attack. " 'Tis the most beautiful place in all of Scotland, not that I have seen all of Scotland, but I cannot imagine any place more magnificent. Why, you can stand on Ben Lomond and gaze far ahead into the bluest loch anywhere on earth. 'Tis like gazing into... Heaven." Without warning, a lump formed in her throat and tears welled in her eyes, making her feel foolish before the other women at the emotion the mere memory of her home roused within her.

The queen came to her rescue. Smiling kindly, she said "I have heard 'tis a wondrous place."

"Did you come to Dunfermline to find a husband?" asked the dark-haired Isobel, the eldest of Margaret's ladies.

The question was a bold one, and since most of them were sent to Malcolm's court to do just that, it hardly seemed necessary to ask, but seeing the women's sudden interest and because she was proud of her intended, she said, "My father selected a husband for me but we are not yet betrothed." Surely the king and queen were aware of her circumstances, but Catrìona had carefully worded her reply should the others not be aware her father was dead.

"Might he be someone we know?" asked Davina timidly. Of all the queen's ladies, the honey-haired woman from Lothian appeared the most soft-spoken.

Catrìona cast a glance at Fia before answering. "Aye," she said proudly. "He is the Irishman from Leinster, Domnall mac Murchada."

Isobel and Audra appeared surprised to learn she was already promised, but their reaction to her mention of Domnall's name told her they were familiar with him.

Davina said nothing but on her face was a puzzled expression.

Before Catrìona could explain, Elspeth jumped in. "You know him, Davina. He is the one who is always with Maerleswein, the English sheriff."

"Maerleswein is no longer a sheriff," corrected Isobel. "He forfeited his lands and title when he led the rebels in York."

"Well, he *was* a sheriff," Elspeth insisted.

"He served William for a time," interjected Margaret. The comment went unnoticed but Catrìona wondered what had turned the sheriff against the Norman they now called the Conqueror.

"Maerleswein and Domnall talk of nothing save ships and trade," said Isobel as if bored by the thought.

"Trade is very important to Scotland," said Margaret. "I have encouraged the king to pursue it for what it can mean for our people."

"Aye, said Fia, "My father is keenly interested in being a part of the king's plans for the sake of Atholl."

" 'Twas a good thing to encourage trade that brings new wares to our shores," said the kind-hearted Audra in defense of the queen's idea. "My father tells me that before you came to Dunfermline, My Lady, the bright colors and fine clothing the merchants bring to Dunfermline were not seen here. 'Twas only a gathering of rough-clothed warriors eating amid dirty rushes."

Elspeth giggled, apparently trying to imagine the scene.

"Is it true, My Lady?" asked Catrìona. "Did you change the way the men and women dress?"

The queen set down her embroidery and gazed toward the window where sunlight was streaming into the small chamber. "When we first came to Dunfermline two years ago, it was a very different place than it is today." She looked around the circle of women. "Malcolm had no queen; his first wife had died. The tower was the stronghold of men, a place for them to sleep and eat before setting out on a raid. The chapel was a dank, dismal place, rarely used."

"The tower was dark and not clean as it is today," said Cristina, the queen's sister, with obvious disdain. Her face twisted into a grimace, an expression Catrìona could not picture on Margaret. "We were raised in the courts of Hungary and England," Cristina continued, "places of great opulence. We were unused to filth."

Margaret interrupted, mayhap to keep her sister from describing all they had encountered. "Once I agreed to become Malcolm's wife, I wanted his court to bring glory to him and to Scotland."

What must it have been like for the young queen amid so many rough warriors? Margaret had changed many things, bringing a civility to Malcolm's court apparently absent before. "He must love you all the more for it."

Margaret blushed. "I am happy he loves me at all, but in truth, he was willing to make the changes because he saw the wisdom in them."

"And because they were important to you," said the queen's sister.

"Well, I for one am glad for the hearty fare your kitchen prepares," said an enthusiastic Elspeth. "I can only imagine what the king's men dined on before you came to Dunfermline."

The queen seemed amused. "They did not use many spices or sauces in those days. The fare was simple and the meat cooked over the central hearth fire and not always well."

The queen's ladies, who had come after the changes were made, laughed at the queen's description of men tearing great chunks of meat off haunches of venison and boar roasted over an open fire in the hall.

Cristina huffed. " 'Twas hardly acceptable."

After that, the women went back to their needlework and Catrìona did the same, enduring the stabs of her needle for more than an hour.

Finally, she looked up at the light coming through the window, thinking it must be time to meet Giric. Desperate for a change and longing for the diversion flying Kessog would bring, she glanced at Margaret whose deft fingers were working small, perfect stiches of golden thread into a large square of ivory silk. *An altar cloth.*

"My Lady," Catrìona said, setting aside her embroidery. The queen paused in her needlework, lifting her brows in inquiry. "Would it be permitted for me to show one of the orphans my falcon? The lad seemed most eager to see it when we broke our fast together this morning."

The other women, Fia among them, kept their heads down, their busy hands pausing only briefly with Catrìona's question.

The queen's sister frowned, clearly disapproving of the request. A few years younger than Margaret, Cristina was fair-haired, but not so pretty or, Catrìona sensed, so kind as the queen. "Your *falcon?* Surely that is no seemly pet for a lady."

"Kessog is no pet," said Catrìona. "He is a wild bird of prey raised to hunt."

Thankfully, the queen was not as rigid as her sister and intervened before an argument could begin. "Of course you may go. While I encourage my ladies in their embroidery to adorn the chapel's altar and to make beautiful their clothing, we do much more than needlework at Dunfermline. In time you will see, but for today, bringing joy to a small orphan shall be your devotional. 'Twas the lad, Giric, was it not?"

"Aye, My Lady."

"He is a most unusual boy," said the queen. "Misfortune has not dulled his young spirit. Your time with him will be well spent."

Catrìona thanked her new mistress and hurried out of the chamber and down the long set of stairs to the hall below. Grabbing the pouch of meat she had earlier begged from the kitchen servants, she raced through the front door where Giric was already waiting.

"I thought ye'd fergot," he said, stepping away from the tower wall. In his voice she heard the resignation of one used to being disappointed.

"Nay, I did not forget. Come," she extended her hand and he took it. "I will show you Kessog. Mayhap we can fly him. Would you like that?"

His eyes glistened in delight. "Oh, aye! Be it allowed?"

She nodded and they walked toward the mews, the boy asking her questions about the falcon, what he looked like, how big he was, how long she had trained him and, finally, "Does he hunt?"

"Aye, of course. For birds, mostly; ducks are a particular favorite of Kessog's." Again, she had the urge to ask him how he lost his parents. She hoped eventually he would tell her of his own accord. Instead, after she'd answered his questions about the falcon, she asked, "Where do you stay?"

"In the village with the others. 'Tis not far." Catrìona had yet to see the village but was glad the boy had company and a place to sleep.

"You will like my brother," she encouraged. "Niall will meet us at the mews."

Niall was already waiting for her as she and Giric stepped into the dimly lit structure that housed the king's falcons.

Machar retrieved Kessog from his perch. "Good afternoon, my lady."

She returned Machar's greeting and said to her brother, "Niall, this is my new friend, Giric."

She was certain she had done the right thing in bringing the boy when he looked up at Niall and enthusiastically asked, "Do ye fly falcons, too?"

Niall tousled the boy's hair. "Aye, 'tis a sport our father favored. Once, we had many more than just Kessog." He shot Catrìona a glance, regret in his eyes, for his own peregrine falcon had been taken as plunder the day of the Norse attack.

Machar handed the hooded Kessog to Niall, who lowered the bird for Giric to stroke the falcon's breast feathers. "Gently," her brother instructed.

Awestruck, Giric said, "He is…" The boy hesitated as if searching for a word.

"Magnificent?" Niall asked.

"Aye!" exclaimed Giric.

Catrìona thought so, too. Kessog was a fine example of a tiercel, brightly plumed and perfect of form.

"I want to see him fly," said Giric.

"And you shall," Catrìona assured him. "But you will have to look sharp. He is very fast in the hunt."

"There is a field not far from the tower," offered Machar. "The burn runs near it. 'Twill have ducks and room for your falcon to hunt."

Thanking him, she took Kessog on her gauntleted hand and left the mews with Niall.

Giric ran ahead. "I know the field!"

She and Niall walked along, at first not saying much. Then Niall asked, "Do you ever think of Deidre? I have wondered about her and the others who were taken."

It had been a year but she did not hesitate. "Yea, she was more like a younger sister to me than a maidservant. Now she would be seventeen." Catrìona felt a pang of remorse and her brow furrowed. "I have oft woken from a bad dream to see her face before me."

"Do you think they have made her a slave?"

Catrìona did not like to think about what had been the fate of the pretty young woman. " 'Tis possible, mayhap even likely."

"I would get her back if I could," he said solemnly.

CHAPTER 4

Steinar rubbed his aching thigh. He'd been sitting in an alcove at one end of the hall all morning, his head bent to the parchment crafting messages Malcolm intended for the mormaers in the provinces. The king was raising an army of foot for a raid into Northumbria. All who were sworn to him would respond with fighting men. Steinar had to acknowledge the king's wisdom. It was best not to allow an army to be idle overlong. Soldiers with nothing to do were likely to drink and gamble and work up quarrels amongst themselves, rather than train to battle the enemy.

Finishing the last missive, Steinar set his quill aside and stretched his neck from side to side, relieving the cramped muscles. With pleasant reflection, he remembered Talisand's priest, Father Bernard, who had been his tutor. Was his graying brown hair now completely gray? He had been too kind to inflict punishment on Steinar when he had forsaken his lessons. The only thing that had brought him back to his studies had been his father's glare the one time he had been caught sneaking out and his older sister's threat that she would best him if he did not practice as the priest urged. So, instead of riding Artair, the black fell pony he had raised from a colt, he had dipped his quill in the ink and begun again.

When he and Rhodri had come to Scotland and he'd recognized the opportunity to serve the unlettered Malcolm, he had silently thanked Father Bernard for his teaching.

Pushing from the bench, he tentatively put weight on his leg. It protested, stiff at first. Slowly he crossed the empty hall and stepped through the door, looking into the cloud-filled sky portending rain.

As he walked, his leg loosened up. He followed the stream away from the tower, the pain lessening as he went. By the time he reached the open field, he was striding apace.

Suddenly, a hawk's cry pierced the air. He looked up to see a small gray speck cutting across the sky like a shooting star. His wings tucked in close, the bird dove toward a flock of mallards on the wing. One duck exploded in a burst of feathers as the falcon slammed his talons into the bird's wing.

A cheer went up and the two birds plummeted to the ground. Clutching the mallard was a small falcon. The granite-colored head and wing feathers and eggshell throat told Steinar it was a peregrine, a male half the size of his kill.

Well done.

A whistle pierced the air. Steiner inclined his head, searching for the source. Standing to one side of the field with her gauntleted hand outstretched to receive the falcon was the auburn-haired beauty he'd seen in the hall just that morning breaking her fast. The same one he had watched the night before. At this time of day, the queen's ladies were usually at their needlework, yet this one had escaped that duty.

How had she managed that?

The falcon flew to her gauntlet and she fed it meat from a pouch on her belt. The young man with hair the same red as hers was standing next to her. He strode off and retrieved the duck. The woman bent her arm to display the falcon to a small boy beside her.

Thinking this was too good an opportunity to let pass, Steinar crossed the field to the small group standing around the falcon.

He recognized the boy. 'Twas Giric, one of the orphans the queen fed. Likely, the cheer Steinar had heard came from him.

As Steinar drew near, the lad looked up and said, " 'Tis the king's scribe."

Steinar bowed before the woman. "My lady, Steinar of Talisand, at your service."

The falcon flapped his wings and his shrewd black eyes scrutinized

Steinar.

"This is Kessog," the woman said, giving him the bird's name but not her own. "My tiercel."

Not the young man's falcon, but hers. Somehow he was not surprised. He had already marked her as unlike the rest of the queen's ladies.

The falcon flapped his wings again.

"Ye've upset 'im," said the boy with a stern frown darkening his young face.

The woman stroked the falcon's chest with the back of her fingers and the bird calmed. Steinar found the gesture oddly sensual and imagined those same fingers stroking his chest.

" 'Tis no matter," said the auburn-haired young man to Giric. "He is still becoming accustomed to this place. In a few days, the falcon will settle." Facing Steinar, he said, "I am Niall of the Vale of Leven, and this is my sister, Catrìona."

Catrìona. The name seemed to suit her. He liked the lyrical sound of it. Rhodri had been right. The two redheads were siblings. "Welcome to Dunfermline," Steinar said, inclining his head. The woman's eyes, as green as the grass on which he stood, examined him much like her falcon had done earlier.

"Did ye see Kessog take the duck?" Giric proudly asked, his chest puffed out as if the falcon were his own.

"Aye, I saw it," Steinar returned. "A very fast strike."

The woman's smile aimed at the bird perched on her fist made her eyes shine like emeralds. Steinar felt a pang of envy because the favor of that lovely smile was bestowed on the falcon, not on him.

He understood by their speech the two redheads were Gaels but he'd never heard of the place the brother had named. "You said you were from the Vale of Leven. I know of Loch Leven north of Dunfermline but not a vale. Where is that?"

"Far to the west," said Catrìona, "next to the loch called Lomond."

"We came most immediately from Dunkeld," said her brother, "the home of our uncle, the Mormaer of Atholl."

Ah, Rhodri was right again. She is a relation of the powerful Atholl. He might have expected as much. Was she another woman come to the king's court to seek a husband?

Turning to his sister, Niall said, "I must leave if I am to retrieve my bow and join the archers." He handed the duck to the boy. "See that Kessog's kill gets to the kitchen."

Giric took the bird, nodding happily.

"You go to practice your skill with the bow?" Steinar asked the brother.

"Aye."

"Then you will meet my friend, Rhodri, the Welshman."

"The bard?" the brother asked.

"Aye, he is the king's bard but you'll not find another as proficient with the bow," said Steinar. "He taught all at Talisand."

"He never misses," said Giric to Niall.

"Where is this place you speak of," Catrìona asked, "this Talisand?"

" 'Tis in England."

"You are Saxon, then?"

He could speak Gaelic now like one of the Scots but he was still English, or had been until the Conqueror had come. "Not Saxon from Wessex, like the queen. I am from farther north, but like the queen, driven to Malcolm's court by the Normans." The words were bitter on his tongue as he remembered the Norman Bastard who had robbed him of his family and his home, leaving him an exile.

With Niall's imminent departure, Steinar said, "Since you are going to join the archers, I will be happy to see your sister safely back to the mews."

Catrìona frowned, then shrugged and nodded to her brother. "Until this eve."

The brother waved to them as he walked off in the direction of the archery field.

Steinar led her to the path that would take them back to the tower.

Giric ran ahead with the duck hanging from one hand, leaving Steinar alone with Catrìona, who carried her falcon on her gauntlet.

"You did not seem pleased with my offer to escort you, why?"

"I can see myself back, 'tis all."

"Ah, but here at Malcolm's court a lady is usually escorted."

She let out a deep sigh, making him ask, "How do you like being one of the queen's ladies?"

"I cannot really say. The queen is very kind, but the role is a new one for me. Thus far, it has been rising in the dark to pray, feeding the orphans and..."—she screwed up her face as if tasting something unpleasant—"needlework."

Steinar hid a smile. If she were anything like his sister, Serena, this woman would soon grow bored with such a routine. "You may find the days a bit tedious, but if you can attend the queen's councils, the ones she has held with the Culdees, you will find her of keen intelligence. She pursues debate on behalf of the Roman church with great fervor. The king attends, oft translating the Gaelic since it is still a new tongue to her."

"I would like to see these councils you speak of."

He chuckled. "I expected you would."

"Do you know me so well, then?" Sparks in her green eyes signaled a challenge.

"I do not know you at all, my lady, but I suspected." He wanted to tell her of his sister, Serena, who was so like her in temperament, but she might not understand he was offering her praise, not criticism. Catrìona was young and, given her station, likely unused to men. As with a wild falcon, he would have to first win her trust.

A look of annoyance crossed her face. "If you do not mind my being so bold, Steinar of Talisand, from what I have observed, you do not have the look of a scribe."

"I assure you I am educated to the role," he said amused.

"Nay, you misunderstand. I did not mean you had not the skills, else the king would use another. But you carry yourself like one of his knights, in form a warrior, not a clerk."

He was pleased she thought him a warrior, but he wanted to continue their wordplay, which he very much enjoyed. "Bold, indeed, to speak of a man's form and bearing."

Her brows drew together and her lips, previously full and lush, pressed together in a thin line. He had been right to think she had a temper. He sensed a fire simmered just beneath the surface. "I only meant—" she started to say.

"I knew what you meant," he interrupted. "In truth, I was injured so that I now wield a quill instead of a sword."

She was immediately contrite. "Oh, forgive me. 'Twas not my part to suggest—"

"I was not offended, my lady. I like spirit in a woman but few men do, especially those at Malcolm's court. They will expect you to be like Margaret's other ladies, quiet and docile."

"They will be sorely disappointed," she said with apparent indifference.

But I will not. The thought made him smile, but she paid no notice. He liked this woman, so different from the others.

When they arrived at the mews, she returned the falcon to his perch. Giric was nowhere in sight.

"I can see you to the tower, my lady, as I must shortly meet there with the king."

She nodded and they walked along speaking of life in Dunfermline. It was pleasant to hear her voice, even more so to watch the expressions that crossed her beautiful face. But he had to remember she was a mormaer's niece and he no longer had the rank to court such a woman. The stark truth of his circumstances rankled.

They approached the tower where a man with dark hair and a beard waited by the door, his arms crossed over his chest and an angry scowl aimed at Catrìona on his face.

"Angus!" she exclaimed before they reached the man.

"Milady, I was concerned," he said, still frowning. "When I inquired about ye, I was told ye were not with the queen's ladies, that ye had left the tower."

"But I did so with the queen's permission," she assured him.

With her explanation, the man's expression softened.

Who is he to her?

"Angus, you have yet to meet the king's scribe, Steinar of Talisand."

Steinar reached his open hand to grasp the man's, showing him he had nothing to hide.

Angus shook Steinar's hand but returned him a skeptical look.

"He happened upon Niall and me when we were flying Kessog. I wanted to show the falcon to one of the young orphans and the queen agreed I could do so."

"Oh."

She turned to Steinar. "Angus came with Niall and me from the vale. He was one of my father's guards."

"Now yers," Angus insisted. Obviously this man considered himself to be Catrìona's protector.

"Thank you for seeing me back to the tower," she said to Steinar.

Summarily dismissed, he bowed and went through the door, heading to his meeting with the king. Malcolm was another willful Scot, but like the woman, one he respected.

★   ★   ★

Catrìona and Fia dressed for dinner in the gowns Audra had told them the queen preferred her ladies wear.

"' 'Tis the court of the King of Scots and we must comport ourselves in a manner to honor him', so the queen told me herself," Audra had said.

Wearing fine gowns pleased Catrìona. There had been so few opportunities to wear silk and velvet at her father's hillfort, no matter he had been raised from thegn to mormaer when Malcolm became king. The vale was remote and far from court. Unless they had visitors, the women, even Cormac's wife and daughter, more often wore serviceable tunics. But if it pleased Margaret, Catrìona would happily don the elegant gowns her uncle had provided her.

The evening was cool and so she reached for the velvet gown, the emerald green one she thought Domnall would like.

She slipped the gown over her head and Fia laced it snug. "I miss my maidservant," said her cousin.

"Aye, 'tis not like being the lady of Dunkeld." Picking up the green ribands Catrìona had set on the bed, she handed them to her cousin. "Only the queen has a maidservant, but that is as it should be."

"The one who tends Margaret is a Saxon, who may have been with her since she came to Scotland."

Fia began to wrap the silk around Catrìona's plaits. "Once I finish with these," her cousin said, "I've some blue ones for my hair. I want to look pretty this eve."

Catrìona tilted her head to see her cousin, wondering at the excitement she saw dancing in her blue eyes. "You are not, by any chance, going to such measures for the handsome bard, are you?"

"No more than those you engage in for Domnall."

Catriona felt her cheeks heat at Fia's words. " 'Tis what we do, I suppose, dress to please a man." But the moment she thought of the man she wanted to please, it had not been Domnall's face that appeared in her mind but that of the golden-haired scribe.

"Fia, have you ever seen anyone with eyes the color of bluebells, or mayhap the color of a blue thistle flower?"

Her cousin pondered the question for a brief moment. "Nay, I think not. Is there someone here who has eyes like that?"

"Aye. The king's scribe introduced himself to Niall and me this afternoon as we were flying Kessog. His eyes are the color of the bluebells in the woods around Dunfermline. Blue thistle eyes. 'Twas all I could do not to stare they were so... beautiful."

"Beautiful? A man's eyes?"

"Yea," she said, remembering the color like none other she had ever seen.

"And the man," said Fia. "How did you find him?"

"As you would expect a scribe to be, educated and well mannered, but this one has the body of a warrior, not that of a man who spends his days bent over parchment." Then she remembered their conversation. "And he is a trifle overbearing."

Fia laughed. "I daresay *all* the men at Malcolm's court are overbearing."

As she helped Fia to dress and wrapped the silk ribands around her cousin's dark plaits, she remembered her last morning with Deidre who had laid out ribands for her to wear that night. What had become of her?

"There," she said, " 'tis done. Your blue ribands are lovely against your hair. Now I must go or I will be late to meet Domnall."

Reaching for her cloak on the peg, Catriona left their chamber and hurried down the stairs. Domnall was standing just inside the tower door talking with Maerleswein, who, it occurred to her, was about the same height as the scribe, but a score of years older.

Domnall bowed, "Catriona, have you yet met Maerleswein?"

"I have not had the pleasure." She held out her hand and the tall man bowed over it. His sun-lightened hair hung just past his shoulders; his darker beard and mustache were neatly trimmed. Garbed in a fine blue tunic, he appeared every bit the nobleman. Domnall, who was slighter of build, a merchant, not a warrior, seemed much smaller in comparison.

"My lady, I bid you welcome to Dunfermline," said Maerleswein. He spoke Gaelic but with an accent that she took as English.

"Thank you," she said. "Have you been long at Malcolm's court?"

"Too long, I think," he said with a laugh. The two men exchanged a glance that told her they shared a secret. When her brows furrowed in question, he explained, "Malcolm is sending me away, albeit with lands and a wife. The king claims 'tis a reward for my battles against the Conqueror, but I suspect he also wants me guarding his southern border for I will be taking my men with me."

Notwithstanding Maerleswein's musings about the king's motives, Catrìona was certain it was happiness she glimpsed in his face. "You are pleased by these developments, I trust?"

"Aye. I have been too long idle. It will suit me to have lands of my own again. It has been many years since my wife died and my only child, a daughter, is now wed." He grinned then. "I rather like the thought of taking a bride."

Maerleswein's face bore only a few lines despite his more than two score years. His body was still that of a warrior. Her own father, the same age, had carried more weight. She could envision the former sheriff siring more children. "Who might your betrothed be, my lord?"

"One of the queen's ladies. I assume you know her being one your-self."

Catrìona was suddenly anxious. She hoped it was not Audra for already she was fond of her and, selfishly, did not wish to see her go.

" 'Tis Davina of Lothian," he said.

Catrìona inwardly breathed a sigh of relief. She did not know Davina well, but remembered the quiet woman with honey-gold hair and soft brown eyes, a woman of few words who was content with her needlework. "She is lovely."

"Aye, she'll do," said the former sheriff, obviously pleased with the match.

"If you will excuse us, Maerleswein," Domnall interjected, "I promised Catrìona a walk ere the evening meal begins."

"Of course." Maerleswein bowed and strode off to join the king's men.

"Come." Domnall offered his arm. "We have just enough time."

She placed her hand on his forearm and they walked out the open door into a summer evening. The sky was gray with clouds and she smelled rain in the air. Angus was nowhere in sight. For at least a little while, they would be alone except for the people who came and went from the king's tower.

She wanted to ask Domnall about his plans for the future and more precisely, when he would speak to her uncle about their betrothal, but she did not wish to appear anxious, or as the scribe would say, overbold.

"You look lovely this evening," he said. "That color becomes you."

He had said as much of her other gowns in former days. She was pleased but it seemed such a common remark when she wanted to hear so much more. "I am glad you approve." If he would speak of mundane things, so would she. "How went the hunt?"

He smiled. "We will dine on roast boar and venison tonight. 'Twas a vigorous battle to bring the boar down. The king loved it. Malcolm is never more content than when he is in battle, be it against the Normans or more natural beasts."

"Aye, he is quite the opposite of Margaret. But I think she complements him well."

Domnall seemed to consider her words. "The Scots have accepted her."

"How could they not?"

"Yea, the Lady of Scotland is well liked. Malcolm made a wise match, gaining a princess as well as a rich dowry."

"I would rather speak of you," said Catrìona, "Will you linger in Dunfermline?"

"For a while yet." The look in his eyes told her 'twould not be long. Mayhap they would marry here and he would take her with him when he returned to Leinster. It was her most fervent wish.

"I am glad. I would not want you to leave." With a laugh, she added, "Unless, of course, you took me with you." When she saw

Domnall's gaze slip to the ground, she instantly regretted disclosing her thoughts.

"In time, Catrìona. All things in time." Then looking up, he said, "You only just arrived. There is much to learn from the queen."

Mayhap the king's scribe had the right of it. She did tend to be too direct. More like her father than her mother. But she was not slow. Domnall had put her off and his words made her squirm inside. Something was holding him back. *What could it be?*

"Are things well with your family?"

He was silent for a moment telling her she had hit upon a sensitive subject.

"My grandsire has passed."

"I am sorry. Were you close?"

"Not for a long time," was all he said. Then he changed the subject and returned to the topic of the day's hunt, describing the fight the boar had given them.

She listened attentively while her mind spun with possibilities.

Finally, placing his hand over hers, he said, "We had best go in."

Again he had refrained from speaking of their betrothal. *Why?*

⋆   ⋆   ⋆

The River Clyde loomed before her, cloaked in swirling mists. A woman's scream pierced the air, raising a scream in her own throat. She tried to run but her feet seemed to be stuck in the sand. With great effort, she pressed forward. And then she was running, running.

Behind her, Catrìona heard the roar of a harsh voice and the panting of a huge beast. On she ran as screams erupted around her.

Suddenly she was grabbed and wrenched to the ground. A brutal hand clenched her arm, dragging her over the sand and pebbles. She fought to break free, kicking out with her feet but was held fast in a powerful grip.

In a tongue she did not recognize, the savage beast shouted and lifted her over the side of a ship, thrusting her to the hard wooden deck.

Sobbing, she scurried away, but the beast leaped over the side of the hull and stalked toward her. Grabbing her, he bound her hands, bruising her tender skin. She cried out and tried to crawl away but was hauled back.

A dark shadow loomed above her.

"Nay!" she cried out, sobbing.

"Cat! Cat, wake up!"

From deep in the dream, Catrìona's mind cleared of mist as Fia shook her awake. Opening her eyes, she stared unblinking into the darkness, her heart pounding in her chest. Soaked in sweat, she panted out breaths as if she were suffocating. "What—?"

" 'Twas only a dream, Cat," said Fia, drawing Catrìona into her arms.

"Oh, God, Fia. 'Twas so real," she gasped.

"You are all right now," her cousin crooned softly, gently brushing the wet strands of hair from Catrìona's face. " 'Tis over."

She clung to her cousin, a tether to what was real. "In the dream," she murmured, as she regained her senses and her heart settled in her chest, "I was one of the captured."

Silence hung in the air, then Fia said, "You only imagine what it must have been like for Deidre and the others."

"Aye," Catrìona said, thinking it must be so. " 'Twas horrible."

CHAPTER 5

After the terrible dream, Catrìona's life settled into a routine of early morning prayer followed by very busy days. Margaret undertook many acts of charity in which she enlisted her ladies' help. Catrìona willingly participated, for the work was to her liking and diverted her mind from the past.

Not every day was she able to steal away to fly Kessog. But when she did, she enjoyed the thrill of the falcon's hunt and the boy's company, savoring the days left before Kessog began his molt and she would not fly him.

On one of their excursions, Giric had taken her and Niall to the village. It was larger than she had expected, the thatched stone cottages scattered on either side of a wide dirt path. A blacksmith was kept occupied, Giric told her, mending mail and making swords and knives. Two taverns served the people and visitors. Some of the king's men were married and had cottages in the village.

She was surprised when the boy led her to a small cottage where several pallets were laid out on the dirt floor.

" 'Tis where I sleep," he said, pointing to a pallet in the corner. Her heart went out to the boy, living in such conditions.

"And the other pallets?" she asked. "Who sleeps on them?"

"The other orphans."

Catrìona shot a glance to where her brother stood examining the broken shutter over the window. "And besides breaking your fast in the hall, who feeds you?" he asked.

"Some of the village women."

"Mayhap we can make this a better place. It must be cold in the winter."

"Aye, 'tis," was the boy's only reply. It tore at her heart to see the orphans living in such poverty. She was certain Margaret did not know of it. Catrìona could feel her resolve to help building within her and vowed to take a hand in the village.

"I will ask the queen to allow me time and servants to make some needed changes here."

Niall turned from the window. "I will help, too."

Margaret had been pleased when Catrìona later asked her for supplies and servants to clean and repair the cottage. The queen had offered to provide clothing and assure the women who fed the children had sufficient stores of food. Catrìona set about seeing the children had new clothes, enlisting her fellow ladies to make the girls pretty tunics, embroidered with flowers. And, because she had suggested the work, Catrìona could hardly fail to participate in the needlework, but the constant company of the chattering women and her frustration at her dismal ability with a needle often left her bored and restless.

A few afternoons later, she had thought the piece she was embroidering was finished until she turned it over. She let out an exasperated sigh when she saw the tangle of knotted thread. It would have to be ripped out and done again. How she wanted to escape the task and the small talk of the queen's chamber to walk alone in the woods.

Her eyes flitted about the small chamber and, not seeing Margaret, remembered she had left to be with her young son. Angus would be busy in the practice yard with the king's men and Niall would be with the archers. A perfect time for what she had in mind.

Leaving the other ladies engaged in their sewing, she left the chamber and, once outside the tower, took the path through the woods, following the burn. It was a glorious day, the sun streaming through the leaves to fall on the yellow flowers growing by the path. Birds sang above her, drawing the chitter of red squirrels.

Giving in to a sudden urge, she slipped off her shoes and stripped her feet of the linen hose, wriggling her freed toes in the grass growing to one side of the path. She relished the way the tender green shoots tickled her feet. Undoing her plaits, she let her hair fall free down her back. Stuffing her hose into her shoes, she clutched them in one arm and began to walk.

And then she ran.

Exhilarated by the breeze on her face and the wind in her hair, she ran and ran until, out of breath, she slowed to a walk. Her heart raced as she deeply inhaled the scent of the pine forest, feeling very alive. Nothing had felt so good in a very long time. It reminded her of those times as a girl she had loved to run barefoot in the vale.

If only those days had not ended so abruptly.

To her right the burn rippled over rocks, making a burbling sound. She looked for a place to cross it. A short way ahead she spotted a tree fallen across the stream. Its trunk appeared wide enough for a person's feet. Determined to cross, she held her skirts away with her free hand and stepped carefully onto the log. With each step she gained confidence. Halfway across, her foot slipped. Hands flailing, she tumbled into the swiftly moving stream with a great splash, her hose and shoes floating away on the current.

"Argh!" Her bottom resting uncomfortably on the rocks beneath the water, she grabbed for the garments slipping away, relieved when she recovered them.

For a moment she just sat there, frustrated and chilled. The burn was not deep, but she was most thoroughly soaked.

A chuckle sounded from the woods.

★   ★   ★

On his way back to the tower from his sword practice, Steinar spotted what looked like a tree nymph darting past him. Running on the path with the abandon of a wild thing, she had not seen him hidden among the trees. But he recognized the slim figure in the leaf-colored gown, her auburn hair, like a crimson banner, flying out behind her catching the sunlight filtering through the trees.

A free spirit alone in the woods to tempt him.

He could not help wondering if, like his sister, Catrìona had been indulged by a loving father who allowed her pursuits that were more properly those of a son than a daughter. Women like Serena were rare and Catriona, so like his sister, called to some part of him long dormant.

Intrigued, he decided to follow her.

When she started to cross the stream, he remembered the moss he had seen growing on the fallen tree. Mayhap she had not recognized the danger, how slippery the growth would be under her feet.

He opened his mouth to warn her just as she gave out a shriek and fell into the water with a loud splash. It had to be cold. But he could not resist a chuckle for her dazed expression as she sat blinking in the shallow water.

"Does your father allow you to run barefoot in the forest and dance across logs?"

She whipped her head around and narrowed her eyes. Her long hair fell around her shoulders like a dark crimson shawl, dripping water onto her gown. And still she was beautiful.

"That is none of your concern, Scribe." With a muffled curse, she struggled to rise. He reached out to help her just as she added somberly, "My father is dead."

The way she had said it, the look of anguish in her eyes, told him she still mourned her father's loss. Mayhap his death had been recent.

"Here," he said reaching toward her, "take my hand and allow me to help you out."

There was fire in her eyes but she took his hand while holding on to her shoes, soaked with water.

He pulled her from the stream, sodden and shivering. It was the first time they had touched and even dripping wet, the feel of her skin caused a surge of desire to course through him. The wet gown clung to her body, revealing her nipples hardened to small buds and her curves in vivid detail. Wet, she was even more alluring than before. He wanted to pull her close, to feel her softness, but instead, he merely steadied her with his hands. "Did you not see the moss that grows on the log? 'Tis quite apparent."

Her brow furrowed. "You might have warned me."

"You fell before I could."

Wiping water from her face, she looked up at him. Her eyes were the green of the forest around them. Light filtering through the trees added a soft glow to her pale, damp skin. His gaze dropped to her lips, the color of wild roses. He ached to kiss them.

Bending his head, he moved his lips closer to hers.

Water suddenly dripped from her hair onto her nose, causing her to sniff and step back.

Still holding her shoes in one hand, she shivered. "I… I must look a mess."

"Indeed not, but you are pale." Recognizing her predicament, he said, "I wear no cloak to offer you, but I can give you the heat of my body." Taking the shoes she carried and dropping them to the ground, he pulled her into his arms and held her against his chest, ignoring the water soaking into his tunic. Her breasts pressed into his chest, warming him as his body responded to the nearness of the woman he could not dismiss from his thoughts. She might be innocent but she possessed a natural seductiveness that promised passion to the man who would claim her. And he wanted to be that man. Every warrior in the king's hall had noticed the girl. Of all the queen's ladies, she was the most talked about. They had taken to calling her the Rose of Dunfermline, a coveted prize for the one who would gain her hand.

He stared into her eyes as he lowered his mouth to hers, waiting for a sign he should stop. She may have been too dazed or too wet to remember the rules. Or mayhap she did not want to. Her breath came out on a soft sigh, telling him she, too, was affected by their closeness. He allowed himself the briefest touch of her lips. They were cool and soft. Drawing her more tightly into his embrace, he kissed her.

She responded tentatively, not with practiced movements but with an enchanting innocence.

He tasted of her, inhaling her scent, not unlike the clean, fresh scent of the woods around them. When the kiss ended, he raised his head. "Can it be the kiss of the king's scribe does not offend the mormaer's niece?"

As if she was rousing from sleep, she blinked, and placing her hands on his chest, pushed. " 'Twas not at all proper."

He stepped away, his lips twitching up in a smile. "Ah, but that is not what I asked you." For a moment he was lost in the green pools of her eyes. He wanted more of her, all of her. But when he moved toward her, she backed away.

"I shall say nothing of our encounter," she said shivering, "and, please, tell no one."

"I would not speak of this to anyone. After all, 'twas only a brief sharing of my body's heat to warm you, nothing more," he lied. The flicker of surprise in her eyes told him they both knew it, but mayhap she needed the lie. He grinned. "I cannot speak for you, but 'tis certain I am warmed."

"You are impudent, Scribe," she said as water dripped from her hair to her face and down her lovely neck.

"Before we go, you must admit you enjoyed that kiss as much as I did."

"I certainly did not. I was merely... allowing you to share your warmth."

He returned her a small laugh. "If you insist." He picked up her wet shoes from the ground and reached out his hand. "Come, I will see you back to the tower."

She pulled away and stared down at her wet gown. "I cannot go back like *this!*"

The gown clung to her slender curves in a most provocative way. He wanted to strip it from her and carry her naked to his bed, but instead, he said, "No, I expect not. We will take the back way to the mews and you can wait there while I retrieve a cloak for you."

"If you ask a servant, she can fetch my cousin, Fia, who will get one."

He chuckled. " 'Tis probably best you not be seen wearing one of mine."

They walked back together on the sun-dappled path. Despite the summer day, she shivered with cold. Taking her hand, he let his warmth flow to her, relieved she had not noticed the sword sheathed on his other side. He was not ready for any save Rhodri to know of his practice in the woods.

★　★　★

Catrìona sneezed. Beneath her robe, her skin was chilled like a plucked goose and her shivering would not stop. "I can... cannot seem to get wa… warm." In truth, she had not been warm since the scribe let go of her hand.

"What were you thinking that you would run alone in the woods?" scolded Fia.

In Catriona's mind, she pictured them as young girls. "Remember when we were children, those sun-filled summers when we ran barefoot in the woods near Atholl?"

"Aye, I remember." Her cousin looked at her askance and, with a disbelieving shrug of her shoulders, chided, "But you are nineteen now, Cat, no longer a child."

"I was missing those days, Fia. I just wanted to be free and without the sad memories or the limitations of life as a lady of the queen. I was enjoying myself until I tried to cross the burn."

"You are fortunate 'twas the scribe who found you."

Yea, very fortunate. She raised her hand to her lips, remembering the scribe's warm lips on hers. It was her first real kiss. She paled at the thought it was not Domnall who had given it to her, but instead, the handsome scribe. Still she would not change what had happened if she could. The kiss had awakened a part of her never stirred before. *Was it a sin to have allowed him to kiss her so? To respond as she had?*

"I hate to think what Angus would say if he knew."

She averted her gaze from her cousin, not wanting Fia to see the flush Catriona could feel rising in her cheeks. "Like you, he would scold."

"And rightly so."

Catriona ran her fingers through her wet hair feeling Fia's eyes upon her. "How can you be younger than me and still act the older sister?"

"Hmm. Mayhap because I would not be so foolish. You had better get dressed or they will be upbraiding us for being late to the evening meal. Here," said Fia, picking up a drying cloth. "I'll help with your hair."

Fia placed the drying cloth over Catriona's head and rubbed vigorously, soaking up much of the remaining water. Catriona's thoughts turned to the scribe and the way his eyes had lingered on her lips. When he had drawn her into his warm embrace, she had melted into the heat of his muscular chest. Even through her wet gown she had been very aware of his body touching hers. His strength had surrounded her. She knew she should have pulled away but, excited by his touch, she had allowed his masculine scent and towering height to engulf her. She had not wanted to flee; she had wanted to stay and draw upon his warmth. She had wanted him to kiss her.

How could that be when I am intended for Domnall?

She and Domnall had yet to experience such intimacy, but there was a shared respect between them and the knowledge he was the man her father had chosen. Surely her father had chosen well. She remembered the proud look on his face when he told her Domnall was an Irishman of noble blood worthy of a mormaer's daughter.

Steinar was only the king's clerk and an impudent one at that. But when his arms were around her, his station did not seem to matter.

Catrìona handed Fia the drying cloth and shook out her hair, stepping close to the brazier. Once warmed, she donned the crimson velvet gown she had chosen to wear. 'Twas a shade she was fond of that did not war with the color of her hair.

"Will you plait your hair?" asked Fia.

"If you would help me, I would plait only the sides and secure them in the back. The rest of it I would wear free. 'Tis still not entirely dry."

"That has always been my favorite way you wear it. I imagine Domnall will like it as well. You have such beautiful hair."

"If you like red…"

"Men do prefer the queen's coloring, I suppose. Margaret's flaxen locks are lovely but your hair is unusual. Men notice it."

Fia's compliment made Catrìona glad they were friends as well as cousins.

While Fia dressed on her hair, Catrìona recalled her meeting with Domnall and Maerleswein. She had forgotten to tell Fia about Davina's coming betrothal. "Had you heard that Davina will be leaving the queen's service to marry?"

"Nay, but then she is not one to speak much. Who is it to be?"

"Maerleswein, the nobleman who was once an English sheriff. Domnall introduced us and Maerleswein told me the king has given him lands in Lothian and Davina for his bride."

"Do you think she will be pleased?" Fia inquired.

"He is a fine looking man, of noble lineage and seems well mannered. He is older than she might have hoped for, but no doubt a better man than some the king could have chosen."

"Mayhap he conferred with the queen. Margaret knows her ladies."

"Whether he did or not, Davina does not seem like one who would object."

Remembering what Audra had told her when they had first come to Dunfermline, Catrìona said, "I expect there will be a new lady joining us when Davina leaves."

"Aye, most likely."

In no time at all, Fia had woven the sides of Catrìona's hair into two narrow plaits and gathered them to the back of her head to entwine together in one long plait resting on top of her free-flowing tresses. The change in the way she typically wore her hair pleased her.

Once Fia was dressed, they left the chamber for the hall where they would meet the other ladies. Uncle Matad had departed for Atholl the day before, but even before he had gone, she and Fia had joined the queen's ladies at one of the tables for meals and no longer ate on the dais. Catrìona was glad for the change. Though she missed Edgar's company, she did not wish to be on display. Sitting with the queen's ladies allowed her to hide among them, hopefully avoiding the leering eyes of the king's men.

★　★　★

Steinar stood next to Rhodri at the bottom of the stairs, swapping stories about their day. Behind them, the hall was already noisy with the crowd gathering for the evening meal. Light from the open shutters spoke of the long summer days that had come to Scotland.

He had not told his friend of his encounter with the auburn-haired tree nymph and her plunge into the burn. He would keep that meeting and the memory of their kiss to himself, delighting in the one thing he had learned: she was not indifferent to him.

As he searched the crowd for the queen's ladies, Steinar heard Rhodri's sharp intake of breath. Following his friend's gaze up the stairs, Steinar saw Catrìona and her cousin slowly descending. Catrìona was clothed in a deep crimson gown that dipped low, exposing her ivory skin and hinting at her enticing breasts, the same breasts he had felt through her wet gown that afternoon. Her long auburn tresses hung free, one thick strand cascading over her shoulder.

Rhodri dug an elbow into Steinar's ribs. "Introduce me to the dark-haired one."

Steinar had noticed the tendre Rhodri held for the girl and was unsurprised at the request.

"Ladies," he said as the two reached the last step. "Might we detain you for a moment?"

The women paused with expectant expressions. "Aye," said Catrìona, her green eyes shimmering like emeralds.

"Allow me to present my friend, Rhodri of Gwynedd, the king's bard and master of the bow."

"Rhodri, this is Catrìona of the Vale of Leven and her cousin, Fia of Atholl."

Each of the young women held out her hand to the bard.

Rhodri bowed low, first over Catrìona's hand. "A rare vixen," he said smiling up at her. Then he took the hand of the dark-haired one and placed a kiss on her knuckles. "The rarest of jewels with dark sapphire eyes. Your midnight hair and fair skin make me think you Welsh, my lady and cause me to long for the land of my youth."

The dark-haired girl blushed, seemingly flattered, as Steinar was certain Rhodri had meant her to be. His friend had won the heart of many a woman at Malcolm's court. But the bard's lingering kiss on Fia's hand and his intense gaze told Steinar this woman was more to Rhodri than just another pretty girl.

"Fia," breathed Rhodri in his deep voice. "A lovely name for a lovely woman."

Ignoring his friend's besotted state, Steinar offered his arm to Catrìona. "May I escort you to your table?"

Placing her hand on his arm, she flashed him a smile and whispered, "How could I refuse a gallant scribe who only this afternoon saved a drowning lady?"

He laughed. " 'Tis difficult to drown in a few feet of water, my lady, but aye, how could you refuse?"

Steinar guided Catrìona to where the queen's ladies were taking their seats at one end of a trestle table set with candles and pitchers of wine.

Rhodri and Catrìona's cousin followed closely behind them.

Steinar leaned down to whisper in Catrìona's ear, "I like your hair like that. It reminds me of how it looked when you ran through the woods." *The way it would look spread on my pillow.*

Before she could reply, he bid the ladies good eve and pulled a reluctant Rhodri toward their seats farther down the table.

On the dais, the king's family took their seats along with Maerleswein and Davina. An older man sat on Davina's other side. On the opposite side of the queen sat her brother, Edgar, and her sister.

"I wonder why Maerleswein sits with the king tonight," said Steinar.

Rhodri leaned in to whisper. " 'Tis the betrothal of Maerleswein and Davina we celebrate. The man on her other side is her father."

A servant set a large platter on the table, drawing Steinar's attention. "That explains our fare. 'Tis not often we dine on more than fish, duck and boar. Tonight they serve us swan and peacocks." The birds, adorned with some of their own feathers, were surrounded by roasted vegetables and flowers set upon large serving dishes. In the rising aromas, he detected garlic and fennel. There were also peas in cream sauce, one of his favorites.

Once the hall quieted, the king rose to his feet, goblet in hand. "This eve we celebrate a great man and his betrothal to a noble Scotswoman. I bid you raise your goblets to Maerleswein and Davina, betrothed this day!"

The hall erupted in shouts as goblets were raised and their contents downed with many smiles, for the two were popular with both the men and the women. The jests, Steinar knew, would come later, after the ladies retired from the hall.

"I'm to sing them a love song," said Rhodri. "Orders from the king. I am quite certain 'tis a match made for land and loyalty but I will try to encourage them to more."

"You have such a song?"

"Aye, a timeless one."

"I can hardly wait to hear it," Steinar teased.

"The queen will like it," Rhodri said with a shrug. " 'Tis all that matters."

"Now you have me intrigued." Steinar waited expectantly but Rhodri said nothing more.

Throughout the dinner, Steinar watched Catrìona, her long auburn hair flowing in waves down her back like a fiery waterfall. Her face glowed in the candlelight, making him want to claim another kiss. But it was the memory of her running in the forest like one of the wild creatures that filled his mind. Then he saw her raising her hand to sound a shrill whistle calling her falcon to her gauntlet as if one with the hawk. Yet with the orphan boy, her words were tender. *A most unusual woman.* And one who stirred his heart as well as his loins.

She laughed at something one of the women said and her laughter made her face shine with joy.

"My friend," Rhodri said in somber tone, "be careful on whom your gaze rests. I have heard she is all but betrothed to Domnall mac Murchada, the Irishman from Leinster."

Inwardly, Steinar scowled. "I have met the man and so have you," he threw back. "I am not fond of his ways. A man who is promised to a lady should not be so quick to indulge in common rutting."

The meal drew to a close as more wine was poured. Rhodri left the table and headed toward the stool set before the dais. On the way, he stopped to bow before Catrìona's cousin, making his interest known to all. There had been other ladies who had garnered the bard's interest in the past, but none like this one. Steinar could only hope Rhodri's attentions to Atholl's daughter did not result in a scolding from the king.

Rhodri picked up his harp and sat on a stool facing the king and queen, the hearth to his back. The fire had died to coals but the flickering torches set the hall aglow.

"In honor of the occasion," Rhodri said plucking a few strings, "I sing an ancient song of love adapted for the betrothed couple." He sang softly in Gaelic, the words weaving their magic as tendrils of ethereal sounds echoed from his harp.

Like a lily among thorns is Davina among women.
Like an apple tree among the trees of the forest is her beloved among men.
Let him lead her to the banquet hall.

And let his banner over her be love.

Your love is more delightful than wine.
Pleasing is the fragrance of your perfumes.
Take me away with you—let us hurry!
For I will praise your love more than wine.

The king whispered a translation to Margaret and Steinar noted the slow smile that spread across her face. When the song finished—and there was more of it—Rhodri sang a song in Welsh, mayhap another love song. Finally, he stood and bowed. The queen gave the bard a knowing smile.

Rhodri returned to their table and Steinar greeted him with, "Very well done." Once his friend was seated, Steinar asked, "Where did you get the song you sang for the betrothed couple?"

"I borrowed it from a very old source. 'Tis Solomon's song. I am certain the queen recognized it. Mayhap she is the only one in the hall who did."

"You are a clever bard."

Rhodri said not a word but the look in his eyes told Steinar he owned the compliment.

★ ★ ★

"That first song the bard sang was somehow familiar," Catrìona said to Fia as she drank the last of her wine, "but I cannot think of where I have heard it."

"They were lovely words and so romantic. Did you see Davina blush?"

"Aye, especially when Maerleswein grinned."

Fia sighed. "The bard is quite talented. And handsome."

Catrìona gave her cousin a sharp glance. "His song seemed to please the queen. Did you see her smile at the bard?" Catrìona had observed the subtle exchange between Margaret and the bard and wondered what lay beneath it. She had also noted the glances Rhodri exchanged with her cousin.

"Nay, I was watching Rhodri."

Catrìona let out a sigh. Fia's attraction for the bard was as hopeless as his was for her. "Do not allow your heart to wander in that direction, Fia. You know your father would have the king wed you to some favored mormaer."

Fia ignored the warning and picked up her goblet of wine. " 'Twas a fine meal."

"Aye, it was." Thinking out loud, Catrìona added, "Margaret lingers in the hall tonight, mayhap for Davina's sake."

"She and Maerleswein are to leave on the morrow to be married in Lothian," said Fia.

Catrìona considered again the vacancy Davina's departure would leave. "I wonder who will take her place."

Fia shrugged. "We can only hope whoever she is, she is as sweet as the lady she replaces."

CHAPTER 6

Catrìona watched Giric stuff a hunk of bread into his mouth and race from the hall, the small gray wiry-haired creature with an uncanny resemblance to the king's hounds following on the boy's heels.

Catrìona rose with the other ladies and decided to get some air before settling into her needlework.

In front of the tower, Steinar stood, talking with one of the king's men. Her heart sped in her chest at the sight of him.

Giric tugged on Steinar's sleeve. "Have ye met my dog?" he asked. The man talking with Steinar laughed and waved goodbye as he walked away.

Steinar greeted Catrìona with a smile before looking down at the dog. One ear of the small hound was cocked up and one folded down as if the animal was uncertain if he should be alert. But his small dark eyes bespoke intelligence.

"If you are referring to that bit of gray fluff that follows you about, yea, I have seen him, most recently under the table when we broke our fast."

"He is ever so clever," said Giric, beaming at the dog. "He stayed out of sight while we ate."

Steinar crossed his arms over his chest and brought one hand up to cup his chin as he studied the boy's new acquisition.

Catrìona took that moment to ask Giric, "Where did you find him?"

Giric scratched the dog affectionately behind one ear. "He followed me to my pallet one night." In response, the small beast wagged his tail and licked the boy's hand.

"I imagine," said Steinar, with a wink to Catrìona, "he has followed you ever since."

Giric nodded.

Catrìona had seen the dog follow the boy into the hall that morning to lay curled up at his feet while he ate. "Like a shadow."

"That's it!" exclaimed Giric, his dark hair falling over his forehead as he inclined his head to look at the dog. " 'Tis what I will call ye."

The dog wagged his tail.

"A good name," said Steinar. "He follows you about like your own."

The dog scurried off, picked up a large stick in his mouth and carried it back to Giric. Taking the stick from the dog, the boy tossed it some distance away. The dog ran to the stick and stood over it looking at the boy.

"Shadow!" Giric called. The dog snatched the stick in his mouth and sauntered over to the boy, dropping it at his feet.

"He seems to know his name already," Catrìona said.

Giric ran off then, Shadow following close on his heels, just as a group of riders crested the rise and reined in their horses in front of the tower.

Standing next to the scribe, Catrìona shaded her eyes from the sun to gaze up at the arriving party. Four men, richly attired, and a woman wearing a dark cloak over a green gown, dismounted.

Steinar bid Catrìona good day, saying he had some work to do for the king. He walked toward the door to the tower, his limp barely perceptible. Her eyes took in his lithe movement, his broad shoulders and his long legs. As he reached the door, it opened and he stepped aside to allow Margaret, followed by Fia and the other ladies, to pass through.

Fia hurried to Catrìona. "We are to meet the new lady, Isla of Blackwell."

Catrìona turned her attention to the new arrivals and particularly the woman, as she and Fia joined the welcoming party.

The king strode through the tower door and went to stand by the queen.

Malcolm greeted the men while Margaret and her ladies welcomed the woman. "Greetings, Isla," said the queen.

The new lady made a brief curtsey, "My Lady."

Catrìona studied her, curious to learn more about the one who would be joining them in service to the queen. Isla's hair was a warm brown and as she drew closer, Catrìona saw she had hazel eyes. She was not pretty like Fia or the queen but her face was still attractive and the fine clothes she wore bespoke wealth.

The king suggested the travelers join him for some refreshments and, readily agreeing, they strolled toward the tower door. The men walked ahead and the queen followed with Isla. The other ladies trailed behind, Catrìona and Fia alone at the end.

"What do you know of her?" Catrìona asked her cousin in a whisper.

"Only what the queen told us after you left the hall with Giric. She is from Ayrshire in the west where her father has much land in oats and barley. He raises cattle, too."

"Ayrshire lies south of the vale on the Firth of Clyde," said Catrìona, idly thinking here was yet another woman to be bartered away by the king. She was glad she would not share such a fate.

Once they were all inside the hall, Isla was introduced to the queen's ladies and Audra kindly offered to show their newest member to her chamber, which the two of them would share.

The king and queen set about entertaining the men. A few minutes later, Catrìona and Fia left for their own chamber to retrieve their cloaks as the queen had told her ladies they would be joining her on an outing that day. As they passed Audra's door, the sounds of an argument could be heard.

"I will not rise before dawn, nor will I feed urchins. And I have no intention of living like a nun. I am here to gain a husband!"

Audra's words in reply were soft and muffled. Catrìona could only imagine what she had said to Isla. Exchanging a look with Fia, she said, "It seems we are in for a storm."

"Aye," said Fia, as they continued down the corridor. "Isla's concerns are all for herself. I pity the man the king gives her to wed."

"If she is unkind to Audra, I may decide not to like her," Catrìona said, wondering how one as selfish as Isla would fare among them. After living as one of the queen's ladies and seeing Margaret give of herself to the poor and the needy, she had come to admire her mistress. Even the early rising and the hour of morning prayer were not so onerous as they had seemed at first.

The queen's errand that afternoon took them to a small hill about a mile south of Dunfermline in the direction of the River Forth. It had rained during the night and the ground was soft and the grass damp.

The queen sat, reading from a small book she carried.

"Does the queen come here to read?" Catrìona asked Audra from where they stood some distance away. Isobel, the most senior of the queen's ladies would know, but Catrìona preferred to ask Audra, who did not seem to mind her many questions.

"She comes here to meet the people, making herself available to any who would speak with her."

Catrìona nodded. She was becoming accustomed to her mistress' unusual behavior. She and Audra found seats on nearby rocks. Fia joined them.

Audra leaned in to say, "Sometimes the queen takes coins from the king's treasury to give to the poor who come."

Catrìona nodded again, remembering a story Steinar had told her of a time he had overheard the king teasing Margaret about her thievery.

"Once he even threatened to have her arrested," the scribe said.

Knowing the king's reputation for being harsh, Catrìona was horrified at the thought. "Would he do that?"

"Nay, but he made a great show of it before erupting into laughter. Knowing Margaret never seeks anything for herself alone, he found her theft highly amusing."

"What did Margaret do?"

"The queen just smiled and reminded Malcolm she had brought him a good dowry and the poor needed the coins more than he did."

Catrìona had smiled to herself at the idea of Margaret admonishing the king, but as she considered it, the queen's logic was flawless.

"I think they both enjoyed the exchange," Steinar concluded.

Catrìona had grown fond of her conversations with the scribe. She had often found herself looking for him when the men came into the hall to break their fast. His manner was easy and he always had something interesting to tell her. She loved his stories of his home and his sister he seemed to admire. After the morning meal, she would stop to talk to him outside the tower. Sometimes Giric joined them, hanging on the scribe's every word, for it was clear the boy admired him.

The king also valued Steinar, ever calling for the scribe's aid in deciphering some missive he had received. Their two heads, one dark, one light, would bend over the parchment and the king would nod his understanding as Steinar read the words. In recent days, messages had come more frequently, making Catrìona wonder what was going on.

The queen spoke just then to one of the ladies, calling Catrìona back to the present, but the thought of Steinar did not immediately leave her. Images of his golden hair shimmering in the light of the sun and the feel of his lips on hers flickered in her mind. She chided herself for thinking of the scribe when she should be thinking of Domnall. He was due back today from a trip he had made in furtherance of a matter of trade for the king.

Her musings were interrupted by a group of women, some with babes in their arms, some with small children tagging along, who walked toward the queen from the direction of the village.

Margaret invited them to join her and greeted the children.

"When is the new prince to be born?" asked one of the village women, who balanced a young child on her hip. The woman's tunic was plain and faded beneath her thin shawl. A simple head covering bespoke her married status.

"In early September," said Margaret, rubbing her hand over her belly.

"Do you hope for another son?" asked one woman who held the hand of a small boy.

Margaret smiled. "I will take whatever the Good Lord gives me. But the king would like another son."

The women smiled their understanding.

As the queen spoke to the women, a group of travelers passing on the road stopped to bid her good day. By their clothing of rough woolen tunics, heavy cloaks and leather satchels the men carried, Catrìona judged them to be pilgrims.

"Where do you come from?" asked Margaret of the man who, leaning on his wooden staff, appeared to be leading the party.

"We come from Dun Edin across the Forth, bound for the shrine of Saint Andrew," said the bearded man. His face was weather-beaten, his dark hair long and tangled.

"Did you have any problem crossing the Forth?" the queen asked.

"Nay but the boat was costly," he replied. Catrìona was aware pilgrims often traveled with little coin and accepted charity where it was offered.

" 'Tis a worthy pilgrimage," Margaret remarked. She stood and walked toward the small party, pressing coins into their hands. "To help you on your way."

They thanked her profusely and departed for the village where they said they hoped to find lodging for the night before they resumed their journey eastward.

As the pilgrims continued down the road, Margaret resumed her seat on the stone, her gaze following them until they disappeared from sight. Then the queen shifted her attention back to the village women. After some conversation, the women also turned to leave.

"Wait," Margaret cried, holding out a hand as if to stop them. Rising from the stone bench, she took off her scarlet cloak. To the woman who drew her thin shawl tightly around her, the queen said, "You have no cloak. Take mine."

"Oh no, My Lady," the woman said, dismayed by the queen's generous offer.

But Margaret would not be gainsaid. "I have others and this one I would give to you."

It was then Catrìona realized several of the women wore no cloaks.

Audra was the first to follow the lead of their mistress, taking her own cloak from her shoulders and placing it around one of the village women.

Seized by a sudden desire to show kindness to the women, Catrìona took off her cloak. Tears came to her eyes as she walked to one of the women whose height was nearly her own and whose rust-colored tunic was simple and could not be very warm. Two young children clung to her skirts. Handing the green cloak to the woman, she said, "It will look nice on you and it will keep you warm."

The woman accepted Catrìona's cloak. "Thank you, my lady. 'Tis very generous."

Catrìona sensed she had changed as a result of Margaret's influence, for while she loved her green cloak, another lay in her chest, while this woman had none. What joy it gave her to give.

The rest of the queen's ladies removed their cloaks and gave them to the women who had none.

All except for Isla of Blackwell.

Isla drew her beautiful blue cloak more tightly around her and turned her head away. Catrìona remembered Isla's heated exchange with Audra that morning and what she had said about why she had come.

As the women and their children departed, Margaret resumed her seat on the flat stone and sat back staring toward the River Forth, a distant look in her eyes.

From where they were, Catrìona could see a slice of blue water above the vegetation in the distance. She and the other ladies resumed their seats around Margaret.

After some time, the queen beckoned Catrìona to her. She did not hesitate and went to sit beside the queen. Without her cloak, Catrìona felt the cold of the stone through her gown as she took her seat and knew the queen had to feel it as well. "My Lady?"

Margaret spoke in a soft voice. "I have been thinking about the pilgrims, Catrìona. I would make their way easier as they journey to the shrine of Saint Andrew."

Catrìona waited expectantly for Margaret to explain, not understanding why the queen had singled her out.

"And I want you to help me," said the queen.

Catrìona considered it an honor to be asked by the virtuous queen to assist her but still the question rose to her lips. "Me?"

Margaret returned her a small laugh. "It has not slipped my notice that of all my ladies, you are the one who is not happy unless challenged." Then with a smile, "Even if you have to wander far afield to find that challenge. You take on ventures no one else would. None of my other ladies own a falcon or seeks out paths through the woods. 'Tis no wonder your father gave you one of his guards."

Feeling heat rise in her cheeks, she dropped her gaze to her lap. "Aye."

"I hoped this might take your mind from the events in the vale, even end the dreams you sometimes have."

"You know about them?" Catrìona said, surprised. She would not have wanted the queen to be aware that the events in the vale still haunted her.

"Your fellow ladies were concerned for you when they heard your screams in the night."

Catrìona dropped her gaze to her hands. "They are less now, My Lady."

The queen patted her hand. "That is good." As Catrìona raised her head, Margaret said, "I seem to recall you have befriended the king's scribe, have you not?"

She nodded hesitantly, wondering what the queen had in mind.

"Assuming I can persuade the king to part with more of his gold, I will need to account for the expenditures and you can work with the scribe to see it done."

Though she was delighted to have the chance to work with Steinar, Catrìona was dismayed at the prospect of spending the king's gold, no matter what Steinar had told her.

Margaret appeared undaunted. "I would have a ferry built to take the pilgrims from Dun Edin across the Forth without cost. I know some shipbuilders who can do it. From Dunfermline to the shrine 'tis thirty miles, which means once they cross the Forth, they still have days of weary travel. I would build lodging for them on this side of the Forth. This, too, I would provide without charge."

"So large a task…" Catrìona said, thinking aloud.

The queen laughed. "Aye, but one that would interest you more than embroidery, no?"

Catrìona nodded, looking at the tips of her fingers still scarred from the many needle pricks. Never had she imagined an undertaking like building a ferry and an inn, but she was quick to catch the queen's enthusiasm. "There are many Saxons who do not yet have work, My Lady. Might they be called upon to serve in your inn? Some might even have skills to build and take charge of it."

"A splendid idea!" exclaimed Margaret. "Of course, I will have to appoint a steward, someone I trust to oversee the inn, but 'tis doable. Nechtan might be of assistance." Then with a small smile, she added, "Using the Saxons to help run the inn and serve the pilgrims should appeal to my husband, assuming I can convince him his people will love him all the more for his generosity."

With that, the queen stood, beckoning her ladies, urging them to return with her to the tower.

On the way back, Margaret filled Catrìona's mind with ideas for the new ferry and the inn to serve the pilgrims. The enormity of the task excited her. Finally there was something for her to do of importance.

*   *   *

That evening, when Steinar came into the hall with Rhodri, his eyes were drawn to the king standing near the tower door speaking with the family that had arrived earlier that day. The man was stout and dark-haired, of middle years. The women with him both had the same nut-brown hair, one older and one younger. Their clothing told Steinar they were people of great wealth. The man's blue cloak was trimmed in gilted leather and the women wore silk gowns trimmed in velvet.

Steinar nudged Rhodri in the ribs. "Do you know those who speak with the king? I missed their names when they arrived earlier and I spent the afternoon holed up writing the king's missives."

"By the way he is dressed, I would say he is one of the king's mormaers, but I do not know either him or the women. I've been on the archery field most of the day."

The king and the family walked to the dais and were joined by the queen.

Steinar took his seat next to Rhodri, noting the young woman sitting on the dais was the same age as the queen's ladies. "Mayhap the woman is the replacement for Davina."

"She is comely enough," Rhodri observed without enthusiasm.

Having found her place at the high table, the young woman's gaze drifted about the hall, her nose tilted up. "Her manner suggests a haughty spirit."

"Whether she is haughty or no matters little," said Rhodri. "If she is to be one of the ladies who serve Margaret, she is likely here at her father's bidding to make a good match. Lands and coin will produce a husband for her even if she is a witch."

Rhodri had the right of it. Since Margaret had become queen, several of her ladies had left to marry one of the king's favored men. Fruit ripe for the picking. As he watched Catrìona, he realized he did not want her to be given to anyone save him, and particularly not to a man such as Domnall. No doubt her powerful uncle, the Mormaer of Atholl, had a hand in the match. Steinar did not want to think of another man touching her, of taking her innocence. But there was little he could say to prevent it.

"Take care lest you become obsessed with the flame-haired one," said Rhodri sliding onto the bench next to him.

"Mayhap you are right." At one time Steinar might have searched the hall for a willing woman to take to his bed. Now he watched only Catrìona. Tonight her face was lit with excitement as she and her cousin spoke in lively conversation. What had given rise to her impassioned mood?

"Her brother practices with the archers every day," Rhodri remarked, distracting him from Catrìona.

"Is Niall any good?"

"Quite good. Like your sister, Serena, skill with a bow comes easily to him and I expect he will ride with the archers on Malcolm's next raid."

"It will not be long now," Steinar remarked. "The king has summoned men from the provinces for that very purpose." Any day, Steinar expected to see warriors pouring in to Dunfermline in response to the king's missives to his chiefs.

The servants began setting pitchers of wine on the tables. Once the king's goblet was filled, he shot up from his seat and raised his goblet in toast to the new arrivals.

"To our guests, the Mormaer of Blackwell and his wife and daughter. Welcome to Dunfermline."

Goblets all around the hall were raised and wine quaffed as shouts of "Aye!" ascended from the crowd.

Servants set haunches of roast venison before them, the spicy aroma making Steinar's mouth water. A Saxon serving wench poured wine into their goblets, aiming a slow smile at Steinar as she did so. Long flaxen plaits complemented her round face and form, but he was not interested. He had eyes for only one woman.

"Will you entertain us this eve?" he asked Rhodri.

"Not tonight." He grinned. "I am to have the evening free." The bard sliced off a piece of meat and brought it to the trencher they shared. "The king has arranged for a group of minstrels for dancing."

★   ★   ★

"Dancing!" Catrìona exclaimed with pleasure. "I have not danced in a very long time. Not since before…" Her words trailed off as she remembered her parents had arranged for music and dancing the evening she and Domnall were to be betrothed. The vision of the planned gaiety faded from her mind, reminding her she and Domnall were not yet betrothed.

Across from her, Fia's blue eyes glistened excitedly. "I can hardly eat for the thought of dancing in King Malcolm's court. Do you think the bard will play with the minstrels? I would so like to dance with him." Her cousin's gaze shifted to where the bard sat with Steinar. "Rhodri is so handsome tonight in his green velvet tunic."

"You will have to wait and see," said Catrìona. "I expect there will be several instruments. Mandolins, flutes, mayhap even drums. He may be asked to join them."

Elspeth, the youngest of the queen's ladies, sat nearby flirting with one of the king's guards and giggling when he returned her smiles with a lusty glance.

"She had best contain her smiles," Fia whispered to Catrìona, "else she will soon be devoured by that one."

Her cousin's eyes were narrowed on a muscled warrior Catrìona had not noticed before, but now she could see there was a fierceness about his person. He had dark, intense eyes and a warrior's chest and arms. His long hair was neither blond nor brown but somewhere in between, held in place by a strip of leather encircling his head. Unlike his hair, his short beard and mustache were red.

"He is Colbán of Moray," said Fia, "captain of the king's guard and a man known for stealing young women's virtue."

Catrìona looked at her cousin. "How could you know that?"

"When you are off with Giric flying your falcon, I hear things and Niall sometimes passes to me what he learns from the men at archery practice. He thought to warn us."

Catrìona watched the one called Colbán as his dark eyes narrowed on Elspeth, like a wolf leering at a lamb. "He appears more man than a silly girl like Elspeth can handle," she whispered to Fia.

"He has an eye for the queen's ladies," said Fia in a low voice. " 'Tis said the king will give him one of us to wed."

Catrìona shrugged. It was no concern of hers, unless he desired her cousin. Inwardly, she feared he might, for Fia was very pretty.

Fia looked at her pointedly. "I have seen him watching *you* more than once."

"He can watch me all he wants," Catrìona pronounced defiantly. "I am promised to Domnall."

When the meal was concluded, the tables were pushed to the walls leaving a large space in the middle of the room for dancing on either side of the central hearth where the fire had been reduced to glowing embers.

Three minstrels took their places in front of the dais facing into the hall where men and women anxiously waited for the music to begin.

They had only begun to pluck at their instruments when Fia nudged her in the side. "Look! Rhodri is not among the musicians. Mayhap he will dance after all."

Catrìona grew anxious as she looked around the crowded hall, searching for Domnall. She had expected him to come to her when the music began, but he had not. "I wonder where Domnall is."

"I do not wish to be the bearer of sad news, Cousin, but look to the end of the dais where the new lady has just stepped down. See who awaits her?"

Catrìona's brows drew together, first in confusion, then in dismay, as she saw her intended kiss the hand of Blackwell's daughter and lead her to a group of dancers. "Why does Domnall seek *her* out?"

"You need look no farther than her father's fortune," came Fia's retort. "My father once told me the Mormaer of Blackwell has much land and many ships."

Would Domnall seek the hand of another for greater fortune? Shamed that the man to whom she had promised her heart had chosen another to partner, Catrìona turned to go. "I cannot stay," she told Fia.

She was in such a hurry to get away she did not see the tall blond scribe step into her path until she nearly collided with him. His chest was suddenly before her face and she came to a stop, raising her head to look into his unusual eyes.

He grinned broadly. "Will you dance with me, my lady?"

Swallowing hard, she blinked back the tears she had been holding in. "Of... of course." She took his offered hand and they joined the dancers forming a circle. His hand was large and warm and his grip sure. Somehow knowing he had hold of her gave her comfort. Too, Domnall would see she was not bereft of admirers.

The steps of the dance took them around the circle to the left. Given his limp, she was surprised how agile Steinar was at the quick steps. The dance forced her to concentrate and she smiled stiffly at the others, for inwardly she was hurting. The pain of Domnall's defection gnawed away at her. Appearing to be gay when she was downcast was not easy, but Steinar's seeming delight at being her partner helped to soothe the hurt Domnall's rejection had caused.

She stole a glance at the circle of dancers that included Domnall and Blackwell's daughter along with Elspeth and the king's captain.

Steinar drew her attention back to him when he said, "I have not had such a beautiful partner since the queen condescended to dance with me some months ago." Catrìona saw laughter in his beautiful blue thistle eyes.

She did not hide her gratitude. "To compare me to Margaret is compliment indeed. You exaggerate, of course." And then with a small smile, "But I will allow it."

The pace of the dance quickened as the minstrels played faster. When Fia and the bard joined their circle, Catrìona reached up to speak into Steinar's ear so he could hear her over the music. "Your friend partners with my cousin."

Watching the two, Steinar said, "Rhodri is much taken with her. He imagines she is Welsh."

"I have not known any Welshmen, save the bard, but Fia's roots are in Alba; she is a true Gael."

"Aye, he knows it, but he is smitten all the same."

Catching glimpses of Fia and the Welshman holding hands and dancing, their smiles only for each other, Catrìona had to admit, "And she with him."

"Rhodri is an unusual man," said Steinar.

"Because, like you, he is educated?"

"That and more. Even I do not know his whole story. He rarely speaks of his past."

The song ended and their hands dropped to their sides as they waited for another round to begin. Without meaning to, Catrìona's gaze caught Isla of Blackwell's hand reaching to Domnall's chest as she laughed. Pulling her thoughts back to the man standing beside her, she listened as he went on.

"Rhodri was in England for several years before coming with me to Scotland."

"Why did he come to Scotland?"

" 'Twas for friendship's sake. I could not stay in England but my wound made travel difficult. Rhodri helped me. I have always known someday he would return to Wales but I would not wish it to be soon."

The music began again and he took her hand, joining with the new circle forming. Forcing her gaze away from the circle where Domnall danced with the woman from Blackwell, Catrìona kept her eyes on the golden-haired scribe and her mind on the steps of the dance.

When the music stopped, she realized Steinar had not limped while they were dancing. "Your leg is better?"

"Aye, 'tis better every day."

The circle of dancers Catrìona and Steinar were a part of made room for the king and queen who had decided to join in the dancing. Catrìona studied the pair. They made a handsome couple with his kingly presence and her graceful bearing. On his dark head, he wore a golden crown. Her flaxen plaits hung long beneath her gold-crowned headscarf. Margaret was years younger than her husband and very pretty as she smiled up at the king. It was obvious they had danced together many times for they moved as one through the steps.

When the song ended, Catrìona was standing near the queen. Margaret put a hand to her chest, breathing deeply. "I am out of breath but I did love it so!"

On Margaret's other side, the king said, "Aye, *mo cridhe*, it has been too long."

A servant brought the king and the queen goblets of wine. Margaret sipped hers. Malcolm took a large swig and handed the goblet back to the servant. Bowing to the queen, the king walked to the center of the room, the eyes of the crowd upon him.

Margaret drew near Catrìona. "You must see this." Then the queen moved to the side of the room, her eyes on her husband.

A servant brought two swords and placed them across each other on the ground in front of the king.

Catrìona felt the anticipation of the men around her as Steinar leaned in to whisper, "The king is going to show us the victory dance he conceived. I'm told 'twas after a particularly bloody battle." When she looked at him in question, he said, "He slew one of Mac Bethad's chiefs and in recognition of his victory, Malcolm laid his victim's sword on the ground, crossed it with his own and danced around and over the naked blades in triumph."

Catrìona vaguely recalled her father, who had fought with Malcolm, telling her of a bizarre dance Malcolm had performed after the battle.

The music began slowly, a single steady drumbeat at first, as all eyes turned to the king. With uplifted arms, he began to lift his legs in high steps dancing around and over the crossed swords without ever touching either of them. For a man of middle years, he was most nimble. The people formed a circle around the king and began to clap their hands in time with the drum. The other instruments joined in as the drum beat faster.

" 'Tis not just a victory dance," Steinar explained, "but a reminder to the men their king is still the virile warrior he was when first he danced over his dead enemy's sword."

"Are not the son his wife bore him and the child she carries sufficient testimony of that?" asked Catrìona.

"Tis a different kind of virility," he said with a smile that made her blush.

Margaret, her hand on her rounded belly, stood silently watching, her face unreadable. She neither smiled at her husband's achievement nor did she look at him with disdain for what the crossed swords symbolized.

Margaret accepts the man she married without asking him to be what he is not. The wisdom displayed by her mistress did not escape Catrìona, yet, in many ways, she believed Margaret had tamed Malcolm and not the other way round.

As Malcolm continued to dance over the swords, Catrìona's thoughts drifted back to the day before when the queen had asked her to accompany her to a place in the woods she liked to go.

"The light is always good there," Margaret explained.

Catrìona quickly agreed and fetched her needlework, assuming the queen meant to do the same. They found places to sit under a tree by the burn some distance from the tower and both had embroidered for a while. Then Catrìona looked up from her needlework to see the queen reading from a small book lying open on her lap.

"What is the book you read, My Lady?" she asked.

The queen closed the book and the shimmer of jewels on its cover caused Catrìona to inhale sharply. The book was encased in gold and decorated in sapphires, rubies and emeralds. Sunlight filtering through the trees made the gems glisten. She had seen scrolls in her father's hillfort and she'd been given a Psalter as a young girl, but she had never seen a book like this. " 'Tis beautiful."

" 'Tis the Gospels I read always. I brought this with me to England from Hungary. 'Twas a gift from my father and my greatest treasure."

"I can see why. Surely it must be very valuable."

Margaret smiled. "It is, but not for the reason you might think. It was once covered in plain brown leather, worn with use, but Malcolm saw how I treasured it and had the gold cover and jewels added. It reminds me of Solomon's temple, bejeweled for God's glory. You see, the real treasure lies not with its cover, Catrìona, but with what is inside."

"I see." And she did. " 'Tis the words you prize."

"Yea, God's words to us."

Catrìona sighed, wishing she could be as devout as her mistress. "I once believed as you do, but that was before... before I lost my family." In between words, she had sobbed, unable to stop the flow of tears. "I have tried… but I find that I cannot accept a God who could allow such evil."

Margaret had set aside her bejeweled book and put her arm around Catrìona's shoulders, drawing her close. It was a tender gesture more like that of the mother she had lost than of her queen. "My dear Catrìona, God knows your heart better than you do yourself. He knows you will heal and return to Him."

Such faith… such kindness!

Catrìona had come to love her mistress and understood why the king loved what was precious to Margaret. For all that he could not read, Malcolm had covered Margaret's volume of the Gospels with jewels for love of his queen.

Catrìona's straying thoughts returned to the hall just as the king finished his sword dance and the hall erupted in shouts of praise.

"Come," said Steinar, "let us get some wine. I have grown thirsty with so much dancing."

Catrìona felt the beads of sweat on her brow and the trickle between her breasts. The hall had grown overwarm with all the people dancing. "Aye, some wine would be welcome."

He guided her to a table where pitchers of wine and goblets had been set out. Catrìona noticed his limp had returned.

"Does your leg pain you?" she asked.

"Only when I forget to rest it. I have so enjoyed dancing with you, my lady, I fair forgot."

She laughed. "Again you exaggerate." From the corner of her eye, she saw Domnall moving toward her, the woman from Blackwell's hand tucked into the crook of his elbow.

CHAPTER 7

Steinar heard Catrìona's sudden intake of breath and turned to see her rigid stance and her eyes staring straight ahead, as if preparing for an onslaught. The cause of her anxious state quickly became apparent as he followed her gaze.

The nobleman from Leinster, Domnall mac Murchada—the one to whom she was supposedly "all but betrothed"—was coming toward them, Blackwell's daughter on his arm.

"Greetings, Catrìona, and to you, Steinar," the Irishman said as he approached. "I understand you have met Isla of Blackwell, Catrìona."

She nodded. "We met earlier today."

He turned his face to Isla. "Well, since you have met Catrìona, allow me to introduce Steinar, the king's scribe."

"My lady," Steinar said, bowing over Isla's offered hand.

Isla gave him a dismissive glance. "How unusual to have a scribe who is not a man of the church."

"Aye," was Steinar's only response. He did not like the superior tone in the woman's voice and he sensed Catrìona was hurt by Domnall's attention to the woman.

Steinar wondered what the man was about. If Domnall was to marry Catrìona, why had he been dancing with the queen's new lady? *Was the man mad?* Surely his actions were beyond mere courtesy to a new arrival.

Steinar forgot the wine they had been about to have, wanting to take Catrìona away from the uncomfortable scene. "If you will excuse us," he said to the pair, "we were just about to go outside."

Domnall did not object. Instead, he bowed to Catrìona as they took their leave.

Steinar guided her through the door and into the night. The sky was the color of pale heather as it often was at gloaming in the long summer days.

Behind them, the door creaked open and Angus, her protector, stepped out and leaned against the stone wall of the tower, crossing his arms over his chest in an unsubtle warning.

They walked a short distance away. "None of the other ladies brings a guard to Malcolm's court," he said to Catrìona. "I think yours mistrusts me."

"Do not mind Angus. He is just doing what my father would have wanted, ever faithful to his oath. He has stood by me since... since my father's death."

Seeing again the pain in her eyes, he did not want to speak of unpleasant things nor embarrass her about Domnall's slight, but he would give her the opportunity to confide in him if she chose. "Did you want to tell me of it?"

"Not tonight," she said somberly, looking at the ground.

Respecting her wishes, he would speak of something else. "The queen has told me of her plans for the ferry and the inn for the pilgrims." And then with a smile, "Your new undertaking."

"Did she?" Catrìona asked, her somber mood appearing to lift.

" 'Twill be the queen's boldest venture yet."

"But a worthy one, do you not think?" In her eyes, he saw a fervor he'd not seen before.

"I do. The pilgrims traveling to St. Andrew's shrine will be forever in Malcolm's debt."

"I rather think the pilgrims will know 'tis the *queen's* ferry they ride without charge," she said, "but I do hope the king will support Margaret in this."

"She can be most persuasive where he is concerned. And you are right," he admitted. "The people will know such charity, if granted, comes from the queen."

"She told me you and I are to help her. Did she say what we are to do? I've not spoken with her about the details, only her vision for the completed work."

"She intends to speak with the king," Steinar said, laying out what the queen had told him. "Once he approves, which I expect he will, Margaret will soon have the men and materials to begin the task."

"That will please Margaret."

"You and I are to be her partners in this new work," he said with a grin.

She shot him a side-glance. "That should be entertaining,"

Her teasing manner told him her mood had improved and he was glad of it. Even if she were hiding her true feelings, he would try and encourage her. "Margaret has much confidence in you. She told me of all her ladies you are the only one she would entrust with such a project."

He was pleased when Catrìona's cheeks turned scarlet, bringing color to her face that had been pale before and hoped she had forgotten the scene in the hall. He felt only disgust for Domnall's actions and what they portended. Steinar suspected his attentions to Isla of Blackwell were more than a kindness to the new lady. He had never considered Domnall worthy of Catrìona. If the Irish noble were no longer in her future, she would be free to accept another. As soon as that became known, Malcolm's men would begin circling like wolves around a stranded fawn. *What will I do if that happens?*

"Let us see about that wine," he said, offering her his arm. And then with a smile, "Mayhap Angus is thirsty."

★   ★   ★

Catrìona had yet to break her fast and was feeding a small girl when Fia hissed into her ear, "I do not know how Margaret puts up with her!"

Isla of Blackwell had turned away from the orphans, refusing to join the ladies in feeding them and walked to the hearth reaching her hands toward the fire. The woman had missed the morning prayers with the queen, keeping to her chamber until it was time to break her fast.

Catrìona did not like to think of Isla else the tears would begin to fall. In the fortnight since the woman had arrived at Dunfermline, things had changed with Domnall. He now paid open court to the lady from Blackwell and she often spoke of him, bragging of her conquest.

Catrìona had believed Isla was unaware Domnall had been intended for her, but when she had suggested as much to Fia, her cousin was quick to disagree. "Oh, she knows you were Domnall's intended. 'Twas common knowledge around the hall. That is why the other men kept their distance from you, well, all save the scribe. And none of the men worried much over him. No, Isla is merely indifferent to another's pain."

To think Isla knew and did not care made it all the worse as the conversation at the ladies' table continued.

"Why, only last eve," Isla said to Audra, "Domnall described his home in Leinster to me and told me how much he wants me to see it. He plans to speak to my father on his way home."

"Domnall goes home?" asked Audra, shooting a glance at Catrìona.

"Only for a time. He has family matters to see to and he is negotiating a trading venture between Leinster and King Malcolm."

That Domnall had shared his business with this new lady—things he had never told her—caused a deep hurt within Catrìona. She felt the tears well in her eyes. Unable to stand more of the woman's boasting, with a hasty apology to the queen, Catrìona fled the hall as her tears began to flow.

She ran from the tower into the forest not realizing she had come to the place next to the burn where she had sat with the queen. The only sounds were those of the water rushing over stones and the birds in the trees above her.

She sat on a fallen log crossing her arms tightly around her, rocking back and forth, as the tears fell. *How could he do this? And without a word to me!*

Hearing footfalls behind her coming closer along the path, she brushed the tears from her face and turned her head toward the stream, hoping whoever it was would pass her by.

"Catrìona."

The queen.

Catrìona turned to face her mistress.

"It occurred to me you might come here. I think I know why you weep but I would listen if you would speak of it," said Margaret.

Catriona got to her feet, unwilling to keep all that was in her heart from the queen. "The man my father chose for me, the man I thought to wed, has now chosen another."

"Ah," Margaret said knowingly as she beckoned Catriona to sit and eased herself down beside her. "Domnall mac Murchada. I have observed his actions toward Isla of Blackwell. 'Twould seem he has at last found someone much like himself."

"What do you mean?"

"In the year he has been in Dunfermline, I have become aware of ill-favored character. He is not one I would have chosen for you."

Catriona drew little comfort from Margaret's words. All she could think of was Domnall's rejection. Beneath the hurt he had caused was the pain from the loss of her parents. The deep wounds had not healed. Mayhap they never would. " 'Tis not just Domnall, My Lady. My heart is broken; I am distraught for all that I have lost."

Margaret took Catriona's trembling hand in hers. "I know you have suffered much, Catriona, and I am very sorry for your pain. It was my hope when you came to us that you would find healing. You will, in time."

Catriona looked into the queen's gentle sky-colored eyes. "I hope so, My Lady."

Margaret gave her an understanding smile. "There is no soul so damaged, no heart so broken, it cannot be healed by God, Catriona."

Tears flowed from Catriona's eyes in a great rush as she turned into Margaret's comforting arms wanting desperately for the words to be true.

The queen stroked her back. "I know what it is to experience loss, Catriona. I was still young when my father died. Then, my country was torn from me and my family's lives threatened so that we had to flee. I know fear."

Guilt crept over Catriona. How could she wallow in self-pity when the queen had lost her father and her home, even her country? Catriona sat up and blinked back the tears filling her eyes. "I am sorry, My Lady."

"Few among us have not known tragedy. I, too, once doubted God."

She could not believe this devout queen had ever doubted God. "You?"

A smile crossed her face. " 'Tis quite human, I have discovered. God understands your grief, Catrìona, as He did mine. Did not evil men kill His Son? But that terrible loss was part of a greater plan."

Catrìona nodded as Margaret spoke, seeing truth in the queen's words.

"God has a greater plan for us, as well. Sometimes His plans are different than ours." The queen looked into her eyes. "We must accept whatever He allows into our lives, trusting Him to use it for good."

It was hard for Catrìona to accept all that had happened as the queen suggested she should, but Margaret's words made her wonder for the first time if mayhap she was not intended for Domnall after all. What if her father had been wrong to choose him? Painful though the possibility was, she had to consider it might be true.

"You knew, of course, that I did not wish to marry," said the queen.

"Aye," said Catrìona, wiping away the last of the tears. "Edgar told me."

"It was Edgar who persuaded me to accept Malcolm's suit. He told me I had to do it for the family's protection and to give him the powerful ally he needed to try and take back England."

"And so you married Malcolm…"

"I did. Out of duty, at first. But I have come to see, 'twas not Edgar who betrothed me to Malcolm. 'Twas God."

At Catrìona's look of surprise, Margaret said, "Like you, the life I once thought to have was not to be. Instead, God gave me a loving husband and a country to serve. A different calling, but one no less worthy."

"You love the king." Why it had suddenly occurred to Catrìona she could not say. It might have been the wistful look in Margaret's eyes when she spoke of her husband.

"Yea, I do. I love my husband and his people, who are now my people."

"I admire all you do for them, especially the poor," said Catrìona. "It has become one of my joys to help the orphans."

Margaret stared past Catrìona to the waters of the burn, flowing fast with the summer rains they had experienced. "I have tried to be a proper wife for Malcolm, to do what seems needful for Scotland, encouraging trade with other countries, bringing to our shores new wares, making the tower a fit home for a king and sharing with Malcolm God's truth. But I ask God, what more would He have me do?"

"Is that what you pray for?" asked Catrìona, curious as to what consumed the queen's prayers when she secluded herself in the cave.

"I pray for Scotland, for her future, her people and for wisdom for my husband to lead them." Tears filled Margaret's eyes as she spoke. "I ask God for children who will serve Him and Scotland after Malcolm and I are gone from this life."

A lump formed in Catrìona's throat as she pondered the queen's devotion to her new country and her husband. "Surely God will honor your prayers. None doubt that the Lady of Scotland loves God and the people."

Margaret smiled. "It pleases me to think so," she said, slowly rising, her hand pressing into her lower back.

Catrìona got to her feet. "Does the child pain you, My Lady?"

"Nay, but sometimes my back aches. 'Tis nothing. Come," urged the queen, "let us return." Smiling, she said, "We have a ferry to build and an inn to see to. 'Tis a challenge worthy of you, Catrìona. And it should please you to know the king has given his consent to all we spoke of."

Encouraged by the queen, Catrìona rose and walked back to the tower speaking of the future that lay ahead. To Catrìona, they seemed like two friends walking the path together.

★　★　★

Catrìona lifted her head from the miserable embroidery she had struggled with all morning. Twice she had torn out a thread to replace it with another. Her flowers, she sadly admitted, looked more like bannocks than blossoms.

The heat in the chamber where the queen's ladies labored was oppressive this summer morning. With a deep sigh, she set aside the odious task and begged leave to get some air. Margaret, always accommodating, gave a gracious nod of assent.

Hurriedly, lest the queen change her mind, Catrìona left the chamber and headed down the corridor thinking she might visit Kessog in the mews to see how his molt was coming along.

Feeling better as she descended the stairs to the hall where the air was fresher, she was nearly at the last step when she looked up to see the captain of the king's guard striding toward her from the hearth. Colbán's long legs quickly covered the distance between them.

She stopped on the last stair, waiting. What could he want?

Her curiosity changed to wonder when, reaching her, he bowed in deep obeisance.

"Lady Catrìona."

The king's captain had never paid her much attention except for perfunctory greetings when she came into the hall with the queen's ladies. But she remembered Fia's remark that he had watched her. "Sir?" she asked warily.

"I had hoped to catch you away from the others."

She waited expectantly, interested to know why he should need to speak to her alone. Except for the servants, the hall was typically empty at this time of the day, as he must have known.

When he hesitated, she stepped down from the stair to the floor, which she immediately realized was a mistake. Now he loomed over her, like a huge bear. And his dark eyes were intently focused on her.

She swallowed. " 'Twould seem your timing is good, sir."

Despite his initial approach, which she judged overbold, he now appeared diffident, confusing her. His brown eyes grew warm as he considered her while anxiously fumbling with a length of copper-colored cloth he carried.

Without warning, he thrust the cloth toward her.

She reached for it with both hands. It was soft, fine wool. A man's tunic mayhap? With raised brows, she looked up at him. "Sir?"

" 'Tis mine," he said. "I know the queen's ladies embroider garments when they devote themselves to their needlework. I would ask you to embroider this for me."

Beneath the request Catrìona heard a tone of command. But then, the king's captain was used to having his requests carried out as ordered and, after all, she was only a woman. "Sir, there are others among the queen's ladies whose fingers are more skillful than mine with a needle. I would be happy to ask one of them—"

"Nay!" he blurted out. Then pausing, he began again. "It must be *your* hand that embroiders the tunic."

Why mine? His intense gaze remained fixed on her, telling her there was no use in arguing. Sighing in resignation, she said, "Very well, if it will please you, I will try."

He flashed her a brilliant smile, his teeth white between his red mustache and beard. "Aye, 'twould please me." With that he bowed, turned and stalked off toward the tower door.

Flustered, she watched him go. *How strange.*

Her original mission forgotten, she turned on her heels and slowly climbed the long set of wooden stairs, casting a glance at her scarred fingertips, hoping she would not bleed all over the tunic when she attempted to adorn it with some sort of design that might please such a man.

★   ★   ★

In the days that followed the celebration of Maerleswein and Davina's betrothal, Steinar watched with interest as warriors flocked to Dunfermline from provinces near and far in response to the king's summons. Many rode horses and carried fine swords. Others were archers skilled enough to garner Rhodri's respect. Still others were men-at-arms pledged to a mormaer.

The village bulged with men overflowing the taverns, keeping the serving wenches busy. Tents were erected to house the soldiers and the night air smelled of their cook fires that illuminated the meadows and trees all around the burn.

Special contingents had to be dispatched to hunt in order to feed all the men. Each evening their captains dined in the hall that swelled with the new arrivals.

With so many warriors in such a crowded area, there were bound to be fights, especially if one of them was full of wine and took offense at something that was said.

Colbán, captain of Malcolm's guard, did not tolerate open fighting among the men and disputes, when they erupted into violence, were quickly quashed. But there was one man who caused more problems than the others, a swaggering braggart named Rian of Lothian.

More than once Steinar had heard the king mutter under his breath that in Rian of Lothian, Maerleswein had foisted off on his king a particularly troublesome piece of flesh.

"Probably laughing at me this very moment," Malcolm had said.

Rian bore scars on his face that announced to all he was a wild brute of a man. Jagged wounds ill healed. His brown hair was always disheveled and his clothing looked more animal in origin than the fine woolens favored at Malcolm's court. He was as wide as he was tall but he had not gone to fat. The braggart was all muscle and sinew.

He had instigated several fights in the village and no father would allow his daughter near the man. It took the constant vigilance of the king's guard to keep the peace when Rian was involved.

That afternoon, as Steinar was returning from his surreptitious sword practice in the woods, his leg paining him for not having rested it, he came upon Rian and his rabble of followers. With ugly jeers and much laughter, they were tormenting Giric's little dog, Shadow.

Rian prodded the little dog with a stick. Shadow's barking merely incited the brute's followers.

"What is that, a barking rat? Smite it harder, Rian!" said one from where he leaned against the stable.

"Just a wee beastie," drawled another.

"Whatever it is, makes an irksome noise," said Rian.

When the dog kept barking, Rian kicked it with his boot.

The dog's yelp brought Giric running. Scooping him up, the boy shouted, "Leave 'im be!"

"Ho! What have we here?" Rian said his eyes narrowing on Giric. "Can this be the master of the rat? Or mayhap 'tis his brother. Both are mangy little scraps. Come here, let me get a closer look at ye." When Giric started to back away, Rian made a grab for the boy's collar and growled in anger when Giric kicked him and, dodging his grip, stepped aside, clutching the whimpering dog to his chest.

Steinar took a step forward, intending to call a halt to the farce, when Niall strode across the open ground and stepped in front of the boy. Gently shoving him aside, he said. "Take him away, Giric. I will handle this."

Niall faced Rian, a slim youth against a muscled brute. "Seems to me you are a bit large to be picking on wee dogs and littlings."

Rian's face twisted into a grimace as he circled Niall while the brute's friends shouted insults.

" 'Tis only a lad hisself," said one blustering fellow.

"I am nae certain 'tis even a lad," taunted Rian. "Might be a girl with that long red hair."

Rian's companions erupted in cruel laughter.

Niall said nothing but stood his ground, his bow slung over his shoulder, his chin jutting out.

Rian glanced over his shoulder at his companions, grinned and charged. His beefy shoulder caught Niall full in the chest, knocking him off his feet.

Niall fell and a loud snap rent the air as his bow broke beneath him. He jumped up, ripped the broken bow from his shoulder and yanked the seax at his hip from its leather sheath.

Rian smirked and slowly pulled his sword from its scabbard, the steel making a cold threatening ring as it slid free. He waved the sword menacingly in front of Niall's face.

The men watching backed away, Rian's followers among them.

Steinar had been watching for Colbán or one of the king's guards, someone who actually had authority over the men, but none were present.

So it must be me.

"Enough!" Steinar shouted, striding into the middle of the rising tension. He stood in front of Niall, facing Rian. "What goes here?"

CHAPTER 8

Catrìona had only stepped though the tower door when the loud shouts of men stopped her. Not far away in the open area between the tower and the outbuildings, a group of men circled around what sounded like a brawl. There had been more instances of such fighting since the new warriors had come to Dunfermline. She often took a circuitous path to avoid them and she would do so now.

She had taken only a few steps when Giric came running toward her, his dog at his side barking furiously. " 'Tis the scribe, my lady!" He grabbed her hand and pulled her toward the circle of men. Through a break in the crowd, she saw Niall standing to one side, his bow broken at his feet and the scribe in front of him facing a thick-shouldered warrior wielding a long sword.

Fear gripped her. What had happened? Was Steinar unarmed against the warrior's sword?

The ring of steel cut through the men's shouts as Steinar jerked his sword from its scabbard and held it before him, his legs slightly apart. *Where had he found a sword?*

The crowd stepped back, murmuring.

Giric let go of her hand and drew closer to the looming fight. She reached out and grabbed him, pulling him toward her. "Stand up here," she told him and led him to a bench he could stand on to safely watch. She stepped closer to watch what transpired.

"Anyone can defeat a youth who carries only a knife," Steinar said to the large warrior whose back faced her. "Let us see how you do against a man who is armed with a sword!" The undercurrent in Steinar's voice bespoke anger but also the confidence of one who knew how to wield such a blade. She understood he had once been a warrior but that had been years ago. What of now?

The two men appeared evenly matched in height but Steinar was leaner and younger. His long golden hair settled on his shoulders, reflecting the sun like a torch, while the mountain of a man who would fight him was dark, his hair shorter and unkempt.

She heard the sneer in his opponent's voice as he pulled his seax from his hip to join the sword he held in his other hand. "This should prove a novelty, cutting up a scribe. But ye need have no worry. I will leave yer right hand should the king find himself in need of a scrivener." The man bellowed his laughter.

Slowly pulling his own short sword from his belt, Steinar said, "If you wish to fight with two blades, I can accommodate you."

Now each man held a sword and a long knife, poised to strike. With growing dismay, Catriona realized there would be no shields in this fight, only blades, and no mail to shield tender flesh. She bit her knuckled fist, tension building inside her. Could Steinar fight the older, larger man?

"It seems I must be the one to teach you manners," Steinar calmly said as he began to circle his opponent. " 'Tis not wise to mistreat those invited to the king's court."

The crowd moved back as the two men circled each other. Through the gaps in the shifting men, she watched the swords and knives poised to strike.

The one called Rian suddenly lunged for the scribe's chest, but Steinar slipped to the side as if he'd anticipated the move. As he did, he sliced the other man's leg.

A line of red emerged on Rian's hosen and the man howled his anger.

The crowd backed away as Steinar took another step, his right leg appearing to falter.

Catriona inhaled sharply, praying he would have the strength to continue. She could not bear for him to be hurt by this man who, she was certain, would show no mercy.

But she need not have feared, for Steinar was ready for the stocky warrior's next strike, beating back the larger man's sword and seax with blows Rian strained to fend off.

The sound of steel meeting steel filled the air as the four weapons clashed in rapid succession.

Steinar's feet moved in a fluid motion. At times his steps were so fast it was difficult to see them. The dazzling display seemed to confuse his opponent who shook his head as if trying to focus on Steinar's blades.

"The scribe can fight!" called out one man.

"Aye and well," said another.

"The scribe is good!" Giric cried out to her. His dog, Shadow, barked each time the crowd grew excited or surged toward them.

Before her eyes, the man she had known only as a scribe had turned into a fierce warrior, his movements sure and practiced, his sword arm strong. At times, the metal flashed so fast the blades were nearly a blur.

Out of the corner of her eye, Catrìona glimpsed the king and Colbán come around the corner of the tower. As they drew near her, the two men paused to watch the fight.

The crowd shouted encouragement to the two locked in a deadly clash of blades, their gazes so fixed on the combat they did not see the king.

Malcolm crossed his arms over his chest and tilted his head to one side, appearing to study the fight with keen interest.

Steinar and his fulsome opponent slowed, circling each other, wiping sweat from their faces with the sleeves of their tunics. It appeared to Catrìona that Rian was starting to tire, his feet faltering in the face of so much skill.

Mayhap he is as surprised as the rest of them that Steinar can wield a blade.

Rian slashed at Steinar with his knife while swinging his sword, but Steinar danced away.

The crowd murmured their amazement at Steinar's ability to repeatedly deflect the blade of a man whose sword they had obviously feared. Catrìona felt relief Steinar was holding his own and pride welled up inside her to think that, even with a wounded leg, he should fight so well. *What a magnificent warrior he is!*

Steinar pivoted to avoid the other man's lunge but one edge of Rian's sword caught the scribe's arm. He winced and shoved his seax into the sheath at his belt.

What is he doing?

Grabbing the pointed end of his own sword with his glove, while holding the hilt in his other hand, Steinar met Rian's next strike with a forceful blow of the blunt side of the blade. His shoulder muscles flexed beneath his tunic with the impact that shoved Rian back.

The larger man stumbled and his sword fell from his hand, clanging as it hit the ground.

The scribe kicked it away. "Do you wish to continue with only that knife?" he asked.

Rian sheathed his seax, his chest heaving with exertion. "Nay, 'tis enough."

"Then concede me the victory," Steinar said.

The brute named Rian wiped his face with the back of his hand. "Ye have won."

Steinar sheathed his sword. "From now on, you will leave the archer alone?" And Catrìona realized Steinar referred to her brother.

"Aye, I'll leave the paltry archer be," Rian conceded with bad grace.

"I'd be careful what you call the king's archers," Steinar cautioned. "Their arrows bear the kiss of death."

The crowd was quiet now, listening with interest.

Giric jumped from the bench and ran to her side, his dog following. "Did ye see him? Did ye see the scribe fight?"

"Aye," she said. "I saw it all."

Rhodri came to stand beside Niall. "I will see you have a new bow, this time a longbow of elm like mine."

Niall smiled his approval.

Catrìona's heart burst with gratitude for Steinar's defense of her brother. But before she could go to him to express her thanks, the king strode into the midst of the crowd, a satisfied smile on his face.

Seeing the king, the crowd of men fell away.

Steinar, whose back had been to the king, whirled around, a look of incredulity on his face. "My Lord."

Malcolm slapped Steinar on the back. "It appears you have as much skill with a sword as you do with a quill."

The men standing around nodded.

"I have need of your sword arm as one of my guards," said the king.

Catrìona's heart lurched. *Oh, God, a guard.* A guard was a man of war like her father, like all of Malcolm's men. Steinar could be injured or killed.

"As for you, Rian of Lothian," Malcolm's tone was harsh as he faced the warrior, towering over him, "if ever I hear of you instigating another fight, you will be gone from my court."

Rian dipped his head, his shoulders slumped. "Aye, My Lord."

"It occurs to me," said the king to Steinar, "if you accompany me to Northumbria, I will have both a guard at my back and a scribe for my messages. 'Twould please the queen." He shot a glance at Rhodri. "A scribe who is a swordsman and a bard who leads my archers. Ha! I shall keep both of you close."

Colbán, the captain of Malcolm's guard, dipped his head to Catrìona as he passed her and joined the king. "We will be glad for his sword arm," he said to Malcolm.

With a satisfied smile directed at the king, Steinar said, "As you wish."

Catrìona could see he was pleased, but she was not certain *she* was pleased. His arm was bleeding from where the ruffian had cut him. The idea of Steinar lying on the ground wounded or worse struck her like a blow. *I care too much to see him hurt.*

Malcolm swept his arm toward the tower in grand gesture. "Come," he said to Steinar and Rhodri, "let us share some wine in my hall. Colbán, you will join us."

The captain of the guard dipped his head to the king.

Malcolm put his arm around Steinar's shoulder and they proceeded toward the door of the tower. Behind the king and Steinar, Rhodri strolled with Colbán.

As they passed, she noted Steinar limped slightly, making her worry all the more. He glanced at her over his shoulder, but if there was a message in his eyes, she could not decipher it.

*　　*　　*

Steinar set down his goblet, content, but feeling the effects of too much wine and no food. The king and Colbán might be at it for some time, but he'd had enough. Across from him, Rhodri had just finished his last goblet. "While I am happy to be joining the ranks of Malcolm's warriors," he said to Rhodri in a low voice, "one more toast and I will be drowning in wine."

"Aye and I've a pretty lass to meet," whispered the bard. "I must go ere I am late."

"You meet Catrìona's cousin?"

"I do," said the Welshman, his deep brown eyes twinkling.

"Be careful, my friend," Steinar cautioned. He hoped Rhodri did not draw the ire of the king for his attention to one of Margaret's ladies.

Ignoring Steinar's words, Rhodri said, "Until this eve!" and hurriedly left the hall.

Steinar sat staring at the closed door, wondering how far things had gone between his friend and the girl. Rhodri had dallied with his share of the ladies who frequented Malcolm's court, always with much success. But this one was different. Fia of Atholl was the daughter of a powerful mormaer. And Steinar was certain the Welshman was in love.

His own besotted state was ever before him. Now that he was again a warrior and one of the king's guards, did he dare think he could win Catrìona's hand? And, with that thought, he began to think of the beautiful firebrand as within his reach.

The king's next words ended Steinar's pondering. "Prepare yourself, Scribe. We ride at dawn."

* * *

Rhodri set out for the place where he had agreed to meet Fia, not far from the tower but still sheltered from curious eyes. With each step his heart beat faster in anticipation of seeing her. They had been careful about their stolen moments. Only Steinar knew they had been meeting in secret.

Never had Rhodri expected to find the woman he wanted at Malcolm's court. He had enjoyed the favors of many since coming to Dunfermline, but none had captured his heart like the dark-haired lass from Atholl. Undaunted by what she believed was a love that could never be, she had allowed their love to grow.

This would be their last chance to be alone before he left for Northumbria. As he came through the copse of trees, he saw her waiting in the lee of a large rock, her long dark hair falling down her back over a sapphire blue gown, the same color as her beautiful eyes.

He stilled when he heard her singing. It was one of his own songs and her voice was sweet to his ears.

"You sing a pleasant melody, my love."

Whirling around, she ran to him. "Oh, Rhodri, I thought you would never come!"

Tortured all morning because he had been unable to touch her, he took her in his arms and kissed her.

Threading her fingers through his head of curls, she pressed her young body against his own.

"I have missed you, my Fia," he whispered in her ear as he showered her forehead and face with kisses.

In response, she pulled his head down to her and kissed him, a wild open-mouthed kiss that left him breathing heavily and his groin swelling.

When their lips finally parted, he said, " 'Tis best we do not continue or I will be taking you to the meadow to make love to you amid the flowers."

"You would not..."

"Nay, but that does not mean I do not think of it." He took her hand and led her to the fallen log they often sat upon.

Changing the subject, she asked, "Why were you late?"

"I would have been here sooner but the king detained Steinar to celebrate his victory over Rian and insisted I join them. Did you see the fight?"

"I did not, but Catriona told me of it. She is very grateful for his defending Niall. She did not say it, but I think she worries about Steinar's joining the king's guard. She cares for your friend, you know."

"And he for her."

"Will you go to Northumbria? Catriona said the king intends you and Steinar both go."

"I was always to go, but now I shall have Steinar with me." Glimpsing the sadness in her eyes, he took her small hands in his. "Will you worry for me while I am gone?"

"I will not!" she said too quickly and tried to pull away.

He held on to her hands, bringing her knuckles to his lips. She turned her head to face him, blushing as he kissed her fingers. "I think you will," he said with a grin. Letting go of her hands, he put his arm around her and drew her close. "Have no fear, my blue-eyed lass from Atholl, I shall return to you."

"You tease me," she said, but did not move from his embrace.

"That is only because you are so serious. 'Tis a good balance you are for me, for I am ever one to play." Then he kissed her again. When the kiss ended, he said, "I will miss seeing your face each day."

"Aye, and I will miss you," she said with a pretty blush in her cheeks.

"I would have a token from you, Fia, one of your ribands to carry with me, one that is the color of your eyes." Many women had given him such tokens but only this one was important. Only this one would he carry next to his heart.

"Aye," she said smiling, delighted at his request. "I will bring it to the evening meal tonight."

"We have but a little time now. You asked before about my home in Gwynedd. I will tell you about it and you can tell me about Atholl. I have seen much of England but little of Scotland and I would know of this land that gave birth to you."

And so he sat next to her and spoke of the land of his birth. " 'Tis a beautiful place, Gwynedd is, with mountains and—as you would call them—lochs. My home lies in the west. 'Tis not so different from Scotland. You would like it."

She turned her face away. "I will never see it."

"Mayhap you will one day. Now tell me of Atholl."

As he listened to her description of her home, he did not tell her all that was in his heart. She was everything he wanted in a woman, in a wife. But to her, he was only a bard and an archer, not one who could claim a mormaer's daughter. He admired her courage in loving a man who was beneath her station. She did not yet know he was more than a bard, more than a warrior. But one day she would.

When she had finished telling him of Dunkeld and Atholl, she faced him, her blue eyes pleading. "Oh, Rhodri, promise me you will be careful in Northumbria."

"I am always careful, my love. Besides, I have one hundred archers under my command, many with longbows like mine. Once we let our volley of arrows fly, we seek cover in the trees to send more arrows into our enemies."

"Is that why you always wear green and brown?"

"Aye, to blend with the forest and the land. 'Tis the manner of Welshmen who are skilled with the bow."

"Does Niall go with you?"

"He does, and most willingly. 'Twill be his first time in battle and he will carry a new bow I will make him."

"Cat will worry."

"You must assure her I will see Niall safely home. He will be at my side and never away from my protection. I will guard him well."

She laid her head on his shoulder. "Oh, Rhodri, what is to become of us?"

He pressed his lips to her forehead. "Have no worry for the future, my Fia. Trust me to have guard over that as well."

⋆   ⋆   ⋆

Early the next morning, before the sun had made an appearance, Catrìona joined the queen and her ladies in the chapel to pray for Malcolm and his men. Her conversations with Fia had told her that her cousin worried for the bard who would lead the king's archers into battle. Catrìona worried for Steinar and the limp that always told her he was weary. Niall, too, would go and she feared for him, as well. She could not lose her brother.

Kneeling, she said her prayers in Latin but the rote words did not echo the cry of her heart. Kings went out to war with little thought for the women they left behind. A woman's only weapon was prayer. But she had learned from Margaret, it was a mighty weapon.

Oh God, please bring them safely back to me.

The mood, as they broke their fast that morning, was somber. Even Giric was subdued as he stared at the men eating in their mail-clad tunics with swords and knives belted at their waists.

The men, eager to ride, were noisy in their leaving as they pushed back the benches, speaking of the coming raid as they headed for the door. Catrìona watched them pass, ignoring their interested gazes. More of Malcolm's men had begun to notice her now that Domnall had openly paid court to Isla.

As the men flowed out the door, she spotted Steinar standing to the side, talking with one of the men. When he was alone, she came to stand before him. He had plaited the hair on either side of his face keeping the hair from his eyes. He wore mail and a sword, marks of his new position with the king.

"Catrìona," he said, looking glad to see her.

His unusual eyes drew her into their depths and suddenly it was hard to breathe. "I... I have yet to thank you for what you did for my brother."

"Niall came to Giric's rescue and I came to aid Niall. I only did what needed being done. I do not think Rian will bother him or the boy again."

"You have my gratitude." *And more.* "I have never seen any man better with a sword."

"I grow stronger."

"But you will be careful now that you serve as one of the king's guards?" She could not bring herself to admit he was going to Northumbria to raid even though she perceived well enough the king's intent.

"I will."

"And I will pray for your safe return."

He smiled at her words. "I am grateful, my lady, and I would ask a favor."

"Anything," she said.

"I understand your cousin has given Rhodri one of her ribands to take with him, a simple token from a queen's lady. Might I beg one of yours?"

It was the gesture of a woman who held a tendre for a warrior to give him a token of her affection. She knew Fia had a fondness for the bard and Catrìona certainly harbored a tendre for Steinar, though she had never told him of her feelings. Still, she did not stop to consider. She would not deny the request of a man riding off to battle, mayhap to his death.

Without hesitating, she pulled an emerald silk riband from her plait and handed it to him. "To remind you that I will pray for your safe return."

He pressed the silk to his lips, then tucked it beneath his mail. "I shall carry it next to my heart, my lady." He bowed and followed the other warriors out of the hall.

She watched him go through the door. *He takes my heart with him.*

As the last of the men left the tower, with a feeling of resignation sitting heavy on her chest, she followed. Just outside, Fia waited with the other women watching the warriors mounting their horses, their shields and helms fixed to their saddles.

At the head of the column, King Malcolm sat proudly on his white charger. Beside him was Duff, Mormaer of Fife, on his chestnut-colored courser. Audra had told them her father's place as leader of the king's army was a privilege granted for Duff's loyalty.

Steinar rode a fine black horse, a stallion strong of bone with a deep chest and long mane. She had never seen him clad in mail and mounted on a horse. Her heart ached to see him depart with Malcolm's warriors, heavily armed for war. But Steinar's expression told her he was pleased to be among them.

Giric appeared beside her and slipped his small hand in hers. "Be he all right?"

She knew of whom he spoke for he and Steinar had formed a bond. "Aye, he will," she said, assuring him as she did herself. *He must return.*

Fia's gaze followed the bard in front of the archers. Still holding Giric's hand, Catrìona put her arm around Fia. "They will return, for the queen prays for them and her prayers are surely of great effect."

Then, spotting Niall behind Rhodri, Catrìona silently prayed for her brother. This was the first time he rode into battle and, though Fia had assured her Rhodri would protect him, Catrìona could only see his youth. God had spared him once. She prayed Niall would be spared again.

Margaret stood with her ladies in the chill of the early morning, a hand raised in goodbye to her husband, as the sun made its appearance silhouetting the men against the gold-tinged sky. The queen's face bore a look of pain. How many times, Catrìona wondered, had Margaret sent the king off to battle? How many times had she waited for him to return?

After the line of men disappeared down the road, Giric raced off, saying he would follow them as they would ride through the village.

Catrìona and Fia turned toward the hall. Angus was standing just outside the door wearing no mail.

"You did not go?" she asked him, suddenly happy that her beloved guard's life would not be risked for such a venture.

"Nay, the king asked fer those willing to stay behind as guards and I stepped forward. 'Tis not Normans I want to be killing, 'tis Northmen."

"It comforts me, dear Angus, to know you remain."

He bowed and opened the tower door for her and Fia.

Domnall came to bid her a hasty goodbye. She could tell he wanted to say more but Isla approached to claim his arm, giving Catrìona a smug smile. Catrìona watched them as they slipped through the open door together, surprised that she felt no regret.

Domnall would leave Dunfermline today, bound for Isla's home in Ayrshire. While he rode west, the king and his men would ride south, first to Lothian and then to Northumbria. Catrìona tried not to imagine the raid. Instead, she set her mind to the new task the queen had given her. There would be much to do if Margaret was to have her ferry and inn ready for the pilgrims before winter.

She would try not to think of Steinar facing the swords of Norman knights. Instead, she hoped her riband kept her in his thoughts for he would surely be in her prayers.

⋆   ⋆   ⋆

Northumbria

Steinar pulled off his helm and wiped the blood from his mail, then accepted the flask of wine Rhodri offered him. Taking a long draw, he swept his sleeve over his mouth. "Much appreciated," he said, handing the flask back to Rhodri. "I was fair thirsty."

Rhodri returned the flask to his satchel and extended his palms to the fire around which Malcolm's men had pitched their tents. "I do not think the king expected the fighting to last all day."

"There were Normans among the Northumbrians," Steinar observed, "trained knights William has placed in the north. Their involvement extended the fight. I took great pleasure in seeing to the end of some." He felt drained by the daylong battle and his leg ached. Seeing the log rolled near the fire, he sank onto it. The heat of the blaze chased away the chill. Riding into Northumbria had affected him more than he had expected. It was not Talisand, which lay to the west, but it was more of England than he had seen in three years.

Rhodri joined him on the log and pulled his quiver into his lap, inspecting his remaining arrows. " 'Twas a wet, dismal day for July," he observed. "The dampness caused my arrows to drop low."

Mist crept along the ground, hiding Steinar's view of the River Tweed. The hills in the distance were shrouded in clouds. He looked at the leather straps crossing his hosen. "I wear as much mud as I do blood." He brushed the dirt and dried mud from his legs.

Steinar thought back over the king's raiding campaign. To his relief, the summer weather had held as they rode south into Lothian, gathering more of Maerleswein's men. Thankfully, Rian had given them no more trouble after the king's scolding.

Once they arrived in Northumbria, the weather had turned foul.

Despite the rain, Malcolm happily took his revenge for the Conqueror's intrusions into Cumbria. Steinar knew from past messages he had composed for Malcolm that the king considered Cumbria and parts of Northumbria to be his.

"Where is Niall?" Steinar asked Rhodri.

His friend tossed a glance over his shoulder. "Seeing to his horse."

"How did he fare today?"

"He did well. As far as I could tell the arrows he launched hit true."

"All to the good. We would both incur his sister's wrath if he were wounded," said Steinar.

" 'Tis not only her brother the redhead has a care for and well you know it. The Rose of Dunfermline favors you."

"Ah, that name. I had forgotten."

A group of young male servants came by just then, pushing a cart piled with muddy mail, shields and leather gambesons. "Can we clean yer armor for ye, sir?"

Aching in every muscle, Steinar rose stiffly and pulled off his mail, handing it to the servant. The green riband Catrìona had given him fell to the ground. He quickly snatched it up, stuffing the silk into his tunic, but not before Rhodri had noticed.

"Ho! You carry the lady's favor. The redhead was wearing ribands that color when we broke our fast."

" 'Twas your idea but it seemed a good one. By her own words, 'tis a reminder she prays for me. Mayhap her prayers will bring me success."

Rhodri gave Steinar a knowing smile. The bard did not miss much, but was friend enough to say no more about Steinar's fondness for the queen's lady.

He returned to his seat on the log. His leg throbbing, he kneaded the muscles before they cramped up on him.

"How much longer do you think we will remain here?" Rhodri asked.

"The king took much plunder today, but he will not turn the men toward home until he has prodded the backside of William's man at Alnwick."

"Gilbert de Tesson?"

"Nay, his son, another William," said Steinar. "Colbán told me Gilbert's son retained the land and the title after his father died at Senlac Hill. Now the son has erected one of those timber castles overlooking the River Aln."

"Like the one at Talisand?" Rhodri asked.

"Aye." Steinar did not like to think of the timber castle that now stood over what had been his home, but he comforted himself with the knowledge his sister, Serena, was happy there with her Norman knight. "The Norman Conqueror insists on his castles wherever he perceives a threat. Maerleswein told me there are now two in York."

Soon, more of Malcolm's men straggled in to warm themselves by the fire and speak of the day's events. They had lost only three, Coinín, Tòmas and Gillis, all good men. But others were wounded, keeping busy the king's physic and the healers who aided him.

This had been only a skirmish. The battle looming ahead—an attack on a wooden fortress full of Norman knights—would be different.

*   *   *

The next morning Steinar left Rhodri and Niall as they sat wrapping linen strips around the tips of their arrows and, donning his helm, urged Artair toward the place where the warriors were gathering.

Colbán rode up to him on his dun-colored horse. "The king has requested you ride at his back today, Scribe."

Steinar nodded and turned his horse toward the front of the column. That the captain of the guard addressed him as "Scribe" did not rankle. Since the fight with Rian, the men spoke the byname with respect, even acceptance, and it pleased him to have regained his place among the men who fought with the king. He might have lost the status of a thegn's son, but at least he could once again call himself a warrior. For too long, the only marks on his hands had been the stains of ink. He was glad his hands now bore calluses from his sword.

Wending his way through the confusion of men and horses, Steinar pulled up behind Malcolm who sat erect atop his white charger. He looked every bit the king, his broad shoulders filling out his mail and his thick dark hair resplendent beneath his gold-crowned helm. Duff rode beside Malcolm, leading the army, his bushy brows showing beneath the edge of his helm.

Malcolm welcomed him with a nod over his shoulder. "We ride to Alnwick to poke at the pride of the Norman whoresons, Scribe. 'Tis a task you should relish."

Steinar smiled. "I do."

★   ★   ★

"Catrìona!" called Audra from the tower's open door. "You are wanted by the queen."

Catrìona left Giric with his dog in front of the tower and ducked back inside the hall. Once there, she went to where Audra stood with the queen next to the hearth. As soon as she glimpsed the queen's face, Catrìona perceived something was gravely amiss. "What is it?"

Facing her two ladies, Margaret said, "I want you to come with me to pray. Malcolm is in terrible danger. I feel it."

The queen had often walked with Catrìona in the woods but she had never before asked her to come with her to pray in the cave. "Of course, My Lady."

Audra nodded her agreement.

They did not even stop to get their cloaks but followed Margaret out of the tower and down the path that led to the cave where, it was said, the queen did her most serious praying.

With so many men gone, the banter and rough speech around the tower were absent, but as they entered the forest, the canopy above them teemed with life. The distinct "kaah" of rooks pierced the air. She looked up to see the black birds with their pale beaks occupying the trees above them.

Margaret, just ahead of her, appeared to falter. Catrìona reached to take the queen's elbow. "Is it the babe, My Lady?"

"Nay. I just need to rest for a moment."

The queen's chest heaved and her brow was furrowed.

Catrìona helped the queen onto an outcropping of rock. "My Lady, should we turn back?"

"I will be fine. I prefer to go to the cave where no sounds distract. Fear for the king grows more insistent within me. He rides into danger this day."

"You should eat, my queen," Audra urged.

Catrìona remembered when the queen and her ladies had broken their fast that morning, Margaret had eaten nothing.

"I will," Margaret assured Audra, "as soon as I have prayed. Now, help me up so that we may reach our destination. Time is short."

Catrìona did not ask the queen how she came by the knowledge the king was in danger and time was short. Mayhap God had called her to pray for her husband. "Yea, My Lady," was all she said as she wrapped one arm around the queen's waist and, together with Audra, lifted her to stand. Catrìona did not let go, but steadied the queen as they continued on their way.

Shortly, the path dipped and finally ended in a small clearing in front of a cave. Margaret did not hesitate but entered the dark opening, Catrìona beside her.

Once inside, Audra lit a candle. The cave was long and narrow. Margaret seemed steadier on her feet now and stepped away from Catrìona. The air was cool. Mayhap it revived her.

Margaret managed to kneel, praying at a makeshift altar of stone.

Catrìona and Audra on each side of her.

Whatever Margaret feared for her husband must have been very real because her whispered prayers had an urgent, pleading tone.

The ground was cold and hard beneath Catrìona's knees as she, too, prayed for the king, reciting the Latin prayers she had come to know. Then she prayed for Niall. When she finished praying for her younger brother, she had a sudden urge to pray for Steinar. If the king were in danger, so might be the scribe, for he now rode with the king's guard. With a fervor brought on by her own fears, she bent her head to pray once again, this time for the man who held her riband and mayhap her heart.

It was a long time before the queen lifted her head and Catrìona and Audra helped her to rise.

"It is done," said Margaret with a sigh. "The king is in God's hands."

CHAPTER 9

The moor they crossed on their way to Alnwick was wild and open, pulling Steinar's gaze to the distant horizon where the sky met the land. To his mind, this level monotonous part of Northumbria lacked the beauty of Talisand with its rolling hills and rivers. Nor did it possess the majesty of Scotland's lochs and mountains.

As he lifted his gaze to the white clouds drifting aimlessly above, he was thankful the day would at least be without rain.

He reached down to stroke Artair's neck as he glanced at the backs of Duff and the king, thinking how it would be to once again face hundreds of Norman swords. The well-trained knights were formidable, but he had learned much in the half dozen years since his first encounter with them at Senlac Hill and no longer feared their blades.

The landscape changed as they approached Alnwick. The moor gave way to grass and shrubs and finally he glimpsed green meadows fringed by dense stands of trees.

It was the middle of the morning when they entered a forested area and the king raised his fist, halting the column of men. In the distance, Steinar saw a timbered castle set upon a grass-covered hill the Normans called a *motte*. He shuddered, for it reminded of the castle the Norman knight called the Red Wolf had built at Talisand.

At the base of the *motte* a palisade fence of wooden posts surrounded the castle and the buildings that supported the knights—at a minimum, a stable, a blacksmith and an armory.

Outside the palisade was a cluster of thatched cottages. *An unprotected village.*

Malcolm turned to Duff. "We will make camp here."

The two rode deeper into the forest where the trees grew in stands, too close in some places even for a horse to pass. Steinar and the men followed, picking their way carefully. As he rode, Steinar assessed their cover, thinking the king had chosen wisely. Their presence was hidden in a forest of trees, thick enough to allow them to remain undetected until they launched their assault.

Between the forest and the village, he could see a river about twenty feet across running in front of the castle looming in the distance. He supposed it was the River Aln the men had spoken of on the journey south. The banks of this river would become their field of battle.

The king dismounted and called for his captains. He then retreated to a small clearing among the trees. Malcolm tossed back over his shoulder, "You, too, Scribe."

Colbán was the first of the captains to ride into the clearing where the king and Duff waited. When the others began flowing into the grassy circle, Rhodri came to stand by Steinar and folded his arms over his chest. " 'Twill not be long now."

Once the dozen men who made up Malcolm's senior captains were assembled, the king addressed them in a solemn voice. "We have come to show the Northumbrians the Normans do not protect them. To remind the Normans they are not welcome here. This is our land and we claim it for Scotland."

The men nodded and "Ayes" were raised in a loud chorus.

Shifting his gaze to Rhodri, the king said, "You and your archers will go before us. Rain fire on the structures. Draw out William de Tesson and his knights." Then Malcolm's eyes scanned the men, considering each face. "If there is plunder to be had, by all means let the men take it from the Norman scum."

The men nodded their appreciation, their faces displaying their eagerness to meet the enemy. With Edgar standing among them, none could forget their queen had lost her country to the Conqueror to whom these Normans swore allegiance.

The group broke apart, each captain returning to his men. Rhodri said to Steinar, "If all goes well, this eve we will dine on fish from the River Aln."

"Aye, and mayhap we will have many Norman swords to add to the king's coffers."

Rhodri nodded and waved goodbye as he went to join his waiting archers.

Soon they would face Norman swords. Some would die, others would be wounded. Steeling himself for the battle ahead, Steinar pulled Catrìona's riband from under his mail and pressed it to his lips, breathing in her woodland scent and seeing before his face her fiery hair. "Soon. I will see you soon," he muttered under his breath. Almost it was a prayer.

An hour later, Rhodri and his archers left the forest, walking on foot ahead of the king and his men. The bowmen forded the river with little difficulty, holding their bows and arrows high. All of the arrows bore the same linen wrapped around the tips and now they appeared to have been dipped in oil. Once they were on the other side, Rhodri ordered them into a single line, standing close together.

Behind the archers, the warriors waited, some on horseback, some on foot, all well armed. Steinar calmed Artair who snorted, restless for what was coming. He was behind Malcolm and Duff and close enough to watch the archers. Colbán and the rest of the king's guard hovered close by.

"Ready your bows!" Rhodri shouted. With their sides facing the village and the castle, the archers held their longbows in their left hand, an arrow in their right. "Nock!" Rhodri cried. In one practiced move, the archers nocked their arrows.

At Rhodri's signal, two men carrying torches, who had been standing at the ends of the line of archers, walked briskly from the ends to the center, lighting the linen on the arrow tips as they went.

Too late, a cry of alarm went up from the palisade gatehouse.

Rhodri shouted "Mark!" and one hundred bows lifted as one. "Draw!" With powerful strokes reflecting a lifetime of training, the men drew back the strings to their ears.

Steinar could taste the tension in the air as shouts rose from the village. The archers waited with their flaming arrows for the next command.

"Loose!" Rhodri roared. Flaming shafts shot into the sky like so many stars before arching and falling, some on the village roofs, some onto the palisade fence posts. Still others speared the roofs of the outbuildings peeking above the fence.

Immediately, the flames caught. Wood and thatch flared. Smoke boiled up.

Rhodri shouted again and another volley of flaming arrows reached into the sky with a loud rushing sound like a hundred birds taking flight.

Rhodri commanded, "Fall back!" and his archers retreated through the ranks of Malcolm's men. Garbed like Rhodri in the colors of the forest, they vanished into the trees.

The king turned to look behind him at his men, a pleased expression on his face. "That should draw them out."

Behind Steinar and the king's guard, hundreds of warriors had fanned out awaiting orders.

They did not wait long. Shouts from the castle filled the air. Villagers scattered in panic, trying to escape the battle to come.

The palisade gate flew open. A stream of mounted knights spewed forth, their silvered helms gleaming in the midday sun and their swords raised in challenge as they flowed onto the wide grassy slope leading to the river.

Malcolm ripped his sword from its sheath and gripped his red and white shield. His voice lifted in a ringing shout. *"Albani! Albani!"*

With a slither of steel, hundreds of swords were pulled from their sheaths and warriors' shouts echoed the king's war cry, the Gaelic word for Scotland.

Malcolm kicked his horse into a charge.

Duff raised his fist into the air and the army of Scots charged forward to follow their king and the Mormaer of Fife as they stormed toward the Normans.

Steinar rode hard behind Malcolm. The familiar excitement surged through his veins just as it had in his prior battles, only this time he had a king to protect.

Malcolm was a strong fighter, moving swiftly through the Normans, slashing left and right, cutting down knights with his powerful sword and using his shield as a blunt weapon to knock heads and block blows.

But the Norman knights and men-at-arms were well prepared. Swords clashed as they fought with skill and vengeance, the clash of metal and men's grunts ringing in Steinar's ears as he fought to guard the king.

From the trees, an occasional arrow hissed by Steinar's head as one of Rhodri's arrows struck home in the body of a foe. Only the Welshman could have launched the precise shots that were too difficult for other archers to make without hitting one of their own. Only he would take such a risk and succeed.

Steinar kept one eye on the king and one on his own flanks. Mounted mail-clad knights came at them from every side only to be beaten back in the clash of steel.

The fighting surged around Steinar with the force of a raging sea. Knights cut down men on foot. Horses fell, screaming and thrashing, taking their riders down with them.

Pikemen grunted with the effort of spearing the fallen into the mud like fish in a shallow stream. The sound of men dying filled the air.

A shout rang out in the midst of the tumult as a group of Norman knights turned their horses toward Malcolm, pointing to the crown on his helm. " 'Tis the Scot king!"

Steinar spurred his horse, blocking their charge, putting himself between the Norman swords and the king.

Colbán rushed to Steinar, adding his strength to the fight.

Sounds of clashing steel rang in Steinar's ears.

The Norman horses reared and plunged as they drove into the midst of Malcolm's protectors. Steinar's horse stood his ground as firm as an oak tree and Steinar sent up a prayer of thanks for Artair's steadiness.

Two of the knights engaged Colbán, drawing him away, but Duff remained steadfast by the king as the two battled on together side by side. Steinar reined Artair around to guard the king's back, cutting a deep gash in the neck of a knight who tried to come at Malcolm from the rear.

Normans surrounded Duff, one knocking him from his horse with a powerful blow, leaving the king exposed. A mounted knight lunged into the gap, swinging his sword like a harvesting scythe, sweeping the king to the ground.

Malcolm sat up, stunned and shook his head. Blood welled on his hosen and ran down his leg.

The Norman slid from his saddle and raised his sword for the killing blow.

Launching himself from his horse, Steinar hit the knight with the full force of his body, pounding his shield into the knight's helm.

The Norman staggered, but recovered and turned again toward Malcolm.

"Nay!" Steinar shouted and blocked the blade intended for the king.

Thwarted, the knight roared his anger and lunged at Steinar. He took the blow on his shield and slipped his sword under it, thrusting deep. The sword point pierced the Norman's mail, sinking into flesh.

The knight fell to the ground, mortally wounded.

As Malcolm struggled to his feet, Steinar stood before him, flashing his sword back and forth.

But the fight to defend the king was not over. One of the mounted knights charged toward Malcolm. Before Steinar could push the king to safety, an arrow, like a hawk after its prey, whirred past his ear. Whipping his head around, he saw the shaft quivering in the Norman's neck. With a gasp, the man toppled from his horse, dead.

Steinar turned to see Malcolm swaying, his wounded leg streaming blood, but he courageously held his sword before him. Steinar breathed a sigh of relief.

Colbán emerged from the fray. "Duff!" he shouted to Steinar. "Where is Duff?"

"I saw him go down—there." Steinar pointed with his sword. "I did not see him rise. Go. I will cover the king."

Colbán kneed his mount to where Duff's horse stood over the wounded mormaer.

Gasping for breath, Steinar surveyed the field of battle. The fighting was waning. The king's guard, freed from their own confrontations with the Normans, joined Steinar, encircling the king.

One of the foot soldiers knelt before Malcolm. "The Normans run back to their castle, My Lord."

"Aye," said the king, lifting his head to watch the Normans retreating, "the cowards flee." Malcolm regarded the field strewn with the fallen. "See to the wounded," he ordered his men.

Steinar nodded at Malcolm's blood-soaked leg. "Sage advice, My Lord. May I suggest you take it yourself?"

Malcolm looked down and staggered in surprise. Steinar caught the king's arm as he shouted for the physic.

* * *

Steinar was still supervising the gathering of prisoners and their weapons when a servant came from Malcolm, summoning him to the king's tent.

Nodding to the posted guards, Steinar entered in time to see the king brush away his physic just finishing with his bandage. In one corner of the tent lay Fife's mormaer on a pallet, his eyes closed beneath his bushy brows.

Steinar turned his attention to the king, awaiting instructions.

Malcolm gave Steinar's leg a harsh glance. "So, Scribe, you think to order your king to take your advice and yet you feel free to ignore it yourself?"

Steinar glanced at his leg, surprised to see dried blood coating his hosen. So intense had been the fighting, so anxious had he been for the king's safety, he had no idea when he had taken the blade.

"It seems we share a wound in common, My Lord," Steinar said. "I had not noticed."

"Well, I noticed," Malcolm replied. "Your wound and much else. We have more in common than a Norman's sword, my English friend." The king accepted a goblet of wine from a servant and leveled a steady gaze on Steinar. "See to the scribe," Malcolm ordered his physic.

The physic knelt to unlace Steinar's leather cross straps and rolled the hosen down, causing him to wince as the physic pulled the linen from the wound. At the physic's instruction, a servant brought water and cloth to cleanse the wound.

"I know what it is to be exiled," said the king. "To see my father cut down before my eyes and be forced to flee my country for my life." At Steinar's puzzled look, Malcolm said, "Aye, you and I share such a past, Scribe. But 'twas England where I took refuge under King Edward's protection and you fled to Scotland where you enjoy mine."

Steinar had known this and yet he had not seen the king as a kindred soul. "But you have come home, My Lord, whereas I never will."

"Scotland is your home, son. Here you can fight alongside me, for we share our hatred for William and his Normans. These things and your loyalty to King Harold were part of why I made you my scribe."

"There was another reason, My Lord?" he asked, looking down at the king's physic coating his wound with some sort of salve.

Malcolm took another draught of his wine and smiled. "Your hand draws a pretty script."

"I have my father's priest to thank for that. But you must know, My Lord, it has been my privilege to serve you, whether as scribe or soldier."

The king sat back, running his hand over his dark beard. "Now it seems I owe you my life. You will find me most generous."

When the physic finished bandaging his wound, Steinar took the seat the king waved him toward and waited for Malcolm to say more.

"As I recall, William gave your lands to one of his henchmen."

"Aye. Sir Renaud de Pierrepont, the one they call the Red Wolf."

"Yea, I have heard of that one. But no matter," the king said, flicking his hand as if brushing off dust. "It so happens that a year ago I lost a faithful mormaer in a vicious attack that destroyed all he held. The lands have since stood without protection, without even a hillfort. I am of a mind to give you those lands on the condition you guard them well and respond to my call for men-at-arms when it comes."

At first, Steinar could not believe the king's words. Lands of his own? Steinar's spirits soared. "I would be most willing, My Lord."

"Aside from your years of service as scribe, you have won the respect of my men," said the king, his demeanor serious. "First you spared one of Rhodri's archers the blade of that bully, Rian, and then you rescued your king from a Norman's sword. There are many who would go with you were they given the chance. I would provide a contingent of warriors and sufficient Saxon servants to help you rebuild."

Steinar moved from where he sat to kneel at the feet of the king, offering his hands in pledge. "My Lord, I pledge my fealty to you unto death."

The king placed his hands around Steinar's. "I accept your pledge. For your service and for preserving the life of your king, you shall have lands in the Vale of Leven and I will bestow upon you the title Mormaer of Levenach."

The Vale of Leven. Catriona's home! And a title! His heart raced in his chest and he fought the rising emotion as tears came to his eyes. Never had he dreamed he would receive such a boon by the king. But as he kneeled before Malcolm, he suddenly realized the mormaer who had been killed was Catriona's father and it had been her home that was attacked. *Oh, my love.*

The king dropped his hands and his dark eyes pierced Steinar where he knelt. "So be it. But say nothing of this yet, Scribe. I will announce it in due time."

Steinar nodded. "As you wish."

Malcolm stood and motioned for Steinar to rise.

"My Lord," Steinar asked the king, "what of Cormac's son, Niall?" He had in mind his own loss of Talisand.

"The young archer? He has yet to become a man and to prove himself. The lands are mine to give as I see fit. You have earned your place among my mormaers. Niall can remain with my archers or go with you, if that be your desire." Then the king turned to face Duff where he lay on the pallet. "What say you of my new liege man?"

"A good choice to replace Cormac."

Steinar was grateful for the affirmation and the approving smile Fife's mormaer gave him.

Steinar did not wish to appear greedy, but he would risk Malcolm's ire if it would gain him the hand of the woman who would render his lands a home. "My Lord?"

The king turned back to him. "You have a question?"

"Aye. Might I not be in need of a wife to raise up sons to serve you?"

The king laughed and Duff joined him, exchanging a few barbs about "the eager scribe" which Steinar ignored.

The physic covered a smile with his hand before closing his leather pouch of medicines, salves and potions and, with a bow to the king, quit the tent.

"Aye, a wife would be in order," said Malcolm. Still appearing amused, he raised a brow. "Have you one in mind?"

"I do, My Lord. And she knows well the land you would give me to hold. 'Tis Catrìona of the Vale of Leven, one of the queen's ladies."

The king turned to Duff. "Is that the redhead?"

Duff grinned, waggling his bushy brows. "Aye, the very one, Cormac's daughter. Audra told me she has become a favorite of your queen."

Malcolm gave Steinar a sharp glance before shaking his head. "Many have asked for that lady's hand, Scribe, including the captain of my guard. I owe Colbán much. He has faithfully served me in defiance of his people who are from Moray, the land of my old enemy, Mac Bethad."

Cruel fragments of hope slipped through Steinar's hands. To gain lands yet lose the woman who would make them a home left him feeling empty, deprived of the light he clung to. But how could the king refuse his faithful captain the woman he wanted? Steinar liked Colbán, a stalwart warrior and a strong leader of men. But he could not picture the rough captain with the free-spirited Catrìona. Steinar's mind rebelled at the idea of another man having her, of fathering her children. He wanted her for his own.

The king must have observed Steinar's dismay, for he slapped him on the back and said, "Cheer up, Scribe. I shall find you a lady to bear you fine sons."

★ ★ ★

Catrìona hurried up the stairs to her chamber, anxious to tell Fia the news. Flinging open the door, out of breath, she shouted, "The king…. he returns!"

"He is here?" her cousin asked from where she sat on the stool combing her long dark hair.

"Nay, but the queen requires us, so do hurry."

"While I quickly plait my hair, tell me what the messenger said."

Out of breath, Catrìona dropped onto the edge of her bed. "I was with the queen going over the plans for the pilgrims' inn when the messenger arrived. The army is but a day's ride away."

Catrìona helped Fia to plait her hair. "Is the messenger still here?"

asked her cousin.

"I do not know. He was to return to the king once he had food and a fresh horse."

Fia's eyes turned anxious.

"Before you ask, there are wounded among them, which is why the main party travels more slowly. Nothing was said of Rhodri." *Or Steinar.*

Knowing her cousin worried for the bard, Catrìona put her arm around Fia's shoulder. "Rhodri may be well. The messenger did not speak of him. He only told the queen Edgar was unharmed. But the king has suffered a leg wound." At Fia's gasp, Catrìona added, " 'Tis not believed serious. God willing, his leg will heal."

Fia tied off her plaits. "Margaret must have been relieved to hear that."

"Aye, but there was bad news, too. Audra's father took a sword in his side."

"Oh, no. Poor Audra," said Fia. "What did the messenger say about Duff?"

"The mormaer complains the king will not allow him to ride his horse, which caused the queen to smile."

Fia's blue eyes met Catrìona's. "The messenger must have talked long for you to hear all that."

"Aye, he did, but 'twas only the queen he spoke with. I only heard because I was sitting with her. When the messenger left, Margaret summoned her ladies to join her in the chapel to say special prayers for the recovery of the wounded."

Fia pushed herself off the bed. "Then we must go."

Catrìona heard the falling rain and went to the window to open the shutter. " 'Tis raining. Best we take our cloaks." She grabbed her cloak from the peg and handed Fia's to her.

As they left the chamber, heading for the chapel, Catrìona's mind turned to the golden-haired scribe. It had not escaped her that the messenger carried no written note. Did the scribe who would have penned such a message yet live?

CHAPTER 10

Steinar's stomach clenched with the rising tension boiling within him as they drew near to Dunfermline. Soon he would see the auburn-haired beauty. Anticipation warred with regret. He had found the woman he wanted and looked forward to their exchanges. And to holding her in his arms. The prospect of losing her to Colbán clouded his mind. How could he let her go? Steinar could only bring himself to give her up if Catrìona herself favored the match. But what if she did not? Would she defy the king's order should he command her to wed his captain? Would Steinar defy the king to whom he had given his oath?

He studied the king's back. Today, as always, Malcolm rode his white charger a little ahead of his guard, impatient to arrive at his destination, but unwilling to drive the weary men harder than they could bear.

The sky above was a clear blue for which Steinar was grateful as some of the men walked and the wounded rode in open carts that slowed their pace. At Malcolm's insistence, Duff traveled in the middle of the army in a cart watched over by the king's physic. But even with wounded among them, spirits were high all around for the raid had been successful.

Next to Steinar rode the king's captain on his dun-colored horse. Was there a hint of a smile on the warrior's face? Was it only the success of the raid that he thought of, or did he know that the king favored his request for Catrìona's hand?

The woman Steinar longed to see.

Colbán was a leader of men: his sword arm strong in battle, his loyalty to the king unquestioned and his voice like brass when issuing commands. And, unlike Steinar, he was a Gael. Mayhap he reminded Catrìona of her father, who had been one of Malcolm's chiefs.

But it was Steinar's kiss she had accepted. Unless there was more between Colbán and Catrìona than he knew. Now that Domnall was courting another, had Catrìona turned her attention to the king's captain? Did she know of Colbán's request for her hand? If she knew Steinar had been granted lands in the Vale of Leven, she might not want to return to the place where she had lost all she held dear. Steinar pressed his hand to his chest where the green riband was tucked beneath mail and tunic, close to his heart. Did Colbán also carry her favor?

As the king rounded a bend in the road leading to the tower, loud cheers ascended into the air from the boisterous crowd lining either side of the road.

Steinar scanned the faces of the women and girls who stood waving and smiling at the returning warriors, disappointed that Catrìona's beautiful face was not among them.

Giric broke from the crowd and ran to him, his eyes shining and his little gray dog barking loudly at his side. "Scribe!"

The crowd's shouts of welcome made it too noisy to converse, but Steinar gave the boy a smile that told him he was glad to see him.

The boy latched on to Steinar's stirrup and walked alongside his horse as they continued on toward the tower. "Yer home!"

The word "home" rang in Steinar's ears. Indeed, Scotland was now and ever would be his home. Somehow he must get word to Serena of his favor with the king.

"Aye, lad, I am home." Reaching his arm to the boy, he said "Grab on!"

Giric took his hand and Steinar lifted the boy into his saddle.

"Oh..." breathed the lad, squirming in front of him. " 'Tis grand from here."

"Your first time on a horse?" Steinar asked.

The boy inclined his head to the side so Steinar could glimpse his face. "Aye."

Giric was not afraid, that much Steinar could see. Rather, he was excited and happy to be riding with him. "Brave lad." Someday, Steinar was certain, Giric would be a bold warrior, a credit to his king.

The tower came into view and Steinar caught sight of the queen and her ladies standing before the carved wooden door, their smiling faces turned toward the returning warriors. Steinar's heart leapt at the sight of Catrìona in a green gown the color of her eyes, her face alight with a glow of happiness.

Was she smiling at him, the king or the king's captain?

The king was the first to dismount and the crowd closed in to wish him well. Colbán followed, slipping from his horse in haste to plunge into the crowd, heading straight for Catrìona.

To Steinar's surprise, Colbán bowed before her and kissed her offered hand. From behind her she brought forth a folded cloth, copper in color, and handed it to him. They were too far away for Steinar to hear the words they exchanged, but Colbán strode into the hall a happy man.

Steinar felt a scowl building on his face as he lifted the boy down and dismounted. Handing the reins to a waiting servant, he took off his gloves and headed to where the ladies greeted the men in front of the tower door. The muscles in his right leg cramped, reminding him he had given the leg little rest in the days he'd been gone.

Giric walked at his side, matching his pace, chattering about the raid into Northumbria. Steinar heard only the last question.

"Was it very bloody?" the boy asked.

Steinar was certain the question was posed in eager anticipation of hearing a story the lad could pass along to the village children.

He tousled the boy's hair. "Wait till we are inside and I've quenched my thirst, then I will tell you."

Confusion reigned in front of the tower blocking his view of the ladies for a moment, but Steinar pressed on, making his way through the crowd to the front door. Catrìona's searching gaze met his. He stepped in front of her and her face lit up with a smile that melted his heart, her eyes sparkling like emeralds. Could it be that Colbán did not yet claim her heart?

"My lady," he said, bowing before her. She offered her hand and he took it, wanting to pull her into his arms, but instead he placed a polite kiss on her slender knuckles.

"I am so glad to see you returned to us," she said, briefly looking over his body as if expecting to find a bandage, but the one he wore, like the king's, was hidden beneath his hosen. "When no missive came from the king, I was concerned something had happened to you."

"You worried for me?" he asked, hoping against hope she favored him despite the intention of the king's captain to make her his wife.

The crowd was loud around them but he leaned in to hear her say, "Aye, I did. We worried for all of you, and prayed much, most particularly for the king. Margaret had a feeling he was in grave danger."

"And so he was," admitted Steinar.

"Tell me, tell me!" cried Giric, pulling on Steinar's tunic sleeve.

"All in good time, lad."

"There is wine and food awaiting you in the hall," said Catrìona as she turned and headed through the open door with the queen's other ladies.

Like Giric's dog pursuing his favorite bone, Steinar followed.

★   ★   ★

Alone in their chamber, except for the physic bent over the king's leg changing his bandage, Margaret closely regarded her husband. His face, now clean of the dirt he had worn home, was lined with fatigue. His long hair was still coated with fine dust from his travels. He sat slumped in his chair, but the glint in his eyes told her his spirits were high.

"The raid went well, My Lord?"

He winced at the ministrations of the physic. "Well enough. Still, we lost some men to Norman swords. And Duff lies wounded."

The loss of his men would weigh heavy upon his shoulders, as would the wounded Duff. The mormaer was not only his loyal right arm, but his trusted friend. "Will he recover?"

Malcolm shot the physic a glance before replying. "Aye, God willing and if you pray for him, *mo cridhe*."

"I shall, My King," she said earnestly. "I have already."

As if wanting to encourage them, the physic added, "Duff's wound is clean and the stars are favorable."

She accepted his words with a smile. "I will keep Duff in my prayers."

The physic finished and gathered up his supplies. "With your leave, My Lord, I would go to the mormaer."

"Aye, see to Duff, then come give me a report on his wound. I would know the truth of it ere I go to him."

The man nodded, bowed and departed.

With the sound of the closing door, Margaret asked, "You count the raid successful?"

"We made our point," Malcolm said in a satisfied tone. "William knows we like not his dreadful timber castles that creep ever closer to Scotland. The one we attacked rises above the River Aln, a blight upon the land."

She poured her husband a goblet of his favorite wine and approached, remembering how the chamber had once looked before she had hung the tapestries. The weapons of war still hung on one wall but the rest bore her softer touch, a melding of their two lives as they had melded their hearts.

Handing him the drink with one hand, with the other she touched his shoulder, wanting to feel the strength of him, wanting to know he was whole. "My ladies and I prayed for you each day." She would not tell him of the dread that had overcome her the day she had summoned Audra and Catrìona to the cave to pray.

Malcolm took a long draw on his wine and set the goblet aside. Taking her hand from his shoulder, he pulled her onto his lap. "It was your prayers, *mo cridhe*, that gave me strength as I rode into battle against the Normans."

She brought his rough warrior hand to her lips and kissed his palm. It would do no good to scold him for attacking William's knights and she never had. She loved him for the man he was. The man God had given her.

He smiled then, his dark eyes twinkling with a familiar desire. "I missed our nights together, Margaret." Placing his hand on her rounded belly, he asked, "How fares the babe?"

"He moves much these days, keeping me awake. Just two months more and, God willing, I will hold him in my arms."

His dark brows rose. "You are certain 'tis a son?"

"He feels much like Edward did, so I plan for a male child. We named the first for my father and the king who gave us both sanctuary. How do you feel about the name Edmund for our second? 'Twas my grandfather's name and he was a king of England."

Malcolm laughed, a deep belly laugh that told her he was pleased. "My wife who always thinks ahead. Aye, another English name will serve well a son who may one day have English subjects."

She thought of the time he had been away, of all he must have seen. It had been years since she had been in England and she was curious to hear of it. "Tell me of all that happened while you were away."

"If you wish to know, I will tell you, but I would see my young Edward ere this day is done. And I must hear of your plans to aid the pilgrims."

"Very well," she said, nestling into the curve of his body like a child awaiting a favored story. "You first."

He launched into a description of his travels, beginning with Lothian. "Maerleswein seems happy with his new bride and your former lady was all aglow."

"I am glad. I believed he would make a good husband for Davina."

"Aye, you did and 'twas a wise suggestion you made."

He began to speak of the raid into Northumbria, his face coming alive as he drew vivid pictures of the archers' flaming arrows and the fighting that followed at Alnwick. "That Welshman is a leader of men, a well-trained fighter, too, not just a bowman. God's blood, some of his shots were like none I have ever seen!"

The story went on and she listened intently, sensing he was leaving something out. "How did you get the wound?"

She could tell he was reluctant to speak of it, but at her prodding, he said, "Sometime in the course of the fight. I do not recall precisely when, but I was suddenly on the ground with the scribe standing over me, defending me against the edge of a Norman's blade like an avenging angel."

A gasp escaped her lips as she imagined Malcolm falling from his horse, vulnerable to the sharp sword of a Norman knight.

He drew her tightly to him and picked up one of her plaits, fingering the pale hair. "'Tis over now, *mo cridhe*, so do not fear for me. My wound is minor. Steinar guarded me well."

" 'Twas God's provision, I've no doubt, and an answer to my prayers. I am glad the English scribe rode at your back."

"For his rescue of his king and for all he has suffered at the hands of William, I have offered Steinar lands in Scotland and the title mormaer. I hope you approve."

"Oh, I do." It seemed right to her that it should be so. "An English thegn's son deserves more than a life as a scribe. He will prove worthy of your trust, I am certain."

"I ordered the scribe to say nothing of the boon I would give him. I want to decide about Colbán first and announce my actions for both at the same time. 'Twould not do to have the scribe favored before my captain."

"Where are the lands you would give Steinar?"

"I thought to have him take Cormac's place. With Steinar's intelligence and breeding, he will be able to forge alliances Scotland needs for the future. The men have come to respect him and willingly follow his command. I would send some of them with him to rebuild the hillfort and he will soon attract others. I like it not that the Vale of Leven has remained a great gaping crevice, unguarded since that Norse raid. 'Tis a back door into Scotland."

"I wish we knew who was responsible for the attack," she said, remembering the terrifying tale Matad had brought them of the slaughter.

"You recall when Atholl first told us of the murder of his sister and Cormac, I sent inquiries to Paul and Erlend Thorfinnsson in the Orkneys. They assured me they had not knowledge of it. I have never known them to lie. After all, they are my own relations and foster my son, Duncan. But mayhap unbeknownst to them, they harbor a villain in their midst."

" 'Twas a terrible thing to lose Cormac and his wife like that. Catrìona and her brother were fortunate to have escaped."

"You remind me," he said, kissing her forehead. "When I told the English scribe I was granting him lands, he made me laugh, saying very seriously he needed a wife to go with them."

"Did he?" She smiled, imagining the handsome scribe insisting on a wife. There would be many women at Malcolm's court who would be proud to accept his suit.

"Aye, he is a bold one. And he was quite certain just who he wanted that wife to be."

She looked at Malcolm expectantly.

"He asked for the hand of Cormac's daughter."

"Catrìona—but why? Because her father's lands were the ones you would give the scribe?"

"Nay, I think not. The look in his eyes told me 'twas the woman herself he wanted. He would have asked for her if I had given him lands in the north instead of the west."

Concern trickled through Margaret. She liked Catrìona and wanted her happiness, but after Domnall's rejection, would Catrìona want any man? "What did you tell him?"

"The truth. I've had many offers for her, including most recently—and most importantly—one from Colbán."

"Your captain wants Catrìona? But is it not Elspeth he favors?"

"The young, silly one? Nay. He may dally with her, but 'tis the red-head he has asked for."

Margaret pondered a match between Catrìona and the captain, to her mind a rough warrior who would do best with a gentle bride. "Colbán is a good man, but I doubt he knows much of Catrìona's strength and her spirit. As I recall, he allows no dissent in the men he commands or the women he possesses."

"That is as it may be, *mo cridhe*, but he has earned such a prize. For some time, I have been thinking to raise Colbán to a mormaer and award him lands. But I would have him close to Dunfermline, not far to the west. 'Tis also possible Cormac's daughter has no desire to return to the place where her parents were murdered. After all, the home she remembers is gone. If I give her to Colbán, he could have the woman he wants and different lands."

Margaret let out a breath. "Oh."

"What is it, *mo cridhe*?" He nibbled on her neck sending shivers down her throat, making it difficult to concentrate. "I have yet to speak to the girl's uncle, which I will do before I give her to anyone."

Margaret considered the possibilities. She wanted to give Catrìona what she never had herself. "If 'twere possible, and each man is acceptable in your eyes, I would let it be the lady's choice."

"Now that would be a bad precedent, Margaret, to let your ladies think they could select their husbands. Can you imagine the chaos that would ensue? Nay, 'tis best I choose them. Besides, since her father's death, the woman is my ward and her lands mine." He nuzzled the tender skin beneath her ear. "Still, you know I always seek your advice."

Margaret tried not to think of his lips sliding down her neck as she pondered the problem. An idea came to her. Running her fingers over her husband's hand now stroking her thigh, she said, "What if 'twere done so that you and I know which man she prefers, but none of the other ladies is aware and the announcement, when it comes, is yours, as always?"

Malcolm laughed. "You are a marvel, *mo cridhe.*" He kissed her on the mouth, a long lingering kiss. Then he lifted his head to stare into her eyes. "Aye, 'twould work." He set her carefully on the bench and stood.

Margaret looked up at him. "I was going to make a trip with Catrìona to the shrine of St. Andrew to select a site for the inn on this side of the Forth and was only waiting for your return. If you agree, I could take both guards with us to observe them with her." To remind him the building of an inn would cost him much coin, she said, "The scribe would also be helpful in accounting for your gold I intend to spend."

Malcolm chuckled. "Clever, *mo cridhe*, but 'tis not the gold I think of. You know I would not send you even to the shrine of St. Andrew without a contingent of my men for protection, especially with the babe's birth two months away. Yea, you can have the two guards and more. Would you take all of your ladies?"

"Nay, only Catrìona and Audra, assuming Audra would be willing to leave her father. Cristina can see that my other ladies are kept busy. My travel to the shrine would also spare Bishop Fothad having to come to Dunfermline to hear my confession."

"Very well. I regret I must stay here to see to my men and the business of the provinces that has accrued in my absence. As well, I must find a new scribe, mayhap one of the Culdee monks who serve in the chapel. How long might you be gone?"

She could see he was anxious. It was all very well for him to charge off to Northumbria to clash swords with the Normans, but he would not want her to go thirty miles to meet with the bishop at St. Andrew's shrine. And she loved him for it. Dropping her gaze to her hands, she said, "We could ride to St. Andrews in but two days' time, except now that I go by cart, I travel more slowly and we will need to make stops to visit the prospective sites for the new inn." She did not look into his eyes until she said, "There and back again might take a fortnight."

Malcolm frowned but, before he could object, she added hopefully, "Mayhap less."

One hand was fisted on his hip as he ran the other through his mane of dark hair. "All right, but do not be surprised if I ride to join you for the return. You have been gone too long from my sight."

Margaret smiled, pleased at her husband's concession. "I would welcome you joining us, My Lord. And by that time I may have learned which of your two guards Catriona would prefer as a husband."

"You can add that to your prayers," he said with a smile. He loved to tease her about her many hours spent in prayer. "And let us hope whichever man the redhead prefers will be acceptable to the lady's uncle. Atholl will have his say, you can be sure."

A knock at the door revealed the physic returned. "My Lord," he said bowing. "God willing, Duff will recover. He is a man of strong countenance."

"Thank you," said Malcolm.

"Oh, and when I left," the physic said, "his daughter was with him."

Malcolm instructed him to see to the other wounded and the physic bowed and left.

Turning to face her, her husband sighed resignedly. "Would that I could take you to my bed, *mo cridhe*, but that will have to await until this eve. There is much to be done at the moment." He held out his hand. "Come, we must visit Duff and the wounded. On the way, you can tell me about the sites you will visit for the new inn. Then I must bathe ere we dine."

* * *

Catrìona sat at one of the long trestle tables crowded with the returning warriors, still coated in the dirt of the road they traveled. They had returned with longer beards and happy faces. The time for the evening meal was not yet upon them, but servants hurried to set platters of cold meat, cheese and bread before the hungry men. Now that they were safely home, the men dove into the food, swapping stories of the raids and quaffing pitchers of honey ale, rarely served in Dunfermline since the king preferred his red wine.

Next to her was Steinar and across from them sat Rhodri and Fia with Giric squeezed in between, his gaze fixed on the scribe. Shadow, the boy's ever-present dog, had taken shelter beneath the table. She could hardly blame him. The hall filled with loud and boisterous exclamations that might frighten such a wee dog, but then again, he might be hoping for a dropped scrap.

Giric sat with his elbows on the table, his head resting on his up-turned palms, enraptured, as Steinar described Rhodri's flaming arrows. The bard downed his ale, blushing as the scribe richly embellished the tale. When the story was finished, Giric looked at Rhodri in awe.

"Ye really did that?"

"Aye, he did," Steinar said before leaning across the table to launch into another story. Catrìona admired the way the scribe gave of his time to entertain the orphan. Giric might have been his own son for all the attention he paid the boy. One day, Steinar would father sons of his own. Might they be her sons? The thought settled into her heart as a happy truth. He was only a scribe, a rebel warrior who had been exiled from his country, but she could not want a better man. At great risk to himself, he had saved Niall from the brute Rian and now he guarded the king. And still, he had time for the orphan boy.

"There I stood before the king," Steinar said in dramatic fashion, "prepared to give my life were it required."

Giric's eyes grew wide and his mouth gaped.

"Just as I was to be speared by a Norman," Steinar spoke slowly, drawing out the suspense, "an arrow whooshed through the air to lodge in the knight's neck." Steinar grasped his neck as if he'd taken the arrow himself. "I heard the Norman gasp as he fell from his horse, dead as he hit the ground."

Rhodri stood and bowed.

Giric clapped his hands together, his face beaming with pride at the feat.

Another story began, this one told by Rhodri. It would be even more fanciful than the ones Steinar had told, she was certain, for the bard was a good storyteller.

Just then, Catrìona noticed Audra rise from the table where she had been sitting to head in the direction of the stairs. The queen's other ladies remained seated but Catrìona expected they would soon follow.

After Rhodri's story ended, Catrìona pushed herself from the bench. "We must go to the wounded, Fia." And then to the others, "The queen has asked us to visit the men who returned bearing wounds. 'Tis our Christ-like duty." She smiled at the scribe and the bard. "Thank you for the most wondrous tales. Mayhap we will see you this eve."

"You will see me afore that, my lady," said Steinar, his blue thistle eyes shining. "We, too, must visit the men above."

Rhodri nodded, his gaze resting on Fia. "Aye, I will join you soon."

With Fia by her side, Catrìona crossed the crowded hall. As she passed the table where Colbán sat with the king's guard, he stood and bowed. "My lady, the stitching you did for me is excellent. It pleases me greatly you chose a warrior's symbol."

Never sure what to say to the man, and mindful his companions who were listening and appeared well into their cups, she decided on a simple acknowledgment, certain he was overstating her dismal efforts at embroidery. "You... you are most welcome, good sir."

She dipped her head and continued on toward the stairs. Fia leaned in to ask, "Does the king's captain refer to that cloth you have been working on? Was that the piece you gave him today upon his return?"

"Aye. Before he left with the king, Colbán asked me to embroider one of his tunics. I was loath to do it, Fia. You know my attempt to embroider scrolls renders them more like twigs gathered for kindling. But 'tis not easy to say nay to that man."

"I find it most interesting he asked *you* to do it."

" 'Tis possible he did not know how terrible I am at the task. I tried to tell him another lady could do a better job."

As they reached the stairs, Fia paused and asked, "Well, how did it look when you finished? He seemed quite content. And what did he mean by a 'warrior's symbol'?"

" 'Twas not like anything I have ever stitched before but the shape of it was something I know well and at least I did not bleed upon the cloth." Catrìona had been most worried she would leave a trail of dark red drops on his copper cloth.

"What did you embroider?" her cousin asked impatiently.

Catrìona began to ascend the stairs and Fia followed. "Falcons, or well, the outline of them with knots for eyes and a feather or two stitched on the body."

"*Falcons*? You embroidered falcons on the tunic of the king's captain?"

"Do not look so surprised," Catrìona protested. " 'Tis an easier shape for me than an intricate flower, and more manly, though I cannot say the birds look much like Kessog, which had been my intent."

"No other man's tunic will bear the falcon, Cat. You will have the king's captain eating from your hand. Truth be told, he was more than a little happy to greet you as we passed."

"Nay, I think not. Colbán would not eat from any woman's hand. Besides, now that I know I can do it, I have a mind to make a tunic for Steinar and adorn it with falcons and mayhap something else." As she had worked on the tunic for the king's captain, she had envisioned making one for the scribe to set him apart, one that spoke of his being lettered as few men were. Aye, she was excited about the tunic.

"I can hardly account for this sudden enthusiasm for needlework," Fia said with mock sarcasm.

Catrìona ignored Fia's remark and, at the top of the stairs, turned down the corridor. She did not wish her cousin to know how she dreamed of Steinar and wanted to do things for him only a wife would do. "I asked Margaret for some cloth and she freely gave it, a rich blue wool that will make a worthy tunic."

"Somehow I do not think this will turn out well," said Fia, her brows drawing together in a frown. "What if all the king's men begin to expect falcons?"

"They will not. My embroidery is not so fine as yours or the other ladies."

Before they arrived at the chamber that was their destination, Catrìona paused in the corridor and looked down at her gown. "We should change ere we go to the wounded, else we decorate our gowns with blood."

"Aye, and quickly," said Fia.

Once changed, they headed toward the first of two chambers Margaret had told them were set aside for the wounded. At the door, Catrìona took a deep breath and entered.

A dozen men were laid out on pallets waiting for the physic and his healers. Servants bustled about bringing water, clean linen and bandages. Not since the attack on the vale had Catrìona seen so many wounded. But at least these had a chance to heal.

Moans from the men echoed around the chamber.

In one corner, the king's physic, a man of middle years with a nearly bald pate, bent over a warrior's arm. On the other side of the room, Audra crouched low over Duff.

Catrìona went toward her and Fia followed. The mormaer lay still, his eyes closed. Placing a hand on Audra's shoulder, Catrìona asked, "How is your father?"

Audra looked up, a small smile on her kind face, which Catrìona took as an attempt to be brave. "He is sleeping now and soon will be taken to the chamber they are preparing for him. He will stay in Dunfermline till he is well." Brushing an errant strand of hair from Duff's forehead, Audra's brow wrinkled in concern. "The wound pains him much, but he refuses to admit it. After the king left, I asked the physic to give him a potion. When it wears off, I imagine he will be blustering about all the attention he is getting, but for now, it allows him to rest."

"I am glad the news is good." Then, pushing up her tunic sleeves, Catrìona asked, "How can we help?"

Audra took in their practical tunics and linen aprons. "The servants have removed the old bandages and cleaned the wounds. The physic has directed the bandages be changed and the servants do that now. If you are up to it, you might help them, but the men like to hear a soft voice and have something to drink. Just to see your faces will cheer them."

"Are the other ladies in the second chamber?" Fia asked.

"All save Isla," replied Audra. "I will join you to help after I see how things are going there."

Catrìona consulted with the king's physic before he quit the room to go with Audra. She and Fia set about the work of helping to comfort the wounded and, where needed, apply clean bandages. The smell of blood was strong in Catrìona's nostrils, but the grateful smiles of the men kept her working.

It was not long before the heat in the room caused the sweat to rise on her forehead. After she had seen to several men and asked the servants to bring them water to drink, she sat back on her heels and surveyed those yet to be tended. Spotting one she recognized, she looked over to Fia. "Is not that one of Rhodri's archers?"

Fia raised her head from where she bent over a man's shoulder and followed Catrìona's gaze. "Aye, 'tis Brian." Tying off the bandage she was working on, Fia rose and walked the short distance to where the archer lay, still wearing the green and brown colors favored by Rhodri's men. "How are you, Brian?"

The archer slowly opened his eyes. "I am well, my lady. 'Tis only my arm that suffered a scratch. 'Twould have been worse but Rhodri's arrow felled the Norman who sought to end my life. The French knight plucked me right from the tree, he did."

"Has the wound been stitched?" Fia asked. At the man's nod, she said, "The servants have gone but I can check to see if 'tis healing."

Catrìona watched as Fia carefully lifted the bandage and then replaced it.

"It seems in good order," her cousin said, smiling at the archer.

" 'Tis only a wee scratch, lady. Were it not for the Welshman and his God-blessed bow, those Normans would have laid me open like a cod, me and many another king's man besides. Rhodri is as slippery as an eel and his aim deadly keen."

Catrìona saw a smile spread across her cousin's face.

"The bard is a wonder," said Fia, lifting a cup of water to the man's mouth. "A voice to soothe a wild beast and skill with a bow to bring one down. A man good at many things."

"Aye, he is," echoed the archer as he laid his head back and closed his eyes. "Aye, he is."

Catrìona pushed to her feet, rubbing the cramp from her lower back and twisting her neck to relieve the stiffness. A feeling of being watched made her look toward the door where the golden-haired scribe stood watching her, his expression unfathomable. Like the sunlight falling on the waters of Loch Lomond, his golden hair reflected the light coming through the window, almost shimmering.

"You make a very pretty picture, my lady. I would ask you to change my bandage but alas, 'tis already done."

Fia snorted beneath her hand and Catrìona shot her cousin a sharp glance.

"I did not know you were wounded," she said, worried he might still be hurt. But there was no evidence of a wound. He stood tall, every bit the strong warrior, yet somehow he seemed a different man than when he left for Northumbria. There was an air of confidence about him she had not seen before.

" 'Tis nothing, yet I would have made much of it to have your gentle hands wrapping linen about my leg."

"If you could see the way I wrap bandages, you might reconsider."

"Is Rhodri about?" Fia interjected, looking at Steinar.

"Aye," he said. "In the other chamber, seeing to some of his wounded archers."

"If 'tis all right with you," Fia faced Catrìona, "since we are done here, I would offer my help in the next chamber."

"Go," Catrìona said. "I will be along shortly. Audra must need help since she did not return."

Steinar moved to one side of the door, allowing Fia to pass.

Now that they were alone, well, except for the sleeping wounded, she remembered hearing some of the returning men speak of the scribe's saving the king's life in Alnwick. "Is it true what they say? That you saved the king?"

" 'Twas my job to defend his back and I did."

"You make it sound a simple thing but the men tell a different story."

He shrugged, apparently unwilling to say more.

"Whatever you did, you have earned the praise of the king's men."

He did not respond to her statement but asked instead, "Must you stay here?"

She gazed about the room. "Most of the men sleep, but I must fetch a servant to keep watch before I could leave them."

"I will fetch the servant," he said. "Then I would speak with you alone."

CHAPTER 11

Steinar did not know what he would say to the woman he wanted, the woman Malcolm intended for Colbán. Since he had turned his horse north from Alnwick, his only desire had been to be alone with Catrìona to see if there was a glimmer of affection for him in her eyes. Beyond that, he now had a pressing desire to know what had transpired a year ago in the Vale of Leven.

Once he had fetched a servant to keep vigil over the wounded, he returned to the auburn-haired beauty who haunted his thoughts. "Will you walk with me outside the tower?"

A faint smile crossed her face. "Aye, that would be most welcome. The air in here is close."

He offered his arm. " 'Tis worse in the hall with its smell of ale and celebrating warriors."

She laughed and took his arm. "You speak the truth."

He glanced at her linen tunic, which lacked the warmth of a velvet gown. "You might want to bring your cloak."

She looked down at her clothing as if she had not remembered what she wore. In one corner of her apron was a bloodstain. "Oh, aye. I will change and get my cloak. I will meet you in the hall."

He waited at the bottom of the stairs. When she finally appeared, his eyes followed her as she descended, suspecting he was not the only man who did so. She had donned a gown and a green woolen cloak over which hung her long auburn plaits.

The tree nymph. He knew then he would never tire of seeing her face, no matter what lines the years would add to it. He only felt complete when she was near.

"I am ready," she said eagerly.

After a fortnight away from her, he, too, was eager. Only he wished they could speak of the future and not the past.

He followed her through the noisy hall and out the tower door, avoiding the gazes of the men still drinking at the tables. One of them might be the king's captain and he wanted no interference from that quarter.

Hoping her burly guard, Angus, had not followed them, he led her away from the tower to a rock outcropping where it was possible to glimpse the blue waters of the Forth a few miles away.

As they drew near the place of clustered stones, he was relieved to see they were alone.

" 'Tis beautiful here," she said, gazing south to where the Forth was visible in the far distance.

Once she had settled onto a rock, he dropped to a large slab of stone across from her, meeting her gaze. "Tell me of your home, Catrìona, and what happened there more than a year ago. How did your father die?"

Frowning, she inquired, "Why do you ask me now?"

"For some time, I have wanted to ask how your father was killed and since I met you, I have been eager to learn about you and your home."

She seemed to accept his explanation. " 'Tis not easy to speak of," she began. " 'Twas a day of great horror. It did not start that way, of course. Angus and I were returning from flying Kessog above Loch Lomond when we came upon Northmen attacking my father's hillfort. I saw it all from the cliffs above." A shadow fell across her lovely face. "In my mind, I can hear the screams of the women and the shouts of raiders as they brutally killed our men. I can see the bodies strewn upon the ground, including those of my mother and father." She paused and looked up, her expression grim. "I still have terrible dreams of that day."

She began to weep and he went to sit beside her, taking her hand in his and placing a protective arm around her shoulders. "Please forgive me. I had no idea you had witnessed your father's death." He let out a breath, wishing he could call back his question. Wanting to let her know he understood, he said, "I know what it is to see your father slain before your eyes. I cannot forget and I expect you never will."

She raised her head to look at him, her green eyes full of tears. "Nay, I cannot forget."

"I understand your dreams, too. For a long time, in my dreams, I relived that long day of fighting on Senlac Hill when the Normans stormed England's shores."

She raised her eyes to meet his, then she looked away, staring into space, mayhap seeing again the terror she had witnessed.

He drew her closer into his chest. " 'Tis all right, Catrìona. We are both far from those fields of death."

She curled her slender fingers around his hand.

"But tell me," he said, "these Northmen, did you know from whence they came? There have been no Northmen attacking Scotland for some time."

"Nay, but because of the banner they flew, Angus believes they might have come from the Orkneys."

"The Orkneys..." Steinar searched his memory for something involving the islands far to the north. "The king has Norse relations in the Orkneys who foster his son, Duncan. From time to time, he exchanges messages with them."

She raised her head and turned to him with sudden interest. "Did you ever pen a message for him about the vale?"

In his mind, he shifted through the missives he had penned pertaining to the Orkneys and the brothers Paul and Erlend Thorfinnsson who ruled the islands. "I do remember something. 'Twas last summer. Malcolm sent a messenger to the brothers and asked me to write a missive for the messenger to carry, inquiring about an attack on one of his mormaers in the west. I had not thought of it because he only mentioned the hillfort's location as being on the River Clyde."

"My father's hillfort was on the River Clyde," she said anxiously. "What news did the king receive back?"

"As I recall, Paul sent a reply saying he had no knowledge of any raid on Scotland and insisted he and his brother were loyal to the king.

They are his stepsons, after all. And Malcolm's eldest son is in their care." Gazing into her anxious eyes, he said, "The king would not hesitate to take revenge for an attack on one of his mormaers if he knew who was responsible."

She looked down at their joined hands, one of her tears dropping onto his hand. "My father was faithful to the king. They fought Mac Bethad together."

He squeezed her hand. "Were any saved besides you and your brother?"

"Angus, of course, and the Northmen spared some of the women, taking them on their ships when they sailed. My handmaiden was among them. She would be seventeen summers now." Her eyes pleading, she asked, "What has become of them?"

He leaned in to press a kiss to her temple. "You cannot think of that now, little one. To worry will not bring them back." He would not tell her the women had likely been sold like so many surplus cattle.

She turned her face and, as she did, her forehead brushed his lips.

"I have missed you," he said, raising her chin with his finger. Her eyes were like liquid emeralds and he could not resist their power. Capturing her lips, he kissed her deeply. She responded, returning the kiss and reaching her hands into his hair.

How he wanted this woman! Not just in his bed but as his partner for life. Keenly aware she was not his to claim, he lifted his mouth from hers, speaking to himself as well as to her. "The king would not be pleased to know I claim your kisses when he may already have in mind a man for you to wed."

She dropped her hands to her lap. "But there is no one…"

Her lips were swollen with his kisses and her eyes a darker shade of green. Wisps of auburn hair blew about her delicate face. Achingly beautiful and so innocent. Apparently she did not know of Colbán's request for her hand. And he could not tell her.

"You do not know that," he said with regret. "The king chooses the husbands for Margaret's ladies. Now that you are free of the Irishman, you will be highly sought after." He wanted to tell her he would ask for her hand but since he had already done so and been turned away, he said nothing.

She shook her head as if unable to accept the possibility. "The queen needs me in her work to build an inn for the pilgrims. Besides," she said, giving him a sharp glance, "would the king not ask if there is one I would want?"

Could she mean him? That she might want him even though she knew him to be merely one of the king's men caused his heart to soar with hope, but it soon died with his memory of the king's words. He could not allow himself to think of having her. In that way lay madness. "The king gives no maiden a choice." When she began to protest, he stood and offered his hand. "All things in time, little one. Come, we'd best return."

⋆　⋆　⋆

Catrìona folded the traveling gowns she would take with her to St. Andrews and Steinar's words came back to her. *All things in time.* The same words of dismissal Domnall had spoken when she laid her heart as his feet. But this was far worse than Domnall, for she cared deeply for Steinar. Once again, she had spoken too soon and received only rejection. He would take her kisses but shun her desire for more, for she would have his heart if she could. Mayhap it was her destiny to be loved by no man. If that were the case, she would rather serve Margaret all of her days than be given by the king to some man for whom she cared little.

Shrugging off the unpleasant thought, she placed her gowns in the small chest, glancing at Fia, trying to decipher her cousin's true feelings about staying behind. She did not appear sad, but Catrìona had to know. "Do you mind awfully not going with the queen?"

Fia looked up from where she sat on the edge of her bed, plaiting her hair. "I do not mind at all, save that I wish you would take Isla with you. Her boasting and arrogance are most tiring, but 'tis possible Cristina will be less indulgent with her than Margaret."

"You may not have to put up with Isla for long. She will depart soon after Domnall returns, do you not think?"

"Aye, mayhap." Her cousin's eyes narrowed on Catrìona, as if watching for a sign of sadness.

"Nay, Fia, I do not wish to have Domnall back. He could not have loved me, betraying me for the sake of coin as he did." What she did not tell Fia was that she had found more comfort in the scribe's arms than ever she had with Domnall's scant attempts to comfort her after her loss.

Rising from the bed, her cousin came toward her and gave her a hug. "Good. I am glad you do not pine for Domnall."

Looking into Fia's eyes, Catrìona said, "It is just as well I go with the queen. Mayhap Domnall will come for Isla while I am away and then I will be free of them both. I will miss you, but at least I will have Audra for company."

Catrìona closed the chest. She had not packed the cinnamon-colored gown she would wear tonight. There was to be a celebration for the king and his returning warriors and she wanted to dress for it. In truth, she dressed to please Steinar even though he had not encouraged her.

Fia resumed her seat on the bed and reached for a second riband to tie off her other plait. "Has Audra said anything about her father?"

"Only that he insists she travel with the queen and since Audra is willing to go, I assume he recovers."

Fia rose from the bed to help her dress. "Just think, Cat, you will be with the handsome scribe all the while you are gone. 'Tis a pleasant thought for you, no?"

Slipping the gown over her head, Catrìona nodded. "Aye." Her cheeks burned with the memory of his kiss, but her countenance fell as she remembered how things had been left between them.

"I am hoping Cristina does not keep us at our embroidery all day while you are away," said Fia. "I want to be able to watch Rhodri at archery practice."

"Do be careful, Fia. Cristina would not approve of your sneaking away to meet the bard."

"Aye, she is a hard one, but more easily fooled than Margaret, who sees into the hearts of her ladies. I think the queen knows I care for Rhodri."

"No doubt she does. One would have to be blind to miss it. 'Tis all over your face when you look at him."

"As are your feelings for Steinar when you look at him. I think he has replaced Domnall in your heart."

She would not deny it. "Aye," was all she said. Then remembering the orphan boy, she asked, "Will you look after Giric while I am gone? I will ask Niall to see to Kessog as well as the lad but you will be there when Giric comes to break his fast. I would not want him to be lonely."

"Gladly. I will enjoy breaking my fast with the boy and his little dog. Shadow never barks at the meal."

Catrìona could not resist the smile she returned her cousin. " 'Tis because Giric feeds the whelp beneath the table. I saw him doing it when the men ate upon their return from Northumbria."

"I should have noticed that, but the lad is quick with his hands." Reaching for her own gown, Fia said, "You and Audra enjoy your travel. I am content to stay in Dunfermline and see to the boy."

Satisfied Fia was not feeling left out, Catrìona helped Fia with her gown and turned her mind to the evening. "There will be a celebration tonight. Mayhap the bard will entertain. There must be many tales from Northumbria he can set to song."

"Aye and some of them could tell of the archers' flaming arrows. My heart pounded in my chest as Steinar spoke of them rushing through the air like a great wind!"

"You are as bad as Giric. His eyes grew huge as Steinar told the stories."

"The lad is very fond of the scribe," observed Fia.

Catrìona reflected on the time they had spent in the hall listening to tales from the raid. "Aye, and with good reason. Both Steinar and Rhodri are warriors and so would Giric be one day if he has his way."

"I wonder what happened to render the lad an orphan," said Fia.

Catrìona had wondered the same thing many times. "The queen never speaks of the orphans' beginnings and I have been too much the coward to ask."

⋆　⋆　⋆

That night, as Catrìona descended the stairs, there was a festive mood among the crowd gathered to celebrate the king's return. Warriors, now bathed and shaved, carried on lively conversations with the women from the village who came to share the meal.

At the bottom of the stairs, the king's captain waited, wearing the copper-colored tunic.

"My lady," he said, bowing before her, "allow me to escort you and your cousin to your table."

An uncomfortable feeling swept over Catrìona as she placed her hand on his offered arm. She was certain his request was in the nature of an order. Shooting a glance at her cousin, she said, "We would be honored."

He deposited them at their table and strode away.

Fia whispered, "I told you those falcons would mean trouble. I have the feeling that man was marking territory."

"Surely you are wrong, Fia. He was merely being gracious to one of the queen's ladies who did him a kindness." Even as she said the words, she hoped she was correct. At first she had been glad he had not found fault with her stitchery, but his attendance on her now caused her to wonder.

While the warriors had been away, Catrìona had begun the blue tunic for Steinar, oddly happy to be sewing for him when she had not liked the task when done for others.

"Apparently the king's captain did not look closely at my stitches," she remarked to Fia, "or he would have been frowning."

"From what I could see," said her cousin, "the work was not lacking. Besides, 'twas not the stitches that garnered his attention, 'twas you."

"But you said he looks at all the queen's ladies. Surely it is Elspeth who holds his attention, not me. He seems to bask in her flirtations."

" 'Tis certain Elspeth showers him with attention, but I cannot imagine a man like Colbán content with her for long."

A few seats away, Elspeth laughed merrily. "She is yet young," said Catrìona. "You remember how we were three years ago."

"Incorrigible," said Fia, "and mayhap *you* still are."

That brought a smile to Catrìona's face. "Aye, mayhap I am."

The food that night was an amazing array of fish, game and roast boar. The kitchen must have been preparing the various dishes since the messenger had come with news of the king's imminent return. Despite that the men had eaten when they returned, they devoured all on their trenchers and consumed many goblets of wine.

Catrìona sipped her wine, catching glimpses of the golden-haired scribe at the other table. His words about her now being free to wed came back to her, causing her to worry. She hoped the king had no plans for her. What would she do if he did?

When Rhodri's entertainment concluded and all the stories had been shared, Margaret slowly rose and, begging leave from the king, stepped down from the dais. Her searching gaze fell upon her ladies and Catrìona rose with the others, relieved to leave the boisterous noise of the male celebration behind her.

★   ★   ★

Steinar checked Artair's saddle and the pack he had slung over the horse's back, eager to be on the road. He had never been very far east of Dunfermline and certainly not as far as St. Andrews, but now that Scotland was his acknowledged home, he was glad for the chance to see more of it. And he was glad to have days with Catrìona away from court even if the king's captain would be accompanying them.

It took some time for the party to be loaded. Malcolm himself insisted on inspecting the cart his queen was to ride in, scolding a servant for insufficient pillows. Once that situation was remedied and the provisions and chests secured, the king settled Margaret into the cart and Colbán assisted Audra to sit beside her.

Steinar was unsurprised to see a servant leading Catrìona's horse from the stable. While Colbán was issuing orders to the other guards, Steinar helped Catrìona to mount her horse next to the queen's cart.

Checking the stirrup, he glanced around but did not see the ever-present Angus. "Your guard does not go with us?"

"Nay," she said settling herself in the saddle, "the king's captain persuaded him that I would be well protected by the guards attending the queen."

"Why do you not ride with the queen and her other lady?" he asked, knowing the answer but hoping he could tease her into some spirited reply.

"I would not be so gently seated." Shooting a glance at the queen whose maidservant was assisting her efforts to get comfortable, Catrìona said, "I can see more from my horse and enjoy the diversions the road has to offer."

"Well, then, you can ride beside me as I'm to lead the party while the king's captain and most of the guard will ride on either side of the queen."

"If I must," she said, as if greatly affronted. Her smile told him she was not.

The queen gave Catrìona an odd look but then Margaret was unused to the back and forth exchanges he enjoyed with her lady.

Today, the weather was warm and Catrìona had chosen to wear a simple linen gown, her cloak slung over the back of her saddle. Her hair was formed into one long plait that hung down her back like a crimson rope, the end of it dangling tantalizingly below the edge of her saddle.

"And what of your falcon?" he asked. "Did you leave the bird behind?"

She frowned, her disappointment evident. "Alas, I must. I just looked in on Kessog this morning. He is never too happy in the middle of a molt but today he was quite disgruntled. His feathers were all askew and he bristled on his perch as I left. 'Twas as if he knew I was going somewhere without him and was chiding me for not taking him despite his untidy appearance."

Steinar chuckled but he well understood the falcon's discomfort. He, too, would bristle should he be forced to wave her goodbye as she hied off to some distant place without him. Nay, he would not think of the day that might come to pass. For now it was enough they rode together. He would relish his moments with her and wait to see if she welcomed the attentions of the king's captain before he lost all hope.

Bowing his head to the queen, he bid Catrìona to follow as he kneed his horse toward the front of the score of riders. Soon, they left the tower behind and took the path leading northeast from Dunfermline.

Above him, the sky was a cloudless blue. The path took them through green meadows edged with wood sorrel and butter-colored flowers. On either side of the meadow tall pines rose high above them. In the distance he could see low hills.

"Where will we lodge tonight?" she asked, her eyes sweeping over the grass-covered hills stretching before them bounded by the deep woods.

"Would you be disappointed if I said in an open field?"

She laughed. "Would you be surprised if I said, 'Nay'?"

"My lady, after your jaunt in the woods and dip in the burn, nothing you do would surprise me. But lest you worry, the king maintains a manor house in Ballingry. 'Tis only a few miles southeast of Loch Leven. From the sketch I looked at of where we were headed, 'twill bring us about a third of the way into our journey."

"I have not had such a long ride since coming to Dunfermline," she said wistfully. "I am enjoying it."

"Then you have no complaints?"

"Quite the opposite, sir. I am pleased beyond measure to be outside, free of the tower's small chambers and, dare I add, free of my needle-work."

He smiled. "You do not love your stitching as the other ladies do?"

"Rarely. But recently I have found a new interest in embroidery, a design of my own."

Immediately he pictured the copper-colored cloth she had presented to Colbán. He had seen the captain wearing a tunic of the same color that evening in the hall, embroidered with what looked like falcons. Only she would have stitched such a design. The thought she might have enjoyed sewing for Colbán made him regret having asked the question.

A short while later, his mood darkening, Steinar called a halt to the procession. "We break here for a short while. The queen will be weary and we've the horses to water." Gesturing to a nearby stand of oak, he said, "There is shade among the trees, my lady."

★   ★   ★

Catrìona could not imagine what had come over Steinar. Without another word, he abruptly turned his horse and swept back toward the queen's cart. The shade of the trees could wait. She would not be directed to the woods when her mistress might need her. Following the moody scribe, Catrìona urged her horse back to where the main group had stopped.

"Allow me to help you," said the king's captain turning to her, hav-ing just helped the queen down from the cart. While Colbán reached to help her down, Steinar assisted Audra. Catrìona fought the feeling of jealousy that washed over her.

Reaching her hands toward the captain's shoulders, she felt his powerful hands circling her waist as he lowered her to the ground. "Thank you, sir. You are most gracious."

"Why not ride in the cart with the queen for the rest of the day, my lady? 'Tis likely more comfortable and you might enjoy the company of the other women. Riding all day on a horse is not for a lady such as you."

She let out an exasperated sigh as she handed the horse's reins to a waiting servant. "Nay, sir. I prefer to ride. I am quite used to it and I daresay, Audra can keep the queen well entertained."

He frowned, his displeasure clear, but he did not challenge her further as they walked together to join the others. A short time later, a cloth was spread beneath the nearby trees and they sat in the shade enjoying a bit of food. 'Twas a small meal but welcome and Catrìona was happy to see the queen ate the bits of cooked game, cheese and berries. Margaret often ate little but mayhap for the sake of the babe she carried, Audra had convinced her to eat.

Beneath the trees, sunlight filtered through the branches, falling onto the small party sitting with the queen. Robins, flitting about in the trees and foraging on the ground, tittered and chirped, making their presence known. Catrìona leaned back on one arm admiring the beautiful afternoon, a breeze wafting through the air.

Several members of the guard had joined them as well as the queen's maidservant, an older Saxon woman whose brown plaits were laced with gray. She was very attentive to Margaret, leaving Audra and Catrìona free to converse with the men.

Colbán eased himself down beside her. "I would sit with you, my lady, if you would allow it."

"Aye, your company is welcome." As long as Steinar was in a mood, she might as well enjoy Colbán's company.

He offered her more ale.

"I will fall off my horse do I drink any more of that heady ale, good sir," she said, declining. "But I thank you for the offer."

He entertained her with stories of his early days with the king. She was not disinterested, but what held her attention even more was the way Audra, sitting a few feet away, stared adoringly at the man. 'Twas the same way Fia stared at the bard. Did Audra hold a tendre for the brash captain? As she listened to the warrior with the red beard and warm brown eyes, who regaled her with tales of his early battles, she pictured a bear, dangerous and cunning, but potentially soft with the right woman. *Could Audra be that woman?*

Out of the corner of her eye, Catrìona glimpsed Steinar snatching glances at her while conversing with Audra. The twinge of jealousy she had felt earlier returned for he appeared to be enjoying Audra's company. She chided herself for it. Audra was kind to everyone, not like Isla of Blackwell. Besides, Catrìona might wish it otherwise, but she had no claim on Steinar.

Still, she watched him, thinking how unlike the other warriors he was. His manners were elegant, he was lettered and he treated her as an equal. She had responded willingly to his kisses, but it was more than attraction she felt for him. She respected him above other men. Few warriors would grant her the freedom to speak her mind as he did. Fewer still cared to hear what she had to say.

If Colbán was a great bear, Steinar of Talisand was a sleek golden panther, both creatures of mythical proportion and neither easily tamed.

★　★　★

Margaret watched her two ladies as they sat eating beneath the trees, drawing the approving glances of the king's guard sitting around them. Each woman was lovely and each had qualities a husband would treasure.

But they are so different.

Catrìona was a spirited beauty, willful, intelligent and courageous, who harbored deep hurts from the loss of her family and betrayal by the man she had thought to wed. Like a fast-moving river, obstacles were nothing to her. She went over them, like water over rocks. Catrìona needed a strong man with a tender heart to love and protect her, but who would not stifle her spirit. One who, after Domnall, would be ever faithful.

In contrast, Audra was a sweet woman, amenable to all, a placid loch that ignored obstacles, consigning the rocks to her deep waters. She would expect less and tolerate more than the fiery Catrìona. But she needed a man who would hold her in high regard.

One would challenge a man; one would bend to a man's demands with never a contrary word.

Would Audra make a better companion for the English thegn's son who had been exiled to a country not his own? A man who harbored his own ghosts of the past? Though Catrìona and Steinar had worked well together on the plans to build the inn, only this morning Margaret had observed the two exchanging words that made her think they did not suit. And now Steinar sat with Audra and Catrìona with Colbán.

The king's captain was strong enough to handle a woman like Catrìona. Both she and Colbán were Gaels, children of Malcolm's beloved Alba. And she had not forgotten that Audra's mother and younger brothers had been killed on the order of Mac Bethad of Moray, the land of Colbán's people. Mayhap she had been wrong in thinking the king's captain might be better served by the gentle Audra.

Margaret vowed to carefully observe them to determine if this new thought was correct. She cared about each of the ladies placed in her charge and she knew from her own experience that the crown of happiness in a woman's life, absent taking the veil, arose from a happy marriage.

CHAPTER 12

Steinar's first glimpse of the king's manor at Ballingry reminded him of his home at Talisand. A two-story light-colored stone building with wooden roof and shuttered windows, it would serve well the king's needs when traveling to St. Andrews if he did not lodge with Fife's mormaer.

Reining in his horse in front of the manor, Steinar dismounted and helped Catrìona to the ground, trying to ignore his body's reaction to having his hands around her waist.

"You seem pleased to be off the horse," he said, returning her brilliant smile.

"I am just happy to reach the first stop on our journey."

He glanced behind him to see Colbán and the other guards assisting the queen and Audra from the cart just as a plump gray-haired man came striding from the manor to meet them. Attired in a brown tunic, he could have been the older brother of Nechtan, the king's steward in Dunfermline.

"My Lady," the man said in gracious manner, bowing before the queen, "welcome to Ballingry. The king sent a rider ahead with news of your coming. Your house stands ready to receive you."

"Thank you, Gormal," said Margaret. "I should have known Malcolm would do that. He worries for my travels, especially now that the child's birth is but a few months away."

Margaret introduced Catrìona and Audra to the steward.

Steinar and Colbán introduced themselves, then followed the queen and her ladies while the rest of the guards went with the servants who were leading the horses to the stables.

As they reached the door, the queen said to the steward, "Your brother sends you his regards."

The steward dipped his head. "And in doing so, Nechtan reminds me I owe him and my nephews a visit."

"His sons grow ever taller," Margaret replied. "Soon, the king will have them joining the ranks of his men."

Steinar entered the manor behind the ladies. Inside, it was laid out somewhat like the king's tower in Dunfermline except it was not in the shape of a square and much smaller in size. Immediately before him were stairs leading to the floor above. The first story consisted of a large room with a long trestle table and benches. An open door at the far end led, he assumed, to the kitchen. The whitewashed walls were decorated with shields and armor, more a man's domain than a woman's.

The steward asked a servant to show the queen and her maidservant to the queen's chamber. "There are refreshments waiting for you, My Lady."

The queen thanked him and headed up the stairs with her maidservant.

The steward turned to Audra and Catrìona, informing them they would share a chamber on the same floor.

"There is room above for some of the guardsmen," he said to Colbán, "but the others will have to bed down in the stables."

Colbán shot a glance at Steinar. "You can share a chamber with me, Scribe."

Steinar was glad he had not been consigned to the stables, for he wanted to be close to Catrìona.

Not long after, they were all settled in and gathered around the long table for the evening meal. Steinar inhaled the aroma from the subtle spices in which the food had been cooked. Platters of fish were served with vegetables, warm bread and butter, and bowls piled high with red berries.

Sitting halfway down the table, the queen took a bite of her fish. " 'Tis very well cooked and most delicious."

The steward beamed. "You are eating trout from Loch Leven, My Lady. The *Keledei,* or Culdees as you may know them, who live on the island in the middle of the lake brought us a fresh catch this morn. They are most grateful you and the king are content to allow them to retain the land."

The queen seemed to ponder Gormal's words. "My husband's family has strong ties to the Culdees. Crínán of Dunkeld, the Culdee abbot, was my husband's grandfather."

"Yea," said the steward, "and a worthy man."

"We worship the same God," Margaret said to Catrìona, "but not always in the same way." Then with a smile, she added, "I have enjoyed my debates with them concerning the observance of Easter."

Steinar remembered the one meeting he had attended where the queen had, with Malcolm translating, forcefully argued the Culdees should make changes in the way they observed Easter and Lent. He had hoped there might be another such gathering for Catrìona to attend, but none had taken place since she had come to Dunfermline. Personally, he preferred the ways of the Culdees, who saw nothing wrong with their taking a wife. Many of them were married.

Catrìona said nothing about the queen's remark but, instead, commented on the food. " 'Tis even better fish than that served in Dunfermline."

Others eating the trout nodded their agreement. Steinar had dined many a night on salmon from the River Lune at Talisand. The rosy flesh of that fish was very different from this trout with its delicate flavor. In his mind, he pictured the green valleys around Talisand, but lest the sadness for loss of his home overtake him, he recalled all he had gained since coming to Scotland, letting go of all he had lost. Had he remained in England, he would never have met Catrìona.

For a long while, the guests chatted amiably with the steward and neither Colbán nor Audra said anything. But Steinar had caught Audra stealing glances at the king's captain, as if she were summoning the courage to address him.

Finally, Audra faced Colbán and said, "I have yet to thank you for your defense of my father in Alnwick, my lord. You risked your life for his. I am ever in your debt."

Colbán, who had kept his eyes turned on his trencher, looked up. " 'Twas my duty, my lady, and I was most happy to do it. Your father is a worthy leader of men. If I could have prevented the wound he received, I would have."

Audra's gentle eyes lingered long on the captain, who seemed unaware of her regard, as he fell again to eating. Those two, Steinar thought, were as much a contrast as Malcolm and his queen.

Taking a drink of his wine, Steinar idly regarded the others sitting around the table. When he came to the queen, he paused. Margaret had grown tired from their journey; every now and then her eyelids drooped. He was unsurprised when she declined a honeyed cake, took a last sip of her wine and rose to retire.

Steinar and Colbán, along with the steward and the men of the guard, stood and bowed to the queen.

Catrìona and Audra quickly followed their mistress and the three women ascended the stairs. The guards who had the first watch of the night dispersed to their posts and the rest retired to their pallets.

After a brief discussion regarding the next day's travel, Steinar and Colbán thanked the steward, bid him good night and repaired to their chamber.

'Twas not unlike the chamber Steinar shared with Rhodri in the king's tower, small but adequate. As he and the king's captain undressed for bed, Steinar commented on trivial events from their day's journey. He received only grunts in reply. Colbán was a man of few words and Steinar missed Rhodri's glib speech. Very quickly, the candle was snuffed.

Sleep came easily to Steinar that night, for the manor was quiet. Even the muted sounds of the night, to which his ears were finely attuned, finally died to silence.

Mayhap it was because he was so aware of her that Steinar's ears pricked the instant he heard the muted scream. *Catrìona.*

Leaping from his bed, not even taking time to don his tunic over his hosen in which he had slept, he ran bare-chested to her chamber door, listening outside the wooden panel. When another scream sounded, he threw open the door and raced to her side.

Still in the throes of the night terror, she tossed beneath the cover.

Easing himself down on the edge of the bed, he pulled her into his arms and pressed her head to his chest. " 'Tis all right, little one. You are safe."

In the bed next to Catrìona's, Audra, roused from sleep by his words, sat up and lit a candle. "What has happened?"

"She has dreams of the attack on her home," he said while rocking Catrìona, whose moan told him she was slowing coming awake.

"I remember some of the ladies speak of it," said Audra. "Poor lass. Can I help?"

"Nay, it will pass, I think."

He knew the minute Catrìona was awake because her arms tightened around his waist. He pressed his palm to the side of her head. " 'Tis me, little one."

Still breathing hard, she said, "It was... oh, my God. I saw him, Steinar. The one who killed my father. I saw him!" She trembled in his arms.

Smoothing the damp tendrils of hair from her face, he said, "Do not think of it. The dream is over and he cannot harm you."

"I will get her some water," said Audra, rising from her bed to don a robe over her undertunic.

When the wooden cup appeared before him, he held it to Catrìona's lips.

She took it and drank. "Thank you, Audra," she said.

As she finished, he set the cup aside and was just laying Catrìona down on her pillow when Colbán appeared at the open door. In the candle's faint light, Steinar could see the scowl on the captain's face. Servants with candles and some of the king's guard, their weapons drawn, crowded behind him.

"What goes here?" Colbán demanded in a harsh tone. "Why are you in the ladies' chamber, Scribe?"

Steinar let out a sigh.

Audra went to the angry captain. Placing her palm on Colbán's chest, she spoke softly. " 'Tis all right, my lord. Catrìona had a bad dream and Steinar came when he heard her scream. She has suffered such dreams before."

The captain appeared to calm at her words and sent the servants and other guards away. "Why does she have such dreams?" he asked shortly.

Steinar squeezed Catrìona's hand and rose from the bed, walking to where Colbán stood next to Audra. "Let us return to our chamber and allow the ladies to sleep. I can answer your questions on the way."

With a rueful glance in Catrìona's direction, Colbán bowed. "I bid you ladies a good night."

★　★　★

The next morning, Catrìona and Audra followed Margaret to a nearby copse of trees where they knelt in prayer, watched over by the king's guard. When they had finished, Margaret took some time to read her Gospels before they returned to the manor to break their fast.

Catrìona's prayers had been disturbed by horrible images from her dream, but once she was seated at the table and looked across at Steinar's smiling face, the images faded from her mind. He had come at her scream in the night to comfort her. She could still feel the warm skin of his bare chest against her cheek and hear his beating heart. The memory caused her own heart to race and she forced her gaze to her gruel. What must he have thought?

After a few bites of the gruel, which sadly lacked raisins, she shifted her gaze to the window where sun streamed in through the open shutters, drawing her attention to the trees outside and the sound of chirping birds. "To where do we ride today?"

Next to her, the queen said, "Today we will see a place Duff believes might serve for the inn. Dalgynch is not far and 'twould be a good halfway point for the pilgrims coming from Dunfermline. The Culdees have a small church there. Duff thought they might be willing to have the pilgrims lodged nearby."

Soon after, they were ready to depart. Catrìona again rode her horse. As before, the queen, her maidservant and Audra rode in the cart. Colbán had tried to dissuade Catrìona from riding, telling her again it was more proper for a lady to ride with the queen, but sensing he did not want to argue with her in front of Margaret, Catrìona prevailed and remained on her horse.

To her mind, the most important person was the queen, who had said nothing of her lady's decision to ride, only giving Catrìona a knowing smile as the captain reluctantly helped her to mount.

She caught Steinar hiding a smile. He shook his head while stroking the neck of his great black horse. "Best to let the lady do as she wishes," he said to Colbán. Then, tossing Catrìona a look of feigned disdain, he added, "She usually does."

The queen looked up, a concerned expression on her face, but Catrìona just laughed. Steinar knew her well. He would never have insisted she sit in the cart with the queen.

Catrìona enjoyed the pleasant morning that took them through green meadows dotted with flowers. Steinar seemed to be in a better mood today as he shared tales of his home and his sister. It seemed Catrìona and Serena had much in common, which the scribe did not seem to mind. He laughed much as he recounted his youth. Catrìona could not help but admire a man who had lost his home and yet could smile.

★   ★   ★

Even traveling at a leisurely pace, as they did, it was only midday when they emerged from the woods and Steinar glimpsed what he assumed was the small village of Dalgynch in the distance.

A short while later, he called a halt to the column and pulled rein in front of a stone chapel. Next to it was a large cottage where, he supposed, the few monks dwelled. In front of the cottage, a too-thin chicken scratched in the dirt. On the other side of the cottage, a reed fence surrounded a garden as large as the chapel. The plants, grown tall with the summer rains, appeared to be thriving. A few gray-robed monks, bent to harvesting turnips, looked up at their arrival. Beyond the garden, a few cows meandered about in a patch of grass.

Before they could dismount, the door of the chapel flew open and a monk, half-tonsured in the Culdee tradition and wearing a gray woolen cowl and sandals, hurried toward them. Behind Steinar and Catrìona, the king's captain helped the queen and the women down from the cart. The monk must have recognized the queen, for he bowed low before her and said, "My Lady, I am Oran. Welcome to our humble abode."

Steinar assisted Catrìona to the ground and she walked the short distance to where Margaret was explaining to the monk their purpose in coming. The monk, a man of middle years with a mild sort of face, appeared delighted with the queen's idea.

"Many pilgrims pass this way and, while we can accommodate them in the chapel, we cannot provide them lodging. An inn would certainly be desirable."

With that, Oran, who was nearly as thin as his chickens, escorted Margaret and the three other women into the cottage.

Steinar followed behind them and stood inside the door, waiting to see if Margaret had need of him.

The monk offered the queen a seat, a cup of ale and some bread and cheese. Fanning herself as if glad to be out of the sun, Margaret gratefully accepted the modest provisions.

Catrìona and Audra took seats on either side of their mistress. The maidservant stood to one side.

Steinar approached the queen. "With your permission, My Lady, I will help Colbán to see the tents raised. If you are agreed, I can show your maidservant where yours will be."

"Of course," said the queen and waved him off. Her maidservant followed him out the door.

Once the horses had been watered and the men and servants occupied with setting up tents, Steinar pointed out to the maidservant where the queen's tent would stand. Then he and Colbán went looking for the queen and her ladies.

"I expect we will find the ladies in the chapel," said Colbán.

"Possibly," said Steinar, but thinking how eager Catrìona and the queen were to see their project made a reality, he said, "or they might already be looking at sites for the inn." His conjecture proved correct as they soon discovered.

The women, accompanied by the monk, were studying a plot of open land lying a short distance from the chapel. On one side, a tree-lined burn, about ten feet across, burbled over rocks as it flowed along.

The queen was deep in conversation with the monk, Audra translating the Gaelic. The Culdee was pointing out various features of the land when Catrìona, seeing Steinar and Colbán approach, came toward them, leaving Audra with the queen.

Catrìona's eyes glistened with excitement. " 'Tis the perfect place for the inn, do you not think?"

Steinar nodded, but he was more interested in her than the ground they were inspecting. Her auburn plaits shone in the sun like burnished copper. " 'Tis most entrancing."

Either she had not understood he was speaking of her, or she chose to ignore it, because she answered her own question. "It will serve the pilgrims well. They will have the chapel in which to pray before going on with their journey, lodging for the night, and vegetables from a larger garden."

"Aye," said Steinar, "all that is possible."

Colbán cast an approving glance at Catrìona. "If the inn is well placed, it can be easily defended."

Steinar observed the predatory look in the eyes of the king's captain, as they narrowed on the woman they both desired. Any man would have noticed the way Catrìona came alive as she described the inn she imagined, her beauty only enhanced by her excitement for the new venture.

"The pilgrims will find a welcome resting spot and the Saxons in Dunfermline with little to do will have a new mission," Catrìona said, glancing back at Margaret, who still conversed with the Culdee. "I think the queen is pleased."

Margaret looked up and beckoned them to her. As they neared, she said, "Did you know there is an ancient stone cross here?" They shook their heads and the queen's blue gaze returned to the monk. "Can you show us?" Audra translated.

"Certainly, My Lady," he said, again with Audra's assistance. " 'Tis not far. It marks the end of the chapel property." Offering his arm, the monk and Margaret strode off, the rest of them following.

The stone cross was immense, taller than any man, and two feet across at the base. It was simple in design with no elaborate carvings, as some Celtic crosses had that Steinar had seen.

Margaret stared at the stone cross for some time before saying, "This must have long been a place of worship to have such an ancient cross. That and your chapel make this the right spot for the pilgrims' inn." Smiling at the monk, she said, "Oh, I am glad we have found it so quickly. God Himself must be directing our steps."

Audra made clear the queen's words for the monk. Next to Audra, Colbán studied the cross, rubbing his hand over his short red beard. "Might be Pictish," he said. " 'Tis old."

"Do you think so, my lord?" Audra asked solicitously.

The king's captain nodded, turning his head to Audra. "Aye, my lady."

Steinar watched the play of emotions that crossed Catrìona's face as her gaze lingered on Audra and the king's captain. Was she jealous of Colbán's attention to her fellow lady? If Catrìona favored Colbán, would Audra's attention to the captain be of concern? Mayhap it would after what Domnall had done. Then, too, Steinar recalled the way Duff's daughter had soothed the captain's anger the night before and wondered whether the gentle Audra harbored feelings for him. And what of Catrìona? Once he and the king's captain were raised to be mormaers, equal in rank, which man would she prefer as husband? The king favored his captain, but did she? He supposed it mattered little what a woman might wish. The king would decide. But it mattered to Steinar.

The queen stared admiringly at the massive cross. Beside her, the monk said, "There is a set of stones that stand in a circle nearby. You might want to see those, too. 'Tis not known precisely what purpose they served though some say the ancients supposed them to be a dancing ring for the fairies." Shaking his head, he added, "We try and dissuade the people from such beliefs."

With Audra's assistance, the queen was made to understand and replied, "Tomorrow, mayhap." Placing her hand on her rounded belly, she said, "For now, I think I shall find my tent and rest for a while."

Audra said a few words to the monk in Gaelic to which he replied, "Of course, My Lady."

Margaret thanked the Culdee and accepted his invitation to dine with him and the other monks that evening. Then she took Catrìona's arm and, together with Audra on her other side, walked toward where the cream-colored tents could be seen beneath the shelter of the trees a short distance away.

Steinar followed. At his side, Colbán said, "It seems we have accomplished our purpose here. Mayhap as soon as tomorrow we can leave for St. Andrews."

"Aye," said Steinar, "if the queen is feeling well enough. She appeared tired to me. The babe might be robbing her of strength."

Colbán nodded.

Steinar thought of what must be done. "If our party is to eat this eve, we'd best hunt or the monks will be serving us one of those meager chickens."

Colbán slapped him on the back. "Aye, a hunt is just what I need."

⋆　⋆　⋆

As the afternoon waned, Catrìona left Audra, who was napping, to check on the queen. Assured by the maidservant that Margaret was resting and did not have need of her ladies, Catrìona headed deeper into the forest to see to her private needs.

Sunlight pierced the dark green canopy of trees, dappling the forest floor, but less so as the stands of trees grew dense before her. 'Twas not unlike the forest in Dunfermline, filled with chattering birds, but there was something more untamed about it.

Having seen to her needs, she carefully stepped around an outcropping of twisted roots. An animal's low growl brought the forest to a sudden silence. She froze, her heart racing, then slowly raised her head to the source of the sound. Above her, a giant cat, gray with black stripes, bared its teeth and hissed sharply while sinking its claws into the thick branch on which it was perched. Its pale green eyes narrowed on her as it spit furiously, poised as if to attack.

Catrìona screamed and reared back just as the wild cat stamped forward, hissing and spitting. She reached for her knife sheathed at her hip.

Strong arms surrounded her, pulling her away from the cat. "I will protect you, my lady." Even without turning, she recognized the voice of the king's captain. Turning her in his arms, he held her to his hard chest. "Do not fear the beast. My sword is yours to command."

She gazed into his brown eyes, seeing concern. "I am grateful, sir." Behind her, the huge cat hissed and growled. She pressed closer to the king's captain. His tunic smelled of an unfamiliar man's sweat but she was too afraid to care. Never had she seen an enormous feline like this one baring its knife-like teeth and claws in such a menacing manner.

Colbán bent his head to bring his lips down on hers, kissing her most forcefully. Jerking her head back, she protested, "Nay, sir. Do not. I may fear the teeth of the wild animal but you are not without teeth yourself."

She looked behind her and, seeing the animal had gone, pushed away from the tall captain. In truth, she feared him as much as the beast.

From the woods came a familiar chuckle. " 'Twas only a wee cat, more afraid of you than you were of it."

"Steinar?" Her eyes searched the thick growth of trees for a head of golden hair. She spotted him standing against a tree, his arms crossed over his chest. " 'Twas no wee cat!" she insisted. "The beast was wild and fierce. It scared me."

Steinar left the tree to indolently stroll toward her. A glance at Colbán told her the captain was not pleased.

"Tell her, Colbán," said Steinar.

"Tell me what?" she asked, her gaze darting from one man to the other.

"Well," Colbán said, shooting Steinar a harsh glare, "mayhap 'twas not so fierce a beast as you thought, but 'twas still wild."

"You mean not as fierce as you *wanted* me to believe?" she said, feeling anger rising within her.

Colbán said nothing, but Steinar laughed. "Anything to steal the lady's kiss, eh Captain?"

Colbán let out a sigh and bowed. "My pardon, my lady. I was sorely tempted."

Having been fooled by the king's captain into allowing him an intimacy she would never have otherwise, she choked back the angry words she was tempted to utter. Too, she was annoyed beyond measure at Steinar's finding it amusing when he should have been at least jealous given the kisses they had shared. She gave them both a "H'mf!" and turned on her heels and stomped out of the forest.

As she left, she heard Colbán say to Steinar, "You might have waited."

"Not likely," came the reply.

"In the future, Scribe, confine your words to your scribbling."

"I am no longer merely the king's scribe. I'm a guardsman now, one of your own."

"Aye," Colbán growled. "And, as I am your captain, you will mind my orders. Where the queen's ladies are concerned, do not oppose me."

* * *

Steinar was more than a little angry but he had to temper his jealousy against what he understood were the king's wishes. His heart lurched as he reminded himself Colbán had asked for Catrìona's hand and the king seemed only too glad to accede to the captain's request. Tempted as he was to raise his sword tip to the back of Colbán's neck when he came upon the captain with his hands on Catrìona, seeing her back away, he had settled for laughter instead.

That night it rained, which fit Steinar's dour mood, and he ate in his tent where he brooded over the situation before sleep overtook him.

The next day had them slogging through wind and rain as they pressed on to St. Andrews, mud splashing to their stirrups.

In the wet weather, his leg took the opportunity to cramp, adding to his displeasure, but Catrìona, uncomplaining, pulled her cloak over her head against the rain and bore the dismal day like one of the men. She declined his invitation to be seated with the queen whose cart was now covered with an oilcloth tent.

What should have been a day's journey turned into two, but finally, the rain subsided and the sun emerged as they reached the coast.

The smell of sea air and cries of gulls welcomed them to St. Andrews, raising his spirits. Catrìona threw her cloak off her head and tilted her face to the sun, her auburn hair glistening like a dark jewel.

Behind the stone church, where Bishop Fothad stood waiting, was the North Sea, its deep blue waters a stark contrast to the ivory sand on the shore and the white clouds billowing above them.

" 'Tis beautiful," she said.

With eyes only for her, he agreed. "Aye, most beautiful."

As they pulled rein, Steinar slid from his horse and helped Catrìona to the ground.

"Have you been here before?" she asked, her green eyes focused on the bishop clothed in a white cowl robe. Behind them, Steinar glimpsed Colbán helping Margaret and Audra down from the cart.

"Nay, but I know Bishop Fothad. He presided at the marriage of Malcolm and Margaret and has come to Dunfermline more than once to hear the queen's confession."

"Those must have been short meetings," she murmured.

He laughed. "You mean the confessions?"

"Aye," she said with a smile he thought winsome. "I look forward to meeting the bishop."

Next to the stone church with its single tower was the Culdee abbey in which the bishop lived, for Fothad was one of them.

Steinar waited until Catrìona had joined Audra and Margaret and the three proceeded toward the bishop. The queen appeared weary. "Does the queen seem tired to you?" he asked Colbán. "More than usual, I mean."

"Mayhap you are right," said the captain.

"I would speak to Bishop Fothad to assure a hot bath awaits in her chamber. Margaret is too gracious to ask but these last few days have been a trial. She needs to rest, and the ladies, too, will want a bath, do you not think?"

Colbán shifted his gaze to study the queen who seemed to be leaning against Catrìona while speaking with the bishop. "Aye, 'tis a good idea. The king would not be happy if he thought we had allowed her to grow overtired. While you speak with the bishop, I will organize the men to raise the tents. I expect the abbey will have room only for the queen, her maidservant and the ladies."

Steinar nodded and strode to where Margaret and the ladies spoke to the bishop.

"Bishop Fothad," he said dipping his head.

"Ah! 'Tis the king's scribe," said the cleric.

"No longer a scribe, Bishop," said the queen. "Steinar is now one of the king's guards."

The monk gave him a long studying look. "Aye, I can see you have changed. Now you have the appearance of a warrior."

As the ladies walked toward the abbey ahead of them, Steinar told the bishop of his concern for the queen. The older man nodded to all his requests. "It shall be done."

Inside the abbey's thick walls, it was cool. Margaret was led to a seat and given a cup of water.

Catriona left the queen to come to him. "Margaret is exhausted from the last few days."

"Aye, I have seen it. The bishop has agreed to ready Margaret's chamber and have a hot bath for her. She can rest ere we dine."

CHAPTER 13

Catrìona popped a last berry into her mouth, noticing the fading light coming through the window. The evening meal was over and intent on having a view of the sea before the sun's light was gone, she asked the queen if she might be permitted a walk outside.

Margaret looked at her with an understanding expression. "Go. 'Twill do you good."

Catrìona thanked the bishop for a fine meal and headed toward the peg where her cloak hung near the door, but before she reached it, the king's captain sprang to his feet and snatched up the green woolen garment and draped it over her shoulders.

"Might I accompany you, my lady?"

She had hoped Steinar would go with her. He had said little since their encounter in the forest and she was hoping for some time alone with him to clear the air between them. The constant rain and wind they had experienced on their way to St. Andrews had left them no time for anything save trying to keep dry. However, in the stern set of Colbán's jaw, she sensed "nay" was not going to be an acceptable reply. "Of course. Your company is welcome, sir." Out of the corner of her eye, she saw the queen smile.

If Catrìona was less than enthusiastic, Colbán did not appear to notice. But she was certain Audra did. A glance in the lady's direction revealed Audra's hazel eyes following her and the king's captain as they left the abbey. To Catrìona's disappointment, Steinar's gaze was focused on his wine.

Outside, she and Colbán strolled in silence beyond the abbey to the edge of the grass-covered land, looking seaward across the sand. Waves gently rushing to shore a stone's throw away hissed as they met the sand, the sound soothing to her ears.

In the distance, darkening clouds hung heavy over the sea. She turned to see the sky behind her. At the horizon, slashes of rose and gold intruded between layers of gray and blue as the sun gave a parting glance to the land.

Taking in the beauty of the setting sun, she turned back to the sea. "I was raised on Loch Lomond and the River Clyde. This is my first glimpse of the North Sea."

Colbán spoke in his deep, warrior's voice. "Then I am pleased you are seeing it with me."

"You are from Moray?" She knew little of his home except it was the land of Mac Bethad, King Malcolm's old enemy.

"Aye. My youth was spent far to the north. But during the last ten years I have served Malcolm, we have sailed many of Scotland's waters together."

Catrìona shot him a sidelong glance, thinking he could not yet have seen thirty summers. "You were a young warrior when you came to Dunfermline?"

He stared into the distance. "Aye, it seems a very long time ago."

"Will you return to your home some day?" she asked, wondering at the same time if she wanted to return to the Vale of Leven. The land was now the king's and there was no home to return to.

"Nay, I think not. I have made my home with Malcolm and my loyalties are here. I expect to serve him for the rest of my days." He turned from staring at the sea to stare at her. Even without looking at him she felt the heat of his gaze. "But I do want a wife and sons."

Slowly, she turned to meet his intense gaze, so like that of the fierce bear she had thought him to be. "Surely the king will honor your wish." To forestall him saying the words his eyes were speaking, she said, "Have you considered Audra? Duff's daughter is a kind woman and her father is a great warrior, favored by the king. She would make a wonderful wife."

"Aye, mayhap she would. I like her well enough. But her mother and younger brothers were murdered by Mac Bethad…"

Catrìona hesitated, the truth dawning on her.

"…of Moray," he finished.

"Oh," she said, and then remembering when it had happened, she added, "But surely Audra would not charge you with their deaths. You must have been very young."

"I was twelve summers that year. I did not fight with Mac Bethad." He turned to face her. "But he was our king and before that, he had been the mormaer of Moray. Many in my family fought at his side. They might have been among the men who killed Duff's wife."

A deep sigh escaped her. What she had seen in Audra's eyes bespoke a longing for the king's captain, mayhap even love, not loathing, but it would take more than Catrìona's words to persuade this stubborn man Audra cared for him no matter he was from Moray.

" 'Tis no matter," he said, interrupting her thoughts, "for I have another in mind to take as my wife."

He paused then, his eyes boring into her and then he stared at her lips. Catrìona sensed he wanted to kiss her, might even try to repeat the demanding kiss he had given her in the woods. She could not tell him her heart belonged to another, one whose kisses robbed her of breath, nor would he hear of Audra's desire for him. It was all such a muddle.

Wanting to discourage him, she said, " 'Tis best to choose one who is willing, sir."

In a tone she had heard him use in commanding his men, he said, "All women are willing in time."

She couldn't resist the laughter that bubbled up in her chest for the arrogance of his pronouncement. "You do not lack for confidence, good sir."

He clenched his jaw and narrowed his eyes. "Confidence, madam, comes from skill, practice and experience, as any warrior will tell you." Raising his head and thrusting his shoulders back, he said, "When it comes to women, I possess all three."

She huffed out a breath. How could she make such a man understand? "I do not think you would like a woman who defies you at every turn," she insisted, refraining from pointing out that she would be just such a woman.

"Nay, I would insist on compliance," he threw back, his forehead furrowing.

She was searching her mind for a sharp retort when, behind him, she saw a pale sail catch the last rays of the dying sun. "A ship!"

Colbán whipped around. "The king's ship."

★   ★   ★

It was gloaming when the king strode down the plank from his ship to meet Margaret who, by then, was waiting on the sand. One of the guards carried a torch, allowing Catrìona to see the gleam in the king's eyes, matched by that in the eyes of his queen.

"My Lord, I had no idea you would sail to St. Andrews!" exclaimed Margaret.

Malcolm swept her into his arms. "*Mo cridhe*, I only wanted to give you an easier ride home, one you could share with your husband."

Margaret's cheeks flushed. "I am glad you came, my husband."

The company that had traveled with the queen had gathered on the shore to welcome Malcolm. At his words to the queen, smiles broke out on every face.

Catrìona felt a pang of envy at the warmth of Margaret's relationship with the king.

"I see you all made the journey," said Malcolm when it became clear he could no longer ignore his men.

"Aye," said Colbán, stepping forward and speaking for the others. "The queen is safely delivered to St. Andrews."

Behind the king, bounding down the plank leading from the ship a score of feet away was Giric, heading straight for Steinar who had come to stand beside Catrìona.

Reaching Steinar, the boy took his hand. "Did ye miss me, Scribe?"

"I might have," Steinar said with a wink at the boy. "How did you talk the king into letting you come?"

With one arm still wrapped around Margaret, Malcolm gave the boy a sharp glance. "He did not ask but sneaked onto the ship as it was being loaded. Small mite that he is, he was well hidden behind a crate of altar cloths. We were already in the Forth when he was discovered."

Margaret smiled at the boy, as if amused by his daring, then looked at her husband. "We only arrived today ourselves."

The king turned to his captain as if for an explanation.

"The weather slowed our progress," said Colbán. "But the queen found what she was looking for."

"Aye," said Margaret, "a proper site for the inn and a church beside it. Come, let us retire to the abbey and I can tell you about it."

Bishop Fothad, who had been standing behind the king's guard, strode forward to offer Malcolm a bow. "My Lord, we have food ready if you are hungry."

"Good eve," said the king to the white-cowled bishop. "Yea, food is welcome. My men on the ship are ever hungry. And I have brought the bard to entertain us."

Catrìona cast her gaze on the ship. Rhodri stood on the deck, his arm lifted in a gesture of greeting. At his side was a grinning Fia.

"I wonder how she managed that," Catrìona muttered to herself.

"What?" whispered Steinar.

" 'Tis nothing." However Fia had done it, Catrìona felt her spirits rise at the prospect of having her cousin with her again.

The king beckoned Rhodri to join him and the bard complied, descending the plank with his harp under one arm and his other hand extended to help Fia.

Once the ship's oars were stowed and the sail furled, the men who worked the lines and rigging joined the party on shore and everyone followed the torch-bearer to the abbey.

Catrìona delighted in the merriment that filled the abbey's large chamber as platters of fish were served to the king and his crew, along with vegetables, warm bread and much wine. After the meal, there were berries and honeyed cakes for all who wanted them.

The abbey's table that had earlier comfortably accommodated the queen's party was now crowded and seating on the benches cramped, but no one seemed to mind. Laughter echoed around the chamber, followed by Rhodri's songs of the seas and ships, which lulled them all into a contented state.

Happy to have been spared the further attentions of the king's captain, Catrìona sipped her wine and leaned toward Fia. "How did you manage to be included while the other ladies were not?"

" 'Twas simple. I asked the king." At Catrìona's look of incredulity, Fia added, "I told him you and I are quite close and I knew you would want to see me. 'Tis true, is it not?"

"Aye, I am glad you are here."

"Then I thought of what *you* might say, so, I told the king that I had never been on a ship and I was certain my father would be pleased should I have the experience."

Barely able to control her laughter, Catrìona exclaimed, "Fia, you did not!"

"I did. 'Tis likely true. And you know you would have said it. Besides, I had no intention of being left behind when the king called for Rhodri. If Malcolm had not given his consent, I might have stolen aboard with the boy." Glancing at the end of the table where Steinar and Giric sat together talking, Fia asked, "What has happened with the scribe? He wears a grim expression whenever he looks at you."

Catrìona shrugged. "In truth, I do not know, but he has been in an unpleasant mood ever since he came upon me in the woods with the king's captain. I was furious with both of them."

Fia raised her brows.

"Not here," whispered Catrìona. "I will explain later when we are alone."

"You tease me beyond measure."

*   *   *

Giric rambled on excitedly about his trip on the king's ship. All the while, Steinar watched Catrìona, desperate to know what happened between her and Colbán before the king arrived. Had she succumbed to the king's captain as so many women did?

Interrupting his thoughts, Giric asked, "Have ye ever sailed with the king?"

Steinar looked down at the boy's face, shining with the joy of his adventure. "Nay but mayhap I will for the return to Dunfermline."

"I would like that. I was not ill either."

"If you are to one day be a great warrior and travel to the distant parts of Scotland, 'tis good you are at ease on the sea." Already, Steinar knew he wanted the boy to come with him when he claimed his lands in the vale, but mayhap Catrìona would want the lad to go with her. Steinar could not bear to think of her staying behind with the king's captain.

★ ★ ★

As soon as the door to their chamber closed, her husband pulled Margaret into his arms. He smelled of salt and the sea and she was very glad to have him with her. His strength was a comfort she had learned to draw upon. "You dismissed my maidservant," she said teasingly, as she fumbled with her laces.

A slow smile spread across Malcolm's face, his dark eyes twinkling. "You will need no servant tonight for I have much experience with your laces, madam." With his arms wrapped around her, he reached behind her to pull the laces free as he kissed his way down her throat, sending shivers coursing through her.

"You will wake the babe," she said in feigned objection.

Malcolm turned her in his arms so that her back was to his chest and placed his large palms on her rounded belly. "Aye, he will have no sleep for a while, *mo cridhe*, for I have learned to pleasure you with only slight jostling of the babe." Sliding her gown from her shoulders, he helped her to step from it as it sagged to the floor and led her to the bed, the bishop's own she suspected, for it was large.

He removed his crown and then hers, setting them and her head-cloth aside.

She sat on the edge of the bed cushion, watching as Malcolm shed his clothes, providing a feast for her starving senses.

"How goes the contest to win the affections of the redhead?" Malcolm asked as he pulled off his tunic and began to unwrap the leather strips crossing his hosen.

"Catrìona and Steinar have exchanged words more than once and, in the last few days, he has paid little attention to her. But just this eve, she went most willingly with your captain on a walk along the shore. It may be that 'tis Colbán she would prefer after all."

"Either man is worthy," he observed.

He pulled his inner tunic off, revealing his muscled chest. At two score years, he was still a warrior to be reckoned with. Margaret's mouth watered as he began to loosen the ties that held his hosen to his waist.

"If I match the redhead with my captain," said Malcolm, slowing his disrobing, which she was certain was intentional, "what think you of Duff's daughter for the scribe? Might not such a gentle woman appreciate his lettered ways and his knowledge of so many languages? Together they could make a formidable pair in winning us the friendship of the western isles."

"Yea, the match could work if Duff would agree to let Audra go so far from Fife. She is his only daughter and dearly beloved."

"I will have a word with him when we return to the tower."

He peeled his hosen from his legs to stand naked before her, his manhood telling her how much she was missed.

Because she perceived he was testing her resolve, she asked blithely, "How fares the Mormaer of Fife? Does he recover?"

"Oh, aye," he said stalking toward her. "To my eyes, he is not well, yet in Colbán's absence, Duff directs the men at their sword practice and vows to lead the next hunt."

She laughed. "A warrior's warrior that one," she said, dropping all pretense of patience and holding her arms open in welcome.

He stepped between her legs and, with a hand beneath each of her knees, pulled her bottom to the edge of the bed, pressing his hardened flesh against her woman's center. "And so am I, *mo cridhe*."

★ ★ ★

Catrìona and Fia followed Audra and Margaret at dawn the next morning as they walked over the sandy ground to the chapel just beyond the abbey. *At least it is not dark.*

The chapel, perched on the edge of a flat bit of land, overlooked the North Sea. The bright circle of the sun rose in a red-gold sky over the calm waters. Small waves met the shore, subdued as if in reverence.

Catrìona had glimpsed the humble place of worship when they arrived the day before. Built in the shape of a cross, the church was simple in design. Its significance, Catrìona knew, was owing to the relics of Saint Andrew long housed here.

She joined the others to silently kneel before the altar to pray. While Catrìona had much to be thankful for, she still wondered about the future. Surely the king would not give her to a rough man like Colbán, but the captain seemed to be focused on her as his choice.

When the queen had finished her prayers, Catrìona helped her to rise and waited with Audra and Fia for their mistress' instructions.

"I am to see the bishop," Margaret said, "but should you wish to make a confession prior to breaking your fast, any of the monks who tend the chapel can accommodate you."

"I will come back later," said Audra and turned to go with the queen.

Fia looked at Catrìona, her brows raised in question.

Knowing her cousin was anxious to break her fast with Rhodri, she said, "Go ahead, I will join you shortly."

Catrìona wanted to stay behind. It was not that she had much to confess, though she was certain she had done something that should be set before a priest, but there were questions she would ask a man of God.

Seeing no monk in the chapel, she strolled outside to gaze at the waters of the North Sea. The vastness of it somehow calmed her. The slope to the sea from where she stood was gradual and easily walked if one did not mind the loose sand. Sparse vegetation grew up amidst the sand with wildflowers making their presence known here and there.

Gulls shrieked as they flew from the rocks to cross her path. On the beach, ringed plovers darted across the sand to forage among the green plants. In the distance, a flock of eider ducks glided over the blue waters, the males with their stark black and white feathers vivid against the blue, like nuns set to flight.

As she stood watching the glorious splendor of God's creative work, she remembered the queen's words. *God has a greater plan for us.* Surely He had a purpose for her and Niall since they were spared when so many were not.

" 'Tis glorious, is it not?" came a soft male voice from behind her.

She turned to see a brown-haired monk in a gray cowl robe, his hands folded in front of him.

"I was just thinking the same thing." She recognized him as one who had dined with them the night before. "You are Caerell?"

"Aye, so I am. Did you wish to speak with one of us, my lady?"

She hesitated, unsure of what to say. "There are things I would ask you if there is time."

"I am here to listen," came his reply. In his soft gray eyes, she saw he was sincere. His manner was kindly. She did not think he would judge her for her doubts, so when he gestured to a large rock, she went.

They sat and watched the birds and she told him of the last year of her life and how she had doubted God for all that had happened to her family and her people.

The Culdee was patient, hearing all. When at last he spoke, his words were as gentle as his voice. "The path to wisdom often leads through the valley of doubt, my child. To lose so much and still desire to trust God tells me you are already on that path. Remember Job's question to his doubting wife, 'Shall we receive good at the hand of God, and not evil?'. It is the work of a lifetime to trust Him through hardship and loss, but that is what we are called to do."

She knew his words to be truth. "Queen Margaret told me I must accept whatever God allows into my life, trusting Him to use it for good."

He nodded. "The Lady of Scotland is a wise woman, someone who has been hurt in the past, yet whose faith remains unshaken."

"I am worried for my future."

"Place your trust in God for that, my lady, and I will pray for you."

The monk placed his hand on her head and prayed. As he spoke to God, Catríona felt a peace such as she had never known.

★　★　★

Steinar had just finished breaking his fast when Malcolm rose from his seat, drew the queen up beside him and turned to the bishop.

"We have availed ourselves of your hospitality long enough, Bishop Fothad. It is time we sail."

The bishop rose, as did Steinar and the king's men.

"It has been my privilege to host you and your lady, My Lord," said the bishop, bowing. "You and Queen Margaret are welcome any time you can be with us."

"Before we go," said the queen "there is something I have for the chapel." A servant, who had been standing behind Margaret, brought forward a carved wooden chest and set it on the table before the queen. She opened it to reveal a jewel-encrusted gold cross. Gasps sounded from those gathered around. Steinar, too, thought it a splendid piece of great beauty, certainly worthy of the simple chapel that housed the apostle's bones. He wondered if the cross had come from Hungary, a part of the queen's dowry.

The bishop was quick to accept the ornate cross Margaret laid in his hands. "My Lady, 'tis a magnificent gift. We are humbled by your generosity."

"The Lord's house should reflect His glory," she said in reply.

Steinar anticipated Malcolm's next words.

"I am for Dunfermline!" the king proclaimed. "Master shipman," he said to the steersman, "make ready my ship." Then to Colbán, "Select those guards you need and send the rest home by land. You and Steinar will sail with me. You, too, Rhodri. And the ladies."

Eager to be away, the men set off to accomplish their assigned tasks.

"What about me?" Giric piped up.

Steinar reached his hand to cover the lad's mouth. "Please excuse him, My Lord."

The king chuckled. "You can see to the pup, Scribe." Then Malcolm paused. "But now that I think of it, I have a missive I need you to draft so it can be dispatched immediately upon our arrival in Dunfermline. Mayhap you'd best leave the boy to the ladies."

Before he left the abbey, Steinar penned the message the king had dictated to him for Matad, Mormaer of Atholl, summoning him to court. No subject was given, only the demand for the mormaer's presence. Steinar broke out in a sweat, his hand that held the quill trembling over the parchment as he forced himself to write, knowing with certainty the mormaer was summoned for his niece's betrothal to the captain of the king's guard.

He had known this day was coming, but that did not help him to accept it.

Once Steinar was free of the king, with a heavy heart, he headed to the shore. Some of Malcolm's men were loading the women's chests, along with food for the voyage home. Those who were to travel with the king waited on shore while the ship was made ready.

He looked for Catrìona and found her standing amidst the golden gorse blooming between rocky outcroppings above the shore. Strands of her auburn hair blew about her face, rendering her achingly beautiful in the morning light as she stood talking with her cousin, the lad and Audra.

She must have sensed his regard because she broke away from the others and came toward him.

Just as she reached him, a white-tailed sea eagle soared across the sky, its huge wings, as long as a man was tall, casting a shadow over the water as it glided close to the surface, then reached its talons beneath the water and snatched a fish. They paused to stare open-mouthed at the magnificent bird and the beauty of the sea.

"I have not seen one of those since I lived in the vale," she remarked, watching the eagle as it disappeared into the distance with its prize. "I have missed them."

"And your home?" he asked. "Have you missed it, too?"

"Aye. Not at first, you understand, but now I do. When I left, I felt only sadness. But now I remember the happier times and the beauty of the vale."

"You seem different today," he said, noting her calm demeanor. Her green eyes, typically flashing like emeralds, were quiet pools. "Has something changed?" He did not like to think she was resigned to Colbán's suit, but mayhap she was. As for him, he could only accept it if it meant her happiness.

She surprised him when she said, " 'Twas a conversation I had with one of the monks. He helped me to see that good can come from loss if we but trust God. The queen had told me something similar and, since then, the truth has settled within me." She laughed then, again surprising him, given the subject. "I have not been on very good terms with the Almighty for the last year."

"I think I understand." And he did. "Edgar and I have shared many a conversation about being forever exiled. But to be angry with God is like shouting at the sky. And revenge is lean fare on which to sustain a man's life."

"What you say is true, yet I long for justice." She gripped the hilt of the knife sheathed at her hip. "And I have learned to carry a knife should I need it."

Trying to lighten her mood, he said, "I would expect no less with fierce wildcats lurking among the trees."

She tossed him a smile. "Aye, dangerous beasts are everywhere."

The king's captain approached just then to escort her to where the queen and the other ladies were climbing up the ramp to the ship. Steinar stepped aside.

Once all was loaded, the queen and her maidservant and Audra retired to the small tent erected midship. Catrìona and Fia joined Rhodri to sit on a fixed bench. The rest of the men scrambled aboard, took up the oars and rowed the ship to deeper waters. Once there, they stowed the oars and raised the huge square sail to catch the wind.

"The wind is from the north!" shouted the master shipman to the king. "We will be quickly home."

They sailed from St. Andrews, heading into the North Sea and then south around Fife toward the Firth of Forth. It was nearly August and the weather was fair. Still, when the wind picked up, it was chill and the waters splashed against the ship's hull, the spray misting over them.

Steinar leaned against the hull, his eyes darting to where Catrìona sat next to her cousin. The two women had drawn their cloaks tightly around them. Rhodri and Giric sat near them, Giric pressed against Catrìona, as if for warmth.

The king prowled the deck like a lion confined to a cage. Malcolm was unused to being in a small space, albeit the deck of his ship was larger than most. Eventually, Colbán drew Malcolm aside for a word and the two stood in the prow talking, their words swept away by the wind.

From time to time, the master seaman would shout a command to come about and the lines connected to the sails were loosened and the huge square sail brought around to catch the wind. The seamen then hauled on the ropes to pull the sail taut and keep them sailing into the blustery wind. He admired the ease with which they handled the ship.

When they were not needed to change the sail, the seamen sat on chests next to the oar holes or leaned against the hull as Steinar did.

It was not long before they reached the wide estuary that was the Firth of Forth. Though the waters were not as rough as the North Sea, it was still difficult for one who was used to land to move around the deck, especially if, like Steinar, one had a troublesome leg.

Watching Catrìona laughing at something Rhodri had said, he decided to join them, avoiding Colbán's harsh gaze following him as he made his way to the bench occupied by the small group.

Catrìona and Fia were listening to Giric's questions about sailing and ships. To Steinar's surprise, it was Rhodri who answered them. The bard, as it turned out, had sailed the waters off Wales as a lad. Rhodri explained, "You cannot grow up in a small country surrounded on three sides by water without learning to sail. And Dublin is only a few hours by boat from Gwynedd."

"If 'tis true," Steinar interjected, "why does the color of your face match your tunic?"

"I said I learned to sail," replied his friend, who did, indeed, appear a bit green, "I did not say I liked it overmuch. My preferred habitation is the forest of which there are many in Gwynedd and Powys."

Ignoring the sharp glances from Colbán, who remained in the prow with the king, Steinar took a seat next to Catrìona with Giric nestled between them for shelter from the biting wind. Rhodri talked on about the small wooden ships his countrymen used to sail the coasts of Gwynedd, holding Giric in rapt attention. Fia, Steinar noted, sat very close to the bard on his other side and not for the chill air, he was certain. Her eyes were fixed on Rhodri and, as he spoke, she listened with the same expression as the boy.

Giric might be between them, but Steinar felt the nearness of Catrìona like a strong pull. The wind brought her scent to him as well as her laughter. Green eyes glistening, she listened to one of Rhodri's tales and said to Giric, "Do not believe all the bard tells you. Fairies do not live in the woods of Wales."

"Are you so certain?" Steinar questioned, for he did love to stir her to argue.

"Not you, too!" she cried.

"Mayhap they only live in Wales," said Giric.

Catrìona rolled her eyes to the heavens and, giving him a side-glance, said to her cousin, "I give up. Mayhap they do have fairies in Wales."

"Mayhap we do," said Rhodri with a wink at Giric.

The sun was high in the sky when Audra emerged from the queen's shelter with the maidservant in tow. Expressing concern that the queen needed to keep up her strength, Audra suggested it was time they ate.

The king took up his wife's cause. "Aye, let's have some food for Margaret and her ladies."

Steinar had no doubt the king, too, was hungry and, since the waters of the Forth were calm enough to allow them to eat before they made port, he thought the suggestion a good idea.

Colbán directed the men to assist and soon a bench was laid with bread, cheese and fruit.

"I expect you are not interested in food," Steinar said to Rhodri.

The bard gave him an uncharacteristic smirk. "I will wait for land ere I dine, thank you." Fia patted his hand and the two exchanged a smile.

"In Malcolm's hall, you will not starve," Steinar tossed back before following Catrìona and Giric to the food.

CHAPTER 14

Catrìona had enjoyed the travel over the water, bringing them home so much sooner, but the ship was confining and, worse, constantly moving beneath her feet. Then, too, being under the watchful gaze of the king's captain made her nervous. The few times she and Steinar had laughed over something Rhodri had said caused the bear of a man to shoot Steinar disapproving looks. She wished Colbán could see the love shining in Audra's eyes whenever she looked at him, but sadly, the man remained oblivious to the lady's affections.

It was afternoon and the sun still high in the sky when the king's tower was finally sighted rising above the trees a few miles north of the River Forth. The sail was quickly furled and the men took up oars to bring the ship to land, just as two longships came into view resting on the sand in the small inlet that served as harbor to Dunfermline.

As the king's ship passed close to the two ships, she studied their form and decoration for anything she might recognize. Many ships looked alike, but she shuddered at dragon heads carved into the stems. The resemblance of these two to the longships of the Northmen who attacked the vale was striking.

"Seems my Orkney relations are paying me a visit," boomed the king's voice from the prow. "Margaret, come see!"

The queen stepped from the tent midship and gazed toward the longships.

"Mayhap they have my son, Duncan, with them," Malcolm said to the queen. " 'Tis time he is done with his fostering."

At Catrìona's side, Giric gasped. She looked down to see his eyes wide and his mouth agape as he stared at the two ships.

She crouched down next to the boy. "What is it?"

"The ba… banner," he stuttered nervously. " 'Tis… 'tis the black raven… like the one on the ship of the man who killed my father!"

Catrìona shielded her eyes and looked again at the two ships. At the top of the mast of one waved a pale yellow banner bearing a black raven in the Norse style, like the one she had seen that day in the vale.

A shudder ran up her spine. *Could it be the same? A relative of the king?*

The king's men, straining at the oars, gave force to the ship so that it glided out of the water and up onto the wet sand. Jumping over the side, they hauled the ship to the broad sandy landing.

Catrìona took Giric's trembling hand and followed the queen and the others from the ship. She bent to Giric and whispered, "Wait till we are in the king's tower, then we will know if 'tis the same man. More than one Northman may fly such a banner." She was trying not to panic but her heart pounded in her chest and her lips trembled.

Giric nodded and tightened his hold on her hand.

As they walked past the prows of the two longships, Catrìona caught a brief glimpse of a woman aboard the ship with the raven banner, but a sharp command from a Northman standing guard had the woman ducking under a tent. Before the woman disappeared, Catrìona saw the woman's tunic was of a Norse design and there was something oddly familiar about her. The dark brown hair was the same shade as Deidre's, only a greater length.

Once inside the tower, Catrìona scanned the hall for strangers, but saw none.

Nechtan, the king's steward, hastened toward their party. "My Lord," he addressed the king, "Paul and Erlend Thorfinnsson have arrived. You must have seen their ship."

"Where are the jarls?" the king asked.

"I have seen them to their chamber, the one they usually occupy. They have brought young Duncan, who awaits you in your chamber."

"Good. The queen and I will see Duncan and then have a bit of time ere we dine with our guests."

As the king reached for Margaret's hand to escort her to the stairs, the steward said, "My Lord?"

The king turned back, "Aye?"

"Your stepsons brought another with them, a distant cousin from Norway who has been sojourning with them for the last year or so. His name is Ivar Kalison. I have put him in the far chamber next to your stepsons."

"My thanks for seeing to our guests," Malcolm said. To Margaret, he said, "I do not know that name. Do you?"

The queen shook her head and they proceeded to the stairs.

Catriona turned to Giric. "Find Niall. I must speak with him. Tell him to come to the hall and wait for me. I must change."

"But what about—"

"Shh!" she cautioned the boy. "We can do nothing until the evening meal when we will see these Northmen. If the one who killed your father is among them, he may be the same barbarian who murdered my parents."

Giric's eyes grew large as he realized the terrible past they shared. "Ye?"

"Aye. Orphaned like you, remember? Go now and find Niall."

★   ★   ★

Steinar watched Catriona flee up the stairs. She had not been aware of him when he entered the hall with the others, which was not surprising given how strangely she was acting. She and the lad whispered urgently to each other as if something of great import was afoot. With the firebrand, he could never be sure what she would get involved in next.

Giric raced past him and out the tower door. Steinar followed, curious to know what mischief the two were up to.

"Giric, wait!" he yelled.

The boy slowed to a walk and slowly turned. He did not look guilty as Steinar had expected. Giric looked frightened.

"Where are you going in such haste?"

"I... I am to find Niall. His sister wants him."

"Why?" The boy struggled with a response, as if uncertain he should confide his mission to his friend. "Come, lad, you know I would never harm you or Catrìona. I mean you only good."

The boy let out a breath and walked to Steinar, looking up at him. " 'Tis the Northmen who've come."

Steinar's brow furrowed. "The king's stepsons, Paul and Erlend?"

"I know not if they be the ones. But one ship flies a raven banner, like the ship of the Northman who killed my father. Catrìona's parents, too."

Steinar sorted through the possibilities and found a reasonable explanation. "Many ships from Orkney fly such banners, Giric." But he could see his words had not calmed the boy.

Giric's eyes grew anxious. "May I go? The lady asked me to hurry."

"Aye." The boy turned and ran toward the archery field, leaving Steinar to wonder why Catrìona would want to see Niall about the Orkney ships.

*　*　*

Catrìona said nothing to Fia, but quickly washed and changed into a fresh gown. "I must see Niall," she said, not waiting for her cousin's reply, and hurried out of their chamber.

In the hall, there were only a few men standing around as the servants bustled from table to table in preparation for the evening meal.

Near the tower door, Niall waited with Giric.

"I am glad you have returned," said her brother, brushing her cheek with a kiss. "Why have you taken me from archery practice? Giric told me to hurry but he would not tell me the reason for haste."

She put her hand on the boy's shoulder. "Aye, I wanted to speak with you first. Come, let us walk outside."

The three of them slipped through the tower door and went some distance before she turned to her brother. "Did you know that Northmen from the Orkneys have come to Dunfermline?"

"Nay. When?"

"Sometime today, I think. The king says they are his stepsons. I have not seen them, but I have seen their ships. One carries the same banner as the ship that led the attack on the vale."

Niall turned to look south, toward the River Forth. "You are certain?"

"I am certain of the banner." Seeing Giric's fearful expression, she added, "Giric recognized it, too." The boy's eyes shifted from Niall to her and back again. "And there is more, Niall. I saw a woman on the ship. I did not get a good look at her but the more I think of it, she could be Deidre."

"Deidre? Did she see you?"

"I cannot say. If she did, I am certain she did not recognize me, but then Deidre would not expect to see me here. The woman I saw was clothed in Norse garb, a brown linen tunic with some kind of Norse designs on it. Her hair was unplaited but 'twas Deidre's color. Think, Niall. It has been over a year. They might have clothed her as one of their own to hide her among them."

Niall seemed to ponder her words as he took his bow and quiver of arrows from his shoulder. "What do you propose?"

"First, we should find Angus and tell him. He will know if 'tis the same man. The Northmen will come to the evening meal. There, we can see them. If they are the ones who attacked the vale, I want to see if 'tis Deidre who is on that ship. If it is, we must save her, Niall."

"Aye, we must."

"Angus will help us," she said. "Then we can deal with the one who led the raid."

A look of concern crossed Niall's face. It was not for lack of courage. "What if he is a relation of the king?"

"If the Northman is the one who murdered our parents, I care not." Then another thought crossed her mind. Turning to the boy, she said, "Giric, do you know the king's son, the one called Duncan? He would be older than you, mayhap ten or twelve summers, not yet a man."

"Nay, but if he comes into the hall I can befriend him. What need ye?"

"I want to know about the girl I saw."

Giric was eager to help. "I will do it!"

★　★　★

Margaret stepped through the door of their chamber Malcolm opened for her. Afternoon sunlight filled the large space. A dark-haired youth dressed in a tunic of Norse design stood with his back to them looking out the window. He turned. Duncan was tall for twelve summers and stood very straight, his features finely carved and his eyes dark like Malcolm's. She could tell he was trying to play the man for his father.

"Good day, sir."

Malcolm strode to the lad. "I'll have none of that, son. 'Tis a man's hug I'll be having from you." He reached down to embrace the slim youth. Margaret inwardly smiled. The two had long been separated because of the lad's fostering and she knew Malcolm had missed him.

When they broke apart, the boy asked, "You are well, Father?"

"Aye, very well, even better now that you are here. I can see I need not ask about you. You have grown like a young oak, sturdy and true. Someday you will make a fine king, Duncan. Did the jarls teach you your letters?"

"A monk taught me both Gaelic and Norse. I can scrive in two languages now," the youth said proudly. "And I know some English," he added with a glance in Margaret's direction.

Malcolm beamed his approval. "That is good." Then he turned. "Greet your stepmother, the queen."

The youth bowed before her. "Greetings, My Lady," he said in the Saxon tongue.

When he rose, she said, "We welcome you to your home, Duncan. 'Tis time you are with us. You must see your younger brother, Edward. He is a year now and soon," she said, patting her belly, "there will be another who will be following you around."

After more questions, father and son filled each other in on the last few years. At times, she heard a Norse word or two. Finally, Duncan said, "Would it be possible to have some food?"

Malcolm laughed. "I have forgotten how hungry I was at your age. Aye, there is food aplenty. Just ask any of the servants in the kitchen to fetch you some and take no scolding for it not being the supper hour." Margaret smiled when he glanced at her. He was aware she did not favor eating all day, but even she made allowances for growing boys.

Duncan raced from their chamber and she went to kiss Malcolm. "I think that went well, My Lord. He is glad to be with you."

"And I with him," said Malcolm, drawing her into his arms.

★　★　★

Torches and candles blazed in the hall that evening as Steinar stood in the shadows, watching Catrìona. Unlike most evenings when she came with her cousin to join the queen's ladies, tonight she came alone and met Angus, Niall and Giric. 'Twas odd to see the boy since he did not typically eat in the hall in the evening, but given what he had told Steinar, he expected they waited for the king's guests.

A moment later, all eyes were drawn to the stairs as the king and queen descended with three Northmen and a youth. The Northmen were of fair coloring except for one who was dark. The two who were fair had shorter hair and could have been twins for they looked much alike. All three had mustaches and short beards. The youth had Malcolm's coloring and his hair was short. A handsome youth, tall and proud in the way he carried his body. *Must be Duncan.*

The king had his arm draped over the youth's shoulder. As they headed toward the dais, Steinar heard the king say, "You will sit beside me and the queen, Duncan."

Steinar turned to see Catrìona. Her face had gone pale and, even from this distance, he could see her expression was hard and her hand gripped the hilt of her knife. Beside her, Angus was reaching for his sword as his eyes narrowed on the Northman with dark coloring.

He is the one! Before Steinar could take a step forward, Catrìona and her companions disappeared through the tower door.

Striding across the hall, he followed outside to see them hurrying in the direction of the harbor where the ships were anchored. *Why?*

The sun, a golden ball over his right shoulder, would not set for hours. He had plenty of light to follow them down the path to the River Forth. Once his leg had warmed to his forced pace, he gained on them.

Angus walked on one side of Catrìona. On the other side walked Niall, carrying his bow and arrows. Beside him was Giric, trying to keep up.

Steinar was tempted to scold Catrìona for whatever she had in mind. Surely the king could handle this. *What can she mean to do?*

Half the way there, Steinar heard footsteps following him and turned to see Colbán closing the distance between them. Steinar stood still waiting for the captain to catch up.

When Colbán reached him, the captain appeared angry and panting for breath. "Do you think to meet the lady in some hidden glen, Scribe? For, if you do, know I will not have it!"

Steinar pulled Colbán to the side of the path where they could not be heard. "Do not be foolish. I merely follow the lady, her guard and her brother who, I am certain, are headed to the ships from Orkney."

The captain looked puzzled. "Why would she come to see ships she saw this afternoon?"

"Because she believes one of them belongs to the Northman who led the attack on the Vale of Leven, her home. What I do not know is why she comes now to the ship since the Northman I speak of is in the hall with the king."

Colbán let out a huff. "Well, that being the case, I will go with you and we will see this mystery solved. I knew little of the attack on the vale; only that it occurred."

As they took the last mile, speaking in a low voice, Steinar told the captain of all that had happened. "Then this afternoon," he said, "Giric told me Catrìona thought it might be the same ship and the same Northman."

"Not Paul and Erlend," Colbán protested. "They are loyal to Malcolm. God's blood, they are his stepsons and Duncan their half-brother. They would never attack Scotland."

"What of the other one?"

"I only met him briefly. His name is Ivar Kalison, some distant relation from Norway. He says little, a very gruff character."

Steinar found the description ironic coming from Colbán, but he only nodded.

By now, they had nearly reached those they followed. Ahead of them, loomed the small inlet where the ships were drawn onto the sand, the king's larger one on one side and the two Orkney longships on the other.

★   ★   ★

Catrìona stood with the others, hidden in a stand of trees on one side of the harbor, her heart telling her the woman she had seen aboard the longship was Deidre. But as she gazed at the ship in the light of the setting sun, fear snaked up her spine. Northmen stood guard over it. For all she knew they might be among those who had attacked the vale. Her fist clenched around her knife hilt. She might be afraid but she would not fail to act.

Giric had learned from Duncan, who had come into the hall looking for food, that the one called Ivar had brought with him a woman. She was assumed to be Ivar's concubine as he had kept her in the stone house he occupied while he was visiting Paul and Erlend in the Orkneys. Duncan had heard her speak only twice.

"Duncan told me 'twas Gaelic she spoke, not Norse," Giric had said, adding, "Duncan speaks both Gaelic and Norse like his father, the king."

Giric had also learned that the one called Ivar intended to take the girl with him to Norway. "Duncan told me 'tis why she is with him now."

Knowing the man who killed her parents was soon to be leaving Scotland made Catrìona desperate to rescue Deidre and see justice done. She did not trust the barbarian not to lie and deny the raid and claim Deidre was some other woman. He might even kill the handmaiden to hide his despicable acts.

As they stood watching the Northman's ship, Angus said, "Ye and the lad stay here, while Niall and I see to the guards. I see none on the second longship but they could be out of sight."

Niall pulled an arrow from his quiver and nocked it.

"Nay!" she protested. "I want Deidre to know I am here. She will be afraid. While you two handle the guards, I can see her to safety."

"I'll not argue with ye, milady," said her guard. "Ye'll stay. 'Tis bad enough ye have come this far."

Catrìona said nothing. Once they disabled the guards, she would be there for her maidservant. She would not fail her.

Angus and Niall crept closer, ducking behind the king's ship for cover.

From behind her, she heard a familiar voice speak. "Did you think Angus and Niall could dispatch those Northmen without help?"

Whirling around, Catrìona faced Steinar. With him was Colbán whose face was set in a harsh frown. "Aye, madam, did you conceive this plan? You should be in the hall with the other ladies."

She let out a sigh. The man was impossible. "My maidservant,

Deidre, is on that ship and I must save her ere the murderer sails with her to Norway."

"Ah, so that is it," said Steinar, shooting the captain a glance. "We had best help them rescue the lass."

"Aye, I suppose we must. Lead on, Scribe."

Catrìona felt a sudden wave of relief wash over her. In truth, she had been concerned for her brother and Angus. They did not know how many of the Northmen guarded the ship, but however many there were, they would be well armed with swords, battleaxes and knives.

⋆ ⋆ ⋆

Steinar crept up behind Angus where he waited with Catrìona's brother, watching the longship. Not wanting to startle them, he spoke in a quiet voice. "You are not alone, Angus. 'Tis Steinar and Colbán come to help you rescue the lass."

To his credit, Angus did not jump but merely looked over his shoulder and smiled. "Ye're most welcome, lads. I was beginning to think I should go fer help."

Niall dipped his head to Steinar and the king's captain.

"How many?" whispered Colbán.

"At least five or six on the longship with the falcon banner," replied Niall.

"We've seen none on the other," said Angus, "but we canna be certain."

Steinar said, "Some of us must get around to the other side so we can come at them from both directions. I will take Niall and go around, crossing where the trees lie close to the path." He was determined to keep Catrìona's brother close where he could protect him.

When the sun was halfway below the horizon, he and Niall managed to cross over the path to wait next to the longship belonging to the brothers, Paul and Erlend. A quick glance over the side told him there was no guard on the deck. The ship with the raven banner lay between this one and the king's ship.

Steinar waved to Colbán, the signal they had agreed upon, and silently crept toward the longship where Catrìona had seen the woman. The king's captain and Angus approached from the other side. As

Steinar neared the guarded ship, he heard a conversation in Gaelic.

"He means to ransom the girl," said one with a husky voice.

"Might have at one time," said another in a lecherous tone, "But I think he's changed his mind. Ivar would have her for himself. She's the mormaer's daughter, after all. But 'tis going to be a cold night once the sun is down and I could do with a woman's warm flesh. What say ye we sample the goods?"

"A fool's thought," said Husky. "For that, Ivar would unman ye. He might share the plunder, but never the women he takes. Besides, this one is still virgin. As long as he thought to ransom her, he did not touch her. He would know if ye were to take her first."

Seeing Colbán and Angus move into position, Steinar gave the signal and the four of them bounded over the sides of the ship. Steinar drew his sword as his feet touched the deck, the steel hissing as it left the scabbard.

Husky and Lecherous leapt to their feet, yanking their swords free, the sound of sliding steel ringing in the air. Three men had been sleeping, but quickly roused to grab their axes and long knives.

"We come for the girl," said Steinar. "She is not your master's to take. She is a Gael and one of ours."

"Ye'll not have her," said Husky, who Steinar now saw to be a large muscled Northman with long scraggly hair and beard.

"As you wish," said Steinar, drawing his short sword from his hip to add to his raised sword.

The one Steinar had dubbed Lecherous—a thin weasel of a man— lunged at him from several feet away. Before his blade struck, Niall let fly his arrow. It sank into the man's neck. The Northman made a choking sound and slid to the deck clutching the arrow.

"One down," said Niall with a smile.

Rhodri would be proud, but Steinar could not allow the youth to remain in the fray. The remaining Northmen charged toward them as Steinar shouted to Niall, "Go to the prow! 'Tis a better place to shoot."

The youth obeyed as Steinar fought off the enraged Husky. The Northman swung his sword, slicing through air as Steinar stepped to the side, avoiding the bulky Northman's blade.

"Ye look like a Dane," said Husky, "but ye do not fight like one."

Steinar heard the sounds of swords clashing behind him. "You face an English rebel in King Malcolm's service," he said as he beat back the man's sword and took a slice out of Husky's unmailed sword arm. "The last man you will see before death."

With an oath, the Northman backed off and leapt over the side of the ship and ran into the woods. *To his master, most likely.*

One was dead and one had fled but there were still three to dispose of. The battle erupted into a clash of metal and men's grunts as the three remaining Northmen, like cornered animals, fought Steinar, Angus and Colbán. The sun was beginning to set and it became more difficult to see. The ropes and tools left on the deck made the footing treacherous and, more than once, Steinar had stumbled. Still, each man fought on, seeking mastery over his opponent.

A shriek from inside the tent when a Northman stepped on it told Steinar the lass was inside and afraid. "Stay down, Deidre!" he shouted, hoping she would draw comfort from his use of her name.

For a time, he and Colbán fought back to back until one of the Northmen lunged toward Niall who stood in the prow nocking another arrow. Steinar raced across the deck and blocked the sword aimed at Catrìona's brother. The Northman turned from the archer to engage Steinar and the fighting continued.

★　★　★

The sounds of battle erupted all around Catrìona, echoing in her ears as they had on the day the vale was attacked, the same sounds she had heard in her dreams. When Deidre screamed, she could be patient no longer.

I must get Deidre to safety.

Bracing herself for what lay ahead, she cautioned Giric, who stood at her side. "Do not board the ship. You must promise."

"Aye," the boy said reluctantly. "I promise." But he picked up some rocks and followed close on her heels as she left her hiding place and ran to the side of the longship where the fighting raged.

She could hardly blame the boy for wanting to be of use, for she did not like standing idly by as those she loved fought her enemies.

Surveying the deck from where she stood, she saw the fighting stretched from midship to the prow. Assuring herself the king's men lived and Steinar and her brother stood strong, she scrambled over the side and hurried toward the back of the tent. "Deidre!" she hissed a whisper.

Her handmaiden emerged and flew into Catrìona's arms. "Oh, mistress," she sobbed. "You found me!"

"I never gave up," said Catrìona. "Come, we must get you away before we catch one of those swords." She pulled Deidre toward the side of the ship, thinking to drag her to safety, when one of the Northmen, seeing them escaping, plunged toward them, his sword flashing.

"And now we have two," he said as he reached them and slowly brought the edge of his sword to her neck, stopping just short of her skin. "Ivar will be pleased."

She froze, afraid to breathe.

Beside her, Deidre cried, "Nay!"

Suddenly, behind the Northman loomed Steinar like a vengeful god. The sword held to her neck flew away with a blow from Steinar's short blade. Dropping his sword, Steinar grabbed the Northman's long hair, drew back his head and sliced across his neck.

Blood spurted onto Catrìona, the smell of it nearly making her retch.

"Go!" shouted Steinar and picked up his sword, turning to confront another.

Catrìona dragged Deidre to the side and they scrambled over the gunwale to the ground. As she looked back, she saw Colbán trip over a body on the deck, leaving his shoulder open to a Northman's blade. He grunted as it sliced through his tunic and he sagged to the deck. Steinar ran to defend him against the killing blow, but before Steinar could reach him, an arrow whooshed through the air and lodged deep in the Northman's chest.

From the prow, Niall shouted, " 'Tis two!"

* * *

Steinar could feel his leg weakening from his many stumbles on the deck, now slippery with blood and strewn with bodies of two Northmen. Colbán was wounded and unable to lift his sword. The two remaining Northmen breathed heavily as they plunged their swords toward Steinar and Angus but the two fought side by side, battling the Northmen back. Niall, unwounded in the prow, nocked another arrow.

'Twas then the Northmen's dark-haired leader made his appearance, leaping onto the deck of the ship. "You would dare take what is mine?" He waved his sword slowly back and forth in front of Steinar. Even in the gloaming, the steel glistened. Beside the man called Ivar stood the one Steinar had dubbed Husky, returned now that he had his master to fight with him.

"She is not yours, Ivar," said Steinar. "Do Thorfinn's sons know you took her in your attack on the Vale of Leven?"

"They know naught of it. And there will be no one to tell them once you and these few with you are dead."

Ivar's arrival had brought a pause in the fighting and distracted the Northman fighting Angus. Out of the corner of his eye, Steinar saw Catriona's guard seize his opportunity and plunge his sword into the man's belly, piercing through his body.

Angered, Ivar and Husky attacked with vengeance, the third Northman joining them, three swords against two. Steinar had been in worse scrapes but he was tiring and liked not the odds. Ivar was skilled and fresh for the fight. But Steinar's determination to kill the man who had destroyed Catriona's family gave him new strength.

From the side of the ship, rocks flew through the air to pelt their Norse adversaries. Out of the corner of his eye, Steinar glimpsed Giric raising another rock. "Get him out of here!" he yelled to Niall.

Niall dropped from the prow and came around the side to grab the boy from his perch.

Steinar and Angus fought on, managing to hold off the three Northmen. It took all of Steinar's strength to keep Ivar at bay, slicing his sword through the air in rapid strikes while dancing to avoid the Northman's skilled blade.

An arrow flew through the air, piercing the chest of Husky, sending him to the deck.

" 'Tis three," came Niall's cry.

"This one," Steinar said, his tone full of scorn as his eyes narrowed on Ivar raising his sword, "is mine." Blocking the sword's blow with his own sword, he sent up a furious attack that backed the dark Northman to the side of the ship.

"And this one is mine!" yelled Angus as he swung his powerful sword at the man he fought. "Fer my lord, Cormac!" he shouted, cutting off the man's head in one powerful stroke. The Northman's body crashed to the deck, his head rolling to hit the side of the longship.

Steinar sheathed his short blade and gripped the hilt of his sword with both hands. "Now 'tis only you that remains," he said to Ivar, disdain dripping from his words. Faster than the Northman could follow with his eyes, Steinar sliced across Ivar's chest, leaving a long line oozing forth blood.

Ivar looked down at the widening streak of red, stunned.

Mayhap he has never been wounded. A weakness Steinar did not have, for he was not afraid to take a blade. With all his strength, he swung and caught Ivar across the throat just as the Northman looked up.

★   ★   ★

Relieved the last of the Northmen had been dispatched to Hades, Catrìona leapt over the side of the ship and ran to Steinar, flinging herself into his arms and kissing him with wild abandon.

"Oh, Steinar!"

From behind her, Angus coughed. She turned to see her guard standing there with a disapproving look and blood coating his tunic.

A movement at the prow drew her eyes to where Niall stood with Giric, smiles on both their faces.

Realizing she had become a spectacle, she stepped back.

"I see," said Colbán.

At his words, she turned to see him sitting against the hull, blood dripping from his shoulder. Guilt gripped her as she remembered the king's captain had taken a blade. Rushing to him, she knelt at his side. "Oh, sir, you *are* wounded."

"Most grievously, madam," he said sarcastically. She wondered if he referred to his shoulder or seeing her display of affection for Steinar. "But the wound will keep," he said. " 'Tis time we return to the king." Colbán struggled to rise. Angus came to help him to his feet. "Malcolm will be sorry to have missed this," said the king's captain. "He does love a good fight."

Colbán sagged in Angus' arms and Steinar rushed to support the captain's other side.

"Mind the rocks Giric has left on the deck," said Niall with a smirk in the boy's direction. Then, more seriously, he added, "They will make it hard going."

Her brother offered to go to the tower to bring horses and a cart. Steinar agreed it would be better that Colbán not have to walk the distance.

Catriona's suggestion she ride in the cart with Colbán was accepted.

When the cart arrived, she climbed in to sit beside the wounded captain, pressing a cloth to his shoulder to staunch the bleeding. Deidre joined her. Steinar and Angus rode on either side of the cart and Niall behind.

The king's captain dozed while Deidre told Catriona of the last year the handmaiden had endured with the Northman named Ivar. "We did not go at once to Orkney," she began. "The Northman, Ivar, made other ports as he plundered his way north. At some, he unloaded men and all the women, save me."

"Why did he keep you?"

"Oh, mistress. You saved me, you did. He thought I was you!" At Catriona's puzzled expression, Deidre said, "Remember, I wore your gown. When the attack came, I was alone in your chamber, packing your things. 'Twas from there I was taken. Ivar could speak Gaelic as some of his men, that is how I learned he meant to ransom me, but then he changed his mind. I heard him tell one of his men he was going to take me with him to Norway. If you had not rescued me from his ship, I might never have seen you again!"

Catriona reached out to grasp Deidre's hand. "I never gave up hope. I never stopped praying you would be found." She could not see her maidservant's blue eyes but she heard the quiver in her voice. Relief flooded her and she thanked God for bringing Deidre back to her.

It was dark when they arrived back at the tower. Much confusion and many questions awaited them but all was delayed when the king saw his wounded captain.

"Summon my physic at once!" Malcolm yelled to his steward.

With Margaret's permission and feeling responsible in some measure for what had happened to the bold captain, Catrìona followed the men carrying Colbán to his chamber high in the tower, leaving Steinar and the others to answer the king's questions.

Audra, her eyes anxious with fear, hurried up the stairs behind Catrìona, saying she might be of assistance to the physic. Remembering the love Catrìona had seen in the eyes of Duff's daughter for the king's captain, she wholeheartedly agreed, urging Audra to come.

Colbán was awake when the physic cleaned and stitched his wound, bearing the pain uncomplaining. The king's captain said little, but his eyes followed Catrìona as she helped the physic, handing him the things he requested from his pouch of medicines. The bear of a man lay back against the pillows, his muscled chest bared for the physic's ministrations.

When the wound was stitched, Catrìona asked a servant to request the Culdee monk, who served in the chapel, to make a plaster for the wound. She had observed his well-kept herb garden and perceived he was knowledgeable in potions. The plaster the woman returned with smelled of mint but the servant told her it also contained yarrow.

"He said 'twill help the wound heal, my lady."

Catrìona thanked her and when the physic was finished, with Audra watching, she applied the plaster to the wound herself.

Colbán gave her a small smile. " 'Tis probably good the scribe was not wounded or I would see little of your care this night."

"You have one better than I, good captain." She looked toward Audra who had been attentive to Colbán's every move. "Audra has taught me much and her heart is ever sympathetic to those in need, which you are, at least tonight. You have my thanks for aiding my guard and my brother."

When the physic had gone, Colbán finally succumbed to sleep and Catrìona got to her feet, wanting to wash and change her bloodstained clothing before meeting her mistress.

While Colbán was awake, Audra had kept a discreet distance, sitting by his bedside. Now that he slept, she took his hand and held it between hers in a gesture, which, to Catrìona, spoke of more than just concern.

Tears began to fall from Audra's eyes as she glanced up at Catrìona. "I will stay with him."

Seeing the love in the woman's eyes, Catrìona nodded, knowing that when she returned in the morning to check on the captain, Audra would still be here. "I will bring you some willow bark tea to give him for pain and a potion for sleep should he not be able to rest the night." Then, thinking of her fellow lady, she added, "And some food for you."

Audra gave her a faint smile. "Thank you."

Catrìona placed her hand on Audra's shoulder in comfort. "He fought bravely. You can be proud of him."

Tears flowing unheeded, Audra said in a whisper, "I am always proud of him."

CHAPTER 15

Catrìona was aware that much happened after the battle on the Northman's longship, but because she had been tending to Colbán, she had been spared the questions of the king and the Orkney jarls. But once she had changed, she went to see the queen, knowing she owed Margaret an explanation.

The queen was mild in her scolding. "You should have come to me, Catrìona, but I can understand your desire to save your maidservant. 'Tis clear that God was protecting you and for that I am most grateful."

The queen was right, of course. To rescue Deidre had been an impulsive act, but she had not trusted Ivar to be honest, even with the king. She regretted Colbán's wound, but she was not sorry for having gone after Deidre, who was now to share the chamber with her and Fia.

The next morning, Steinar assured her that he and Angus had answered all to the king's and the jarls' satisfaction. "Truth be told," he said when they broke their fast, "I believe Paul and Erlend were embarrassed to have one such as Ivar living in their midst, hiding his perfidy behind their hospitality. They made excuses for not having spent much time with Ivar. It seems he was gone much of the time and now they know why."

During that day, Colbán remained abed and Duff, still recovering from his own wound, rarely moved from his chamber. When Audra was not with Colbán, she was seeing to her father, running between the two. Catrìona worried for the lady's well-being and frequently checked on her, offering help where needed.

Often, when Catrìona came to see the king's captain, he would be protesting his confinement. "I should be on the practice field with my men!" Catrìona was unsurprised. Such a man, used to being outside, commanding his warriors, would rebel at having to remain abed.

Both she and Audra ignored his complaining.

The next day, Catrìona came to check on Colbán's progress. When she approached his chamber, she found the door ajar.

His voice boomed in command. "Leave me, woman, I am nearly well!"

Audra's soft voice drifted to the corridor. "I will not leave you, my lord."

Catrìona peered through the small opening to see Audra handing the captain a wooden cup. " 'Tis something that will ease the pain."

To Catrìona's surprise, the gruff warrior took it and drank, but afterward said, "I would rather have the king's wine or even the ale we are sometimes served. This has a bitter taste and does little to improve a man's spirits."

Catrìona silently chuckled. *The bear growls.*

Audra's words in response were murmured. "I will see you have all you desire, my lord."

Colbán's dark eyes searched Audra's face. "You are very kind, putting up with my many grumblings. Do you forget from whence I come, madam?"

Catrìona could not see Audra's face, but she heard the sincerity in the lady's voice as she gently protested. "Oh, no, my lord. I am well aware you are from Moray. But if you knew how high is my regard for you, you would not doubt my desire to see you hale once again. Why, I think you are the most courageous, honorable and true of all who serve the king."

Colbán drew his head back and studied Audra for a moment, his brows drawn together. "Would your father think the same, my lady?"

"Aye, my lord. I know he does."

Catrìona smiled to herself and turned to tiptoe away. After that, she no longer worried for the king's captain and came not again to see how he fared.

★ ★ ★

A few days after Deidre's rescue, to Catriona's delight, her uncle, Fia's father, arrived at the tower. He was glad to see his daughter and niece, but they had only begun to speak with him when the king swept the mormaer away, calling for wine and telling the steward they must not be disturbed.

Catriona and Fia looked at each other and shrugged. They would see Matad at the evening meal.

That same day, Domnall returned to Dunfermline with the news that Isla of Blackwell's father had consented to his suit. Catriona had hoped he and Isla would already be gone before she returned from St. Andrews, but she had not been so fortunate and now all the ladies were forced to listen to Isla's wedding plans.

It was early afternoon when Catriona finished the blue tunic she had been stitching for Steinar. She held it up to the light from the window in her chamber, admiring the silver and gold stitching that had taken her many hours of laborious effort. Behind her, Fia and Deidre happily sorted through gowns the queen's sister thought might fit the hand-maiden.

Carefully folding the tunic and placing it in her chest, Catriona told the two women she would return shortly. 'Twas August and Kessog should be coming out of his molt. She would find Giric and they could pay the falcon a visit.

She entered the hall to see Steinar standing near the hearth fire.

He waved and she went to join him, but before she could speak, the king summoned him. "Scribe, I would have you read this missive the Irishman has brought me from the Mormaer of Blackwell."

She waited by the hearth fire as the two men spoke, hoping to learn of the message's contents. Steinar must have realized her intent. When he finished with the king, he came to her.

" 'Tis done," he said. "Blackwell comes in two days' time and they will marry in the chapel. Then presumably, both will leave Dunfermline, hopefully not to be seen again."

Catriona sighed in relief and not just for herself. All of the queen's ladies would be glad to see Isla go. She thanked Steinar and told him she was off to find Giric. As she was about to invite him to come with her, the king called Steinar back for a word.

"I will find you later," he said and returned to the king.

Slipping through the tower door, Catrìona considered where she might find the boy. He sometimes watched Angus at sword practice, or he might be at the archery field where Rhodri put the archers through their paces. But more often, she could find Giric and his dog, Shadow, in the village at this time of day. She decided to go to the village since she wanted to see the changes that had been made to the orphans' cottage. Then she would find the boy, wherever he was, and they could visit Kessog together.

She walked past the stables with only pleasant thoughts in her mind. She had received justice for the death of her parents, Colbán had finally seen Audra's true affection and, soon, the man who betrayed her for another would be gone.

As she strolled along, she did not pay much attention to the few people coming and going, except to return a smile of greeting. Suddenly, a hand reached out and grabbed her, pulling her into the shadows.

"Domnall!" she cried out when she recognized who it was. "What can you mean by this?" She yanked back her arm, but he held it fast. "Unhand me!"

He moved closer, his face inches from hers. "Nay, not until you hear me out."

He smelled of some scent and the shoulders of his tunic were richly embroidered with flowers. It was as he had always been but now she found his flowery scent and his embellished tunic disgusted her.

Heart pounding in her chest, she spit out, "Say it then and be gone!"

He lifted his finger to her jaw and slowly slid it to her chin. She stiffened at the unwanted touch. "I have always found you a seductive woman, Catrìona. It was not for lack of interest I gave you up for Isla, you know."

"That is no concern of mine now, Domnall. You have your betrothed. See to her and leave me alone."

"Nay, I would still have you in my bed. You could not be my wife, but you could be my mistress. What say you?"

She huffed out a laugh. "Surely you jest!"

He looked at her, affronted. "I am most serious. You have no dowry to speak of and no rich trade to offer as you once did."

"If I did not come to your bed when I was your intended, do you think I would do so now when you have spurned me? You are beyond contemptible!"

Without warning, he dropped her hand and drove his chest into her, forcing her against the side of the stable, the rough boards bruising the tender flesh of her back. "I will have you, as I always wanted." Without pretense of gentleness, his mouth came down hard upon hers, forcing his tongue into her mouth.

She pushed against his chest with her hands but she could not move him. With one foot, she kicked at his shin as hard as her shoe allowed in the tight space.

Raising his mouth from her abused lips, he said, "I always did like your fire."

A hiss of steel was followed by the flash of metal as a sword tip slid before her eyes to hover next to Domnall's cheek. "Take your hands from her or I shall scar you for life, you dishonorable cur."

Steinar! Her chest heaving, she turned to look into his beautiful eyes, relief washing over her.

"Has he harmed you, little one?"

She pressed her lips together trying to hold back the tears filling her eyes. "I am fine."

Domnall backed away from the sword but the blade followed to remain close to his face. "What business is this of yours, Scribe?"

"You, a man betrothed, would force yourself on one of the queen's ladies? Get you gone, Domnall. See to your own lady!" In a tone of disgust, Steinar added, "I wish you well of her."

Domnall glanced again at the blade, barely a breath from his eye, and fled.

Steinar sheathed his sword and pulled Catrìona into his arms. " 'Tis over, little one. He is gone."

For a moment she was content to be held. Wiping the tears of relief from her eyes, she tilted her head up to look at him. "You saved me."

"Aye, lass, and I always will."

Steinar did not speak the words to Domnall that had been in his heart. "She belongs to me!" he had wanted to shout. But how could he claim a lady the king intended for another?

When the king had called him back for a word, it was to tell Steinar that he was still considering what lady he might give him for a wife and expected to make his choice soon. The conversation that followed left Steinar despairing of hope.

"It will not be the redhead you asked for," said Malcolm. "Still, I've a fine lady in mind."

"But Sir, 'tis Catrìona I love."

His face stern, the king shot back, "Love has little to do with raising sons to serve your king, but I will think on it."

Steinar believed it more likely the king would quickly dismiss Steinar's plea from his mind. Thus, he had not claimed her before the despicable Domnall. But he could protect her and vow to always do so. And as long as a glimmer of hope remained, as long as she had yet to be betrothed, he would seek her company.

"Do you go in search of Giric?" he asked her when she had calmed.

"Yea," she said. "I had thought to find him in the village and was on my way there."

"If it pleases you, I would accompany you." He was not about to leave her alone to be found again by the loathsome Irishman.

She tossed him a smile. "Aye, it would please me."

They continued down the path that led to the village and she told him of all she had done with Margaret's permission to improve the cottage where the orphans lived. As she talked, she seemed to shake off the incident at the stables.

"The queen sent some of the Saxons who are skilled in building to repair the cottage so it will be warm for winter. And I have enlisted some of the women to make it more of a home. Margaret gave me the services of a dear woman, Aeleva, who now cares for the orphans. She cooks and keeps house for them. They seem to love her."

Catrìona's green eyes sparkled as she spoke. He was glad to see Domnall's attack did not affect her enthusiasm for what she had done for the orphans. "I expect the queen is delighted," he said, trying to encourage her.

"I think she is. Margaret had always believed the village women cared for the orphans and they did, after a fashion. But not like Aeleva does now. She is more a mother to them and the young ones especially need that."

At the cottage, he and Catrìona stopped to admire the changes. The stones were whitewashed, the shutters new and flowers formed a pretty border on either side of the door. A fair-haired Saxon woman, rosy-cheeked and plump, came out to greet them. "Good day to you, sir, mistress."

"Good day to you, Aeleva," said Catrìona. "This is Steinar, one of the king's men."

Aeleva curtsied and Steinar wished the woman a good day and then asked her, "Is Giric about?"

"Just around the side," Aeleva said, pointing, "working on the pen for the chickens."

They found Giric building a reed fence on the far side of the cottage where fat chickens were pecking at seed tossed on the ground by a small girl, younger than Giric. The boy looked up at their appearance and beamed. "Is it not grand?"

"Aye," said Steinar. "And now you would be a builder besides a warrior?"

"I shall be both!" he announced, puffing out his small chest. The girl giggled, her fawn-colored curls falling onto her round cheeks.

Steinar laughed at the boy's audacity but when he thought of all that would be required to make a home in the Vale of Leven, he reconsidered. "Indeed you shall be."

"If you have the time, oh master builder," said Catrìona in feigned sarcasm, "I would invite you to go with us to see Kessog. With all that has happened, I have not looked in on him since I returned from St. Andrews. He will be feeling slighted."

Pounding in a last branch, Giric said, "Aye, I will go! And might there be food in the hall? Mayhap Duncan is there."

Steinar said, "I've no doubt there will be food and"—he winked at Catrìona—"if the lady agrees, mayhap we might fly the falcon."

Giric beamed and waved goodbye to the girl as he rushed to join them.

★   ★   ★

Catrìona was glad neither Domnall nor Isla was in the hall as they crossed the large space to the kitchen. Sickened by what he had attempted, she did not want to see either of them.

Sitting on a stool in the kitchen, they found Duncan nibbling on cheese.

"You and the king's son," the round-faced cook said to Giric, "are drawing down our reserves of cheese." With a smile for Catrìona and Steinar, she added, " 'Tis regrettable the lads' stomachs need constant refilling, but 'tis always the way of it."

"Ye will not tell the king, will ye?" asked Giric.

"Nay," the cook assured the boy, "but 'tis not the king you need worry about, 'tis the queen. She is the one with strict rules about eating before the evening meal."

"Oh," said the two lads in unison, looking very worried.

Catrìona laughed and reached to where she knew they kept bits of raw meat and put some in her pouch for Kessog.

"We are on our way to the mews," she told Duncan. "Would you like to come with us to visit my tiercel and see the king's hawks?"

The youth jumped up from his seat. He was twice Giric's age, but the two could have been brothers. "I would!"

It was late in the afternoon when they entered the dim light of the mews. Machar was feeding the falcons and seemed happy to see the visitors. "Your tiercel has been pining for you, my lady, but I have kept him fat to hasten his molt. See," he said, taking Kessog from his perch, "his tail feathers are all in now."

"But he does not look ready to hunt," she said with disappointment as she cast a glance over his still ruffled plumage.

" 'Twill not be long now. Mayhap another sennight," said the falconer.

Duncan and Giric spent some time looking at all the hawks. Catrìona stood next to Kessog's perch stroking his feathers as she marveled at Steinar's patience with the boys. He listened attentively to their questions, answering them when he could. Machar, with his greater knowledge of the hawks, answered some.

Finally, Steinar looked up at her with raised brows as if he had read her mind.

"Aye," she said, "we had best be off. The evening meal will soon be upon us and the king will be asking for his son."

She waved goodbye to Giric, who ran off toward the village, and headed toward the tower, Steinar and Duncan talking of the changes Margaret had made since coming to Dunfermline. Catrìona marveled at the friendship between the golden warrior, once a scribe, and the dark-haired youth who was destined to one day be king. Would Steinar serve Duncan as he had his father? Would she be by his side if he did?

★   ★   ★

That night, when Catrìona and Fia arrived in the hall for the evening meal, the dais was crowded with persons of high rank and the hall filled with warriors in the service of the king and his esteemed visitors.

On the king's left sat Matad, Mormaer of Atholl, Fia's father. Next to him was Duff, Mormaer of Fife, still recovering from his wound gained in Northumbria. It would be awhile before the one who led the king's army sat a horse.

On Duff's other side was the king's young son, Duncan.

Edgar helped the queen into her chair beside the king and then sat on her other side. Beside Edgar were the king's stepsons, the Jarls of Orkney, Paul and Erlend Thorfinnsson.

"Your father sits next to the king," Catrìona said to her cousin as they joined the other ladies.

Fia spoke into her ear. "Aye and Rhodri will entertain them all. He has prepared some special songs that tell of Alba's deep past."

Catrìona had told Fia of Domnall's disgusting behavior earlier that day and, though Fia was horrified, she was not surprised. "Isla and Domnall deserve each other. He will never be faithful and she will never let him forget it. They will soon be a pair of squabbling ducks."

"Aye, mayhap you are right," said Catrìona. "I wish them well of each other."

Not far away sat Steinar and Rhodri, who dipped their handsome heads in greeting when she looked their way. She had been so happy to be with Steinar that afternoon. It had helped to lessen the impact of her encounter with Domnall. But when she thought of what the Irishman had done, her anger returned. She did not like to think of what might have happened had Steinar not come. The golden-haired scribe had become her champion and, if her prayers were answered, one day, he would be more. He might be without land and title but he had courage and honor the king would not fail to reward. Audra might be wrong in thinking Colbán was more courageous and honorable than all the king's men. Catrìona believed Steinar could well hold that place.

The meal of roast pheasant and boar was delicious and she vowed to save for Giric a few tasty morsels of meat and whatever sweet they would be served, for the boy would be dining on plainer fare. When she saw a platter of berry tarts arrive at the table, she snatched one up and set it aside to keep for the lad.

Finally, it was time for the entertainment. Rhodri took up his harp and walked to the front of the room, a signal to all to quiet in anticipation of the bard's songs.

Suddenly, the tower door burst open and in stepped a tall man clad in unusual garb with a longbow and a quiver of arrows slung over his shoulder. He was flanked by two burly guards in similar attire who also carried longbows. The tall man's tunic was dark green in color, his hosen dark brown, heavier than that worn by Malcolm's men and loose about his legs. Over all of it, he wore a sleeveless fur cloak that fitted his body but was open down the front. His curly brown hair reached only to his nape and was confined by a leather thong circling his head like a crown.

His eyes scanned the hall, his scrutiny finally alighting on the king.

"Come forward, stranger!" shouted Malcolm.

The man spoke a word to his guards, who remained at the door, and strode toward the dais. Once there, he took his bow and quiver of arrows from his shoulder and bowed, all eyes upon him.

Rhodri, who was standing before the king, moved to one side, an expression of keen interest on his face as he regarded the stranger.

"And who might you be, good sir?" asked Malcolm, seemingly amused by the intrusion.

"I am Cillyn ap Cynfyn," he declared, "brother to Bleddyn ap

Cynfyn, the King of Gwynedd and Powys in Wales." After he'd said this, Catrìona heard him repeat the message in the Saxon tongue while looking at the queen. Then the Welshman took from his cloak a parchment and handed it to Malcolm. "A letter from my brother, the king."

"You are welcome in my court," said Malcolm, setting the letter aside. "The Welsh are our friends. What has brought you to Dunfermline?"

"I come for my nephew, Iorwerth ap Bleddyn."

The king retuned him a puzzled look. "We have no man here by that name."

"Most respectfully, I disagree, My Lord. I expect you know him by another name." Shooting the king's bard a glance, the Welsh nobleman said, "I am told he took the name Rhodri when he decided to defy his noble father and go off adventuring with his harp some years ago."

All eyes turned on Rhodri, whose gaze never wavered from the Welshman who claimed to be his uncle.

At Catrìona's side, Fia gasped.

"You did not know?" she whispered to her cousin.

Fia shook her head. "Nay, but I always knew he must be more than a bard."

"Rhodri," said the king. "Does this man speak the truth? Are you his nephew, son of the Welsh king?"

Rhodri said, "He is, indeed, my uncle and he speaks the truth, My Lord. I was young and impulsive. My father and I had a disagreement over my interest in poetry and the harp."

"Hmm," muttered the king, rubbing a hand over his beard. "And what is your purpose, Cillyn ap Cynfyn, save to see your nephew?"

Cillyn drew himself up, his head raised in noble fashion. "My older brother, the king, summons his son home. His words to me were, ' 'Tis time my son takes his rightful place; one day he will share the crown with his brothers'."

The king stepped down from the dais and offered the Welshman his hand. "I would have your friendship, Cillyn ap Cynfyn. In truth, I would have more. Your country and mine both loathe the Norman invader. I would have an alliance. Would your brother, the king, agree to such?"

The Welshman appeared to consider Malcolm's question for a moment and then said, "He might be so inclined if I were to return with my nephew. We have long sheltered the Norman's enemies, including the English rebel, Eadric the Wild, who allied himself to my brother when he was the Prince of Gwynedd. As you say, our countries are friends and we have a common enemy."

Catrìona squeezed her cousin's hand, knowing Fia was in love and it would break her heart if Rhodri left Scotland.

Malcolm turned to the bard. "I do not like to think of you leaving my court, Rhodri or Iorwerth, however you are called. By which name should we henceforth address you?"

"Rhodri, My Lord. 'Tis a name of great renoun in Wales and my own ancestor. I have become used to the sound of it."

"As you wish. So, Rhodri, do you agree to return with your uncle to Wales and seek this alliance with Scotland?"

The hall was so quiet not even the hounds in the corner stirred as all waited for Rhodri's answer. Only the hearth fire, which burned low, made any sound at all.

Rhodri's reply, when it came, echoed through the hall. "I agree... on one condition."

Malcolm and Cillyn turned their gazes on the Welshman once considered a bard and a bowman but now recognized as the son of the Welsh king.

"And what is that?" asked Malcolm. "Come, do not keep us in suspense."

Rhodri shifted his gaze to the dais where Fia's father sat. "I would ask the Mormaer of Atholl for the hand of his daughter, Fia, for I will have no other as my wife."

Catrìona turned to her cousin. Fia's cheeks were streaked with tears, but it was not sadness she saw in her blue eyes; it was joy. "Oh, Fia."

"Fia of Atholl, come forward!" shouted the king. Then turning to the Welsh lord, Malcolm said, "A troublesome thing this tendency of my men to demand the bride of their choice."

Catrìona saw the queen roll her eyes to the roof above and remembered that Malcolm had once demanded his choice of a bride.

Addressing the Mormaer of Atholl, who frowned from the dais, the king said, "You'd best join us as well, Matad. It seems the whole kingdom is to witness this conversation."

Fia went forward to stand by Rhodri. Her father stepped down from the dais to join the king next to the Welsh lord, who was as tall as the king but more slender of build.

To Matad, Malcolm exclaimed, "By all the saints! I want this alliance for Scotland!"

Matad remained silent, watching his daughter.

The king frowned at his mormaer. "Rhodri is a good man, a fine warrior and plays the music of Heaven. And, above all that, he is a king's son. What more could you want in a son-in-law, Matad?"

Fia's father stood with one hand on his hip. "All you say is correct, My King, but I do not like the thought of my only daughter going so far away. 'Tis not even Scotland."

Rhodri took Fia's hand and the two gazed longingly at each other. Catrìona knew then Fia's father would not be able to say her nay. Nor would he deny the king an alliance he badly wanted.

"Gwynedd is not far, my lord," said Cillyn to Matad. "A short sail north to the River Clyde and then a few days' ride east to Dunfermline or Atholl. I came that way but a sennight ago when my scouts returned with word my nephew was here."

"And I would promise to bring Fia to see you," encouraged Rhodri.

Through the whole conversation, Catrìona saw the queen anxiously observing from the dais. Her mouth moved though no words could be heard. *She prays!*

"Do you love this man?" Matad asked his daughter.

"Oh, aye, Father, I do. Ever since I first glimpsed him. I would willingly follow him to Wales."

" 'Twas the same for me, my lord," said Rhodri to Fia's father. "I vow to love her and treasure her all of my days." When Fia's father remained silent, Rhodri said, "Would it help if we named our first son Matad and agree he would foster with you?"

The king chuckled.

Fia's father let out a breath even Catrìona could hear. "Aye, it might," he said shortly. "But I would have you linger awhile in Dunfermline and wed here."

"I would not think of taking Fia back to Wales except as my wife," said Rhodri.

The king breathed an audible sigh of relief and, on the dais, the queen smiled. " 'Tis agreed," Malcolm said. "The two will tarry awhile in Dunfermline, as I trust will you, Cillyn, and before they depart, there will be a wedding. More than one if my calculations be true."

CHAPTER 16

In the sennight that followed, Steinar had more than enough to occupy his days. In addition to sword practice with his fellow guards and the occasional hunt, Paul and Erlend Thorfinnsson had given him Ivar's ship and skilled workmen from their own longship to have it properly fitted out.

Out of the hearing of others, Malcolm had told Steinar, "Ivar destroyed Cormac's ship, so 'tis right you shall claim the Northman's. My mormaer in the Vale of Leven should have a ship. And, should you not yet know, I have asked Paul and Erlend to hunt for the other women taken from the vale."

"Catriona will be happy to hear it," he had told the king.

Steinar was overjoyed at the news of the ship, but he wondered what Catriona would think of it. Because the king had sworn him to silence, he did not tell Catriona why he was the one to oversee the work on the longship and she did not ask. But one of the first things he did was to have the dragon heads on the stems removed and the wood sanded smooth.

Fortunately, the king made Paul and Erlend aware of his plans for Steinar, whereupon the brothers offered to sail the ship, once re-fitted, to the Vale of Leven with whatever supplies Steinar would need for the hillfort he would build. On the way, they would stop along the coast where they thought Ivar might have left some of his men and the women he had taken from the vale. Since the two brothers from

Orkney were to leave when the ship was finished, they had assured him he would see it in the vale ere long.

Catrìona, he had noticed, was occupied with many things, foremost being the queen's plans for the pilgrims' ferry and inn.

"Margaret has pilfered much gold from the king's treasury for all she has planned for the pilgrims," Catrìona told him one evening. "But then you must know since you account for it."

"Malcolm does not seem to mind," Steinar had replied. "When I show him the mounting costs, he just shrugs. Mayhap he thinks 'tis a reasonable penance for his raids on Northumbria."

"The queen would tell him he should do it for love of God and as a kindness to the pilgrims," Catrìona had said, "but I think you have the right of it. The king would see it as penance."

The revelation concerning Rhodri's origins, about which Steinar teased him much, soon spread to all in Dunfermline. Aware of his noble lineage, they now stumbled over addressing him as "my lord", which Steinar found most amusing. If Rhodri must leave Scotland, at least he would leave with honor and acclaim and his choice of bride. Steinar had heard Catrìona and her cousin making plans for the wedding and Rhodri spoke often with the king and Cillyn about an alliance with Wales.

Three days after Rhodri was declared the son of a king, the Mormaer of Blackwell returned to court and his daughter, Isla, and Domnall were wed. A brief celebration followed and the next day the three left for Ayrshire in the west where the newly married couple planned to sojourn before sailing to Ireland. All at court were to glad to see them go, most especially Steinar, who was relieved the Irishman who had acted so dishonorably toward Catrìona was gone from her life.

By the time Domnall left, Colbán was up and about, though not yet swinging a sword with the guards. Audra, Steinar noticed, was equally attentive to the king's captain as she was to her father, who was managing to move about the hall with more ease each day. Colbán no longer cast possessive glances toward Catrìona. Mayhap he was confident that the king had granted his request for her hand. Steinar did not like to think of it and turned, instead, to the work on what was now his ship.

Rhodri still trained Malcolm's archers, but now he openly paid court to his betrothed. He and Fia were so happy at times it was difficult to be around them. "Must he look at her like that?" asked Giric one morning as they broke their fast. " 'Tis as if he is suffering a spell."

"Aye, lad, love is like that." He glanced at Catrìona, sitting a stone's throw away, and inwardly pined. If Giric could see on Steinar's face what was hidden in his heart, the boy would think him ill. Indeed, he was sick at heart. It was only a matter of time before the king announced his decision and Steinar dreaded the coming day.

Another sennight passed when, deep in August, Maerleswein returned to court in a cloud of dust, thundering up the slope to the tower with two of his men. Steinar had just returned from the River Forth where his ship was nearly finished, when the small group of riders pulled rein in front of the tower.

Maerleswein swung his leg over his saddle and dropped to the ground, his two guards doing the same, as he handed the reins of his horse, blowing and lathered, to a groom.

With a wave to Steinar, Maerleswein jerked open the tower door and strode into the hall. Steinar followed, curious to know what produced the frowns on the faces of the three and their hurried manner.

"I must see the king at once!" Maerleswein yelled to Nechtan, the steward, who came running.

"Aye, my lord. He is with his Lady. I shall advise him you are here."

" 'Tis urgent!" the former sheriff called out to the steward's back.

A moment later, Malcolm stomped down the stairs, relaxed until he looked at the men, ruddy cheeked and wiping sweat from their brows. "What brings you from Lothian in such fevered haste?" Before Maerleswein could answer, the king demanded, "What is it?"

"My Lord," Maerleswein said, not taking time to bow, "William and his army of French knights ride into Scotland. They will cross Lothian tonight if they keep to their pace."

The king cursed beneath his breath. "What has stirred the nest of Norman vipers, I wonder?"

"William has always seen you as a threat," replied the tall, stately man who had once been the Sheriff of Lincolnshire. "I am certain he has in mind your raids on Northumbria."

"What took the Bastard so long?" asked an exasperated Malcolm, running his hand through his hair as he paced.

"Last year, you will recall, he was taken up with mutilating the prisoners he took at Ely. The first part of this year, I am told he was called to Normandy. Only now is he free to seek revenge on us. Knowing William as I do, I would say he sees you as the last and greatest threat to his crown."

"Aye, I have known it. 'Tis a shame both Duff and my captain still recover from wounds and my army has been disbanded these last many weeks."

"There is also the matter of your marriage to Margaret and your aid for Edgar's claim to the throne. William has not forgotten the rebels who rose in York but two years ago."

"The ones you led?" Malcolm said, his mouth twitching up in a grin.

"Aye, he still fears the queen's brother. Edgar is popular with the people."

"As is only right." The king called for wine and food for the men. The three who had ridden so fast to Dunfermline appeared weary. "I suppose you rode straight through?" inquired the king.

Maerleswein brushed the dust from his tunic. "Aye, I came as soon as I had the news."

"Sit and eat." Malcolm looked about the hall and seeing Steinar standing to the side, beckoned him. "I need your scribe services. Join us and bring your quill and parchment."

Steinar did not need to hear the urgency in the king's voice to know this was a perilous situation. Hurriedly, he fetched the requested items and took his place beside the two men, the guards who came with Maerleswein sitting farther down the table.

A servant set goblets of wine before them and platters of bread, cheese and pears. "How many ride with William?" asked Malcolm who ignored the refreshments.

Maerleswein reached for a goblet and a hunk of cheese. "The reports say he rides with hundreds of mounted knights as well as men-at-arms following on foot. 'Tis the same way he came upon York. But there is more."

Steinar watched the king, who appeared to be bracing for a storm, his expression dour. "What more?"

"Ships have been sighted off the coast of Lothian heading north toward the Firth of Forth."

Malcolm cursed and slammed his fist on the table, causing the platter to jump. "Would the Bastard have the intention, do you think, of sailing to my very threshold?"

"Or farther north," Maerleswein suggested. "If they sail to the Firth of Tay, he would have his ships behind you and his army before you."

" 'Tis just like the Norman invader. He would surround the lion's very lair."

"Delay would be our friend just now," suggested Maerleswein as he gulped the wine.

"Aye, I must delay the invaders until I have my army with me." Then turning to Steinar whose quill hovered over the parchment, the king said, "The missives you sent before for the raid on Northumbria. We must have them again, only this time, summon only the mormaers who are within a day's ride. I would have all the men they can gather, not just a tithe. They must ride for Dunfermline with all speed when they get the message. Our future depends upon it."

Steinar nodded and began to write with fury.

"Will you stay the night?" the king asked Maerleswein.

"Nay, I must return to Lothian. Davina is with child and happily so. I have sent her to safety, but I must join my men and those of her father to see what can be done. Mayhap the Normans do not look to plunder Lothian but we must take all steps to see they do not. I worry our coast is vulnerable."

"If William's army rides fast, they may pass quickly through Lothian on their way to me. Mayhap you will be spared."

The two men grasped forearms and met each other's gaze. "Godspeed," said Maerleswein.

"Godspeed," echoed the king.

Steinar was still writing when the tower door thumped closed and the king turned to him. "When you have finished, summon my guard. And best include Colbán. He will be offended if I think him too weak to have a role in this fight. I will go and see Duff about what part of my army lies close."

Steinar stood from his writing and bowed. "As you wish, My Lord."

Then he returned to his seat and took up his quill. He would finish and dispatch the missives and then go for the guard. Out of the corner of his eye he saw Malcolm whip around and head toward the stairs. When the king reached them, he looked up and into the face of his queen.

★   ★   ★

Margaret walked up the stairs with her husband and waited until they were in their chamber and the door closed before turning to look into his troubled eyes. "My Lord?"

Gently, he laid his palm on her belly. "Your time draws near, *mo cridhe?*"

She stared into his warm brown eyes wondering, with Scotland at stake and the Conqueror at their doors, why he would choose now to ask. "Mayhap a month, no more."

He sighed and led her to sit beside him on a bench. The responsibility for his people weighed heavy on him. Even his shoulders, normally so straight, appeared to sag. "I would not be at war when the lad is born. This battle must be over soon."

Rising, he reached for his sword and belted it on, adding to his clothing other weapons he customarily wore, including the long seax he sheathed at his hip. "I'd best keep these with me now."

Her heart raced thinking of his blood being shed again by a Norman sword. She had only one chance to call him back from the brink of death and it was now.

"My Lord, will you not first count the cost?"

He cocked his head to one side and raised a brow. "*Mo cridhe?*"

"If you do battle with William, your warriors may send the Normans from our land, but I would risk my husband and the Scots their king. Though he seems to love it, I cannot believe William wants such a war. Scotland is no easy prey. Our warriors are as fierce as the Picts that preceded them. Soon, autumn comes and winter close behind it. His knights would be mired in mud and snow. They do not know the glens like you do."

"What is it you suggest?"

"If you but seek terms, you may give up little to gain much. Send him from our border with only words to carry home to London."

Malcolm came to her then and she stood, reaching her hands to his shoulders. "Let us have our years together, my love, so that God might give us more sons for Scotland."

"You would have me *negotiate* with the Norman Bastard?"

She raised her head as the queen she was, the queen he had made her but a few years before. "Yea, I would. And, if you do this, my ladies and I will fast and pray for all the hours you are gone."

Malcolm left her and walked to the window, gazing south, seeing in his mind as she did, the Normans marching toward them, their numbers too great to count.

Letting out a sigh, he turned to face her. Gone was the warrior whose mind was set on battle. In his place was the wise king she had come to love. "Your counsel is prudent, *mo cridhe*. I will speak with Duff and Matad. Should they agree, I will seek a meeting with William." He smiled then and hope rose within her. "He thinks me to be wily, or so I have heard. If there is to be a meeting, I shall not disappoint. Pray God helps me."

She went into his arms and embraced him, pressing her cheek to his broad chest. His strong arms tightened around her and the babe she carried. Tears filled her eyes as she looked up at him, "I shall, My Lord."

*   *   *

In his camp in Midlothian that night, William stood by the crackling fire outside his tent, gazing north. His back rigid and his smile tight, he was vaguely aware that Eadric, the one called "the Wild", had come to stand beside him.

"We have no desire for a pitched battle in Lothian, Eadric. Truth be said, we do not consider ourselves in Scotland until we have crossed the Forth."

"Your orders, then?"

William was unsurprised by Eadric's lukewarm attitude toward their current endeavor given the Saxon's history. At the outset, he had joined with his Welsh neighbors to inflict great damage on Herefordshire. He had only become William's man two years ago, and that forcibly. "By the splendor of God, tomorrow our army will cross the Forth near the place they call Strivelyn, east of Dunfermline. We will meet our ships on the Tay, deeper into Scotland than Malcolm will have imagined, and there we will engage the wily Scot."

Eadric remained silent, but it mattered little to William. The Saxon had no alliance with the Scots and would offer no objection.

"We will yet have all of this island in our grasp," said William. He could taste the fruit of his ambition. He had not conquered England to lose this northern bit. But, as he reflected on the vastness of this northern land, he thought again, frowning as he stared into the fire. Malcolm Canmore was not a foe so easily conquered as the rest. Even the Romans had feared the Picts.

★   ★   ★

By the time of the evening meal, all of Dunfermline had heard of the Conqueror's march on Scotland. Steinar listened to the men speculating on where the battle would be and the numbers of Norman knights they would face. Fear among the women was tangible and worry etched deep in their faces. He looked often at Catrìona, trying to tell her without words to have faith.

The queen and her ladies were the first to depart the hall that night. Catrìona darted a glance at him as she rose to leave. He gave her an encouraging smile, which she returned. They both knew what lay ahead.

Once the ladies had departed, the steward drove everyone from the hall, save those the king desired to speak with in private council.

Gathered to the king were his closest advisors, the mormaers whose lands were nearest, who had ridden with all haste at the receipt of the king's summons, bringing a large portion of the king's army with them. In addition to his guard, the king had also invited Rhodri and his uncle, Cillyn, to stay for the meeting, presumably because of the Welsh hatred for William and the alliance Malcolm hoped to gain. Among the highest ranking, Steinar knew Duff and Matad best, but there were others he had seen only once or twice.

They sat at one of the trestle tables, the king in the center and the others around him, some sitting, and some standing. The hall grew quiet; the king had their attention to a man. Steinar was curious to know what Malcolm's strategy would be.

"I have a proposition to discuss with you," the king began. "It is my intention to keep William waiting wherever he alights until the rest of our army can reach us. In a day or two, when they have arrived and William, ever impatient, is cursing me beneath his breath, I would send a messenger asking for a meeting to discuss his *requests*."

Mumbles echoed around the table as the men considered the king's plan.

"Do you intend to submit to William or grant him some part of Scotland?" asked a disbelieving Duff, his bushy brows drawn together in a frown, his hazel eyes so like his daughter's suddenly looking fierce.

"Nay," said a smiling Malcolm. "I intend to give him nothing but a few scraps from my table."

"What might those be?" asked a serious Matad.

"I have lands in England and others in Cumbria and Northumbria granted me by King Edward. Mayhap William can be satisfied to have authority over those. In truth, I would not oppose granting him such if, in return, I can gain something I want, which is more land."

"And what about Scotland?" asked the Mormaer of Ross, father of the queen's lady, Isobel.

"What of it?" the king tossed back. "Do you think I would give that loathsome usurper any part of Alba? Nay, never think it. I will not!"

Steinar listened to the murmuring that was set off by the king's suggested course of action. All were skeptical, untrusting of the Norman who had stolen Edgar's crown. But eventually, heads began to nod.

Duff spoke for all of them. "Aye, 'tis worth a try. But the army must be at your back, My Lord."

"You will not ride with me, old friend," the king said to the Mormaer of Fife. "I would that you heal. Days in the saddle would only slow your progress."

Duff opened his mouth to protest but the king raised his hand. "Nay and let that be an end to it." The king shifted his gaze to Colbán. "You, too, shall remain behind, my captain."

Colbán nodded, his expression showing he was disappointed but resigned.

Steinar spoke up. "I would lead your guard for Colbán, should you desire it, My Lord."

"And I would lead your army in Duff's absence," said Matad.

The king returned them a tight smile. "Then I look only to the one who leads my archers," said Malcolm. "Rhodri?"

"I am yours to command, My Lord," said Rhodri, bowing his head.

Cillyn interrupted. "Nay! My nephew will not be a part of this. I have only just found him and would not risk his life when a kingdom awaits him in Wales. Not until my brother, the king, agrees to the alliance shall my nephew fight again with the Scots."

Rhodri looked to Malcolm.

The king said, "Aye, have it your way, Cillyn. I would not risk an alliance with Wales. But if I am to be deprived of my best archer, I might ask you to suggest another, Rhodri."

"A name immediately comes to mind, My Lord, though he is young, not yet seventeen summers. But that is the age at which I first commanded my father's archers. Niall of the Vale of Leven is very good and his arrows always straight and true. The men like him and he would eagerly serve, should you command it. In the ranks of your archers are others who are older and would aid him."

"So be it!" exclaimed Malcolm. "We will wait till our army is here and then see what can be gained when the Scottish lion seeks a meeting with the French leopard."

★　★　★

Crossing the Forth at a narrow point, William led his army northeast, skirting Dunfermline that lay to the south. He passed Loch Leven without a thought to the monks who dwelled there and rode through lands that some might think possessed great beauty, paying little attention to what surrounded him. He was intent on only one thing: reaching the Tay and there doing battle with his enemy who had harbored the English rebels. Malcolm Canmore was the last obstacle to his dominating all of Britain and William was certain the Scot, who had battled his way to the throne, would not fail to accept the challenge.

The sun was low in the sky over his left shoulder as he sat atop his Iberian warhorse, the same stallion he had ridden up Senlac Hill at Hastings, and looked at the broad River Tay. It was the furthest point north to which fate had brought him. The church tower that rose seventy feet in the air in the village of Abernethy would stand as landmark for the battle to come.

"A fitting place for us to meet, is it not?" he asked Eadric. His men on either side of Eadric nodded their assent, but Eadric remained silent, granting the king he now served only a shrug.

★ ★ ★

The next afternoon, Margaret was sewing with her ladies when word came the Normans were camped on the banks of the Tay.

"Will there be a great battle?" Elspeth asked anxiously for the Tay ran through her father's lands.

"I pray not," said Margaret, "but I have told the king we will fast and pray for him and his men while they are gone."

"Steinar is to lead the guard in place of Colbán," said Catriona. "And my brother leads the archers."

"My father will head the king's army," said Fia.

Each of her ladies had a man close to them whose life would be risked in the next few days. Margaret had thought to distract them with their stitchery but soon came to realize they had set aside their embroidery for their trembling hands were not up to the task.

She wanted to give them hope but would not mislead. "The king will talk of peace before he resorts to war, but William has thrown down the gauntlet at Malcolm's very door."

"Does the Norman think to build timbered castles all over Scotland?" asked Audra.

" 'Tis said there are hundreds in England now," said Cristina, the queen's sister.

"The people suffer for he has burned crops and salted land to discourage rebellion," remarked Isobel of Ross.

"Let us not think of England," said Margaret. "We can thank God we are not there and pray Scotland never sees such a thing come to pass."

The chamber door opened and Margaret's maidservant said, "My Lady, the king asks for ye."

Margaret rose. "I will return when I have news. The men will not leave for a day or two. As soon as they do, we will go to the chapel to pray."

Swiftly, she walked the small distance to her bedchamber. As she opened the door her gaze met Malcolm's across the room. Light streamed in from the window adding hints of gold to his brown eyes. She saw the excitement in them and realized his course was set and he was eager to get to it.

"William is holed up at Abernethy on the River Tay," he said. "As soon as I have my army, or all that can be gathered with so little notice, I will go to meet him but first I had to see you."

She went to him, needing to touch him to draw from his strength. "Abernethy is not far, My Lord. You can feed the Conqueror your few promises and soon return to me."

"Aye, 'tis interesting he has stopped at the Tay. I wonder if he knows it was once the abode of the Pictish kings and a reminder to all that Scotland has fought off invaders before."

"I will pray he leaves without a fight, My Lord, beaten by your wisdom."

Malcolm chuckled. "Aye, mayhap. But he is no easy foe and he comes with knights and ships prepared for battle." Then fixing her gaze with his dark eyes, he said, "There is one thing he will want above all, *mo cridhe*, and I think you know what that is."

She waited, dreading what he would say.

"William will want to make sure he does not again face a challenge for the crown he has seized and defended these last many years. There is only one whose claim to the throne of England is and always has been greater than William's."

"Edgar" she breathed out.

"Yea, 'tis Edgar, now old enough to wear the crown. At the very least, William will want my vow not to aid him again. Are you prepared for that, *mo cridhe?*"

She said nothing, only looked at him, seeing sympathy in his eyes. He knew, as she did, how her brother had longed to take up his legacy.

"When Edgar urged my suit upon you," he continued, " 'twas in part to win my support."

"Much has changed since then…"

"Aye, after York, he and Maerleswein returned with defeat in their eyes. I saw it."

"Should I speak to Edgar about what may be asked of him?" she asked.

"Nay. If you did, he would willingly give up his claim to spare us the war, but 'tis best if it comes to him. And if it does, we shall see. Edgar is more an exile than any of us, a king denied his throne by one grasping for plunder, lands and power like the Northmen from which the Normans hail."

★   ★   ★

Catriona stood in front of the tower, her arms wrapped around her as if she could hold in her anxious thoughts and her many fears.

The queen and the other ladies stood nearby, watching the men depart for Abernethy. The king sat atop his white charger. Beside him was Fia's father.

Catriona reached out to take her cousin's hand.

"At least I do not worry for Rhodri," Fia said.

It was not the same for Catriona. This time, all the men she loved rode with Malcolm, mayhap to a bloody battle. Steinar, at the king's back, led the guard. Niall rode at the front of the line of archers, an older bowman next to him. And Angus rode with Malcolm's mounted warriors, waving to her as he passed by.

Steinar had come to see her before he departed, telling her not to worry. But how could she not? This time he had not asked for a favor to carry and he did not speak of the future, yet she still harbored hope that one day she would belong to the golden-haired warrior. The words Rhodri had spoken of Fia rang in her ears. *I will have no other.*

When the men were out of sight, the queen called them to prayer. "We fast and pray until they return." Not a lady spoke against it, but of one accord, they turned and followed Margaret to the chapel.

★   ★   ★

It was very late in the day when the men returned. Gloaming still colored the sky shades of gray, rose and heather. Margaret looked down from the window in her chamber that overlooked the front of the tower. At the head of his men, Malcolm wearily swung from his horse and met his young son, Duncan, who had waited in front of the tower for his father's return.

The words of the men dismounting were muffled but Margaret could see there had been no battle. No blood covered their mail and the horses appeared calm.

A few moments later, the door of their chamber swung open and Malcolm stood before her.

She wanted to run to him, to thank God for the war that would not be, yet his forlorn look told her all was not well. "Did you agree on terms, My Lord?"

Running his long fingers through his dark locks, he came to her, kissing her cheek before he slumped into his chair. "Aye, we have agreed on terms, though I like not all of them."

One hand on her rounded belly, she eased herself onto the bench next to him. "Tell me, my husband."

"I have secured my lands in Cumbria but allowed William's authority over them. He is to leave Scotland with no demands on her and no taking of plunder or rapine by his army as they go, but I expect he will allow them free rein once they cross into Northumbria."

"To submit only for your lands that lie so far south of Lothian is not so grievous as it could have been, My Lord."

"Aye, mayhap, but the rest of it you will like less well." His disquieting gaze told her what she would hear would be dark news, indeed. "As I anticipated, Edgar will not have my support again for a try at England's throne. William would prefer your brother leave my court, but I agreed only to convey that request to Edgar. I refused to demand it of him."

"I think even Edgar anticipated William's concern for his crown."

"Aye. Not all are content with his ruthless domination of England, and well he knows it."

She sensed from Malcolm's somber mood there was more. "What else?"

"He required a hostage to seal my bond."

"Who?"

"Duncan."

She gasped. "But you have only just gotten him back and he is but a youth."

"Aye, *mo cridhe,* but he is my heir and the Norman Bastard sees only that. If I know William, he thinks to make a Norman of my son. You must set your prayers against it."

"You and I were both raised in England, My Lord, you away from your beloved Scots and I away from Hungary where I was born. Yet here we are, both in Scotland, committed to her cause. Surely Duncan can spend the rest of his youth in England and return a Scot to lead his people."

"Remember, *mo cridhe,* it was pious Edward's England where you and I spent our youth, I in Cumbria and you in Wessex. The Norman king is not Edward. He is treacherous and will try and deprive me of my eldest son by making him like one of them. I can only warn Duncan of what William no doubt intends and hope the lad's heart is not turned."

She took Malcolm's hand and kissed the back of it, covered in scars from his many battles. A warrior but with a father's tender heart. "You did what was right, My Lord. This may be a hard ending, but is it not better than war?"

"Aye, that is what I tell myself, though my sword cried to be unsheathed the whole time I listened to the pompous Frenchman spout his demands."

"When is Duncan to go?"

"Tomorrow. I will take him to the narrow place in the River Forth where the Normans will cross on their way south."

"My prayers will go with you and Duncan."

★   ★   ★

A solemn cloud hung over the hall the next morning as Steinar broke his fast with the king and his men. The court ate in silence, all knowing the king would soon leave for the place where Duncan was to be handed over to the Normans. Duncan ate only at the urging of his father.

"You must keep up your strength, my son."

To Steinar, the youth appeared near tears, but he blinked them back and reached for a piece of bread. 'Twas a dark day for Duncan who was saying goodbye to his Orkney half-brothers as well as his father.

This time, Colbán would lead the guard and Steinar would join them. Duff insisted on riding the short distance to stand with his friend, the king, in his difficult hour and Malcolm had allowed it.

The ride was slow, in part due to the pace set by Malcolm for Duff's still healing wound, and in part for the reluctance of the king to be about the task at all.

When they reached the bank of the Forth where William waited with his army stretched out behind him, Malcolm dismounted, pulled Duncan from his horse and walked to one side with the youth, away from the Normans but not so far that Steinar, Colbán and Duff could not hear.

"You know I would not ask this of you, son, but standing as hostage spares Scotland a war with these French who have taken over England."

"Aye, Father. I know." The youth was the image of his father and just as courageous.

"Not that it will change the result, but I must know. You are willing?"

Duncan, brave through it all, looked up at his father. "I am willing, sir."

"For my sake, they will treat you well, Duncan. They know should any harm come to you it would mean war, not just any war but one of vengeance such as they have never seen."

Duncan nodded, seeming to take it in.

"I was your age when I was exiled to England and I returned to reign as King of Scots. Let them educate you, my son, teach you your letters and how to fight like a knight. But do not let them poison your mind to their Norman ways. Always remember you are a Scot, the son of a Scots king and the grandson of another, the one for whom you were named. One day you will return to Scotland to rule our people as King Duncan, the second of that name. Learn what you must to prepare for that role and put aside all else the Normans may try and teach you. William would rule all of Alba if he could. May God never allow it."

"I will remember, Father."

Tipping the boy's chin up, the king said, "I love you, my son. You will always be in my prayers and Margaret's. And know this. I will raise your brothers, the one that is born and the others who will follow, to know you will reign ahead of them."

Duncan reached for his father and buried his head in the folds of

Malcolm's tunic, for the king wore no mail this day. Malcolm grasped the boy around the shoulders and held him fast. Steinar saw the tears filled the king's eyes, but Malcolm raised his head, calling them back. He was a king first, noble in bearing and manner. But he was also a father. Steinar's heart reached out to him. He had lost his own father to William the Conqueror.

At last, Malcolm set Duncan from him. "Go, my son and God-speed."

CHAPTER 17

Steinar turned when the tower door suddenly opened and a man he recognized as one who had ridden with Maerleswein strode inside. Steinar rose and, going to the man, accepted the parchment he thrust at him.

He meant to carry it to Malcolm where he and the queen ate on the dais, but the king shouted, "Read it!"

Steinar glanced toward Catrìona where she sat eating with the other ladies before opening the sealed parchment. Scanning its contents, he raised his voice so all in the hall could hear. "The Normans have crossed back into Northumbria. All is well in Lothian."

The hall erupted in loud exclamations of joy.

With a glance at his queen, Malcolm stood and waited for the din to die down. When he had their attention, the king said, "There has been enough sadness. And enough of the Normans' threat hanging over us. 'Tis time for happy entertaining of our guests from Orkney and Wales and for some rewards I have been planning. This I will do tomorrow night and we will celebrate but lift now your goblets and drink with me!"

All rose from their seats and downed a drink of wine and the hall erupted in loud cheers as the tension hanging over them for so long dissipated.

Steinar went to where Catrìona sat with the ladies. "Tomorrow, the king will determine your fate, I think."

She looked up, her expression confident. "Nay, 'tis only God who will determine my future, as He will yours."

Steinar bowed and walked away, admiring Catrìona's faith but despairing for what he believed the king's decision would be. He would fight for her if a battle would win her hand but how could he defy the king to whom he was sworn?

★   ★   ★

The next evening the hall was crowded with their many visitors as well as those eager to hear of the king's rewards for those he favored. The moment it was explained to Steinar what the seating on the dais would be, he understood the king's decision had not altered its course.

Colbán was to have Catrìona and, as it was explained to Steinar, he was to be given Audra of Fife. Much as he admired Duff's daughter, his heart sank at the wrong of it. He loved Catrìona and wanted only her. In his heart he had long known there would never be another like his high-spirited tree nymph.

The king's captain escorted Catrìona to the dais to take her place between Colbán and the Mormaer of Atholl, her uncle, who sat next to the king. From the anxious looks she gave her cousin, Steinar understood the auburn-haired beauty had not been privy to the king's decision to give Colbán her hand. She must know she could not say nay to the king if he decreed she should wed his captain. A queen's lady went where the king commanded.

Steinar helped Audra to take her place on the dais between him and Duff, who sat next to the queen. Audra had the look of a startled doe, understanding slowly dawning as she darted glances from Steinar to her father, who sat in stony silence, his bushy brows framing his steady eyes as he gazed into the hall.

Colbán had barely taken his seat before he propelled himself up by his good arm and strode to where the king sat sipping his wine. The captain bent to whisper in the king's ear. The king's brows drew together, as he listened intently. After a few moments, he beckoned Duff to him from where he sat on the other side of the queen.

The three conversed in whispers, oblivious to the interested stares of those in the hall. Food was served and savory smells rose in the air from the elaborate feast of swan, partridge and roast boar, but no one ate. All waited upon the king.

When the three at the dais finished their conversation, the king nodded to Colbán. Duff raised his bushy brows and shrugged. Colbán and Duff went back to their seats and the king leaned into the queen, saying something only she could hear. Then Malcolm shifted in his chair toward Matad and whispered yet again; this time the conversation took a longer span of time.

By now, the entire hall was quiet and staring at the dais, watching the bizarre series of whispers, curious to know what was afoot.

When the king and Matad finished their whispers, Malcolm shot to his feet, goblet in hand. "Tonight we have much to celebrate!"

Steinar cringed, his stomach rolling as he awaited the announcement ending his dreams of happiness. On the other side of the dais, Catrìona looked about to cry. But oddly, the queen was smiling.

"First," said the king, "I have two warriors to reward with lands and a title."

"Rise, Colbán of Moray!"

The king's captain stood, straight and tall, his long hair confined by a leather strip at his crown and his red beard neatly trimmed for the occasion.

"Colbán, ever-faithful captain of my guard, you have served me long and well. Hereafter, you shall be Mormaer of Strivelyn, with all those lands surrounding, close enough to Dunfermline should I need you to come quickly. You are charged with building a large fortress to garrison some of my men. There I intend to visit often."

A loud cheer went up and the captain bowed. "You are generous, My Lord."

Colbán returned to his seat and the king turned to face Steinar.

"Rise Steinar of Talisand!"

Like the captain before him, Steinar stood and faced the king. "For the English thegn's son who became a rebel and defied the Norman tyrant, then became my trusted scribe and saved the life of his king, you shall hereafter be the Mormaer of Levenach and shall have lands in the Vale of Leven. You are charged with building a hillfort and guarding Scotland's western border. Your new ship should help in these efforts."

Steinar bowed and gave the words of assent and thanks, as he must, even as Catrìona gasped. It must have come as a shock to learn he would have her father's lands and a ship besides. It broke his heart to think she would not be with him when he claimed them.

Loud praise sounded around the hall, for the king's pronouncements were popular among all those gathered. Goblets were raised and wine quaffed.

The king raised his hand and the hall quieted. "There is more, good people of Alba. Audra of Fife, please rise." Audra, dutiful and looking as if she feared the worst, slowly rose, her eyes fixed on Malcolm as he walked to where she stood next to her father. The king took her hand and escorted her to the other side of the dais where Colbán sat. The king's captain rose and accepted her hand. "Today these two are betrothed," announced the king.

Loud cheers erupted.

Steinar sat, confused and amazed. *Colbán is to have Audra?*

Tears streamed down Audra's face as Colbán bowed over her hand. "My lady, I hope this pleases you, as it does me."

"Oh, aye, my lord, it does," she said, joy evident on her face.

Sitting beside Steinar, Duff smiled.

A few bawdy jests sounded from the men before the king quieted them with a loud "Hist!" When the hall was silent, Malcolm said, "That leaves me with the prize long sought by my former scribe, now Mormaer of Levenach. Catrìona of the Vale of Leven, your uncle, the Mormaer of Atholl, has agreed with my decision to betroth you to Steinar." Without waiting to hear Catrìona's choked reply, the king raised his goblet and loudly proclaimed, "So be it!"

Everyone in the hall raised their goblets and quaffed their red wine before slamming their goblets down on the tables and shouting the king's words. "So be it!"

Steinar leapt to his feet, ran to the other end of the dais and pulled a startled Catrìona into his arms, kissing her soundly in front of all. "My love," he said to her tear-streaked face. "It was always you and only you that I wanted. Will you happily be my bride?"

"Aye," she said. "Oh, aye."

"Heirs by next summer!" someone shouted from the rear of the hall and the chant was picked up and carried around the room.

On the dais, all three ladies blushed scarlet, even the queen.

★   ★   ★

That night was a blur for Catrìona as her wedding and that of Audra's were added to Fia's and the three of them spoke excitedly of their future. She had slept little for the joy that filled her heart at being betrothed to the man she loved. *And with lands in the vale!* She had not anticipated all the blessings that were now hers. But she was not slow to thank God for all He had done.

That morning, many prayers of thanks were spoken. And after, Margaret, beaming with happiness, said, "I could not have asked God for more than to see the three of you happily wed." Then looking at Isobel and Elspeth, the queen added, "Now I must pray for husbands for you two and the ladies who will join you in the future."

In the hall, Catrìona broke her fast with Steinar. Before she could tell Giric, he came running in shouting, "I heard ye will wed the scribe!"

"Aye, 'tis true," she said, glancing at Steinar who wore a broad grin.

Giric joined them to eat. After the meal, they went about their separate tasks for there was much to do before the weddings that were to take place the next day.

Catrìona and Fia worked to embellish the gowns they would wear and Audra, who now occupied her chamber alone, came to join them.

That afternoon, servants bustled about calling for more tables and benches, village women flowed into the hall carrying baskets of flowers, and wonderful smells wafted from the kitchen to the second story, making Catrìona's mouth water.

Early in the afternoon, Steinar knocked at her chamber door and suggested a walk to the village to see Giric.

"Giric was excited about our marrying," she said as she walked with Steinar down the stairs to the hall. "Have you spoken again with him?"

"Aye," he said throwing her a look that told her he would say more.

"And?" she asked, raising her brows.

He opened the door of the tower and let her pass through. "He worries for our leaving." She walked a little ahead of him. He caught up to say, "I wanted to ask you before I talked with the lad." From the corner of her eye she saw him snatch a glance at her as if checking her mood. "I would like to take the boy with us to the vale and, if you are willing, raise him as our own."

A smile broke out on her face and, unbidden, tears filled her eyes. "Nothing would please me more than to have Giric with us and I think he will not want to be parted from you." She hoped one day God would give them children but to have Giric as their own child now was a great boon.

He stopped in the path and turned to face her, ignoring the looks of those passing by. Taking both of her hands in his, he said, "We are of one mind, little cat. 'Tis a good sign of the days to come, is it not?"

She kissed him on the cheek, a light peck. "A good sign, yea." Then, thinking of the name he had called her, she said, "You called me 'little cat'."

"Aye, 'tis how I think of you. 'Tis an affectionate term. Should I call you something else?"

"Nay. 'Tis the name my father called me. I have always loved it."

"Then little cat you shall be." He squeezed her hand, kissed her on the forehead and ignored the knowing smiles of those passing them as they held hands and continued down the path.

"What of Angus and Niall?" she asked, just realizing she had yet to speak to either about returning to the vale.

"I assumed you would want both to go with us so I asked if they would come."

Her anxious gaze met his.

"They said yes; they will both come."

"Oh, I am glad!" she exclaimed.

"Niall wants to be near Wales to visit Rhodri, and both miss the vale as much as you do. Except for Niall, who used his time here to perfect his skill with the bow, I think neither is fond of life at court. And Angus has a fancy for your handmaiden. Did you know?"

"Nay, Deidre has been most secretive about who she steals away to see, but Angus is a fierce protector and I can see how she would respond to him. Mayhap she liked him before and I just did not see it."

When they got to the village, the men and women greeted them with broad smiles. " 'Tis one of the brides," said one woman, waving from where she swept the short path leading to her cottage.

At the door of the orphans' cottage, fair-haired Aeleva welcomed them. "All the women are picking flowers for the chapel and the hall."

"Everyone knows they are invited?" Steinar asked.

"Aye, 'tis going to be a grand celebration. The women who were in Dunfermline ere I came say nothing like it has occurred since the king wed Lady Margaret."

Happiness welled up inside Catrìona. She would share one of the most important days of her life with Fia and Audra, as well as the queen who meant so much to her.

"Is Giric about?" Steinar asked, peering around the side of the cottage at the now finished chicken pen. "We have something to tell him." He squeezed Catrìona's hand, sending tingling sensations through her body.

"Let's see," said Aeleva, one fist braced on her generous hip. "After doing his chores, the boy skipped off. Said something about finding the two of you and flying the falcon."

They thanked her, said they would see her at the wedding and went in search of Giric. They found him in the mews.

"There ye are!" said Giric, rushing to them.

Machar congratulated them on their betrothal and took Kessog from his perch. "Once the lad came, I thought you would be here soon," he said to Catrìona. "Your tiercel is just ending his molt and is anxious to fly."

Giric jumped up and down. "Oh, can we?"

Catrìona looked at Steinar and seeing him nod, she said, "Aye, we will fly him and we have something to ask you on our way to the field."

When they told the boy of their desire to take him with them and raise him as their own, he stopped and stared, great tears falling from his thin face before they crouched before him and he leapt into their open arms. "I had hoped ye would," Giric said. "I even asked the queen if she would pray for me. And she did!"

The hours they spent with Giric in the meadow that day were ones Catrìona would always remember. The sky above was a brilliant blue, the grass a deep emerald green, the flowers yellow and white at the edge of the forest.

Kessog flew from the gauntlet, happy to be streaking through the air once again, searching out a mallard.

Steinar wrapped his arm around her shoulder and drew her close as Giric stood nearby watching the falcon.

"This is all I desire, little cat. You and the home we will make together."

" 'Twas my dream, too, even when I thought you only an English scribe." He slapped her bottom and though she properly chided him, she was secretly happy, remembering the time she had seen Malcolm do the same to his queen. Then remembering the tunic she had made, she said, "I have something for you when we return to the tower."

★   ★   ★

A feeling of exuberant joy seemed to permeate the very walls of the tower on the day of the wedding. Everyone's face bore a smile.

Catrìona's work in the village had brought her many friends; Audra's kindness garnered the people's love; and Fia was admired for having snagged the bard all the women wanted, many saying the fairies must have aided her.

When Catrìona told Fia of the rumors, she laughed. Rhodri, when he heard of it, vowed to compose an ode to the fairies that had helped him win his bride.

In her chamber, Deidre and a servant, sent by the queen to help the brides, brought out the gowns they had decided to wear: sapphire for Fia because it was Rhodri's favorite color for her and matched her eyes, gold for Audra for it brought out the gold in her hazel eyes and green that was the color of the forest for Catrìona because Steinar told her he would ever think of her as his tree nymph.

Each wore a circlet of silver and gold around her crown, gifts from the queen, leaving their long tresses free down their backs. After this day they would wear the circlets over the headscarves that would mark them married women.

The night before, Catrìona had given Steinar the blue tunic she made for him, embroidered with silver and gold falcons and quills. " 'Tis the color of your eyes," she told him as she proudly placed it into his hands. "It may not be the fine stitching of the other ladies, but know that I did it myself."

"In truth, I was worried when I saw the tunic you embroidered for Colbán," Steinar had said. "I believed it a sign you agreed with his request for your hand."

"At the time, I knew nothing of it," she had assured him. "Colbán asked me to embroider the tunic. His request, so unforeseen, quite startled me. But the doing of it gave me the idea to make this one for you." She looked into the face of the man she loved. "The one for Colbán was something I did as one of the queen's ladies. This one I did for love of the man who would wear it."

Beaming, he had held it up and studied the silver and gold threads that marked the quills and outlined the falcons, filled in with flaxen thread. She had labored much to get the design just right. "You are too modest, little cat," he had said. " 'Tis truly magnificent. I will wear it proudly."

★   ★   ★

Margaret stood with her husband, watching her three ladies and the men who would soon be their husbands take their places in front of the chapel door. The Culdee monk in his gray cowl robe who was to perform the ceremony seemed a bit overwhelmed by having to wed three couples, but he managed, in spite of it, to pronounce the words that saw them wed.

All of Dunfermline looked on, smiling their pleasure.

As the couples walked back to the tower for the feast that would follow, Margaret slipped her arm through her husband's and leaned in to ask in a whisper, "What was it Colbán said to you that made you switch the brides at the last moment?"

"He apologized for being remiss in telling me that Audra had declared she loved him no matter he was from Moray. It seems he returns her affection."

"What about Catrìona?"

"At the same time he became aware of Audra's feelings, he realized the redhead favored the scribe. Colbán's words were, 'Hurled herself into the scribe's arms when he rescued her from the Northman, not a glance for me though I lay wounded and bleeding on the deck!'."

"Ah," said Margaret, "so my first instinct was correct. 'Twas Catrìona for Steinar all along."

He pulled her close and kissed her on her cheek. "Just so, *mo cridhe.*"

The celebration that day brought a warm gladness to Margaret's heart, seeing her ladies happily wed to good men. And that night when she said her prayers, she had much to be thankful for.

★　★　★

The feasting had gone on for some time when, ignoring the jests from the men in the hall, Steinar led Catrìona to the stairs, eager to be alone with his bride. The celebration in the hall would continue late into the night but not with them. Looking over his shoulder, he saw Rhodri and Colbán coming behind him, their brides in tow.

Catrìona's hand was cold in his as they ascended the stairs. *She is nervous.* He gave her a reassuring look. "Trust me, little cat. I will see my beautiful bride happy this night."

"You promise?"

He expected to see mirth dancing in her green eyes but, instead, he saw uncertainty and, mayhap, a little fear. "Aye, I promise. Have I not waited months for you, desperate to have you for my own even though I believed the king would give you to another?"

"Yes." Her green eyes sparkled like jewels. "Oh, yes, you did."

"Then trust me to be patient this night and make our joining a sweet one."

They turned down the corridor, her smile telling him all he needed to know.

When they reached the chamber assigned to them, he was glad to see all had been made ready. Candles and a fire in the brazier warmed the room, dominated by the bed, much larger than the one he normally slept in. For that he was grateful. 'Twould give them more room to move about.

His eyes followed Catrìona as she went to the small table set with a pitcher of wine, two silver goblets and a trencher of bread, cheese and fruit. "I love pears and cherries," she said, idly fingering one of the pears.

My innocent firebrand is stalling. He smiled to himself, knowing he would make it good for her.

Casting her gaze about the chamber, his bride looked at the two chests at the foot of the bed, hers next to his. "My chest," she remarked.

"Aye, my love. While we were being wed, the servants moved all of our things here. See, your cloak and mine hang on pegs next to the door. 'Twill be our chamber until we leave for the vale."

He came up behind her and slid his arms around her slim waist, pulling her back against his chest, loving the feel of her and her scent, as fresh as the forest. Running his lips down the side of her neck, he felt her shiver. "Do not be afraid, little cat. Have I not held you before? And do I not love you?" He turned her in his arms and met her emerald gaze. "Since the king gave me your hand, I have dreamed of this night. Truth be told, mayhap even before."

Her cheeks flushed. "I, too, have dreamed of this night, though 'twas all shrouded in mist. I knew not what to expect. The queen had a few words with the three of us yesterday and that helped calm my fears."

He drew her close and nibbled at her ear. "Would you like some wine?"

"A sip, mayhap," she said, stepping back.

He poured her some wine and handed her the goblet. As she reached for it her gaze fixed on the gold band on her finger.

"The ring is a sign to all you are mine." He took her goblet and set it aside and pressed his lips to the back of her hand, then pulled her into his arms and brushed his lips over hers. They were soft and warm and tasted of the wine. "Let me show you the joys of love."

He turned her slowly so he could unlace her gown, brushing aside her thick auburn hair to kiss her neck from ear to nape.

"Ah," she breathed, inclining her head and giving him greater access to her neck. "You give me shivers."

"My intention exactly," he said, running his tongue around the edge of her ear.

Soon he would have her naked and next to him but he intended to take his time, winning her trust, stroking her like a wary falcon.

Once he had removed her belt, he pulled her gown from her shoulders and let it slide to the floor. While he doffed his own tunic and loosened the cross straps around his hosen, she kicked off her shoes and removed her stockings. The glimpses he caught of her bare legs made him eager to touch them. Now she was left in only her undertunic and he in only his hosen.

Her eyes darted to his bare chest reminding him that she had never before seen him like this.

"Aye, I know I have a scar or two. 'Tis a warrior's fate."

"I do not mind," she said. "To me you are beautiful." She came near and reached out her hand to run her fingers down a scar that crossed one side of his chest. Her eyes grew wide and the pupils darkened when her fingers brushed his nipple causing it to harden.

He covered her hands with his. "I love your fingers on my chest, little cat, but if you continue to touch me like that I may lose the control I vowed to have this night." Taking her hand, he led her to the bed and pulled back the cover. "In you go. Our nest awaits."

She climbed in, carefully it appeared to him, as if unsure of the bedding. When she lay back on the pillow and gave him a small smile, his heart melted. "From the first time I glimpsed your fiery red tresses, Catrìona of the Vale, I was lost."

Climbing onto the bed, he lay beside her and drew her length against his.

She placed her hand on his shoulder, her lips close to his. "You were only a scribe to me then, but I wanted you, too." Her hand moved over his shoulder and even her tentative touch made him harden in anticipation. "You are warm," she said, looking into his eyes.

"You have no idea, my love." Unable to hold back all he was feeling, he kissed her, relieved when she pulled him closer and slipped her hand behind his neck as if to hold him to her.

She returned his kisses, moaning softly.

Desperate to know the feel of her, he ran his hand over her breasts, her waist and her hip. The soft curves of her flesh he felt beneath her thin undertunic were so enticing he had to remind himself to take his time.

He slipped his hand beneath the thin linen and ran his fingers over the skin of her slender thigh. When her hands gripped his shoulders, his body responded and his hand crept higher. He was heading toward the juncture of her thighs but there were too many clothes between them. Tugging up her tunic, he began to remove it. Discerning his intent, she helped him pull it over her head and tossed it to the floor.

Before him lay his beautiful bride revealed in candlelight, her skin like cream and her breasts perfect with nipples the color of wild roses.

Shyly, she tried to pull the cover over her.

"Nay, do not cover yourself. I would see the beauty I have only imagined, the woman who is mine."

Laying the cover to one side, he peeled off his hosen. Now, as naked as she, he lay alongside her, letting her feel all of him. Slipping one of his legs between hers, he drew her thighs apart, while he cupped her breasts and licked her nipples to hardened buds.

"Oh," she sighed, her hands holding his head to her breasts.

Her breathing came faster and when he looked up, her eyes were dark with passion and her lips open for his kiss. " 'Tis meant to bring you pleasure and ready you for our joining."

He pulled her close and kissed her, then slid his hand to the nest of dark red curls at the juncture of her thighs and felt her delicate folds, already wet. His aroused flesh pressed against her thigh, his body urging haste. He stifled the desire to mount her and gently circled the bud he knew would bring her near her peak, but he had no intention of allowing her to find release before they were joined as one.

She began to move against his hand and he obliged her with strokes designed to raise her passion. His own was racing and his breathing heavy. Finally, sensing the time was right, he rolled on top of her and let her feel his hardened shaft against her wet flesh.

She raised her hips in invitation and moved against him while he kissed her.

He raised his head. " 'Tis time, my love."

"Yea," she whispered and reached again for his kiss.

Positioning himself over her welcoming flesh, he slid into her tight sheath, filling her completely.

A deep moan sounded from her throat as he claimed her. He stilled, relieved he had not hurt her. It might have been all her riding around the vale or falling off logs into streams, but the little blood he knew they would find in the morning would not be that of a maiden roughly used, but one who was prepared and gently loved.

Her passion did not subside but rose with his and soon they were moving together. "Oh, Steinar," she gasped as her breath came more rapidly.

The pressure rose, leaving him unable to speak. His heart pounded in his chest and their sweat mingled, making their bodies slick against each other.

Sensing her release drawing near, he whispered, "Just let go, my love."

She expelled a breath and her muscles clenched around him, giving him a pleasure he had not known before and demanding his own release. A last deep thrust and his seed flooded her womb.

For a moment, joined together, her arms tight around him, he seemed to float, utterly content. Catrìona was finally his. *But why was this so different?* " 'Twas love," his mind silently whispered. Not just the joining of two bodies, but of two souls.

He rolled to lie next to her and pulled her into his side, feeling the length of her soft warm body as she laid her head on his shoulder.

She placed her palm on his chest, still damp with sweat. "Was it all right?" Her voice sounded unsure.

"Aye, little cat," he said, covering her hand with his and kissing her temple. "It was much better than that. I cannot even describe how wonderful it was, but 'tis clear our nights will bring us much joy and should God bless us, many children."

"I would like children," she said, entwining her fingers in the hair on his chest. Then as if she thought she had forgotten something important, she said, "I enjoyed our joining."

He chuckled. "I could tell that you did."

The candles burned low but there was sufficient light for him to see her smiling. "Steinar," she said.

"Aye?"

"You are mine, are you not?"

"Aye, lass, only yours and forever." Behind him was England and a past he could not, did not, want to bring back. No longer the exile, he now had a home. He belonged to Catrìona and she to him. And both of them belonged to Scotland. "Sleep, little cat and know I will hold you. I vow you will have only good dreams this night."

CHAPTER 18

Sunlight filtering through the shutters awakened Steinar the next morning. Next to him, curled into his side, lay his sleeping bride, her auburn hair spread across the pillow like strands of dark fire. He gently placed a kiss on her forehead and carefully rose so as not to wake her. He had made love to her again in the night when the candles had burned to near nothing and dawn was not yet with them. She would need her rest.

He rose and washed, donned his hosen and sat at the table nibbling on chunks of cheese, basking in his good fortune. He had a wife he loved, lands of his own where he would build them a home and a noble king to serve.

"Steinar?" she murmured from the bed.

"Aye, love, just here."

Rising up on one elbow, tousled from their night of lovemaking, she grinned.

"Happy are you?" he asked.

"Aye," she said, "very."

He could feel himself harden at the sight of her auburn hair falling around her pale shoulders, the cover slipping dangerously close to revealing one perfect breast. "Do you wish me to return to our bed or are you hungry for more than me?"

She laughed. "Conceited rogue. Might you bring the food here so that we can dine on it *and* each other?"

"Ho! My bride learns fast." Picking up the trencher, he reached the edge of the bed in two long strides, his leg bothering him not at all.

He fed her the cherries one by one, then licked the juice from her lips. That led to other delights, which continued until a knock sounded on their door.

★   ★   ★

"Mistress?" Catrìona recognized the voice as her handmaiden.

" 'Tis Deidre," she said to Steinar, moving his hand from her breast. "What is it?" she said to the door.

Through the oak planks, her handmaiden said, "I would not disturb you, milady, but I thought you would want to know that last night the queen had her babe. 'Twas early… a son! The king is ever so pleased. The babe is to be named Edmund and the queen asks you and the other two ladies to stay for the christening."

At Steinar's nod, she said, "Aye, we will."

Hearing Deidre's footsteps retreating down the corridor, Catrìona lay back on the pillows and looked at her new husband, who was smiling at her as he rose up on one elbow, his golden locks loose about his muscled shoulders, his blue thistle eyes gazing at her, a pleased expression on his face. "Should we go congratulate the king and pay tribute to the queen and her new son?"

"Aye," he said, " 'tis best. We have played the slug-a-beds long enough. And we have our nights. The christening will not be for a few days."

★   ★   ★

Three days later, Margaret and Malcolm's babe was christened and Steinar made ready to leave Dunfermline with his new wife and those who would travel with them. Outside the tower door stood the king and queen and a group who had assembled to bid the travelers God-speed.

Rhodri, Fia and Cillyn, headed for Wales, would join their party until they reached the River Clyde where Cillyn's ship awaited him.

Paul and Erlend had left before the three couples were wed, telling Steinar his ship would arrive in the vale ere long with all the supplies he needed. With the dowry Catriona's uncle had provided, and the king's generosity, Steinar was rich with coin.

"I've a new scribe," said the king to Steinar as he watched their chests being loaded into the cart, "so I will expect regular missives from my lettered mormaer."

"As you wish, My Lord," Steinar said. "And should you call, I will come."

Margaret kissed her new babe and handed him to his nurse. A second nurse held her first son, Edward. Coming up to Steinar's bride, the queen said, "I will miss you, lovely Catriona. Things will be a bit dull for a time without my lady who flies falcons and sneaks out to run in the woods."

"I will miss you greatly, My Lady," Catriona said. "You have taught me so much, your life speaking louder than your words."

"I am glad," Margaret replied. "You are still young, but you have grown wise and helped me much. I will let you know of the progress of the ferry and the inn." Then turning to Catriona's cousin, the queen said, "You have your bard, Fia. One day you may wear a queen's crown. Do not forget to wear a cloak of humility as well."

Catriona's cousin curtsied before the queen. "I shall not forget, My Lady."

"Do not forget me!" piped up Giric, running to the queen. His small wiry dog, Shadow, let out a yelp as if demanding to be recognized along with his master.

"I will not forget you, little Giric," said Margaret, reaching down to hug the lad. Then turning to Steinar and Catriona, she said, "He is the son of a Culdee monk, did you know?"

"Nay, I did not," Steinar said.

"Nor I," said Catriona. "He will be like our own son."

Margaret said, "I believe he will prove a worthy one." And to Giric, the queen said, "Did you hear that? You have new parents who love you. Be a good son to them, aye?"

Giric nodded solemnly.

The queen went back to stand with Malcolm and their two young sons.

Angus helped Deidre into the cart where she would ride and came to bow before the king and queen. Taking Giric by the hand, he said to Steinar. "With yer permission, sir, the lad can ride with me."

Steinar nodded and as Angus walked away, Catrìona laid her hand on Steinar's arm. "He is no longer my guard. Now, by his own decision, Angus serves you, the Mormaer of Levenach."

Steinar touched her hand. "I am glad to have so faithful a man."

Rhodri came to pay his respects to the king, bowing low.

"You are a king's son, Rhodri," said Malcolm. "One day, should God will it, you may be a king. Forget not Scotland where you sojourned. I expect to hear of that alliance we discussed."

"I shall speak of it to my father when I arrive in Wales, My Lord."

Steinar watched as Catrìona's uncle came to say his goodbye. He kissed and hugged his daughter, then his niece, and said to Rhodri, "I will hold you to the promise to bring my daughter to see me." And to Steinar, he said, "I want to see my niece, as well."

Steinar nodded, as did Rhodri.

Colbán and Audra emerged from the tower together with the queen's two other ladies. Colbán seemed very content with his new bride and she with him. The captain had told Steinar 'twas his intent to stay for a while to see the guard settled with another captain before he and Audra left for Strivelyn to the west. " 'Tis not far so I can come and go while our fortress is being built."

"I am thankful for our time serving together in the king's guard," said Steinar. And he meant it. Colbán was a faithful leader of men and he knew the two would remain friends.

Colbán slapped him on the back. "I have a feeling we will see each other more often than we might think."

Finally they were ready to leave and had said all their goodbyes.

Steinar led the procession away from Dunfermline, waving goodbye to those watching from the front of the tower. Seeing the sadness in Catrìona's eyes, he said, " 'Tis hard to leave, I know, but happy are the days that lie ahead, my love."

She smiled then, her green eyes flashing. "Aye, and I go home with a full heart and a husband besides."

"One who loves you very much, little cat."

EPILOGUE

The Vale of Leven, Strathclyde, Scotland 1087

Catrìona stood at the top of the rise, shielding her eyes against the summer sun, anxiously waiting for Steinar's golden head to appear. He had sent word of King Malcolm's victory over the Moray rebels in the north, but she would not be at peace until he was safe in her arms.

In the fifteen summers that had passed since they had returned to the vale, much had happened to make her content. But not when her husband rode to battle, as he had seven years after the Treaty of Abernethy when, to no one's surprise, Malcolm again raided Northumbria. She worried then and she worried now. There were always men who did not return. And so she had come to understand the pain she had seen in Margaret's eyes all those years before when Malcolm rode off with his warriors, wearing mail and helm.

The hillfort that stood behind her was the one Steinar had built that first fall. It was larger than her father's and not in the same place. Wisely, Steinar had decided they would live higher above the vale, where she had flown Kessog that day so long ago, the day that changed her life forever.

From here, they could see the deep blue waters of Loch Lomond in one direction and the River Clyde in the other. On the shore of the River Clyde, where her father's hillfort had once stood, there was now a chapel next to the many graves. She could not see it from here, yet she knew it well. Steinar, Niall and Angus had built the chapel and invited

Caerell, the Culdee monk she had met at St. Andrews to live in the vale. To her delight, he had accepted the invitation.

Other graves had been added over the years to those that stood witness to the Northmen's attack, including that of a babe she and Steinar had lost that first year, a girl child. That was before God gave them five strong sons.

She had wanted a love like her parents had and, with Steinar, she had found it. In the years that had passed, her love for him had grown, mellowing like a fine wine aged with time. They did not always agree. Sometimes, she thought Steinar actually started arguments for he seemed to love the debate that followed. Always they came together in the end.

She thought of Deidre, her faithful handmaiden. How she missed her. Two years after they returned to the vale, she had finally consented to marry Angus, who was, like Malcolm, nearly twice the age of his bride at their wedding. Each consoled the other for what they had lost that day of the Northmen's raid. The next summer Deidre gave birth, but did not survive childbed, dying in Angus' arms. Their daughter, who Angus had named Deidre, was the joy of her father's life.

Catrìona had promised Angus she would be a mother to the child and she had kept her word. The winsome, dark-haired girl had filled the hole in her heart left by the death of her own child.

A year after Rhodri and Fia had gone to Gwynedd, his father, the king, had died. Rhodri, or Iorwerth, as he was known to his people, now shared control of Powys and Gwynedd with his brothers, as Cillyn had said he would. Though Rhodri was never able to persuade his brothers to make a formal alliance with Scotland, he maintained good relations with Malcolm. Several times, he and Fia had come through the vale on their way to visit Fia's father in Atholl. Fia had given Rhodri three daughters and then two sons. Their oldest son, Matad, fostered with his grandfather. The two were inseparable.

Sometimes, Niall traveled with Rhodri and Fia back to Wales. One year, Niall returned home with a Welsh bride, Aneira, a lovely girl, who now lived with them in the hillfort.

Catrìona smiled to herself thinking of Giric. He would be returning with Steinar and Niall this day and there were many lasses in the vale who would be happy to hear it. The orphan had become a true son to her and Steinar, the only one of their six boys old enough to go to war with his father. At one and twenty summers, Giric had become the warrior he had vowed to be, tall and proud of bearing and skilled with a sword.

Giric's dog, Shadow, had died three summers ago and the king, inquiring about Giric's sad face on their trip to Dunfermline that year, gave him a whelp from one of the royal hounds. Giric had named the gangly dog *Sealgair*, or Hunter. The hound followed him everywhere. Not to be outdone, Steinar had asked the king for a pup and now a female hound stood guard at the hillfort.

Last year, Davina had lost her beloved Maerleswein to a winter sickness after he'd come home soaked to the skin, caught in a deluge with some of his men. He had lived into his sixth decade and fathered two sons in Scotland who would live after him. 'Twas a full life by any man's standard, yet Catrìona's heart went out to Davina, for whom she prayed every day. But at least in Lothian, Davina had her people around her.

Catrìona supposed Audra was as happy as any of them for she had both her husband and father to fuss over. Colbán protested much but it was apparent to all he loved his doting wife. On their way to Dunfermline, Catrìona and Steinar often stopped to visit them in the large fortress built on a hill at Strivelyn overlooking the lowest crossing point on the River Forth.

In his fifth decade, Audra's father, Duff, still fought at the king's side. According to Steinar's message, Duff, his two sons and Colbán had led the battle against the rebels in Moray.

Margaret had given Malcolm five sons, then two daughters and, finally four summers ago, little David. They still resided at the royal seat in Dunfermline but there was talk of building a fortress at Dun Edin on the other side of the Forth.

Catrìona knew Margaret missed her brother, Edgar, who had eventually made peace with William and left Scotland to seek his fortune in Italy. At more than thirty summers, he had yet to wed. Whenever Catrìona thought of him she would experience a deep sorrow, remembering the handsome young man who had charmed her that first night in Dunfermline. He deserved so much more.

As for Duncan, the king's eldest son was still in England, trained as a Norman knight and, to Malcolm's dismay, serving in William's campaigns. Nearly thirty, Duncan had yet to be released from his obligation as hostage.

The queen had seen her ferry built and the pilgrims now regularly traveled over the waters of the Forth on their way to St. Andrew's shrine, staying at the queen's inns, for Margaret had built one on either side of the Forth. Catriona smiled, remembering that summer she had traveled to St. Andrews with the queen. Sometimes, on winter nights as they sat around the hearth fire, she and Steinar would speak of it and laugh about the wildcat that had frightened her so.

As for Kessog, though an old falcon, he still hunted over the waters of Loch Lomond, taking a duck now and then for their table. Niall was expanding the mews to house the falcons he and Giric had trained.

Ahead, Catriona spotted Steinar atop his black horse leading a band of warriors up the hill. Niall rode on one side of him and Giric on the other, his hound trotting beside him. They looked weary and dust-covered, but their smiles told her they were happy to be home.

Heart racing, she picked up her skirts and ran toward them, over-joyed to see they were whole. Behind her, she heard the pounding of little feet following her down the path.

And so, in the end...

Malcolm Canmore, King of Scots, had his queen who he adored.

Maerleswein, the former Sheriff of Lincolnshire, found love a second time and lived to father two sons.

Colbán, captain of the king's guard, found redemption in the arms of a gentle woman whose love forgave even the murder by his people of her mother and younger brothers.

Rhodri, the Welsh bard and master of the bow, regained his noble heritage because the woman he loved was willing to follow him wherever his path led.

And, Steinar and Catrìona, having once lost all, found a love for the ages.

POSTSCRIPT

Sometimes, we authors discover real history intersects with our fictional imaginings in what might have been called "whate" centuries ago and today is thought of as "fortunate serendipity". So it was with *Rebel Warrior*.

After I had already done considerable research for this novel, decided on the main characters and written the first scene in the Vale of Leven, I discovered something most interesting.

There is a tradition that says the Earls of Lennox are descended from a Northumbrian named Arkil, who took refuge in Scotland in 1070 after the Conquest. For his loyalty to King Malcolm Canmore and his resistance to William the Conqueror, Arkil was given lands in the Vale of Leven in recompense for the lands that William took from him and he was granted the title Mormaer of Levenach, which eventually migrated to "Levenax".

In the 12th century, the Mormaers of Levenax became the Earls of Lennox, which became part of the Royal House of Stewart. I like to think that the male descendants of Steinar and Catrìona became those earls and served well the future Kings of the Scots.

Since I plan a series set in 12th century Scotland, featuring the origins of Clan Donald, you might even encounter one of Steinar's descendants in a future novel. And, there is also the real possibility that Steinar himself may appear in my next novel, *King's Knight*, the story of the Red Wolf's son, Alexander, set some twenty years after *Rebel Warrior*.

I invite you to visit my Pinterest board for *Rebel Warrior*, pinterest. com / reganwalker123 / rebel-warrior-by-regan-walker. There, you can view maps and pictures of the places referred to in the story, see the characters as I do, glimpse the flora and fauna of the time and the books I relied upon. It's my research in pictures!

I love to keep in touch with my readers. You can contact me via my website and sign up for my newsletter there, too. www. ReganWalkerAuthor.com.

If you enjoyed my story, please write a review!

AUTHOR'S BIO

Regan Walker is an award-winning, bestselling author of Regency, Georgian and Medieval romances. She has five times been featured in USA TODAY's HEA column and four times nominated for the prestigious RONE award (her novel, *The Red Wolf's Prize* won Best Historical Novel for 2015 in the medieval category).

Regan writes historically authentic novels with real history and real historic figures where her readers can experience history, adventure and love. She lives in San Diego with her Golden Retriever who she says helps her to smell the roses every day.

BOOKS BY REGAN WALKER

The Medieval Warriors series:

The Red Wolf's Prize
Rogue Knight
Rebel Warrior
King's Knight (coming in late 2016)

The Agents of the Crown series:

To Tame the Wind (prequel)
Racing with the Wind
Against the Wind
Wind Raven
Echo in the Wind (coming in 2017)

Holiday Stories (related to the Agents of the Crown):

The Shamrock & The Rose
The Twelfth Night Wager
The Holly & The Thistle

www.ReganWalkerAuthor.com

CPSIA information can be obtained
at www.ICGtesting.com
Printed in the USA
LVOW04s1544140616

492558LV00036B/798/P